SANDY River

The Marble Falls Legacy - Book 2

by
Bruce Judisch

DEDICATION

To Gabriel and Isabelle, wherever they might be

Acknowledgments

A special thanks goes out to several people who contributed their personal time and interest in helping me craft *Sandy River*.

Taffy Davis, Farmington Historical Society, who patiently sacrificed hours watching me pore through volumes of historical documents, guiding me through the Titcomb and Octagon Houses, and answering countless follow-up questions I neglected to ask while I was there. I couldn't help but write her into the story. I hope she took that as a compliment …

Candace Calvert, my go-to expert on emergency medical procedures, accomplished fellow author, and tireless encourager.

Jan Bell, RN, Director, ICU/MED-SURG, who provided essential details regarding local emergency processes and procedures at Franklin Memorial Hospital.

Belinda Mansfield, my local expert on all things Rangeley, Maine, the town Marble Falls is based upon.

Lora Doncea, my intrepid editor, whose patience and attention to detail are second to none.

Jeannie Judisch, the best wife and beta reader a writer could ask for.

Lynnette Bonner, who captured the essence and feel of *Sandy River* with a terrific cover design.

A blast of wind sideswiped the Corolla, wrestling for control of the steering wheel from her grasp. Gwen's heart lurched as she corrected and backed off the accelerator. Steeling herself against early-afternoon drowsiness, she groped for a Styrofoam coffee cup in the console and sucked lukewarm dregs through a lipstick-stained sip hole in the plastic lid. She adjusted the rearview mirror and grimaced at the disheveled face blinking back at her. Bloodshot hazel eyes and wisps of blond hair tangled from repeated finger rakings gave witness to little sleep and a burdened mind. Yawning, she leaned forward and squinted into the dizzying wash of snow flurries obscuring traffic on southbound I-95. The cheerful sign welcoming her to Massachusetts passed almost without notice.

Despite the adrenaline surge and caffeine jolt, only a couple of miles passed before the highway's white divider strips began to blur again. More than once, the horn of a passing motorist startled her back into her own lane, and she nearly missed the exit onto I-93 South toward Boston altogether. But then, almost before she realized it, she was veering into the driveway of her two-story beige brick home in Medford, the tired sedan's worn brakes grating to a halt.

Switching off the engine, she lowered her forehead against the steering wheel, sighing in gratitude that she'd survived the journey and in sadness at why she'd embarked upon it. When she looked back up, the dark house loomed through the sullen grayness of a waning afternoon. Her throat tightened at the last memory of her father's slouching silhouette framed in the upstairs window as she backed out of the driveway two months ago. That night, the notion that they might yet reconcile—perhaps rekindle some of the warmth they'd shared when she was a child—was cut short by the figure turning away and the curtains falling back into stillness. During the hurried journey back to Marble Falls, she'd reassured herself that as soon as the pressing matters calling her there were resolved, she would return to Medford, sit with him, work things out. Somehow.

But present urgencies buried the past, and a promising future with her boyfriend, Brent Newcomb, submerged it further. Self-made promises withdrew to the back of her mind, much as her father had withdrawn into his in the years following her mother's death. Then her cell phone chirped one frigid December morning, and those promises died.

The family attorney was kind, but brief. He regretted the sudden passing of her father, suggested she return at her earliest convenience to settle his estate.

Convenience?

The lawyer's droning explanation of the circumstances faded into numbness. Something about the lady from the cleaning service discovering her father's body, an impending autopsy, execution of the will.

"Ms. Kelly? Are you there?"

"Yes … I'm sorry."

"Please contact my office at your convenience to review the will."

That word again. An unfinished chapter of her life had slammed shut, and she would seal it forever as a matter of convenience.

She reached for her seat belt buckle, still staring glumly at her childhood home, dark and silent. If she had anything to say about it, once her legal obligations had concluded, she would never again set foot in this house. Ever.

But now there was closure to find, memories to be laid to rest. And for that, there was only one place to begin.

***

Thirty minutes later, her things settled in her old bedroom and a teapot slowly heating on the stove, Gwen stood at the top of a pull-down ladder on the second-story landing. Sweater tucked close against the musty chill, she surveyed the darkening attic. Snow-filtered light squeezed through louvered windows at each end of the garret, sending fading shafts of gray across a dusty array of cardboard boxes and black plastic bags. All lay silent except for the steady *click-click-click* of a rusted wind turbine embedded in the roof.

She reached up and tugged on a cotton string, and a solitary lightbulb crackled to life, casting a jaundiced glow into the gray twilight. Gwen scanned the remnants of her heritage, mind full of reminiscence. Nearest the ladder, a random collection of odds and ends lay strewn across plywood sheets spanning the joists. A couple of old suitcases, a veneered pressboard filing cabinet supporting a teetering stack of cardboard document boxes, a miscellaneous array of swollen black plastic bags tied off at the top. Halfway across the low-ceilinged space, two garment bags hung from nails in the ridgepole. One held her father's navy uniform, the other her mother's wedding dress. Around them lay a jumbled pile of Christmas decorations that hadn't welcomed the holiday since she was twelve years old, the year her mother fell from the second-story landing while stringing garland, marking an abrupt end to Gwen's childhood. Just beyond them rested a dusty cedar chest containing family mementos.

She stepped up onto twin planks running the length of the attic and edged along the narrow walkway, ducking low rafters and dodging wisps of cobwebs. Skirting the garment bags, she stopped beside the cedar chest. As she paused, subliminal whisperings rose from somewhere in the back of her mind. Voice-like, but unintelligible, they pulled her attention to the trunk. Gwen frowned, shook her head, and began to move on, when her foot slipped from the edge of the plank. As she fought to regain her balance, her leg bumped against the trunk's metal hasp, and it fell open. The sharp crack of the metal against the front of the trunk resounded like a gunshot. In the startled quiet that followed, the whisperings intensified, echoed, demanded. She closed her eyes, hands pressed to her ears, and the voices silenced.

When she opened her eyes, her gaze landed on the trunk. She knelt. Fingered the hasp. Lifted the lid. Musty air billowed out and a sneeze escaped as she peered into the trunk's dim interior. To the left lay a linen wrapping around what would be Grandmother Kelly's needlepoint. Next to the linen, a red enameled music box, its lid supporting a ballerina in mid-pirouette, lay buffered by a crocheted afghan, another one of grandmother's endeavors. Photo albums stacked side by side filled the remaining space. She lifted out an album and cracked opened the time-worn cloth cover. The first page held a wedding napkin embossed with her parents' names, an infant's pink hair ribbon—hers? The pictorial journey progressed backward in time through subsequent albums. Color snapshots browning with age gave way to black-and-white photos of generations of Kellys smiling, then mildly tolerating, then simply peering stoically at the camera. She smiled at a 1959 playbill from the opening-night Broadway performance of *Gypsy* folded beneath the images of her grandparents. Odd how their stern expressions created so stark a contrast against the gaiety of the playbill, as though denying they'd had anything to do with such frivolous amusement.

Gwen flipped gently through the pages toward the back cover. As she reached the end, she was about to close the volume when a startling image caught her eye. She pulled the album closer and lifted it to the light. Fastened to the black cardstock page was a lithograph of a curly-haired girl in a form-fitting dress with a pleated white bodice. Flashing a coquettish smile, she beckoned the viewer with a flirtatious forefinger. Gwen gasped. It was identical to the lithograph sewn into the lining of the steamer trunk in Margie's antique shop that had created so much turmoil in the quiet village of Marble Falls only two months prior.

Trembling, she eased the brittle paper from its tabs. She turned the image over and her throat went dry. Penned in graceful calligraphy was a single entry.

Irma Louise (nee Kelly) Jones. Marble Falls, Maine. 1867.

In Marble Falls, Officer Brent Newcomb closed the door behind himself and stamped the snow from his boots. He brushed a melting layer of snowflakes from his coat sleeves, hung his coat, hat, and gloves in the foyer, and blew warmth into his stiff hands. Stepping into the living room, he propped fists on his hips at one of the saddest sights a true outdoorsman could behold. A cold fireplace. He clomped across the rough-hewn wooden floor, and moments later, a pile of kindling sputtered to life at the touch of a matchstick, and a comforting warmth bathed his face and arms as he piled wedges of oak onto the growing flames.

Closing the wire mesh screen, he turned and scanned the room. All that was lacking now was a hot meal on the coffee table and Gwen snuggled up beside him on the couch—not necessarily in that order. But ski season was in full swing, and the three-man Marble Falls Police Department had its hands full, so Chief Lawson had denied his request to accompany Gwen to Medford. The chief was more concerned about rescuing inexperienced drivers from snowy ditches, calming landowners irate over snowmobilers overrunning private property, and quelling alcohol-fueled altercations between regulars and vacationers at the Sports Pub & Grill. So Brent watched Gwen drive alone up Main Street, his heart sinking as the car climbed the hill and disappear from sight. Now, despite the warmth of a crackling log fire, the prospect of another solitary evening left him cold on the inside.

Stomach churning, he wandered into the kitchen and rummaged through the refrigerator. A pint-sized Tupperware tub near the back of the fridge caught his eye, and he reached for it. He popped off the lid, winced, and jammed it back into place. The rank odor billowing out from the fuzzy green contents killed any desire to solve the mystery of what it might be. Stifling a gag, he strode to the back door and pitched the container into the trash bin beside the porch.

Back in the kitchen, he'd just opened the freezer compartment in search of something less volatile to eat when a familiar ringtone sounded. He grabbed his cell phone from his belt.

"Hey, Gwen! You have no idea how much I miss you."

"You must be looking for something to eat."

"That's purely coincidental."

"Right."

He laughed. "Seriously, I didn't realize how empty Marble Falls would be without you. Please tell me you're coming back tomorrow."

"Well, I hoped this would only take a day or two, but … "

"But what?"

"Apparently there are some unresolved issues with Daddy's will. I meet with his lawyer tomorrow morning." She paused. "And there's something else."

"Something else?"

"I'm going to text you a photo of something I found in the attic. I'm interested in your reaction."

"Can't you tell me any more than that?"

"And spoil the surprise? Nope. You'll see what I mean when—oh! The phone beeped. It's the attorney's office. They're probably confirming tomorrow's appointment. I'll call you back."

"Okay. Love you."

"I love you too."

Brent disconnected the call and went back to foraging. He grabbed the two remaining eggs from their carton, praying they were newer than whatever was in the Tupperware. Soon, angry hissing and spitting from an overheated frying pan joined the scratching of a ballpoint pen as the grocery list he'd procrastinated on making took form.

Back in front of the fire, he laid the phone on the end table and took a bite of fried eggs on ketchup-slathered whole-wheat toast. No sooner had he begun to chew when his phone signaled an incoming text. He tapped the screen and stared at the image that flashed onto it. Setting down the sandwich, he picked up the phone and enlarged the image. Smiling back at him was the face of the model from the lining of the bridal trunk.

Gwen's message read, "Meet Irma Louise Kelly Jones, my great-great-great-grandmother."

***

"You've got to be kidding." Brent shifted the phone to his left shoulder while he wiped grease splatter from the stovetop.

"It shocked me too," Gwen replied. "Did you notice her surname?"

"Sure did. Isn't Jones the name of the Confederate prisoner who drew the smuggler's map?"

"Yes, Francis Xavier Jones. Do you suppose he had the picture sewn onto the trunk lining? And if so, how did my grandmother meet up with him?"

"Yeah, and something else just occurred to me. If your grandmother did marry Francis Jones, and John Smith was also Jones' descendent, that would make—"

"Don't say it." Gwen's voice shuddered through the speaker. "The thought that I might be any relation to that ... that horrible kidnapper ..."

Brent chuckled. " 'Nuff said."

"Thank you."

"So when are you coming home?"

"I'll know more after tomorrow's appointment."

"Hope it's not long. You're talking to a really lonely guy."

"Stay lonely until I get back. Promise?"

"Don't need to promise. I can't imagine life without you."

A brief silence, then a soft reply crept from the receiver. "That's the nicest thing anyone has ever said to me."

His tone matched hers. "It won't be the last."

3

Following breakfast the next morning, Gwen poured a second cup of coffee and leaned onto the kitchen table, head propped on the palm of her hand. The family photo album lay on the placemat with Irma Louise Kelly smiling up at her. Gwen frowned back. A further search of the album had yielded nothing more regarding her mysterious ancestor. If only there were a note or a caption to provide context. But no, the beguiling pose offered the only glimpse into the young woman's curious personality—which, by all appearances, was not a traditional one.

She sipped her coffee and reflected on the first time she saw that image. Hadn't it seemed vaguely familiar, even then? Gwen must have looked through the family album sometime in her youth, but any such memory was lost. She set down her cup and stared up at the ceiling. If the chest in the attic held no more clues, this would be the end of it. But if it did … She pushed back from the table, coffee forgotten. The only certainty was that the mystery wasn't going to be solved down here in the kitchen.

Back in the attic, Gwen stood over the heirloom chest, fingertips against her cheek. *Please let there be something more. Anything.* She dropped to her knees, opened the trunk, and pulled out the remaining photograph albums. After setting them onto the floorboards, she began to close the lid, then paused. Could there be something in the trunk other than the photo albums that might be helpful? She slipped her hand beneath her grandmother's needlepoint and swept it along the smooth bottom, then back again. At a back corner, her fingers bumped into something solid. She shifted the linen aside, uncovering three small books. Scooping them up, she held them to the light. Bindings split and peeling, their frayed leather covers bore the stenciled words *My Journal*. Beneath the titles were the numerals "1," "2," and "3" penned in once-black ink now purpled with age.

Gwen peered closer at the top journal. Inked into the cover above the numerals were the faint initials "ILK." *Irma Louise Kelly?* Her heart skipped a beat, and she clutched them to her chest. *Oh please, Lord, let it be her.*

The photo albums and open trunk forgotten, Gwen scurried down from the attic and laid the aged journals onto the kitchen table. She gazed at them, fingers tented to her lips. The questions that had flooded her mind that morning resurged. Would the diaries commend or condemn her enigmatic grandmother? Had she been part of a Civil War conspiracy, or innocently entangled in one? Unexpectedly, Gwen's heart warmed as Irma Louise Kelly transformed into more than a face on an ancient lithograph. She was *family*, a real person whose distant blood flowed through Gwen's own veins. Although she had yet to read a single word, her grandmother's memory blossomed, became more than a vague figure of family lore. So, just as a primitive camera had captured Grandmother Irma's image, these journals offered a record of her innermost thoughts, emotions important enough to be preserved. Gwen thought back to the photo album and smiled. The lithograph's enticing pose had accomplished its purpose in drawing her close. Regardless of what the books might reveal of her ancestor's Civil War sympathies, Gwen would be her advocate, her ally. Her friend. Why? Who knew? Maybe a rebellious gene that had traveled from grandmother to granddaughter through the family DNA. Or perhaps simply because, even over the ages, blood was thicker than … well, than pretty much anything.

***

Brent awoke from a shallow nap at his cell phone sounding off. He covered a yawn with one hand and groped on the end table with the other.

"Hey, Gwen."

"You've been sleeping."

He sighed. "How can you tell?"

"Women's intuition."

He rubbed his eyes. "Yeah, okay."

She giggled. "Besides, you yawned between 'Hey' and 'Gwen.'"

"I did?"

"Yup."

He grinned. "So much for women's intuition."

"Don't dismiss it too quickly, mister. I also know you had a rough day at the office."

"How did you know that?"

"I'll never tell."

"That's not fair."

"And it never will be."

He chuckled and stretched. "I suppose not."

Her voice softened. "It looks like I might be in Boston a little longer than I thought."

He sat up. "Why?"

"I still have the appointment at the law office tomorrow, and … I've come across more information on Grandmother Irma."

"Really?"

"I found her journals."

"That's great, but can't you bring them back to Marble Falls with you?"

Her impish smile lit up the phone line. "Why, are you still trying to find something to eat?"

He smiled. "Funny. No, I miss you, and I want you back even if I never eat again."

"I miss you too. But I still have to arrange Daddy's estate, and that may take longer than I originally thought. Plus, there may be more I can learn about Grandmother Irma in this house. It's just that … for some reason, she's become really important to me." She paused. "Please understand."

He allowed a none-too-subtle sigh to escape. "I get it."

"Thank you. I knew you would."

"Don't stay any longer than absolutely necessary though."

"I won't."

"Because I really am running short of groceries."

"Brent!"

He laughed and disconnected the call.

4

Gwen tucked her legs up and snuggled against a mohair afghan draped over the back of the family room sofa. The hiss of a gas-fueled flame against concrete logs in the fireplace danced as the Mormon Tabernacle Choir's rendition of *Be Still My Soul* serenaded her from her father's vintage stereo console. The house lay still except for the faint clatter of freezing rain gusting against the window beside the hearth. She closed her eyes and sensed a vague aroma of pipe tobacco—her father's Cherry Blend?—wafting through the room. Real, or nostalgia? It hardly mattered. Either way, the effect was so strong she half expected to open her eyes to him hunched in the doorway with his terry cloth bathrobe hanging open to a dingy T-shirt and striped pajama bottoms, hair mussed, eyes vacant. How he looked the last time she saw him. She blinked away the mental image and reached toward the end table for the first volume of her grandmother's diary.

She opened the book, wincing as the brittle spine crackled. Carefully, she smoothed the first page and Grandmother Irma's delicate handwriting saw light for the first time in who knew how long. She gently stroked the page with her fingertips, eyes misting as something deep inside her reached out to the last person who had touched this paper.

After allowing a moment for her heart to calm, Gwen began to read.

Sunday, July 29, 1860.

So, a journal is it? As though I have nothing better to do than sit and write of things I'd rather be doing. Of course, it isn't your fault, little book. Although you mean nothing by it, you're simply another attempt to chain me to the house.

***

The lazy charm of an 1860 Bostonian afternoon draped Mt. Vernon Street in a cloak of respectable lethargy. But for the occasional clopping of unhurried horses' hooves on weathered cobblestones, dignified silence reigned along the stately red-brick houses on Beacon Hill's South Slope. For over a century, the upper crust of Bostonian society dubbed the Brahmins had valued that tranquility above all, save family honor. Such sentiment did not hold true of Beacon Hill in its entirety, though, for lying over its northward crest was the South Slope's elder sibling, aptly the North Slope, and a stronger contrast between the two could scarcely be imagined. There, alleyways carved dark paths between dingy red-brick tenements of the seedy Charles River waterfront that had attracted British soldiers and sailors with its tawdry offerings before and during the Revolutionary War. After the Colonial victory, the battered legions of the King's finest disappeared over the Atlantic horizon, leaving a void now filled largely by freed and escaped slaves whose cause threatened the young country with yet another war. A war that would shake life on both sides of the Hill.

But our story picks up back on the South Slope, where upscale row houses shared the manicured streets with the few remaining free-standing mansions. It was in one of these dignified residences, designed by no one less than the preeminent Charles Bullfinch, that the Kelly family settled in 1846. Their patriarch, Byrne Patrick Kelly, had seeded his fortune in Fall River's textile mills and nurtured it through a series of ventures, some speculative, some pragmatic, but all profitable. So, he brought his wife Kate and their four-year-old daughter, Irma Louise, to a new life among Boston's elite.

It wasn't long before the serene neighborhood began to take notice of its *nouveau riche*, if for no other reason than the frequent clashes between the headstrong girl, precocious in childhood and nearly impossible in her teens, and her equally stalwart father. Irma was both the apple of and a stye in Byrne's eye, and more than once he'd been heard declaring that, although she filled his very life, she would likely also be the death of him.

Mercifully, the neighborhood had been spared disruption on this particular Sunday. The Kelly mansion was bathed in peaceful sunlight that filtered through lace-lined curtains covering a second-story bedroom window and cast a soft luminescence over a white canopy bed with a rose-colored coverlet folded at the foot, and silken floral wallpaper gracing the walls. Only the ticking pendulum of a glass-domed clock on the mahogany dresser broke an otherwise absolute stillness. Or better put, a deceptive stillness. For across the bedroom, a soundless but intense battle raged.

Seated before an ornate Victorian vanity, eighteen-year-old Irma Kelly glowered into an oval plate glass mirror, in combat with an errant brown curl invading her forehead. Despite multiple tactics levied against it, the maverick wisp resisted all attempts to be tamed, much like its mistress. Irma had finally reached the point of exasperation and was reaching for a pair of scissors, when—

"Irma Louise Kelly!" her father bellowed from downstairs.

Her shoulders slumped. *Oh, what is it now?* She forced a light tone and leaned toward the open bedroom door. "I'm here, Father."

Silence.

She heaved a sigh, frowned into the mirror at the victorious curl, then rose and stepped into the hallway.

Her father stood at the bottom of the staircase, arms folded across his barrel chest. "You have some explaining to do, young lady."

Irma blinked. "Whatever do you mean?"

"You know very well what I mean."

Eyes rounded in innocence, she cocked her head.

"My study," he said. Turning on a heel, he marched through a doorway to his right.

Rolling her eyes, she permitted herself a dramatic moment, then calmly descended the stairs. On the bottom landing, she paused to smooth her dress and steal a look into the hallway mirror. Tucked a strand of hair behind an ear. Picked a bit of lint from her shoulder. Suddenly, she leaned forward and lifted a fingertip to her cheek. Was that a blemish forming? *Oh, please—*

"Irma!"

She jumped. "Coming."

"So is Christmas, but I find myself wondering which of you will arrive first."

Pursing her lips, Irma stepped through the doorway to her father's inner sanctum and drew in a halting breath of the tobacco-tinged air. The spacious dimly lit study had witnessed many a terse conversation between father and daughter over the years, and this encounter held little promise for a calmer exchange. She clasped her hands at her waist. "You wished to speak with me?"

Her father regarded her with narrowed eyes, hands folded on a leather-lined blotter topping his walnut desk. Deafening silence was a favorite tactic, and his skill in executing it was flawless.

Taking advantage of the momentary silence, she surreptitiously sought out an anomaly in the pristine orderliness that ruled the study, her father, the family. Her life. A wayward speck of tobacco ash on the desktop, a fountain pen whose nib had gone unwiped, any abnormality might betray a lapse in his fixation for detail. And therefore an advantage.

On his desk, a mahogany-handled letter opener and matching magnifying glass topped the spotless blotter, aligned and perfectly centered between two neat stacks of papers that lacked any evidence they'd been read. An oil-fueled desk lamp to the left flickered a weak yellow flame from which a faint ribbon of black smoke dissipated as quickly as it cleared the rim of the glass canopy, as though not to draw undue attention to itself. To the right, the stem of a briar pipe protruded from a glass ashtray, its leather tobacco pouch lying to the side cocked slightly at an angle. A short stack of envelopes—what? She flashed back to the misaligned pouch. And smiled inwardly.

His deep voice reclaimed her attention. "I believe you to be aware of why I've summoned you."

"Honestly, Father, you have me at a disadvantage."

He leaned forward, unclasped his hands, and his fingertip began tapping the blotter.

She shifted her stance. *Oh, dear. He is genuinely upset.*

"You were at the negro house again."

"By whose word?"

"It doesn't matter by whose word. The fact is, you defied my instruction not to go there again."

"Did Gerald tell you this?"

"Do you deny it?" The tapping fingertip accelerated its tempo.

"Because if he did—"

He rose to his feet, arms stiffened against the blotter. "Do you *deny* it?"

She stepped back and abandoned all thought of the skewed tobacco pouch. "Father?"

The muscles at the corners of his cheeks twitched.

She dropped her gaze. "I do not deny it."

"Why?"

His question offered a legalistic feint. Why did she disobey him, or why did she go to the African Meeting House? But her quest for leverage faltered, since the answer to both questions was the same. "Because I must."

"You must."

"I see no difference between the negro and us except the color of our skins. And yet, in our arrogance, we have demeaned them to some kind of sub-species solely because we possess the power to tear them from their homeland, their people, and their families at the point of a musket and ship them into forced servitude under conditions worse than those we grant to dumb livestock." She looked up. "I would ask you the same question you asked me. Why? Under God, what gives us the right to shackle other human beings simply because they do not resemble us in appearance?"

"It is the law of the land."

Irma's jaw dropped. "The law?" she blurted. "Under Roman law it was legal to torture and murder Christians. You are a church elder, Father. Would you argue that such actions were justified simply because it was expedient to the state, that it was the law?"

Irma flinched when her father slapped the palm of his hand against the desktop. "You will not presume to lecture me on matters of the law!"

"But—"

"Nor will you disobey me again regarding the North Slope." He straightened, fingertips pressing into the blotter, gaze boring into hers. "There is more to it than you realize."

She locked gazes with him, eyes ablaze. "What more could there be?"

A sudden sheen of moisture in her father's averted eyes extinguished the fire in hers, and her frown evened. "Father?"

He exhaled. "My immediate concern does not pertain to the morality of slavery. Indeed, I applaud your passion. However, I am concerned for your safety." He paused. "You are a remarkably beautiful young woman."

Irma's cheeks warmed, and she dropped her gaze.

He continued. "The streets of the North Slope are dark, and there are scoundrels there who would force themselves upon you without a second thought."

She lifted her head. "I can take care of—"

"You *cannot* take care of yourself. Don't you see?" He closed his eyes, drew a deep breath, slowly released it. "I have no doubt you would prevail in a debate of logic with any ruffian." He opened his eyes and leaned forward. "But ruffians do not debate, and they care nothing for logic. They carry knives, and they prey on those they believe to be weaker than they. And they will deem a young woman in South Slope finery to be weak every single time."

Irma swallowed.

Her father's jaw tightened. "My greatest fear in life is to find my precious daughter's body bloodied and violated in a back alley because her stubbornness overcame her common sense."

Eyes wide, Irma stepped backward and folded her hands over her bodice.

Byrne lifted a hand. "I regret the harsh words, but I have come to believe that such language may be the only way to get through to you."

"Not all on the North Slope are vile, Father."

"They are not. But it takes only one, and the soil there is fertile."

She dipped her head.

Her father settled into his chair, signaling the discussion was coming to a close. "Still, I am not so naïve as to think this conversation will dissuade you from visiting the African Meeting House again. Therefore, I am willing to meet you halfway."

Irma looked up. *A concession? From Father?* "And halfway would be … ?"

"If you find yourself irresistibly drawn there again, I insist that you travel with a trustworthy escort."

"You mean Gerald."

"Gerald is as trustworthy as any."

"He does not share my ardor for the negro cause."

"But he loves you, and he will protect you regardless of the cause."

They regarded each other for several moments. Finally, she straightened her shoulders. "Very well, I accept your condition."

He lifted a brow. "You 'accept my condition'?"

Irma smiled. "With gratitude." She curtsied, smile broadening. "I love you, Father."

She pivoted and flitted into the hallway, pausing at the foot of the stairs long enough to catch a heavy sigh floating through the study doorway, followed by a faint, "If you only knew how much I love you, my daughter."

She swallowed past a lump and slowly climbed the stairs.

Back in her bedroom, she sat again before the mirror, chin propped on her palms, ignoring the rebellious curl. At the side of her vanity, a small book rested on a sheet of wrapping paper, its arresting twine dangling over the edge. An ornately gilded fountain pen and glass jar of ink lay next to it. A gift from Gerald, one that certainly carried her father's blessing. She sighed glumly. *A diary. How cliché.*

She lifted the journal. Turned it over and inspected it. Began to set it down, then paused. A coy smile curved her lips. She opened the book and reached for the pen.

They want me to write? Very well, that is exactly what I'll do.

Irma uncapped the inkwell, dipped in the pen, then touched its nib to the page.

Sunday, July 29, 1860.
So, a journal is it? ...

***

Gwen smiled. *I love her already.* She carefully flipped through several more pages, some filled with text, others revealing only a few lines. She looked at the other two volumes sitting on the end table. What kind of story would they tell? A yawn swelled her chest as the grandfather clock in the hallway toned eleven o'clock. She folded her hands over the diary, rested her head onto a throw pillow, closed her eyes and imagined herself tucked in Brent's strong arms. His head nods, his warm brown eyes focused patiently on her as she excitedly told him about her grandmother. He would listen intently, maybe have some insightful thoughts, but most of all, he would share in her excitement. His loving face filling her mind, she drifted off.

5

At 9:30 the following morning, Gwen pulled into a vacant parking spot across from the office building of the Kelly family's lawyer. Stepping out of the car, she zipped her coat up to her chin and pulled her knit hat down over her ears. She squinted up to the third story where the roof of the turreted brown-brick edifice faded into a snow-laden haze. A stiff breeze tunneled down High Street, prickling her cheeks and forehead with tiny ice crystals. Shoulders hunched and hands jammed into her coat pockets, she hurried across the street and into the warmth of the of the historic professional building's foyer. A directory listed the office of *Henry Forbson, Attorney at Law* on the first floor. She loosened her coat as she walked through an attractively decorated atrium and along modern fluorescent-lit hallways. When she reached his office suite, she pulled in a deep breath, opened the door, and entered.

The small waiting room was a conservative classic, unlike the modern appearance of the outer hallways. She walked up to the receptionist's desk and gave her name. The legal assistant—Mona Stillwell, according to the enameled nameplate on her desk—offered her something from the coffee bar. Gwen politely declined, her stomach not quite settled, and eased herself onto the settee. She scanned an array of magazines on the low glass-topped coffee table centered in the seating area, finally selecting a past issue of *New England Home.*

A few pages later, the magazine lay on her lap, forgotten, as her thoughts circled around conversations with her father that she should have had. The click of a doorknob pulled her back to the present. A short, dark-haired woman entered from the hallway. She stopped short at the sight of Gwen, then nodded at Mona and took a seat across the room, focusing her attention on the newscast playing quietly on a flat-screen TV mounted to the wall.

"Ms. Kelly?" A thin, middle-aged, balding man in a pinstriped gray suit walked out from an inner doorway. His gaze flicked momentarily to the dark-haired woman, then immediately back to Gwen. "I'm Henry Forbson." He extended his hand. Thin, only an inch or two taller than she, and slightly stooped, he regarded her with piercing dark eyes.

Gwen laid aside the magazine, rose, and shook hands with him. He motioned toward the inner doorway. "Please come this way."

She followed the attorney into a large office lined with bookcases and glass-doored cabinets topped with assorted memorabilia. An array of marksmanship trophies on a nearby cabinet seemed rather odd for someone who seemed so formal.

He closed the door, rounded a massive executive desk, and gestured toward an overstuffed chair. "Please sit down."

"Thank you." She sat on the edge of the chair, purse clutched on her lap.

The lawyer took a seat in a high-backed leather chair and folded his hands on the desk. "I'm sure you're anxious to settle this ... unfortunate event."

She nodded.

He cleared his throat. "But of course you are." He hesitated, then dropped his gaze and began absently shuffling the papers in the folder.

Gwen shifted her weight. "Mr. Forbson, isn't a will normally mailed to the beneficiaries? Why the formality?"

His fingers stilled, and he looked up. "I knew your father well, Ms. Kelly. We were members of the same social clubs and engaged in pistol competitions together. My wife and I shared many dinners with your parents before ... " His jaw twitched.

"Before my mother died. Thank you for your sensitivity."

He nodded. "I asked you here because there is a codicil attached to your father's will. One I had no part in preparing."

"A codicil?"

He lifted a document from his desk and offered it to her. "Perhaps you should read it."

Gwen accepted the paper. After a moment, she leaned against the back of the chair and looked up, shocked. "Are you telling me … I have a *brother*?"

He shook his head. "No, your father is telling you that. I had no knowledge of any offspring other than yourself."

"But how? Why didn't I know?"

"I'm afraid I haven't any way of knowing. In any event, your father intends for your brother to receive an equal share of his estate."

Gwen stared at the desktop, voice hollow. "The estate is the least of my concerns. I have a brother … " she reread the document, "named Simon Hardy."

"Apparently."

"How can I find him?"

He shook his head with a slight shrug.

***

"What?" Brent pushed back from the kitchen table and pressed the cell phone to his ear.

"You heard right. His name is Simon Hardy." She paused. "And I haven't a clue where he is."

"Your lawyer had no contact information for him?"

"No, he was as surprised as I was."

"Well … " Brent hesitated.

"Well what?"

"Does it strike you as odd that your brother has a different surname than you do? Why isn't he Simon Kelly?"

Gwen's voice crept quietly through the receiver. "What are you saying?"

Brent measured his words. "Is it possible your mother might not have known about him?"

"Brent!"

"Hold on a minute. Please don't shoot the messenger. What's the date on the codicil?"

"January 14, 2004."

"Was that before or after—"

Gwen's voice quavered. "It was after Mother's death."

"I'm sorry, Sweetheart."

"Oh, how *could* he have?"

"Let's not rush to judgement. How much do you know about your father's life before he married your mom?"

"Not a lot. He grew up in New Hampshire, went to the Naval Academy, then spent six years on active duty. He was on aircraft carriers, I think. Or maybe submarines."

Brent chuckled. "Kind of a big difference there."

"He never really talked about it, Brent."

"Sorry, bad time to joke. When did he meet your mom?"

"He left the military in 1987 and hired on with a financial management firm in Boston. That's where he met Mother. She managed a team of actuaries."

"Wow. Brainy lady."

"She was. Anyway, they got married the next year."

"So, he could have met someone while he was in the Navy, well before he met your mom."

"I suppose." She paused. "I wonder if Simon even knows about this."

"Good question."

"I have lots of good questions, just no answers. I don't even know where to start."

"Codicils go through the same legal process as the basic will, so there had to be witnesses."

"I saw that, but I didn't recognize any of the names ... except maybe one."

"Who?"

"Teresa Hardy. Do you think it's a coincidence that she has the same surname as my brother?"

"I'm not big on coincidences. Why don't you scan the codicil and email it to me? I'll see what I can find out. You're busy enough handling the estate."

"Which will probably get tied up in probate if I can't find Simon." She sighed. "I was so hoping this would be simple, and that I could close the estate quickly."

"Maybe you still can. Let's take it one step at a time."

"Thanks, Brent. You're the best."

"Anything to get you back home."

-6-

That evening, Gwen sat in a rose-colored terry cloth bathrobe, absently combing through her shower-damp hair. She had emailed a copy of the codicil to Brent that afternoon, and he signed off with a sentiment that brightened her eyes and warmed her cheeks. Could this be the same man whose harsh words had heated those cheeks with anger when they first met at Margie's antique shop only two months ago? Her mind raced through the rollercoaster of emotions she went through that autumn. After feeling so alone in the world, she had discovered so many unexpected blessings—love and friendship, an awakened faith, and hope for the future. A sudden urge to forget the whole legal mess, throw together her suitcase, and drive back to Marble Falls nearly took her breath away, and she lowered the comb to the vanity. But Medford held family obligations that could not be ignored.

On the vanity, her father's will and her grandmother's diary pulled her into an emotional tug-of-war between present and past. She looked at the legal document, then the old journal. Her gaze lingered. Nothing could be done about the codicil until tomorrow. But the diary? She picked up the aged book.

Leaving her comb on the table and her hair to finish air drying, Gwen rose and crossed over to the bed. Flicking on the bedside lamp, she stretched out on the quilted bedspread and opened to the next page. A few lines into the entry, she widened her eyes, sat up, and pulled the lamp closer.

Thursday, August 2, 1860.

Of all things! What could Father be thinking? An excursion to Maine, the middle of nowhere? And where on earth is Marble Falls?

***

Irma sulked while her father laid out upcoming travel plans that would take his family—take *her*—into the unknown wilds of the northland. Finally, he paused and eyed her. "Will you stop grousing? You may find that you like Maine."

"What's to like? It's no different than Massachusetts other than being colder, if that's possible." Irma dropped onto a chair, arms crossed, legs stiffened in front of her.

Her father sighed. "Talk to her, would you, Kate?" He strode from the dining room, muttering something about if they'd only had a son.

Her mother looked up from her needlepoint. "Hardly a ladylike pose, Irma."

Irma broke an impish smile. "I suppose not. It was more for effect than decorum."

"I'm sure it was, but the object of the effect has left the room." She lowered her craft. "Please comport yourself."

Her daughter straightened, drew her knees together, and clasped her hands on her lap. "Really, though, Mother. Maine?"

"You know how your father loves fishing."

Irma rolled her eyes. "Ugh!"

Kate responded with a gentle smile. "He has an opportunity to acquire some land in the Marble Falls region. I understand it is a very beautiful area." She cocked her head. "Perhaps you could give it a chance?"

Irma huffed. "Very well. I promise I won't complain aloud."

"That is not what I asked."

"But, Maine? Fishing?"

"Indeed, Maine and fishing. Do it for your father. Heaven knows he does everything imaginable for you."

Irma hunched a defeated shrug. "Very well, I promise to give Maine a chance. I can't promise the same about fishing though."

Kate nodded, smile undiminished. "Fair enough." She went back to her needlepoint, seemingly oblivious of another heavy sigh from her daughter.

***

... and so we leave tomorrow. Marble Falls won't be Boston, but perhaps if Mother is right, it won't be too bad either. We shall see.

Gwen lowered the journal. Here was the first connection between her family and Marble Falls. Would it lead to Irma's provocative lithograph taken there years later? The digital clock flipped silently to the midnight hour, and she set the journal aside. She crawled beneath the bedcovers and turned off the lamp.

Fragmented dreams and snippets of disparate conversations looped through her mind while she tossed and turned. The diary, the codicil, finally the weighty anchor her father's estate had tethered to her mind and emotions. Casting a weary glance at the alarm clock at 2:45 a.m., she threw off the covers and padded to the window, where she hugged her waist and stared into silver-blue moonlight glimmering over shallow crests of snow covering the backyard. She touched fingertips to the frost-laced glass. The house was as cold and lifeless as ever. The restlessness that had pushed her away to college, and ultimately to Marble Falls, renewed itself, and she ached for the moment she would see this house in her rearview mirror for the final time. She turned and trudged back to bed, exhausted, but bereft of sleep.

The following morning passed in glum lethargy while she made phone calls to the funeral home, the veteran's cemetery, and her father's creditors. The afternoon was consumed in researching prospective real estate agents and estate sale brokers, finally culminating with an overdue trip to the grocery store. Despite a renewed pantry, dinnertime found her lacking the energy to prepare anything more than tea and toast. Eight o'clock heralded in her final yawn, and she plodded back upstairs.

Lost in emptiness, she undressed, stumbled into bed, and stared at her cell phone lying on the bedside stand. Maybe one more call would put her mind at rest.

7

Brent stretched out on the sofa, fingers laced behind his head, legs propped up on the far arm rest. Shadows danced across the floor from a hardwood fire that crackled, snapped, and sizzled bubbles of sap in the stone fireplace, now framed with pine garland and holly. He closed his eyes and imagined Gwen at his side, her petite frame curled against him, hazel eyes sparkling up at him, wavy blond hair tickling his chin when he leaned over to kiss her. Sighing, he surveyed Gwen's thoughtful effort to bring cheer into the house, reflecting on how her suggestion to decorate for Christmas had caught him off guard.

"I hadn't really thought about it."

"It's after Thanksgiving. How could you not think about decorating for Christmas?"

"I haven't done much decorating since … well, since Janet died."

"Oh, Brent, I'm so sorry. How insensitive of me."

"No, it's fine. I think the decorations are in the guest room closet."

"Do you mind if I look?"

"Not at all."

He'd followed her into the guest room, but stood back while she rummaged through the stuffed closet. An hour later, a white-laced linen runner hand-embroidered with holly and red berries draped the fireplace mantle under two bayberry-scented candles, joining a few other seasonal reminders that adorned the room. She'd left for the evening with a promise to finish the next day. Then came the lawyer's phone call and her sudden departure for Boston.

His gaze settled on two cardboard boxes against the wall. One held Christmas tree ornaments, among them a double-hearted brass frame with his and Janet's first-anniversary photos mounted inside. His lips twitched. It might be a good idea to find another home for it before Gwen came across it.

As he reached for his mug of coffee on the end table, his cell phone's ringtone announced she'd also been thinking of him.

"Hi, Gwen."

"I called to say goodnight."

"I'm glad you did."

She paused. "What's wrong?"

"Nothing."

"You sound down."

He tried to lighten his tone. "I'd be better if you were here."

"It's not that, though, is it?"

Brent drew a steady breath. "I'm fine, really. Mellowing out by the fire."

"If you say so."

"So, any more revelations from your grandmother's diary?"

"Actually, yes. I came across the first reference to Marble Falls."

"Really?"

"August of 1860. Apparently her father was considering buying some land there."

"Did it say where exactly?"

"Not yet—Brent, what is it? Something's not right. I can tell."

He closed his eyes. "I was looking at the Christmas decorations you placed over the fireplace. They haven't been out of the closet in four years, and seeing them again got me thinking."

"I'm sorry. I shouldn't have pushed you to decorate. They probably hold difficult memories for you."

"They do, but it's not that."

"What then?"

A huskiness overtook his voice. "I never thought I would love anyone again as deeply as I loved Janet."

Her voice took on a hint of uncertainty. "I see."

"I don't think you do. The fact is, I'm sitting here realizing that I've never ached for a woman as much as I ache for you right now."

Silence.

"Gwen?"

A tender smile warmed her tone. "Hush. I'm wrapping my heart around what you just said. Don't interrupt."

He chuckled. "Seriously, I'm glad you put the decorations back up. This will be a great Christmas."

"I'll do everything I can to make it so."

"So will I. Goodnight."

***

With a smile, Gwen disconnected the call, turned off the lamp, and snuggled between flannel sheets beneath her quilted bedspread. Brent's loving words colored the present, while Grandmother Irma's echoed from the past. She watched through weary eyes as the alarm clock flipped over minute to minute.

At 11:30 p.m., she surrendered to her restless mind and groped for the lamp switch. She fluffed her pillow, propped it up against the headboard, and reached for Grandmother Irma's diary.

Wednesday, August 15, 1860.

Well, here I am in Marble Falls. We followed the Sandy River nearly the entire carriage ride, and it was lovely. The gentle rushing of water over rocks and boulders almost lulled me to sleep, but I didn't want to miss an inch of its beauty. Still, the remoteness left me strangely unsettled. I became hopeful when we passed through the quaint town of Farmington, less so with tiny Phillips. But when the carriage stopped in Marble Falls, I wondered how the driver even knew we had arrived. Some farms, a sawmill or two, a few homesteads scattered about. Father can't be serious about buying land here. I would starve for civilization.

8

Irma accepted the carriage driver's hand and stepped down onto the dirt roadway. Her first act upon touching Marble Falls soil was to swat a mosquito. A large mosquito. She grimaced at the residue left on her palm and brushed the afternoon's dust coating her dark gray dress, taking care of two problems at once. After stretching a nagging ache out of the small of her back, she fluffed her skirts and looked past the team of horses.

Her mother, a vision of freshness, stood a pace behind her father's shoulder while he conversed with a stranger. Her mother listened quietly, a gentle smile gracing her lips, her skirt showing scarcely a wrinkle. Irma frowned as she scratched at the mosquito bite on her neck. *How does she* do *that?*

Her father introduced his wife to the stranger, who tipped his hat. Her mother dipped a gentle curtsy. When her father turned and beckoned Irma to join them, she lifted the hem of her skirt and stepped forward, striving to mimic her mother's finesse.

"Irma, this is Mr. Abner Toothaker. He is the gentleman we came to see."

Abner nodded. "Miss Kelly." Irma dipped an unsteady curtsy, ankles wobbling on the uneven turf.

Byrne continued. "He has offered to put us up for the night, as there are no suitable accommodations this side of Phillips."

"Can we not return to Phillips then?" Irma asked.

Her mother glanced sharply at her. "Irma!"

Abner chuckled. "No offense taken, Mrs. Kelly. My eldest daughter, Mary Jane, grows equally longin' whenever Phillips—surely any place but Marble Falls—is mentioned."

Kate flashed him a grateful smile.

He turned toward Irma. "Problem is, Miss Kelly, Phillips is over an hour away. They've but two hotels, which fill up quickly this time o' the year."

Irma's cheeks warmed. "Of course, sir. I sincerely apologize. I did not mean to imply your offer of hospitality was in any way lacking."

She glanced toward her mother, who acknowledged the recovery with a thin smile.

Abner continued. "We built a cabin behind the house for my wife's parents, who'll move here after summer season. Ye're are welcomed to stay as long as ye like. However, I'll understand if ye choose to seek more elegant accommodations elsewhere."

Byrne lifted a hand. "Your offer is more than kind. We won't be in Marble Falls for more than a day or two. I'll be pleased to pay a fair price for our stay."

"I'll be acceptin' no payment. Ye're our guests."

"Very well, thank you again." The men shook hands. "Let us unload our baggage. Then I'd like to see this tract of land before night falls." He turned toward his wife. "You don't mind settling us in, do you Kate?"

"Not at all."

Abner bowed to the women and led Byrne toward a stable next to the house. "The land's not far from here. Have ye heard of Quimby Lake?"

***

From the cabin door, Irma watched the cart carrying her father and Abner Toothaker disappear around a curve in the road. Frowning and looking skyward, she waved off another mosquito buzzing incessantly around her head. *Is there no end to these pests?*

Her mother's voice interrupted the skirmish. "Irma, you haven't finished unpacking."

"Coming." She turned, then drew up at the sight of a young woman around her age standing under a fir tree a short distance away. Fair-skinned with wavy brown hair cascading over narrow shoulders, she wore a plain brown homespun dress and matching bonnet. She stared at Irma, hands pressed to the tree trunk.

Irma cocked her head with a smile. "Hello."

The young woman shifted her weight, then took a tentative step forward. "Ye must be Miss Kelly?"

Irma laughed. "I much prefer 'Irma' to 'Miss Kelly'."

The woman returned a cautious smile and relaxed her stance.

Irma stepped forward. "Am I correct in assuming you are Mary Jane?"

"How d'ye know my name?"

"Your father mentioned you." Irma extended her hand. Mary Jane grasped it firmly, and Irma's eyebrows arched. "Oh, my. You have quite a grip."

Mary Jane froze, cheeks flushing. She quickly released Irma's hand with a backward step. "I'm sorry. I didn't mean to—"

Irma laughed again. "I meant nothing by it. In fact, I admire you for it."

"Ye do?"

"Very much so. A strong handshake means a strong constitution." She closed the gap between them and reclaimed Mary Jane's hand. "Unfortunately, such constitutions are rare among women in Boston."

Mary Jane's eyes glazed over. "Boston! Oh, please tell me of Boston."

"What would you like to know?"

"Everything. What be the fashions? What plays at the theater?" She glanced toward the main house and lowered her voice. "Are all the men as handsome as I imagine 'em ta be?"

"Well, I suppose there is much to tell—"

"Irma?"

She jumped at the sound of her mother's voice behind her and turned. "Mother, this is Mary Jane. You recall Mr. Toothaker speaking of her?"

Her mother smiled. "Hello, Mary Jane."

Mary Jane dipped her head and attempted a curtsy. "Good day, Mrs. Kelly."

Irma and her mother briefly met gazes, eyes twinkling. Kate stepped past her daughter, took Mary Jane by the shoulders, and gave her a gentle hug. Mary Jane's eyes widened over the elder woman's shoulder.

Irma giggled. "Mary Jane, you simply must relax. We're quite ordinary."

Kate released her. "We are indeed. Please allow me to thank you for hosting our visit."

Mary Jane blushed. "We've not much chance ta meet fine people here in Marble Falls."

"I'm sure there are many fine people in Marble Falls."

"O' course. I meant … " She glanced at Kate's billowing skirts, as her hands brushed the folds of her own coarse housedress. "We're plain folk."

Irma spoke up. "From what I've observed, plain folk have much to commend them."

A smile tickled Kate's lips. "Well spoken, Irma. Perhaps there is hope for you yet."

Irma frowned, but her mother turned back to Mary Jane. "Why don't you two get acquainted? I'll finish unpacking."

"Oh, would you, Mother? Thank you." Irma took her new friend by the arm. "How much of Marble Falls can you show me before nightfall?"

It was Mary Jane's turn to laugh. "All of it, probably twice over. An' with time ta spare."

Irma giggled, and they walked off arm in arm.

***

I made a true friend that day. One of my very few. Perhaps Marble Falls holds more of value than a few fish in Father's creel.

Gwen closed the journal and replaced it on the bedside stand. Yawning, she reached for the light switch. As she tufted her pillow, Brent's smiling face loomed in her mind. But it was a young Grandmother Irma's mental visage that accompanied her into a dreamful sleep.

*

Late-afternoon shadows crept up the walls of wooden buildings clustered behind a sturdy rail fence. To the right nestled a white farmhouse, modest in decor, exuding an alluring coziness as it soaked in the remaining rays of sunlight filtering through tall trees. A lazy wisp of smoke curled from the stone chimney into the cooling air. Apple trees, heavy laden with summer fruit, fronted the grounds nearest the road, and beyond the house, a tack room shared space with an array of storage sheds clustered around a large barn. Somewhere, a horse neighed, startling a flurry of sparrows into the refuge of neighboring trees.

31

Across the twin-rutted dirt road, her fingertips pressed into the rough bark of an oak tree, and her hungry eyes devoured the pastoral setting of a bygone era. She breathed in the pleasing aroma of baking bread, the headiness of fresh-mown hay, and the earthiness of natural fertilizer. Her ears struggled to catch words murmured by translucent figures huddled near the homestead.

The group separated, two women walking toward the house followed by the carriage, two men toward the stable.

*

Gwen rolled onto her side and hugged her pillow.
The vision wavered, then dissolved.

9

Activity in the Marble Falls Town Office was nearly at a standstill, most of its workers plying the ski slopes of Saddleback Mountain or on snowmobile trails that crisscrossed The Mountain's forested landscape. In the breakroom, the ambulance crew of the Franklin Emergency Medical Services played cards near a portable radio from which Buck Owens confided that Santa Claus looked a lot like his daddy. Only one person in the room bent hard at work in front of a computer. Or tried to.

Brent leaned back from the monitor and took in the radio through the corner of his eye. *Seriously? This is the best you can do?* Then he permitted himself a grudging smile. Okay, it was a cute song. Still …

He glanced up as Chief Lawson's voice suddenly boomed from the doorway. "You still here, Newcomb?"

"Apparently so, Chief."

"Don't get funny."

He grinned. "Sorry, sir."

"What're you doin'?"

"A little research."

The chief grunted. "Finish up and get some rest. The church folk have their Walk to Bethlehem tomorrow, and I don't want anybody gettin' run down by a tourist who don't know how to snowmobile."

Brent laughed. "C'mon, Chief. That's *never* happened."

"Always a first time." The chief stuffed his hat onto his head and stepped back into the hallway.

Still chuckling, Brent jotted a final note on his notepad and logged off the computer. An hour searching for leads on Gwen's brother had produced a nugget or two, but not much more. He checked the clock. She would have made the final arrangements for the funeral by now.

Not being there for her was galling, but it was the worst possible season for taking time off. He reached for his coat and hat. Maybe a call to Medford after dinner would help his mood.

***

Gwen settled onto the family room sofa with a cup of hot chocolate and reflected on the somber day. It had begun with a call from the funeral home informing her that everything was in order for tomorrow's ceremony. The news, although expected, shortened her breath.

"Are you there, Ms. Kelly?"

"Yes, I'm sorry. Everything is still so … so …"

"We completely understand. We'll take care of the details. Please don't worry."

"Thank you."

"We'll see you at six o'clock then?"

Had she replied? All she could think of was the stark mental image of her father's casket sitting cold and lonely in an undertaker's storage room.

The remainder of the morning had passed with vague memories of sifting through her father's papers. At lunchtime, the oppressive atmosphere became too much to bear, so she threw on her coat and drove to CambridgeSide mall, a favorite haunt during her teenage years. She walked the floors, barely noticing the displays and the crowds, stopping midafternoon for a plastic plateful of fast-food Chinese. As she was walking toward the exit, a modest black dress in a festive window display came into view. She slowed her pace as it occurred to her that she owned nothing suitable for tomorrow's funeral. The enticement of a new outfit, bolstered by a sign announcing a sale of 60% off, lured her through the door.

Fifteen minutes later, clutching the shopping bag under an arm, Gwen left the store. Although she'd done serious damage to her budget, sometimes a girl had to do what a girl had to do.

She just got in the house when her phone sounded Brent's ringtone. Dropping the bag on the dining room table, she answered.

"Hi, there."

"Hey, kiddo."

"Kiddo? I'm twenty-six. I'm not *that* much younger than you are."

"In 'dog years' I have you by thirty-five."

"Really? Hmm, so why am I hanging around such an old geezer?"

34

"Hey!"

Gwen giggled. "That'll teach you."

"It sure will." Brent chuckled. "So, have you uncovered any more information on your Grandmother Irma?"

"A little. She made a friend on her first trip to Maine. A Mary Jane Toothaker. Her father's name was Abner."

"Abner Toothaker? He's a well-known figure in Marble Falls' history."

"I also found out where the land was that Irma's father purchased. Are you ready for this? It was near Quimby Pond."

"Interesting."

Gwen shifted the phone to her other ear. "What about you? Have you found the notary or the witnesses from Daddy's codicil?"

"Not much luck there, I'm afraid. The notary apparently worked at a bank in Burlington, Vermont until about five years ago when she retired. The bank manager said she passed away the same year. Cancer."

"Oh, what a shame. But why would Daddy travel all the way to Burlington to have his will amended?"

"Good question. One of the witnesses was a junior loan officer who left the bank in 2012. The manager had no idea where he went."

"That's not much help."

"No, but I'll keep looking. The other witness is a little more interesting."

"How so?"

"She wasn't associated with the bank. I don't know why she happened to be there or why she witnessed the signing."

"Can you find her?"

"I'll try."

"Thanks, Brent. You're great."

"Even for an old geezer?"

She giggled. "Only if you're a dog. And I'm pretty sure you aren't."

They ended the call, and Gwen went upstairs. She quickly removed the sales tags and hung up the dress, envisioning how well that cute pair of heels on display near the fitting room would match. Maybe they were worth another look-over tomorrow morning.

When she at last climbed into bed, the journal whispered to her from the nightstand. But it was late, and she needed rest, so she turned off the lamp and tucked herself under the covers. But sleep proved elusive. She tossed and turned, her grandmother's written words looping through her mind. Finally, she sat up and turned on the lamp. Pulling the diary onto her palm, she opened to her bookmark and began to read.

-10-

Friday, August 17, 1860.
Where has the time gone? Have we truly been in Marble Falls two whole days? There is so much beauty, and Mary Jane has become such a dear friend. I find myself asking her as many questions about Marble Falls as she asks me about Boston. Well, perhaps not quite so many, but almost so. The village has assumed a surprising quaintness. Who knew the wilderness could hold such allure?

***

Irma stretched out on the small wooden-framed bed, tipped the rear of the fountain pen to her chin, and stared into the darkness beyond the halo of her bedside candle. The cabin lay mostly quiet, only her father's muffled snores disturbing the night. An owl hooted outside, and a light rustling of the straw-tick mattress against the far wall suggested her mother was not yet asleep.

Irma laid the pen onto the journal. "Mother?"

"Hush, dear. You'll awaken your father."

Irma returned a muffled giggle. "Father could sleep through a hurricane."

Her mother's tone carried a smile. "Very well then. What is it?"

"Must we leave Marble Falls tomorrow?"

"Why do you ask?"

"Well, the carriage ride back to Farmington is a long one. I thought that after coming all this way, we might tarry a while longer."

"Am I speaking with the same daughter who dragged her feet here the entire way from Boston?"

Irma smiled. "Perhaps my feet require more time to recover."

Her mother laughed softly, and the snoring sputtered. The bed creaked, and a louder wheezing soon resumed. Her mother continued in a whisper. "I assume this is about Mary Jane. You're quite taken with her, aren't you?"

"Very much so. She's like the sister I never had." Irma gasped. "Oh, Mother. That was horribly insensitive of me."

The response was barely audible. "It's all right, dear. It was a long time ago."

"But time doesn't heal all wounds, especially losing a child. Please forgive me." Irma sniffled. "I so wish I didn't blurt things out like I do."

"But if you didn't, you wouldn't be our Irma, would you?" The smile had returned to her mother's voice.

Irma's cheek warmed. "I suppose not."

"Mary Jane is a lovely girl. I'm glad you've found a friend."

"A friend I hate to leave so quickly."

"We can't stay here indefinitely."

Irma rolled onto her side. "I know." She sighed. "It doesn't seem fair."

"Your father has decided to purchase the land at Quimby Lake. That should bring us back to Marble Falls on occasion."

"Bring *him* back, more likely," Irma grumped. "He won't want me tagging along on his fishing trips."

"He might if you were to show interest."

Irma perked up at the thought. "Do you think?" Then the idea of handling a squirming fish puckered her lips. "Oh, dear. I simply don't understand the attraction."

"You're an adventuresome girl, Irma. Think of the challenge of probing an underwater world and luring one of its inhabitants into your own. Through the ages, such conquests have meant life or death for men and their families. Although such means are not necessary to sustain us today, perhaps your father is responding to a primitive urge to provide for his family outside the confines of his executive boardroom."

"I've never thought of it like that."

"And, of course, there is simply the sport of it. I've seen your father release more fish than he kept."

Irma knit her brow. "You've been fishing with Father?"

"In days past. Not as an active participant, but as an appreciative and supporting wife." Her mother's voice lowered. "I couldn't stand to touch one of the slimy things either."

Irma clapped a hand over her mouth to suppress a laugh. Her father snorted, and the bed creaked again. The women quieted until his breathing evened.

"I suppose I could try," Irma said. "It might give Father and me a less controversial topic for discussion than the ones we normally find."

"That would be a victory, wouldn't it?" Her mother reached across the narrow gap between their beds, and Irma squeezed her hand.

"I love you, Mother."

"And I you. Now go to sleep. In the morning, we'll see how Father responds to the idea of lingering a day or two."

"Goodnight." Irma blew out the candle, and her thoughts soon dissolved into dreams.

11

Brent disconnected the phone call and scraped fingernails through his hair in frustration. The manager of the Burlington bank had been polite, even apologetic, but totally unhelpful. No, she had no idea who the mysterious signatory was on the codicil, and, with the notary now deceased, she was afraid there would be little chance of tracking her down.

He reviewed his notes. *So, Teresa Hardy, are you Simon's mother? If so, why was he included in the will, but not you?*

His phone beeped, and he absently reached for it, still frowning.

"Brent Newcomb here."

"My goodness, how formal." Gwen giggled.

Brent laughed. "Sorry, I was concentrating on something else. Your ringtone didn't even register."

"Oh dear, concentrating on something other than me?" A teasing sigh crept through the receiver. "Out of sight, out of mind."

"You're never out of mind."

"Really? Tell me more."

He grinned. "Not over the phone."

"Brent!"

"I can tell you that I just got off a call to the bank in Burlington. Dead end."

Her tone dropped. "So, is that the end of it?"

"No, I have a couple of other things to check out. I'll keep at it."

"Thank you." She paused. "I've been reading more of Grandmother Irma's diary."

"Anything enlightening?"

"Yes, with every page. I so wish I could have met her."

"Have you found anything that sheds light on how her lithograph ended up stitched into the lining of that trunk?"

"Not yet, but her association with Marble Falls is becoming clearer. That's a step closer."

"I'm sure you'll figure it out."

"I hope so. But now I'm just reveling in her story. She was so … I don't know … like me in some ways."

"How so?"

"Do you remember me telling you about going to the pistol range with Daddy in order to be close to him? To show interest in something he loved to do?"

"Yes."

"Grandma Irma was in the same situation with her father, but his hobby was fishing."

"I like him already."

Gwen laughed. "I thought you might. Anyway, she also tried to draw closer to him by adopting a sport he loved. Curious how she thought the same way I did."

"Then I like her already too."

Gwen smiled. "I miss you."

"Not nearly as much as I miss you. I have a special reunion in mind for when you return."

"Oh, you do? Should I arrange for an escort to protect my honor?"

Brent laughed. "Wow, you *have* become steeped in the Victorian Age, haven't you? Don't worry, your honor is safe with me."

Her voice softened. "I know it is. I look forward to the day when an escort would no longer be needed."

"That day may not be far off."

Gwen swallowed and closed her eyes. *Oh Lord, what did I do to deserve such a man?*

"Come home soon."

"As soon as possible."

"Good. I'm waiting, but not patiently."

***

Gwen stretched out under the feather comforter and lost herself in a blank stare at the plaster texturing on the bedroom ceiling. Her fingertip brushed over the phone's screen, still warm from her call to Brent. She smiled, cozying into the thought of being enveloped in his arms, loved, protected. The power he exuded one would expect of a former Marine, perhaps, but restrained by a gentleness that melted her heart. She turned her head and reached for the diary on the end table, running her fingers softly along the binding. *So, Grandmother, when and whom did you love? You've written little of Gerald so far. Will there be more? And if you ended up with Francis Jones, how did that happen?* She laid her head back and closed her eyes. *And were either Gerald or Francis as wonderful as Brent?*

After a moment, she refocused on the journal. So much more to learn.

Tuesday, August 21, 1860.

Although it's difficult to write as the train car weaves and clatters so, I must record my thoughts while they are fresh. It was such a marvelous visit to Marble Falls! I am so glad Father agreed to delay our return to Boston. If he hadn't, how would I have learned what I did?

***

Irma descended the path to the shore of Marble Lake, arm in arm with Mary Jane. "Are you sure you won't get into trouble?"

Mary Jane shook her head. "I finished my morning chores quick so I'd have time to spend with ye."

"I'm so glad you did. This trip would have been unbearable if I hadn't met you."

"Do ye mean little backwoods Marble Falls would have been unbearable?"

Irma turned and blinked. "Of course I didn't. I meant—"

Mary Jane burst out laughing. "I'm kiddin'."

Irma leaned into her friend. "You have learned how to tease me, haven't you?"

"Well, t'wasn't difficult, ye know."

Irma halted and stared at her. "What do you mean by that?"

Mary Jane laughed again. "See?"

Irma broke into a giggle. "Very well, point taken."

They reached the end of the path and settled onto a fallen log by the lakeshore. The waters spread before them like an azure carpet, its wavelets glistening with dancing points of late-afternoon sunlight. "How heavenly," murmured Irma.

"I never tire o' the lake, the mountain," Mary Jane said. "Despite bein' so far from everythin'."

"It's beautiful."

" 'Tis."

Irma glanced at Mary Jane, whose eyes had gone dreamy.

"Mary Jane?"

"Aye?"

"Am I wrong in thinking there is more to your mountain than the lakes and forests?"

Mary Jane averted her eyes and reached for a wildflower. "What more could there be?"

Irma bit her lip. "What's his name?"

Her friend's eyes widened. "Whatever d'ye mean?"

Irma laughed. "Oh, come now. Who is he?"

Mary Jane's cheeks reddened. "Is it so obvious?"

"To one who also longs for love, perhaps."

Mary Jane flashed a tentative smile. "His name's Hiram. He lives in Strong. Oh, how my heart nearly broke from my chest the first time I saw 'im." Her voice faltered. "I s'pose that sounds foolish."

"Not in the least. In fact, I desire for such emotion to overtake me."

"But ye're so beautiful. Surely there's someone who's noticed ye, someone who … I'm sorry, I'm bein' rude. 'Tis not for me ta ask."

Irma touched Mary Jane's hand. "Of course it is. I have a fiancé. His name is Gerald." She tipped her shoulders. "He is a good man, and I'm quite fond of him, but I still await a stirring of passion such as you feel for Hiram."

"I see." Mary Jane's tone quieted. "My problem's a bit the opposite."

"What do you mean?"

"Hiram's very kind, but … "

"But?"

Mary Jane glanced back up the trail toward the homestead. "We've met three times now. This last time, he seemed … intense."

"How so?"

"He acted a gentleman, but the way he looked at me was unsettlin'."

"Do you mean … ?"

"Aye. I sense he longs for me in that way. But that's not the worst of it."

"What is?"

Mary Jane lowered her head. "I 'spect I should feel indignant at what his eyes say ta me." She looked back up. "But I don't. In fact, it excites me." Her voice trembled. "I wonder if I might succumb, if he were ta make an advance."

"Oh, Mary Jane."

"I know what ye're thinking. I'm horrible just ta think of it."

Irma moved her hand to her friend's wrist. "That is not at all what I was thinking. We are in the prime of our lives. Such inclinations are natural."

"So ye feel them too?"

Irma sat back. "Not toward any man I've met thus far. But longings and stirrings are close cousins."

"What am I ta do?"

Irma shook her head. "I cannot counsel you on matters of the heart, for I have no experience with them. I do encourage you to consider life beyond the moment, though. If you succumb, how will you view yourself when Hiram returns to Strong? How will it affect your relationship with your family? For although they may not know of your experience, you surely will. And if a child were to result … "

Mary Jane drew a deep breath. "I've asked myself the same questions many times over."

"I'm certain you have."

"I've no desire ta hurt my family."

"Of course you don't."

"As much as I love Marble Falls, thoughts of escapin' still haunt me. Strong's no more sophisticated, but it's … it's … someplace different."

"Do you know for certain that receiving Hiram's overture would necessarily lead to the escape you seek?"

Mary Jane tipped her head. "I can hope."

"I cannot empathize with your life in Marble Falls, but it fails me to think that so drastic a measure would inevitably lead to a happier estate."

"I cannot expect yer empathy." She lifted her eyes, gaze intense. "But then, ye've got Boston."

Irma's cheeks warmed. "I do. But do not make the mistake of assuming that a big city necessarily brings joy and contentment. It is not geography that defines one's situation. It's one's outlook on life."

Mary Jane smiled. "Ye're a true friend. I will consider your counsel, though ye say ye have none."

Irma squeezed her friend's wrist. "I'm so happy we met."

Mary Jane returned the sentiment with a hug. "I too." She cocked her head. "How will we stay friends when ye leave?"

"I will write you every week."

"An' I'll write ye too."

"Settled, then." Irma rose from the log and smoothed her skirts. "Father has purchased land near Quimby Lake, so we will certainly see each other again. And with his love of fishing," she rolled her eyes, "perhaps fairly often."

"I truly hope so." She jumped at the sound of her mother's voice calling from the house. "Bless me, afternoon chores. I near forgot."

Irma giggled. "I'll race you back." She gathered her skirts and sprinted up the path while Mary Jane was still rising from her seat.

"Hey! That's not fair." Mary Jane laughed and set off in pursuit.

***

And so I worry over what Mary Jane and Hiram may do in an unguarded moment, although it is not my concern. I pray he is the gentleman she believes him to be.

Gwen slowly closed the diary and laid it on the bedside stand. The clock glowed 2:48 a.m. She tugged the chain on the lamp and eased her head back onto the pillow, staring dreamily at a narrow shaft of light stretched across the ceiling from a hallway nightlight. Her imagination filled the gaps in her grandmother's written account with sights and sounds of the girls' lakeside perch. Their heads bent closely together while they confided their most intimate secrets, oblivious to the breeze rustling tree leaves above their heads and wavelets lapping gently at the shoreline. The air might carry the faint wail of a loon echoing across the water from Maneskootuk Island, its lamentation accompanying the waning sunlight into evening dusk, but would they even hear it? She blinked at the blurring shaft of light. How could a few lines written in a journal over a hundred and fifty years ago evoke such vivid mental images and awaken so strong a desire to have met their author? To touch her hand, share a secret, perhaps a hug.

Gwen's eyelids fluttered, and the image of a teasing Irma Louise Kelly beckoning from a fading lithograph ushered her into a shallow sleep.

*

From behind a sumac bush up the trail, the scene felt familiar. The sparkling lake, the whisper of a breeze through thick branches of tall trees, the earthy aroma of pine needles and moss.

The women huddled on an ancient log by the lake, Grandmother Irma's back to the water, Mary Jane's to the bush. Hushed tones, tittering words scattered themselves between the log and the sumac. Oh, to hear what they were saying, to join in. To become three.

But stepping out from behind the bush would surely snap the moment like a dry twig, even if it were possible.

Wouldn't it?

Then Grandma Irma looked past Mary Jane. Directly at the sumac bush.

And she smiled.

*

Gwen's eyes blinked open, and she sat up, pulse accelerated. It was only a dream. But ...

Grandmother Irma smiled at me.

12

The next morning, Gwen sipped her coffee during an early call to the lawyer's office. So far, her questions regarding other aspects of her father's estate had gone unanswered, other than affirming that it would go into probate should her brother not be located.

She rubbed her eyes, musing again over the startling revelation of a long-lost sibling. Her mind painted a gallery of images of what he might look like. Was he as blond-haired and fair-skinned as she, or were his features darker or perhaps ruddy as the Anglo-Scottish surname Hardy might suggest? A dozen possibilities paraded past her mind's eye when suddenly the lawyer's raised voice pierced her reverie and the images evaporated.

"Miss Kelly, are you there?"

"Yes, I'm sorry. You were saying?"

"I'm afraid I don't have the resources to assist you in your search. I can only advise you of the legal implications."

"I understand. Thank you."

"Of course. Good day."

She disconnected the call in glum reflection that this good day would end with her father's funeral. It was the final event demanding her presence in Medford, as the sale of the house and the estate sale could be arranged from Marble Falls. But she was no closer to solving the mystery her father had left behind. There had to be evidence of Simon's life somewhere. The notion pushed her upstairs and into her father's study. As she flicked on the light, she looked around, sighing. It was as orderly and pristine as she remembered it always being. Solid oak desk neatly arranged, marksmanship trophies aligned on a matching file cabinet, an overstuffed leather chair next to a reading table—her father's pipe and tobacco pouch still arranged under a shaded lamp.

On the wall, framed diplomas, professional certificates, and various photographs were hung in perfect formation. In the center was a family portrait taken on a Cape Cod beach the summer before her mother's death. Gwen leaned forward and gently touched her mother's beaming face, her strawberry-blond hair flailing in a stiff Atlantic sea breeze. She was hugging her eleven-year-old daughter close to her side. Gwen's finger lingered, but her eye shifted to her father. He also smiled, arm around her mother's waist, caught unexpectedly by the camera in an adoring sidelong look at his wife. Gwen's eyes misted. *Who were you, Daddy? And who is Simon Hardy?*

She brushed moisture from her cheek and settled slowly onto his office chair. Where to begin? She pulled open the lap drawer, but there was nothing more than a few writing implements, an address book, and a pad of legal paper. She carefully searched the three drawers on either side of the desk. Ten minutes of rummaging through ranks of hanging file folders, three-ring binders, a stack of past-years' pocket calendars, and an assortment of manila envelopes revealed nothing of interest.

Hope fading, she stood and turned toward the file cabinet. The top two drawers held more files that included stock-market reports, brokerage-house prospectuses, and the past several years' worth of income tax filings. But when she knelt and opened the bottom drawer, her breath caught. Covering the bottom of the drawer was a disorganized mass of memorabilia, a startling contrast to the obsessive orderliness of everything else in the study. She sifted through a random assortment of photos, some only of her parents, a few others including her as an infant, others with vaguely recognizable relatives and family friends.

Against the back of the drawer stood another couple of file folders propped up beside a rectangular purple-velvet-covered box with the gilded letters *MOTH* emblazoned on the lid. It looked like a jewelry box, but what was MOTH? As she reached in, her cell phone sounded faintly from the kitchen table downstairs. She closed the drawer, grabbed her coffee mug, and hurried down. The call was from the funeral home director with some last-minute questions and recommendations for the evening's ceremony. She thanked him, disconnected, and glanced at her watch. 10:30 a.m. Still plenty of time, but there were errands, and this was not a day to be running late. The search for evidence of her brother would have to wait.

***

The day passed more quickly than expected, for which Gwen was grateful. The busyness allowed her to focus on everything but the funeral looming ever closer. She busied herself with odd chores, but when the grandfather clock chimed the fifth hour, she trudged upstairs. The new black dress and heels waited patiently on the bed while she refreshed her makeup and rearranged her hair. Thirty minutes later, she was backing out of the driveway, dreading the hour ahead.

At the funeral home, Gwen fidgeted through unfamiliar protocol, though kindly aided by the perceptive funeral director, as people filed into the tastefully designed parlor. Hopelessly longing for Brent's supportive arm, she endured the ceremony, although pleasantly surprised at the number of people in attendance. Her father was apparently well thought of, a fitting legacy for the man she remembered during her childhood. They were kind. Comforting smiles, gentle and sympathetic words, mostly from unfamiliar faces. Mr. Forbson was among them. He introduced his wife—Annette was it?—who patted Gwen's hand and whispered condolences. Gwen nodded absently, smiling her thanks. A young man she loosely remembered as a member of her father's shooting club held her hand and said all the right things, but as he turned to go, brushed up against her and slipped a card with his phone number into her palm. She swallowed back a wave of nausea, flicked the card into a potted plant behind her, and wiped her hand on her dress.

What seemed like hours later, she was staring blankly at a portrait of her father in his navy uniform on an easel near the casket when the funeral director gently touched her arm. She jolted and scanned the room behind him. It had emptied.

"Is there anything else we can do for you, Ms. Kelly?"

"No, thank you. You've been very kind."

He offered a slight bow. "We'll deliver the flowers to your home."

She shook her head. "Isn't there a hospital or a nursing home somewhere that could use them?"

He nodded. "I understand. Please allow me to escort you to your car."

Back home, Gwen changed into her pajamas and robe, then went downstairs to the family room, stopping by the kitchen for a glass of Chardonnay. She eased herself onto the settee, closed her eyes, and took a sip. Then a deeper sip. Warmth radiated from her empty stomach, and the tension from the evening softened. The third pull delivered a tingle to her forehead and offered an easy temptation to drain the glass and go back to the refrigerator for more. She rubbed her eyes and fixed a dull stare into the clear liquid. Who could blame her? Her fingertips whitened against the stem. Who would even know?

As she lifted the glass to her lips, Brent's ringtone blared from the phone on the end table. She jumped, sloshing wine down her chin and onto her robe. She hurriedly set down the glass and grabbed a Kleenex from the table. Dabbing her chin, she drew a deep breath and reached for the phone.

"Hey."

"How are you doing, sweetheart? I'm so sorry I couldn't have been there for you tonight."

His loving voice dissolved the alcohol-fueled temptation, and she nudged the wineglass further away with her fingertips. "I survived."

"You can tell me about it later, if you'd like."

Gwen dabbed at the drops of wine beaded on her robe "I probably won't."

"I get it." His tone lightened. "So, tell me you're on the road back to Marble Falls and that I should scold you for using your phone while driving."

She sputtered a laugh. "It's not against Maine law to talk and drive, Officer Newcomb."

"It's against my law, Ms. Kelly. The moose on Route 4 don't care what's distracting a driver."

"If I were distracted, it wouldn't be because of my phone."

Brent chuckled. "That was the perfect answer."

"I learned from the best."

He laughed.

Gwen cleared her throat. "I spoke with Mr. Forbson earlier today, and he can't help in the search for my brother. All he could do was describe was how much of a probate hassle it will be if we don't find him."

"Figures."

"It's not only about the will. It's … well, I still can't get over the fact that I have a brother out there somewhere. I'd sign my whole inheritance over to find him."

"I'm sure you would."

"Have you had any luck on your end?"

"Not yet. Neither of the witnesses appears to have a criminal record, or at least not under the names they used on the codicil. Today's been pretty busy, so I'll get back to it tomorrow."

"I understand. I've done some homework on arranging an estate sale and finding a realtor, but I can't do anything more until we locate Simon."

"Is there anything in your father's personal effects that might hold a clue as to who or where he might be?"

"Not yet. I've gone through his financial paperwork, like income tax records and household receipts. I did find the deed to the house. It's paid off, which is a relief."

"You may want to check on property taxes. It's the end of the year and they'll be due if he hasn't already paid them."

Her heart lurched. "I didn't even think of that. What if he hasn't paid them yet? Can I access his bank account before we find Simon, or will it be frozen in probate too?"

"You're the executrix, right?"

"Yes."

"Shouldn't be a problem paying debts against the estate, especially taxes. The government isn't going to delay getting their cut over an issue as minor as probate. But check with your lawyer to be sure."

"Thanks. I will."

"On to more pleasant subjects. How are you getting on with your grandmother's diary? Anything interesting?"

"It's *all* interesting. But no connection to Francis Jones or a Jenny Lind trunk yet. I'm close to the end of her 1860 entries, so it's a little early for them to have met. She does have a fiancé, though, did I tell you?"

"No."

"His name is Gerald. So far she's mentioned him briefly. Maybe I'll find more on him later."

"I'm looking forward to reading the journals when you get back to Marble Falls."

Her voice teased. "Oh, I fully intend to monopolize your spare time for quite a while. You may have to be patient in meeting my grandmother."

"I can deal with that."

She paused. "Love you, Brent."

"Love you more."

"No you don't."

"Yes I do."

"Well, if you say so."

"Hey, you're supposed to keep arguing."

She giggled. "I thought guys liked to win arguments."

"I wouldn't exactly call that a 'win'."

"I would."

Gwen lingered, fingering the phone on her lap for several minutes after ending the call … heart warm, but aching. When the hallway clock struck the fifth hour, she rose and padded into the kitchen. Twenty minutes later, she was back in the family room with a mug of chicken soup and cup of spiced tea. She was just about to sit when the headlights of a passing vehicle flashed across the wall. She looked through the front picture window. All was dark, except for giant snowflakes swirling almost ghostlike through the halo of a wrought-iron lamppost beside the driveway.

Setting the food on the end table, she walked to the window and gazed into a wintry scene worthy of the finest Hallmark Christmas card. The front lawn hibernated under a thick blanket of snow, its surface rippled with ice-glazed drifts sculpted by a gusty northeasterly wind. The stiff breeze whistled through a rank of icicles fringing the eaves, and eddies of snow danced across the driveway to the music. Suddenly, she was seven years old again, watching her father hunched against the cold changing out the white lightbulb for a green one, wrapping the post with pine garland, and tying a large red bow onto a sign suspended from a crossbar that announced a happy Kelly family lived here. Slowly, the vision melted into the later years, the house growing as cold as the outside weather … Christmas decorating forsaken, holiday cheer a dimming memory.

As she began to turn from the window, something caught her attention. In the deepening twilight, footprints marked a trail from the street toward her house. Although they were partially buried by the drifting snow, she was able to track them until they disappeared around the corner of the garage. *Who would be out at this hour in this kind of weather? And what are they doing in my yard?* Memories of last October's near-fatal events in Marble Falls resurfaced, and she hugged her shoulders against a chill swelling from inside. After a moment she took a full breath and shook away the angst. It was probably just a neighbor taking a shortcut across the lawn.

As she turned from the window, remnants of the vision of past Christmases led her into the hallway. She looked up the stairway at the attic access. This would be the final Kelly Christmas in this house. Perhaps it would be nice to decorate, to pass it to the next family on a positive note. A resolute smile warmed her face. Yes, tomorrow the attic decorations would see the light of day and herald in the Yuletide. One last time.

Her steps were lighter when she returned to the sofa. She settled in front of the fire and drew the soup mug to her lap. When she reached toward the end table for her spoon, her hand bumped against her grandmother's journal. It looked back at her expectantly. She shook her head. "Not now, I'm hungry."

But not that hungry, I'll wager.

Gwen allowed a grudging smile. "You know me too well."

Indeed I do.

Gwen laughed to herself and reached for the book. "All right, you win. But you'll have to be patient. I'm still going to eat."

That's my girl.

She propped the book open and reclaimed her spoon. As she sipped the broth, she read.

13

Tuesday, October 23, 1860.
The clock has chimed eleven, but the excitement of this evening denies me sleep. How fortunate to witness Caroline Dall present "The Progress of the Woman's Cause" at Tremont Temple, despite the horrible weather. I cannot adequately express my joy in hearing so eloquent a champion of a cause I hold so dear. Perhaps it was all the more joyful, given the difficulty I had in securing the opportunity to attend.

***

"But Father—"

"I'll hear no more of it! Mrs. Dall is a Unitarian, a Transcendentalist, and an apostate to the faith. I'll not have her filling your impressionable young head with such balderdash."

"Much of New England has embraced Transcendentalism."

"The Kelly family did not embrace it, does not embrace it, and will not embrace it as long as I am its patriarch."

"You really have no need to fear. I am well acquainted with its precepts, and it is more a philosophy than a religion. If I were inclined to embrace it, I would have done so by now."

Her father narrowed his gaze. "You are acquainted with Transcendentalism? How, pray tell, did this come about?"

"Please, Father, I'm not a child. In any event, Mrs. Dall is not speaking on matters of religion. She is addressing women's rights."

He lifted an eyebrow. "It seems we still lack common ground."

"Very well, she is also a staunch abolitionist. In that respect, we certainly can agree."

"That alone does not earn her my esteem."

Irma chanced a demur smile. "But surely I enjoy your esteem?"

Byrne heaved a sigh and turned an exasperated look toward his wife sitting quietly by the window, hands folded on her lap. "Kate, you're a woman."

"Why, thank you, Byrne."

Irma giggled.

Her father did not.

"You know what I meant. Will you please speak to her?"

"Of course, dear." She regarded her daughter with a gentle smile. "What draws you so fervently to Mrs. Dall, Irma?"

Irma turned. "As a woman, how can you ask such a question?"

Kate tilted her head and met her daughter's eye.

"Forgive me, Mother." Irma swallowed. "It seems to me that society would be so much the better with the benefit of women's active participation. Carolyn Dall has mustered the courage to advance that notion through thoughtful journalism and oration. She is neither a fanatic nor is she radical in her representation, rather merely—as you say—fervent. Although she is often vilified for her views, she presses forward irrespective of the criticism piled upon her." Irma shrugged. "I simply believe she deserves a respectful audience."

Byrne huffed. "I have met Mrs. Dall, and she seemed to me rather overbearing."

Irma turned toward him. "Perhaps she has discovered such a demeanor necessary to effectively deliver her point, especially in Boston's present social climate." She paused. "I recall a conversation in this room not long ago when you adopted a rather overbearing rhetoric regarding my safety on the North Slope."

He stiffened, his ruddy complexion deepening.

Her mother's firm voice broke through the tension. "Irma, guard your tongue. Mrs. Dall's and your father's sentiments align neither in substance nor in motivation. I'll ask you to consider more closely your own rhetoric, lest you dishonor his love and degrade her cause."

Irma drew a deep breath. "Again, please forgive me, Mother." She lowered her head, adding, "And Father."

He remained still, shuffled a short stack of papers on his desk, stilled, pressed whitened fingertips onto the blotter.

Kate spoke softly, concern edging into her voice. "Byrne?"

Irma lifted her head, eyes rounding at the twitching muscle in her father's jaw, the bulging vein in his forehead.

He straightened and tugged on the hem of his waistcoat, meeting neither of the women's eyes. "Very well. Gerald is to dine with us this evening. He will accompany you."

"But Gerald holds no interest in—"

"Irma!" Her mother's rebuke jolted her.

Byrne continued as though there had been no interruption. "As I have clearly lost whatever influence I may have once had in the affairs of this household, I will ask you to make the arrangements, Kate." He nudged his desk chair neatly into position, then reached for his cane.

Kate rose from her chair. "What do you mean by that?" She cast a terse frown at Irma, then resumed attention to her husband, who was buttoning his coat.

Irma's cheeks flushed at her father's stony expression. "I apologize if I ... " Her words faltered as he moved around the desk, walked past her into the hallway, and retrieved his top hat from a peg on the hall tree.

Kate hurried across the study, reaching the hallway as her husband opened the front door. "Byrne, where are you going?"

His tired voice floated over his shoulder "I shan't be late, but do not hold dinner for me." With that, he pushed his hat onto his head and stepped out into the rain.

***

"A wonderful dinner, Mother," Irma said.

Across the table, Gerald touched his napkin to his lips, folded it, and laid it aside. "I wholeheartedly agree. I always delight at an invitation to dine at your table, Mrs. Kelly."

"Thank you, Gerald. I will see your compliments are relayed to Mrs. Callaghan."

"She is indeed an accomplished cook. "He paused. "My singular regret is Mr. Kelly's absence."

Kate lifted her coffee cup. "I will inform him of your thoughtfulness."

Irma averted her eyes.

When Kate finished her coffee and laid her napkin on the table, a servant immediately began to clear the dessert plates. She resumed her attention toward Gerald. "I do apologize for the change in plans this evening. I hope the early dinner hour did not inconvenience you."

He lifted a hand. "Not in the least."

She turned toward her daughter. "Isn't there something you would like to request of Gerald?"

Irma folded her hands in her lap. "There is."

Gerald's countenance warmed. "Simply ask, my dear."

She looked at him, gauging his possible response to her request. The deep green of his eyes appeared even more vivid than usual against his dark hair and smooth complexion. He had straightened in his chair and appeared eager to please, so she carefully chose her words.

"There is a speech I would like to attend." She gave him a beaming smile and lightly touched his hand. "I wonder if you might escort me."

He arched a dark brow. "A speech?"

She nodded confidently. "Carolyn Healey Dall is at Tremont Temple this evening. She will address the issue of women's rights."

His smile waned. "Mrs. Dall?'

"One and the same."

"She has a reputation for … "

Irma leaned forward. "A reputation for what?"

Gerald cast a questioning look at his future mother-in-law, then returned his attention to Irma. "She is rumored to hold very strong views."

"Who without strong views is worth listening to?" Irma tipped her head. "And, since you speak of rumors, am I correct in assuming you have not personally met her?"

He frowned. "I have not."

She offered another warm smile. "Then perhaps she deserves the benefit of the doubt?"

He chuckled. "She does indeed."

Irma breathed a sigh of relief. "So we shall attend together." She flashed a victorious smile at her mother. "As Father wished."

Her mother returned an even gaze, but her expression had clouded. "As he wished," she echoed quietly.

***

The only damper on the evening was retiring before Father returned home. I do find such exaggerated strife difficult to comprehend. Our exchange in the study seemed no more contentious than others, but something happened this evening. Never before has he abandoned his position so abruptly and with so little decorum.

But tomorrow is another day, and although I still consider my argument to be with merit, I shall seek whatever remedy is necessary to restore normalcy in our household.

14

Thursday, October 25, 1860

The pen lies heavy in my hand. Perhaps I should not attempt to record feelings with which I have not yet reconciled myself. But I feel I must, in hopes that recording them will hurry along that reconciliation.

I did not see Father yesterday, and therefore had no opportunity to assess his mien. At breakfast, Mother appeared subdued, I discerned a redness in her eyes and a huskiness in her voice, perhaps an illness threatening? She remained silent when I inquired as to her health, only sipped her coffee.

Then I inquired as to Father's disposition.

***

"Father is normally at breakfast by now. Is he still upstairs?" Irma laid her napkin on her lap and reached for a white porcelain creamer.

Her mother set down her coffee cup. "He has departed for his offices."

Irma looked at the grandfather clock in the corner of the dining room while she stirred her coffee. "So early? I had hoped to speak with him this morning."

"Concerning … ?"

Irma laid her spoon on the saucer. "I thought he might be interested in a summary of Mrs. Dall's address."

"You do?"

Irma lifted her chin. "You do not?"

Her mother folded her hands on the table. "Surely you credit me with more intelligence than this."

Irma sat back. "Mother?"

"Your reply is as insulting as it is untruthful."

"I beg your—"

"You may enjoy verbal jousting with your father, but it does not settle well with me. I asked you a forthright and honest question, I expect a forthright and honest answer. What is it you wish to discuss with your father?"

Irma's attempt to meet her mother's eye weakened. Words spoken in such a tone were foreign to any conversation they'd ever had, and this strained encounter so soon after the previous day's unsettling conversation with her father was unnerving. "I … I perceived that I upset him yesterday."

"You perceived well."

Irma drew up. "My point was valid."

"Valid, but poorly argued."

"Poorly argued? I prevailed, did I not?"

She jolted as her mother's abrupt rise from her chair rattled the china on the table, sloshing coffee from her cup onto the tablecloth and toppling a candle from the centerpiece. Over her shoulder, Mrs. Callaghan appeared in the doorway dish towel in hand, eyes wide. "So, am I to understand that to prevail is paramount, regardless of the means employed?"

"What I meant was—"

"That in order to win your point, you can justify throwing your father's devotion into his face?"

"Of course not—"

"That social grace and respect for common courtesy are expendable in establishing a woman's 'rightful role' in a society seemingly in peril of losing those very virtues that make it tolerable?"

Irma stared straight ahead, jaw working, but no words offering themselves.

"That in order to gain equality with a man, you must become as boorish as one?"

"Mother, stop!" Irma covered her face with her hands, shuddering.

Her mother's next words came quietly. "I engaged in a lengthy discussion with your father last evening, and briefly again this morning. He will be taking dinner at his club this evening. The conversation you desire with him must wait."

Her mother's chair creaked, and her footsteps faded down the hallway.

***

That evening, Irma and Gerald shared a quiet moment over tea in the sitting room. She strove to remain engaged in their conversation, but her mother's parting words still haunted her. She set her tea on a low table before the settee and shifted toward her fiancé. "Do you consider me boorish?"

His eyes widened, and he lowered his teacup. "Boorish?"

"Boorish."

He set down the cup and saucer, a bemused smile lightening his face. "I can think of very few descriptions that would be less fitting for you, my dear. Why on earth would you ask such a thing?"

"You're being honest?"

The smile faded. "You should never question my being honest with you."

She lowered her gaze and fingered a lace hankie on her lap. "I fear I may have alienated my father in an unguarded moment, although that was not my intent."

"How so?"

"During our discussion regarding Mrs. Dall's address on Tuesday, we exchanged terse words. I'm afraid I may have become unnecessarily harsh in defending my position." She sighed. "He received it poorly and departed rather abruptly." Her eyes moistened. "I've not seen him since."

Gerald knit his brow. "He isn't missing, is he?"

"He is not, but I do think he is avoiding me."

He smiled. "Surely you are mistaken. Your father loves you deeply."

"Mother reminded me of that."

"Well, then. There you are." He patted her hand and reached for his teacup.

"Then why did he walk out on our conversation, remain away from home yesterday, and depart this morning before I arrived at breakfast, which he has never done before? And this evening he is taking dinner at his club, depriving me of yet another opportunity to make amends."

Gerald sipped his tea and shrugged. "Perhaps there are extenuating circumstances, such as problems at one of his mills or strategies to discuss with his board over the upcoming presidential election."

"Neither matters of commerce nor politics have ever before driven him from our dinner table." Tears threatened, and she sniffled. "I cannot help but fear I have damaged our relationship."

"Now, now. I'm sure you're overreacting to a simple misunderstanding. All will correct itself soon."

"Do you really think so?"

"I know so."

Irma lifted her head with a tentative smile. "Thank you, Gerald. You always know the right thing to say."

He returned the smile and took another sip of tea.

She reached for her teacup. "So, now that you've mentioned the upcoming election, does its outcome concern you?"

"I favor Mr. Lincoln politically, but I am apprehensive about the South's reaction if he is elected President."

"Do you think they will secede from the Union over the slavery issue?"

"I am convinced of it, although it is a bit more complicated than just slavery."

"It is an abominable practice."

"However so, if the South does secede, Washington will not stand for it. War will certainly follow." He clasped his hands over his knee. "How many men will die and how many lives be destroyed over a practice that would surely suffocate over time under its own weight?"

"But how much time would that suffocation require? And how many negro lives will be destroyed before it does so?"

"That is the question, isn't it? New industrial inventions are ever on the increase. If we could put our brains and our fortunes toward innovation instead of war, I believe slavery could soon become irrelevant."

"If only others saw it that way."

"Perhaps they will."

A sudden fear prickled Irma's forehead. "What will you do if war does come?"

"I will serve the Union cause."

She sat back, eyes widened. "You would go to war? As a soldier?"

He chuckled and cocked his head. "Your surprise is rather disconcerting, my dear. Do you not think I have the substance to serve in such a capacity?"

Irma's cheeks warmed. "Of course I do, but … a soldier?"

He leaned close and lifted her hand to his lips. "Let's pray it does not come to that. You need not worry your pretty head over such things."

The grandfather clock struck the ninth hour, and he rose. "I fear I have overstayed." Laying a gentle kiss on the back of her hand, he bade her goodnight.

Irma watched him depart, but as though through a cloud. Propping her elbow on the arm of the settee, she rested her chin on her fist and stared out the window into the waning twilight.

***

… and so I could do little else for the remainder of the evening but ponder the fate of my country, my family, and my life.

15

Irma stood at the top of the stairs and bent an ear toward the murmur of conversation drifting through the study doorway below. The men's voices were hushed, but not enough to obscure their words. And when the tension peaked, all concern for discretion appeared to vanish.

"You know what this means, don't you Byrne?"

Irma paused at the voice of Henry Wilkinson, the chairman of her father's board of directors drifting up the staircase.

Her father's gruff response sounded tired. "Of course I know what it means. With Lincoln in Washington, it's a matter of time before the South bolts."

"And our mills rely on Southern cotton."

"Which is the reason I counseled stockpiling cotton in our warehouses months ago. Counsel against which I believe you led the opposition, am I wrong?"

Henry's voice rose, its strain palpable. "It was counsel we were ill-prepared to act upon months ago. Do you intend to waste valuable time pointing fingers at the past when we have real concerns for the future?"

"Not as many concerns as you think."

"What do you mean by that?"

"What I mean is we have a sufficient supply of cotton warehoused in Connecticut to sustain us until supply is reestablished."

Henry paused. "And where did this supply come from?"

"I authorized stockpiling from a separate account when the board's shortsighted argument plunged us into irresponsible action."

"You did what?" Henry shouted. "You circumvented a decision by the board of directors?"

"Of course."

"You had no right to do that!"

"It's my company, Henry. Besides, do you intend to waste valuable time pointing fingers at the past when we have real concerns for the future?"

"Do not dare use my words against me."

"No? If I had not acted, the firm would be on the verge of collapse. Because of my foresight, you and the rest of the board still have an income."

Irma tiptoed down the stairs and reached for her coat on the hall tree as Henry renewed his bluster. "What do you think the board will do when they hear of this?"

"Thank me, if they have any sense." The sound of a match scraping across emery punctuated the awkward silence while Irma buttoned her coat.

"You won't get away with this, Byrne, not this time," growled Henry.

"I already have. Now all that remains is to watch and plan smartly. You can do that, can you not?"

A cloud of pipe smoke wafted through the doorway, and Irma slipped out the door, latching it silently behind her.

***

Lamplight filtered through the arched windows of the African Meeting House, casting a yellow aura over Smith Court and the whitewashed safe house across the street. Irma pulled her collar close, stepped up to the front door, and knocked. It opened, and a massive negro man loomed in the doorway. He leveled a narrow stare at her, then broke into a smile.

"Miz Kelly! What're you doin' out so late?"

Irma smiled. "Hello, Gabriel."

He stood aside. "Ain't fittin' weather for you to be out in."

She lifted a warm smile, stepped through the doorway into the shallow foyer, and removed her bonnet. "I trust Frederick Douglass still plans to speak this evening?"

"Yes'm." He peered out the door. "Where's Mr. Fairchild?"

She looked down as she tugged on her gloves. "He is otherwise occupied, so I decided to come on my own this evening."

He frowned. "Ain't safe, Miz Kelly."

65

Irma flashed another smile. "But I've arrived, haven't I?"

He gestured toward a winding stairway to his left. "Folks is already here."

"Thank you." Loosening her coat, she mounted the steps into the upper level, where a slanting phalanx of wooden benches three rows deep overlooked the meeting hall floor. Below, an orderly array of painted pews sprouted from uneven planks of rough-hewn timber, only a few empty spaces remaining. In an alcove niched into the front wall, a plain wooden rostrum stood in dim lamplight. A low murmur of voices filled the room as people filed in through a rear doorway, energizing the air with expectancy. She scanned the balcony seats and spied a half-empty row at the back that offered an excellent view. Wending her way forward, she settled onto the pew and smiled at a petite mulatto woman sitting next to her. The woman returned a tentative smile, then focused on the scene below, as did Irma. Three men huddled on the steps leading up to the lectern. She immediately recognized the imposing figure of Mr. Douglass among them. The men clasped hands, and he took his place behind the podium.

The hall grew quiet.

Irma leaned forward to catch every word, although she needn't have. The former slave's booming voice resonated into every corner of the hall, perhaps aided by the alcove's acoustics, perhaps not. She fancied his deepened brow and fiery countenance kindled by his rude eviction from Tremont Temple, which had been the original venue for this speech. Again, perhaps not. Maybe this was simply Frederick Douglass.

His speech did not disappoint. More than once, Irma found herself on the verge of tears, shaking her head and whispering snippets of indignation to the mulatto woman at their speaker's stark portrayal of families destroyed by slavery and a supposedly free nation indifferent to such a heinous practice. Enrapt, time passed without notice.

Finally, the address completed, she departed the gallery with Douglass' words echoing through her mind's ear. Back in foyer, Gabriel dipped his head and opened the front door. "I can send for a carriage, Miz Kelly."

Irma retied the bonnet strings beneath her chin. "Thank you, but that won't be necessary. It's a short walk over the hill." He frowned, but nodded as she stepped out into the evening damp.

Hunching her shoulders, Irma hugged the building fronts and set a brisk pace to the corner, then turned up Joy Street toward the crest of Beacon Hill. Above the inky cityscape, a sullen sky drained itself in a near-freezing mist that swirled through the streetlamps' light, coated the sloped pavement with a slippery glaze, and chilled her to the bone. She stared down at the sidewalk, thinking ahead to the warmth of her fire and softness of her bed.

At the top of the road, a gravelly voice slithering from an alleyway startled her. "Well, who's this then?"

Irma's breath caught as a man stepped out from the shadows, blocking her path. A slouched hat darkened his face, and his hands were buried in the deep pockets of a ragged overcoat. He stepped forward. "Lost, are we?"

Her chest heaving, she drew up and forced confidence into her quavering voice. "I am not lost. Let me pass."

He tipped his head back and laughed. "Strong words from such a pretty lit'l lady." He took another step forward, and pulled his hand from a pocket. A steel blade flashed in the dim lamplight. "A lady who might carry a heavy purse, no?"

Irma stepped backward and bumped into someone behind her, sending her heart into her throat. She spun around and came face-to-face with a half-toothed grin spreading from beneath the whiskers of a grimy face.

The second man laughed hoarsely, his rancid breath bringing a gag to Irma's throat. He reached up and fingered a curl hanging from beneath her bonnet. "A purse and maybe more."

"Unhand me, you scoundrel." She tried to slap his hand away, but he grabbed her wrist.

"You best behave, missy. Or sumthin' bad might happen to you."

Irma gritted her teeth, struggling to free her wrist. "Let. Me. Go!"

His grin widened, and he looked past her. "Horace, keep an eye out, would ya?"

Horace snickered. "Sure, Dirk."

Dirk yanked Irma into the narrow alleyway and slammed her up against a brick wall.

She gasped.

He leaned forward until his face was inches from hers. "Maybe a kiss would calm ye down, eh?"

She closed her eyes and turned her head to the side, holding her breath.

"C'mon, lass. Don't be—"

Suddenly, her accoster screamed and fell backward. She stared down at her assailant was writhing on the sidewalk, Gabriel standing over him wielding a thick cane. "Run, Miz Kelly!"

A shadow loomed behind him as Horace lunged with his knife.

"Gabriel!" Irma screamed.

Gabriel pivoted and blocked the thrust. "I said *run!*"

Irma edged along the wall until she cleared the melee, then turned and fled up the street. A hurried look over her shoulder caught Horace in another lunge, his knife arcing down toward Gabriel's chest.

Back on Mt. Vernon Street, Irma stumbled up her mansion's front steps, threw open the door and rushed in, slamming it behind her. Breathlessly, she leaned back and sank to the floor, hands covering her face, sobbing.

"Irma?" Her mother's voice barely penetrated the ringing in her ears. "Whatever is wrong?"

Irma's throat constricted, and she shook her head.

A gentle touch on her arm, and she looked up at her mother's pinched face through a blur of tears.

"Oh, Mother," she gasped. "I fear I have killed a dear friend."

***

Oh, dear Lord, what have I done? What can I do? I can never go back now. And Father must never learn of this. For if he does, what will he think of me? What might he do?

16

Tuesday, December 11, 1860

I must record my thoughts before I go out, for if I wait until I return from the North Slope, I may never address this journal again. I dread what news may await of Gabriel, but I simply must learn of his fate. Why did he have to follow me? Yet if he had not, I would surely not have survived. More so, why did I have to disobey Father and travel the streets alone?

Irma looked up at a knock on the bedroom door. She set the pen down, smoothed back her hair, and drew a deep breath. "I'm here, Mother."

The door opened, and her father stepped into the room.

She shot to her feet, rattling the dressing table and scattering toiletries across its surface.

"Father! I–I didn't expect … I thought you had left for your office." She hugged her waist and stared at the floor.

"Your mother said there was something you need to tell me." He paused. "I infer from your demeanor that the subject is less than sanguine."

Irma swallowed. "Did she tell you anything else?"

"She did not."

She shuddered and reached up to brush a curl from her forehead, but his hand intercepted hers.

"You're trembling." Knitting his brow, he inspected her wrist, where a bruise had formed from Dirk's grasp. His face went dark. "Who hurt you?"

Irma's chin quivered and her eyes brimmed, then overflowed. "Daddy?" she choked. She pushed forward and pressed her face to his chest. He held her close as she drained her tears.

When her shuddering subsided, her father took her by the arm and led her to the bedside. She cupped her face with her hands when he sat down beside her. His words came tenderly. "You have not called me 'Daddy' since you were a mere child. What has happened?"

She wiped a tear from her cheek. "I–I disobeyed you, and someone very dear to me has been hurt because of it."

Her father slipped a handkerchief into her hand. "Explain."

"I went to the African Meeting House yesterday evening to hear Frederick Douglass speak."

He exhaled slowly. "Without an escort."

She nodded and dabbed moisture from her cheeks. "Gerald is in Concord on business, and I couldn't miss the opportunity."

"Continue."

Her voice quavered. "Upon returning home, I was accosted."

"What?" Her father turned her toward him, face turning to stone. "Who accosted you?"

"Two ruffians. A friend rescued me at the last moment. He saved my life, but … " she broke into sobs, "it may have cost him his."

Her father pulled her close and caressed her shoulder while she spilled more tears onto his starched collar. After a moment, he nudged her face up by the chin. "Who was this friend?"

"His name is Gabriel. He followed me from the Meeting House."

"Are you sure he perished?"

"I don't know how he could have survived. I saw one of the men attack him with a knife."

Her father set his jaw and rose. "Take a moment to collect yourself. Then come downstairs."

She looked up. "Father?"

He strode toward the door. "Do not dally."

***

Irma and her father stepped up to the door of the safe house across from the African Meeting House. He rapped on the door with the head of his cane. Irma hunched at his side, face shadowed beneath her bonnet. The door opened, and a robust negro woman filled the doorway. He grasped the lapels of his silk overcoat. "We require access."

She crossed her arms. "Oh, ya do? Why?"

"Isabelle?" Irma said, looking up.

The woman's eyes rounded. "Miz Kelly? Is that you?"

"This is my father. We have come to—"

"I understand you have a man named Gabriel here," he interrupted.

Isabelle glared at him. "We might."

"How is he?" Irma burst out. "Is he alive? I've been so afraid."

"Irma," her father said. "Let me address the issue." He turned back toward Isabelle. "Where is this man?"

Isabelle cocked her head, but remained silent.

"Please, Isabelle," Irma said. "I must know."

"It ain't good, Miz Kelly."

"Oh, my Lord, no." She buried her face in her hands.

"Let me then *request* access," her father said. "If there is anything left to be done."

Isabelle inhaled, then turned and gestured for them to enter. She led them up to the second floor and down a narrow corridor to a dark doorway. "Stay here."

She opened the door and stepped inside. A moment later, the door reopened, and a tearful young mulatto woman emerged carrying a bowl of red-tinged water and a bloody towel. She paused and met Irma's eye as she passed. Irma reached for her arm, but the woman slipped aside and continued down the hallway.

Isabelle reappeared and held the door open for them. They stepped through.

Inside, Irma gasped at the sight of Gabriel's sweat-beaded face, head pressed against a gray pillow, right shoulder covered in blood-soaked strips of cloth. An older negro was dabbing the big man's forehead with a damp cloth.

"Isaiah's the closest we got to a doctor," Isabelle said. "He does what he can."

Byrne addressed his daughter. "This is the man who followed you?"

Irma nodded.

Isabelle swung on him. "Followed her? What do ya mean by *that*?"

Byrne ignored her. "Then we must act."

"What *is* this?" Isabelle shouted. "Get out o' this buildin'!"

"Isabelle, wait," Irma said.

"Wait fer *what*?"

71

Byrne faced her. "Isabelle—"

" 'Mrs. Jones' ta you!" she growled.

Byrne tipped his head. "My sincerest apologies. Mrs. Jones, I would like to put the services of my personal physician at your disposal to attend to this gentleman's wounds." He turned toward Isaiah. "With your permission, sir."

The medical attendant widened his eyes and nodded.

Irma grasped her father's arm. "Father, do you mean it?"

He patted her hand as he locked eyes again with Isabelle. "Furthermore, I understand from my daughter's account that at least one of the men who accosted her suffered greatly from Gabriel's intervention."

Isabelle nodded. "Fact is, neither of 'em will be botherin' anybody for a spell."

"And they were white men."

Isabelle nodded again.

"Then you may also require the services of my attorney, should the scoundrels be foolish enough to press the advantage."

Isabelle's eyes took on a sheen. "I don't know what ta say, Mr. Kelly."

"On Gabriel's behalf, you can accept my eternal gratitude for preserving the honor and life of my well-meaning—" he turned and frowned at Irma, "but impetuous daughter."

Irma's cheeks heated, but she offered no defense.

He continued. "Mrs. Jones, I also assume you will be in regular contact with my daughter, so you can communicate through her—or her *escort*—should those legal services become necessary."

"Yes, sir."

"As for my physician, we must summon him posthaste if he is to be of any help at all. Good day, Mrs. Jones."

"And a blest day ta you, Mr. Kelly. I'll see you ta the door."

***

I thought I knew Father so well. But there appears so much more to learn about him, and so much more to learn about myself. Oh why do I insist on vexing him so? Why has it been so difficult for me to see the love and compassion behind his brusqueness? More so, how can I show him what I have learned?

17

Friday, December 21, 1860

So it has begun. As joyful as we were at Lincoln's election to the Presidency, equally fearful were we of how the Southern states would react. True enough, yesterday South Carolina voted to secede from the Union with several states poised to follow. And there is talk of war which terrifies me, as Gerald has resolved to enlist. What will such a war do to our country, to our family? To my future?

***

Irma perched on the edge of the settee beside her mother, face pinched at the terse conversation underway between her father and Gerald.

"The Union cannot dissolve, sir," Gerald said.

"Of course it cannot," her father replied. "But that is not my most pressing concern at the moment."

"What could be more pressing?"

"You are."

"I am?"

"You are betrothed to my daughter. Your future is very much my concern."

"You refer to my intention of enlisting in the Union's cause?"

"I do."

Gerald frowned. "Surely you understand a man's duty to his country."

"There are many honorable ways to perform one's duty, and serving as an infantryman is only one. There are valuable support positions in which your talents would be much more useful."

"Such as?"

Bruce Judisch

"You would make an excellent adjutant counsel in the War Department. General Scott would benefit greatly from your sharp mind and knowledge of military law."

"It appears likely General Scott will not remain in his post much longer, and I have no idea what his successor will require. I do know, however, that my penchant for military affairs can be honed through active service, and empathy with the common soldier would be invaluable in maturing it."

Byrne scraped fingers through his thinning scalp. "Confound it, man! You need not break your leg to know that it hurts, as you need not experience the battlefield to know that it kills. You can be of considerably more value advising the command staff than in a trench with a Springfield musket."

Gerald softened his voice. "With all respect, sir, this does not sound like the staunch patriot I know you to be."

Byrne reddened and turned his attention to his pipe and tobacco.

"What is it, sir?"

"It is simply common sense," Byrne replied, opening the pouch.

Kate spoke up. "Byrne, perhaps you should tell him."

Irma turned toward her mother. "Tell him what?"

"Just a moment, dear."

"I echo Irma's question," Gerald said. "What is it that drives such a fervent protest to my desire to serve?"

Byrne's chest expanded and he set aside the tobacco pouch. "My father served with Andrew Jackson at New Orleans."

Gerald smiled tentatively. "A momentous battle for the United States. You must surely be proud."

Byrne shook his head. "Over two thousand British soldiers perished in that battle."

"And less than fifty Americans. How glorious a victory!"

"My father was among the fifty."

Gerald's face slackened. "I am … very sorry, sir."

"The Treaty of Ghent ending the war had been signed nearly a month earlier. Two thousand British and fifty American men died needlessly, leaving behind wives, sons, and daughters who should have celebrated homecomings, but instead mourned irreplaceable losses." Byrne's voice tightened. "Some of those wives never recovered."

Irma spoke up. "Is that why Grandmother Kelly … "

74

Kate patted her daughter's wrist. "It is, Irma. Let Father finish."

Byrne continued. "War brings out the best and the worst of men. But it never apologizes for its wanton destruction of lives beyond those of a soldier's, to people innocent of its atrocities and unappreciative of glory." He met Gerald's eye. "There is no more joy in sending a mini-ball into the gut of another man than receiving one into your own."

Gerald leaned forward. "I understand, sir. But it is neither joy nor glory I seek. God willing, this impending conflict will be resolved short of the need for mini-balls. But if it does not, I must honor my commitment to a country that has blessed me with the opportunity of a secure and promising future." He smiled at Irma.

Her cheeks warmed, and she fingered a lace hankie on her lap.

Byrne sighed. "I understand, and I respect your sentiment. We shall pray it does not come to that."

Gerald nodded. "We shall pray."

***

I cannot help but admire Gerald's resolve, yet I remain perplexed. For though my heart warms at his adoring attentions, my body's desire remain cool. Why is this so? And should I even be writing about such a thing? Perhaps I shall never know.

Gwen closed the journal and laid it on the bedside table, mind in turmoil. It was certain that the mysterious bridal trunk had belonged to her grandmother, and that she had eventually joined her life with Francis Jones. So what happened to Gerald?

She turned off the light and snuggled into her pillow, but her eyes remained open. A full moon cast a vivid white streak down the bedroom wall, flickering through the heavy curtain of swollen snowflakes drifting past the window. The undulating reflection lulled her into a stupor, and the room blurred.

But the relief of deep sleep was long in coming.

18

The next morning, Gwen awoke with a start. Bright sunlight glaring off of the waxed hardwood floor revealed the sun had begun the day without her. She reached to the end table and turned the alarm clock toward her. 9:47 a.m.

She threw off the covers and grabbed her robe. After a quick shower and an even quicker makeup application, she pulled on a pair of sweats. In the upper hallway, the attic access demanded her attention. She set her jaw. Today the house would don its first Christmas decor in fifteen years.

Forty-five minutes and a dozen dust-induced sneezes later, an array of splitting cardboard boxes and bulging plastic bags were stacked against the wall of the stairway landing. Most of the aged masking tape labels on the boxes lay curled on the floor, making the boxes' contents a mystery. She puffed a blond curl from her forehead and smiled. After all these years, the containers would hold as many surprises as the Christmas gifts of her childhood had.

But where to start? Inside or outside?

Outside. The neighbors would learn the Kelly family had not completely forsaken the season, despite its long delinquency.

She opened a box labeled "OUTSIDE GARLAND." As she extracted a strand of plastic pine needles embedded with tiny white lights, a distant memory glistened her eyes. This was the garland that had spiraled the lamppost beside the driveway. She recalled her mother's soft hand resting on her shoulder while they watched her father braving the elements to mark the celebration of their Maker's birth. Gwen subconsciously reached for her shoulder as she brushed away a tear.

She carried the garland to the hallway and donned a heavy coat, woolen scarf, and gloves. Maybe her father had challenged the biting wind in little more than a fleece-lined coat, but that didn't mean she had to. She pushed through the front door, traipsed down the driveway, and honored her father's dedication to his family and his Lord. She plugged the strand of lights into the socket at the base of the post and squeaked through the dry snow back to the house, anxious to see if the tiny lightbulbs had survived their exile in the attic.

The garland sprang to life at the flick of the light switch. Spirit buoyed, she remounted the stairway. She carried the dried, cracking box it was packed in downstairs, through the back doorway, and dumped it in the trash bin. When she turned, she suddenly drew back. Another set of footprints in the snow, shallow and crusted in contrast to her fresh prints, rounded the corner of the garage toward where she stood. But no trail led away from the porch.

***

Brent peered through the cruiser's windshield at a man staggering down the icy steps of the Sports Pub & Grill. Face obscured by a baseball cap pulled low, the inebriated patron grasped the metal railing when his feet shot out from under him, and barely managed to pull himself upright. He finally reached the sidewalk where he groped in his coat pocket and pulled out a set of keys. Several thumb-jabs on the electronic key fob finally found their mark, and a vintage Chevy Tracker at the curb flashed its lights. The man struggled onto the driver's seat and the engine sputtered to life. The vehicle skidded sideways on the snow, tires spinning in a vain attempt to gain traction up Main Street.

Brent sighed, turned on his flashers, and pulled out behind the helpless vehicle.

When the driver cut his engine, Brent exited the cruiser and strode up to the driver's side. The window lowered to a grinning face.

Brent rolled his eyes. "Hello, Howard."

"Hello, Officer Newcomb. Good to see our vigilant police department on top of things."

"So, how many spoofs does this make now?"

Howard arched a thoughtful brow. "I do believe I've lost count."

"I should run you in for wasting valuable police time."

"Valuable police time? Isn't that like an oxymoron or something?"

Bruce Judisch

Brent narrowed his gaze. "Don't push it, Dobbs. You're on thin ice."

"Appropriate for Marble Falls in winter, don't you think?"

Brent straightened. "We're done here. Move along."

"Are you sure? Shouldn't you do a breathalyzer test on me to make sure I don't represent a dire threat to the fair citizens of Marble Falls?"

"And waste more resources?"

Howard shrugged. "How could protecting our citizenry be a waste of resources?"

Brent leaned on the vehicle's roof. "I'm not sure whether to recommend you for a Hollywood screen test or a psychiatric exam, but I'm leaning toward the latter. In either event, you need to stop baiting Chad and me with your stunts. We have better things to do."

Howard tipped his hat. "Duly noted, Officer. I live to please."

"Of course you do, Howard, of course you do." Brent stepped back as Howard restarted his car, swerved up Main Street, and disappeared around the bend. He was heading back to the cruiser when his cell phone chimed.

"Hey, Gwen. Tell me you're on the way back to Marble Falls or I hang up."

"You better not."

"I'll take that to mean you're almost here."

"I wish I were."

Brent's smile thinned. "You don't sound like your usual self. Is something wrong?"

"Not really."

"That doesn't sound very reassuring."

"It's probably nothing."

"Famous last words."

She responded with a light laugh, and he smiled. "That's a little better. What's up?"

"I was in the backyard a little while ago, and I saw footprints leading up to the garage. I didn't see a set tracks going away, which is a little freaky." She paused. "I'm probably being paranoid."

"After what you went through a couple of months ago, a little paranoia is understandable. Maybe even a little healthy."

"I suppose so."

"Were the tracks fresh?"

78

"They didn't appear to be."

"It couldn't hurt to have the police take a look around, just to be sure."

"They'd think I'm being silly. There's been no break-in or anything else suspicious." Her voice lightened. "Anyway, that aside, I decided to decorate for Christmas."

"You did? That's great."

"Yeah, but it's bringing back memories that are affecting my mood and maybe my judgement. The tracks are probably from the trash collector or a neighbor kid. I'm making too big of a deal out of it."

"If you're sure."

"I am. Oh, someone's beeping in. It might be the lawyer's office. I better take it."

"Call me right away if you have any more concerns. Or for any other reason." He paused. "Or for no reason at all."

"I will. Love you."

"Love you too." Brent disconnected the call. Despite his best intentions, the search for Gwen's missing half-brother had languished under the demands of ski-season duties. It was time to turn the heat back up. The sooner she was back in Marble Falls, the better.

Gwen accepted the call that had interrupted her conversation with Brent. "Hello?"

"Am I speaking with Ms. Gwen Kelly?"

"You are."

"This is Sgt. Mark Ferguson of the Medford Police Department."

"What a coincidence. I was just thinking of calling the police."

"Why, is there something wrong?"

"Nothing serious, I'm sure. Sorry, I didn't mean to concern you." She cleared her throat. "What can I do for you?"

"First, let me offer my condolences on the passing of your father. I'm sure this is a difficult time for you."

"Thank you." She paused. "But how are you aware that I lost my father?"

"The medical examiner's office contacted us regarding his autopsy."

"Why would they do that?"

"Because ... well, I'm afraid there are some puzzling aspects."

Gwen straightened. "What do you mean?"

"They stated that it took an abnormally long time for your father's blood to clot after his injury. The blow to his head wasn't that severe, but the hemorrhaging it caused was excessive. I'm wondering what caused the blow in the first place and why the excessive bleeding."

"I don't understand."

"Did your father use any prescription drugs that may account for dizziness or hemophilia-like symptoms?"

"Not that I'm aware of."

"Would you permit me to inspect your residence? I have no basis for a search warrant, so this would be purely voluntary on your part.

There may be a simple explanation, but given the autopsy findings, it would be advisable to perform at least a preliminary investigation to discount foul play."

Gwen gripped the phone. "Foul play? Do you think somebody may have hurt my father?"

"I have no evidence to suggest that. There could be a simple explanation. I just want to get closure on it."

"Thank you, Sgt. Ferguson. I would be pleased for you to investigate. When would it be convenient?"

They agreed on ten o'clock the next morning and ended the call. Gwen set her phone on the table, mind racing. *Suspicious circumstances? Daddy?* His emotional withdrawal after her mother's death offered at least a little room for questioning, but what could symptoms like this mean? Surely not drugs ...

Worry drove her to the upstairs bathroom where she rummaged through his medicine cabinet for anything out of the ordinary. It held little more than a styptic pencil, a small box of Band-Aids, and a generic statin for cholesterol sitting next to a bottle of low-dose aspirin. An uneasy relief eased her mind, mitigated by frustration over not finding anything to allay the officer's unsettling words. She went back downstairs to the pantry and scanned the shelves. Plastic bottles lined the wall on the second shelf—vitamins, fish oil, and a ginseng herbal supplement. All seemingly harmless. Stepping farther in to the pantry, her toe bumped into a cardboard box on the floor. She knelt and flipped it open. It held more bottles of the ginseng. Further searching revealed nothing more threatening than macaroni and cheese and a couple of cans for tuna, so she closed the door.

The suggestion of pasta awoke a carbohydrate craving, and she checked her watch, surprised to see that dinnertime was already upon her. Breakfast had been light and lunch nonexistent, so she searched the fridge for something more justifiable than mac and cheese. It offered nothing of interest, but as she closed the door, an advertising magnet for Pinky's Famous Pizza caught her eye. She smiled at something Brent had once told her. *"Pizza, nature's perfect food."* The mac and cheese forgotten, she retrieved her phone and placed an order.

Forty minutes later Gwen paid the delivery man, carried the pizza into the family room, and settled onto the sofa. A moisture-beaded glass of Diet Coke waited on the end table, Grandmother Irma's diary lying next to it. The gas fireplace contributed to the ambiance, but added little warmth, so she pulled the crocheted afghan across her lap. She opened the diary and scooped a slice of pizza onto her palm. *Pizza, family lore, and a warm afghan. What more could she ask? Well, other than Brent, of course.*

She picked up where she'd left off in the diary. Had Grandmother Irma reconciled with her father? And what had become of Gabriel? She took a bite of pizza and began to read, then perked up halfway through the first paragraph.

Tuesday, December 25, 1860.

Celebrating the birth of our Lord normally brings reflection, gaiety, and joy. But this year, sabers are rattling in the South, and I fear more states will soon secede. And though this evening's conversation was weighty, it did not completely dampen the joy of a most special gift from Gerald.

***

"Oh Gerald, it's beautiful. Wherever did you find it?"

"It pleases you?"

"Of course it pleases me." Irma brushed her fingers across the smooth lacquered veneer of a new steamer trunk, tracing its leather strapping and bronze hasps.

"Do you recognize the design?"

"It's a Jenny Lind trunk, isn't it?"

He chuckled. "I knew I could never slide something like that past you."

She patted his arm. "And consider it a lesson never to try again."

"Lesson learned."

She returned an adoring eye to the trunk. "Father paid dearly for our tickets to hear the 'Swedish Nightingale' in concert. How divine she was. It was my debut formal outing." Irma smiled up at him. "And how kind of you to bring me so wonderful a remembrance."

Her mother spoke up from across the room. "It was very thoughtful of you, Gerald."

"Thank you, ma'am."

He lifted his betrothed's hand and kissed it. "I intend it as a bridal chest, something to hold your dearest possessions in preparation for our life together."

Irma smiled, but lowered her gaze back to the trunk.

"Well done, Gerald," Irma's father said, seated at her mother's side. "You are a man of sensibility and honor."

"Your daughter has a gift for bringing out the best in me."

"Indeed she does." Byrne drew his tobacco pouch from his pocket and filled his pipe, turning toward Irma. "Memories of this Christmas will certainly rank among the highest."

Gerald quieted. "I pray it will be so. With the current state of the Union, there is no telling where we shall find ourselves twelve months hence."

"Oh, please let's not spoil the day with talk of politics," Kate said, setting down her coffee cup.

Gerald dipped his head. "My apologies, Mrs. Kelly. You're right, of course."

"But neither does ignoring reality honor the season," Byrne interjected. He struck a match and held it to the bowl of his pipe. "The first Christmas was not without political intrigue."

Kate gave him a pointed look. "Israel was indeed enmeshed in political turmoil, but very little conversation around the manger appeared to have been devoted to it."

Irma flashed a teasing smile. "I believe she has you there, Father."

Byrne gave her a narrow frown. "Please ask Mrs. Callaghan to refresh our coffee, Irma."

Still smiling, she rose from the settee.

Gerald came quickly to his feet. "I'll assist you."

***

Although I shared Mother's desire not to ruin the festiveness of the holiday, Father's words echoed through my mind, as did Gerald's question. Where indeed will we find ourselves next Christmas?

-20-

Brent had just reached for his coat when his phone rang. He fumbled the device from his belt, pausing to admire the photo of Gwen beaming at him from the screen before accepting the call. "I can't stand much more of this, you know. I'm about to drive to Medford and kidnap you."

Gwen giggled. "Oh, dear. Inducing an officer of the law to commit a felony. What a horrible influence I must be."

"You're worth it. When are you coming home?"

"You keep asking me that."

He tucked the phone against his shoulder while he pulled on his coat. "And I'll keep asking that until I see a blue Corolla with a blond driver coming up Main Street."

"Hmm, what are the chances of another blonde with a blue Corolla deciding to spend a couple of days of ski season in Marble Falls?"

"Less than zero, as far as I'm concerned."

She laughed. "Again, you have the right answer."

He shifted the phone to the other shoulder and zipped up the coat. "So, to what do I owe the pleasure of this call? Do you miss me, or is there something else?"

"Yes and yes."

"Go on."

"Remember when I received a call during our conversation yesterday, and that I thought it might be the lawyer's office?"

"Yes."

"It was from the Medford Police Department. They said there were some anomalies in Daddy's autopsy."

"What anomalies?"

84

Gwen related the oddity of the abnormal bleeding, ending with the officer's plan to visit the following morning.

"Good. Maybe you can mention the footprints in the snow."

"We'll see."

"Do it, Gwen. You observed evidence of suspicious activity, and then the police call saying there's something curious about your father's death. Things are beginning to look a little odd, don't you think?"

"You're starting to scare me."

"I don't mean to scare you, but I do want you to take this seriously." He paused. "Do you want me to come down there? Maybe I can convince Chief Lawson there's good cause for my absence."

"As much as I'd love you to be here, I can't justify pulling you from Marble Falls if the local police are offering to help. I promise I'll mention the footprints."

"I want to know what they say. In fact, I wouldn't mind talking to them myself."

"I'll let them know that."

"Good. Keep me posted, no matter how trivial the details might seem."

"I will—oh, there's the doorbell. It's probably them now."

Brent quieted his voice. "I love you. You know that, right?"

"Yes. But don't ever stop saying it."

He disconnected the call, stepped into the frigid morning air, and peered into a crisp sky. *Lord, I really need you to watch over Gwen. Please?*

***

Gwen opened the door to an imposing plainclothes officer peering down at her with deep blue eyes. Broad shouldered and easily six-and-a-half feet tall, his bulk obscured the outside view from her five-foot-four vantage point. Her eyes widened. "Sergeant Ferguson?"

"Yes, ma'am." He produced an identification card. "May I come in?"

"Of course." She stepped aside as he scraped his feet on the welcome mat and ducked through the doorway.

Once inside, he removed his hat. "Thank you for your cooperation, Ms. Kelly. I'll try to make this as quick as possible."

She gawked at his towering figure. "May I take your coat?"

He removed his overcoat, which barely diminished his size.

She hung it and his hat on the coat rack. "Where would you like to begin?"

"Perhaps where the body—I'm sorry, where your father was found."

Gwen led him into the kitchen and stood aside while he surveyed the room.

"When did you arrive back in Medford?" he asked.

"A couple of days ago."

"Then I assume you've cleaned the kitchen."

"Nothing other than wiping down the counter and washing what few dishes I've dirtied."

He opened the pantry door and peered inside. "The housekeeper wasn't very helpful with details in her report."

"Our lawyer told me it was she who found Father." Gwen paused. "Which puzzled me a little bit."

"How so?"

"He never said anything about taking on a housekeeper, and when I went through his paperwork, I found no record of a housecleaning service."

Sgt. Ferguson closed the pantry door. "Did you mention this to the police?"

"No. I only went through his paperwork this morning." She averted her gaze. "Father and I haven't been particularly close as of late. I assume he didn't think to mention it."

"I'll check the housekeeper's statement again. There's probably a simple explanation."

"You sound just like my boyfriend."

He lifted an eyebrow.

She smiled. "I live in Marble Falls, Maine. I've been seeing a police officer there."

"Marble Falls? What's his name?"

"Brent Newcomb."

He laughed. "Oh, so you're *that* Gwen."

" 'That Gwen'?"

"Brent and I served together in Afghanistan. We still touch bases once in a while, and he told me about this incredible woman he found who he can't brag enough about."

Gwen's cheeks warmed, but she put on a mock-stern expression. "Oh really? He 'found me' and he 'brags' about me?"

The officer hesitated. "Not like that. I meant—"

She burst into laughter. "I'm teasing. I brag about him too, so I can't very well complain, can I?"

Sgt. Ferguson smiled. "Well, knowing him, and now having met you, I can see where you both have something to brag about."

"You're very sweet."

He cleared his throat. "To the matter at hand, you said you searched your father's records for a housekeeping service, correct?"

"Yes, and his recordkeeping is … was very precise. It seems I'd have found something."

Sgt. Ferguson pulled a pad from his shirt pocket and jotted a note. "Do you mind if I look around?"

"Not at all. Oh, and this will probably seem silly, but would you mind checking the garage too?"

"Sure. Why?"

"When I was throwing out some trash this morning, I noticed footprints in the snow leading up to the door, but none leading away." Her face warmed at his quizzical expression. "Never mind. I'm sure it's nothing."

"Have you noticed anything else out of the ordinary?"

"There was a similar set of tracks yesterday, but then they were probably the same ones. I don't really know."

"I'll be happy to check it out."

"Thank you."

He cocked his head. "Are you nervous about staying here alone?"

"I don't think so."

"You don't think so?"

She shook her head. "I'll be fine, thank you."

He searched her face for a moment, then replaced his note pad and walked toward the staircase.

A half-hour search of the house revealed nothing out of the ordinary, so he went to check the footprints. He assessed them for approximate size, looked for a distinctive tread, and measured the distance between them as a clue to the owner's height, but the wind had eroded them to the point that not much detail remained. Nothing inside the garage appeared to have been disturbed. When he reported his findings, Gwen nodded. "I didn't think it was anything. I'm sorry to have taken up your time."

"It's no problem at all."

She saw him to the hallway. "Thanks so much for coming out."

After pulling on his coat, he handed her a card. "Please call if you have any concerns. I want to check a couple of more things at the station, but would a return visit be okay with you if I see a need to follow up?"

"Of course."

Brent frowned at the computer screen, tapping an impatient finger on the desktop. The lack of success in tracking down the people involved with the codicil was bad enough, but worse was the Internet server's sluggish response to his queries. Whoever decided that little circular arrow going round and round was a good idea deserved lynching. He was seriously considering thrusting his boot through the monitor when his cell phone launched into a serenade. He grabbed it off of the table.

"Wow, two calls in one day. What a treat."

She giggled. "Still looking for something to eat?"

He closed the lid of an empty pizza box and nudged it away. "Of course not. I'm providing for myself quite nicely, thank you."

"Another delivery from the Red Onion, right?"

He rolled his eyes. "How do you know these things?"

"I repeat, I'll never tell."

"So what's going on in Medford?"

"I met a friend of yours."

"Who?"

"A Sergeant Mark Ferguson."

"Mark? Where did you run into him?"

"He's the policeman who called yesterday."

"Really? Last I spoke with him, he was working South Boston."

"He said you'd been in touch."

"On and off."

"Uh huh. Enough 'on' to—let's see, how did he put it?—'brag' about 'finding' me."

"No apologies here. I brag on you every chance I get—and I did find you. That is, I found you incredibly attractive."

"Oh, you're really good."

He chuckled. "You inspire me. But, back to business. Did you tell Mark about the footprints?"

"Yes, and he looked around, but he didn't find anything unusual. I told you it was nothing."

"I'm not convinced."

"You're going to make me sorry I said anything."

Brent frowned. "Okay, I'll back off. But I don't like this."

"It'll all be over before you know it, and I'll be back in Marble Falls."

"Promise me at the next sign of anything strange, you'll call me."

"Of course. Sgt. Ferguson said the same thing." Her voice took on a tease. "Plus, he's kind of cute."

"Cute? He's the Incredible Hulk minus the green."

She giggled. "You're terrible."

"It's true. You should see him in desert camo and a T-shirt—wait, on second thought, never mind."

"Careful. I was getting a visual there."

Brent laughed. "Besides, good luck luring him away from Cassie."

"I have no intention of luring anybody away from anybody, but who is Cassie?"

"His girlfriend. It would be easier to separate conjoined twins."

"Then I like him even better." She paused. "How is the search for Simon going?"

"A few rabbit trails, but no rabbits. I'll keep at it."

"Maybe something will turn up."

A movement at the door drew Brent's attention. Chief Lawson was beckoning from his office across the hall. "Gotta go. Don't take any chances."

"I won't."

***

Gwen spent the afternoon separating the salvageable Christmas decorations from those that had succumbed to time and finding the right spots for the survivors. She stepped back to look at the results. A pine-scented candle nestled in a wreath of berry-laden holly lay centered on an embroidered runner spanning the dining room table, an Advent candle set adorned the entryway table, and a five-foot artificial Christmas tree flanked the family-room fireplace, its twinkling multicolored lights flashing off of handmade ornaments. Each ornament had lingered a moment in her hand, stirring her memory with distant moments from childhood and tugging on her heart. She called it quits at twilight, replacing the empty boxes and bags in the attic, and headed to the kitchen for dinner.

She microwaved the surviving half of last evening's pizza and carried it into the family room with a cup of iced tea and her grandmother's diary. Arranging herself on the settee, she again immersed herself into another world.

Saturday, January 12, 1861.

The world is ending, the Union collapsing. As I feared, Mississippi, Florida, and Alabama have followed South Carolina into secession. Worse, Gerald remains firm in his resolve to answer a call to arms, should it come. And Governor Andrew seems equally firm in his resolve that such a call will come. Indeed, how can it not? I dread that our world is about to change so tragically.

-22-

Irma propped her chin onto her hand and stared out the window, mindlessly stirring her tea. The gray afternoon cast a sullen pallor through frozen mist coating the pane. It seemed even the heavens could not veil their despondency over the state of the American Union.

Her mother sat across the room, a copy of *The Pilgrim's Progress* in hand. "You're going to stir that tea to a chill, Irma."

She laid her spoon on the saucer. "How can people be so callous as to enslave others and then threaten war when that callousness is challenged?"

"Economics, dear. The South has built a dependency upon slavery to sustain its economy, and therefore its solvency. To surrender it is to risk collapse."

Irma returned a terse expression. "Economy? Surely you're not suggesting expediency of commerce is an excuse for human maltreatment."

Kate closed her book. "I'm not suggesting anything. I'm simply answering your question."

Irma rolled her eyes. "You can be so frustratingly objective sometimes."

"You might try it for a change."

Irma sniffed and sipped her tea. "Objectivity never accomplishes anything."

Her mother smiled. "And subjectivity leads to wars, such as the impending one you now lament. There is a healthy balance between the two that mankind seems intent on avoiding." She set the book down. "On other matters, have you heard anything more about the man who rescued you on the North Slope?"

"I have not. He is healing from the knife wound, God and father's physician be praised. I fear, though, that there may yet be legal reprisals from the men who attacked me."

"Surely they have no legitimate basis for complaint."

"They do not, but the Fugitive Slave Act makes it easy for such men to press even contrived charges."

"Is Gabriel a fugitive slave?"

She averted her gaze. "I neither know, nor do I care."

The women jolted at a rapid knock on the front door. Irma creased her brow, as a manservant passed the library on his way down the hall. A moment later, he reappeared at the doorway. "Miss Kelly, you have a visitor."

Irma rose and hurried to the door, finding Isabelle Jones hunched on the top stair with a shawl draped over her head. "Isabelle! What on earth brings you here?"

"Please forgive me, Miz Kelly. I know I shouldn't come—"

"Nonsense. Of course you should."

Kate appeared at her side. "Irma? Who is this?"

She turned toward her mother. "This is Isabelle Jones. She's a friend of Gabriel's."

"Heavens' sakes, Irma, ask her in."

Irma moved aside. "I'm so sorry, Isabelle. Please come in."

Isabelle shook her head. "T'wouldn't be proper."

Kate reached out and drew Isabelle in by the hand. "Oh, the devil with propriety. Any friend of Gabriel's is a friend of this family's."

Irma stared at her. "Why Mother. I've never heard you—"

"Hush. We have a guest to attend to." They led Isabelle into the foyer, where Irma offered to take her wrap. The negro matron hesitantly loosened her shawl and surrendered it. When it was hanging neatly over a peg on the hall tree, the matriarch of the Kelly household ushered her into the sitting room and settled her onto the settee nearest the fire. "Irma, please ask Mrs. Callaghan to prepare some tea and biscuits."

"Missus Kelly, please," Isabelle protested. "I don't want ta cause no work."

"Am I to understand you do not like tea and biscuits?"

Isabelle's eyes rounded. "No, ma'am. It's just that—"

"Very well then." Kate turned toward Irma. "Ensure the biscuits are fresh and warm."

Irma smiled and departed for the kitchen. When she returned, her mother was seated next to Isabelle as their distraught visitor spoke. " … so we thank God an' Mr. Kelly for Gabriel's healin'." Her eyes welled. "The wound was too much for us."

"I can speak for Mr. Kelly in conveying our gratitude to Gabriel for intervening on our daughter's behalf. Offering our physician's services was the least we could do."

"Not to us, Missus Kelly." Isabelle shook her head. "Not to us."

Kate grasped Isabelle's hand. "But I sense that is not what brings you here."

At that moment, Mrs. Callaghan entered with a tray of tea and warm biscuits. She set the service on the coffee table, and after a terse glance at Isabelle, pivoted and left the room. Irma poured the tea and offered the first cup and a biscuit to their guest.

Kate continued. "You were saying?"

Isabelle's teacup rattled on the saucer. "Mr. Kelly also said we should watch out for the law, that they might come for Gabriel."

"And have they?"

Isabelle nodded. "We hid him away, but we don't know what ta do if they come back. An' sure as anythin' they will."

Irma spoke up. "Then you must bring him here."

Kate turned a serious expression toward her daughter.

Isabelle's eyes widened. "We can't do that, Miz Kelly."

"Why not? This neighborhood is the last place they would think to look. And we have plenty of room."

"And if they do look here?" asked Kate. "What then?"

Irma lowered her voice. "We have the basement alcove beneath the fireplace."

Her mother pursed her lips, and Isabelle arched a questioning brow.

Irma leaned forward. "The architect who designed this house included a niche beneath the chimney flue. It offers the perfect place to hide."

"It's filthy down there," her mother said.

"No filthier than where Gabriel would end up if they take him. And we can clean it up. In fact, I'll do it myself."

Her mother's lips quivered to a smile. "Your expertise with a mop and wash bucket is somewhat underdeveloped. Are you sure you'd know which end of a broom to hold?"

Irma lifted her chin. "I can learn."

A muffled laugh escaped Isabelle, then she hunched her shoulders. "I'm sorry, Miz Kelly."

Kate made no attempt to stifle her laughter, while Irma crossed her arms and frowned.

Isabelle sobered and cast an imploring look at Kate. "If there's a way ta save Gabriel, I'd be glad ta clean, or cook, or … well, do pret' near anythin'."

Kate rose to her feet. "Irma and I will tend to the cleaning. Your job is to get him here undetected."

Isabelle quickly set down her teacup and stood. "I don't know how to thank you, Missus Kelly." She paused. "But what will Mr. Kelly think?"

"Irma and I will tend to him too." Kate took Isabelle's arm and ushered her into the hallway. "Now, if the situation is as dire as you say, there's no time to lose. We'll expect you soon."

When Isabelle departed, Irma embraced her mother. "Thank you so much."

Kate patted her daughter's shoulder. "Don't thank me until we see how your father reacts. That will be the test."

"Surely he won't mind. He is as beholden to Gabriel as we are."

"Sympathizing with the negro cause and harboring a fugitive slave are two different things. He'll be putting his reputation and his business at risk should Gabriel be discovered. There are penalties."

"I never said he was an escaped slave."

"Unless he has written proof of his freedom, it hardly matters." Kate turned, and Irma followed her back into the sitting room. "And, if he were to be discovered here, how would he explain having gone into hiding if he is a freeman?"

"He won't be found."

Kate smiled at her daughter. "I'm sure he won't."

They settled onto their seats, and Irma reached for a biscuit. "So, what do we do now?"

Kate warmed her tea from the pot, eyes twinkling. "We teach you how to use a broom."

Irma covered her nose and stepped back from the low entrance to the basement alcove. The broom slipped from her grasp and clattered onto the hard-packed dirt floor, as the close mustiness sucked the air from her lungs and left a wave of lightheadedness in its place. Visible in the dim lantern light, cobwebs draped the rough red bricks lining a dank niche blackened with soot from the fireplace above.

Her mother's voice prodded from behind. "Well, let's get started."

"Are you sure we can't find someone to do this, Mother?"

"As few people as possible must be aware of what we're doing. To ensure our privacy, I gave the staff the afternoon off, save Mrs. Callaghan."

Irma sighed. "I suppose you're right." She lifted the lantern and gauged the height of the low opening. How could anyone of Gabriel's size fit into in such tight quarters? "Maybe this wasn't such a good idea after all."

"Come now. Surely a little dust shan't dissuade you from aiding a friend."

"Of course not." Irma met her mother's gaze. "I'm only afraid he'll suffocate down here."

"Air flow is the reason the alcove was built. It provides an updraft to carry the smoke from the fireplaces."

Irma coughed. "It doesn't seem to be doing a very good job of it."

"Scrape the cobwebs from the arch with your broom. That will be a start."

She stepped forward, poked at the opening, and immediately gagged at foul residue that coated the straw bristles. "This is disgusting."

"But less disgusting than seeing such debris coating Gabriel?"

Irma frowned over her shoulder. "You certainly know how to make me feel terrible, don't you?"

Her mother arched her eyebrows, smile undiminished. "I don't know what you mean."

Irma sniffed. "I'm sure you don't."

An hour later, the two women, soiled and clammy with perspiration, climbed the stairs to the first floor coughing and rubbing grime from their foreheads.

Kate sputtered a laugh. "I never thought I'd see the day you would crawl into a dirty hole and scrub at filth most of Mt. Vernon Street doesn't even know exists."

"Please don't remind me. I had my eyes closed most of the time."

"As did I."

Irma giggled. "If only Father could see us now."

"He may if we don't hurry. It must be close to dinnertime."

At the top of the stairs, the women set their cleaning implements aside and bustled into the hall stairway. As they neared the foyer, a voice from behind startled them. "There ye are, Mum."

They spun around, and Kate brushed a tangled wisp of hair behind an ear. "Mrs. Callaghan. You startled me."

"Apologies, Mum. I wanted to tell ye I'll be settin' an extra place at the table this evenin'. Mr. Fairchild will be joining you."

"Gerald?" asked Irma, clasping her filthy hands behind her back. She puffed at a stray curl on her forehead and attempted nonchalance.

Mrs. Callaghan pursed her lips. "Aye, Miss Kelly. One and the same."

Irma narrowed her gaze. "Then I best retire to prepare, hadn't I?"

When the servant turned back toward the kitchen, Irma and her mother exchanged smiles and hurried up the stairs.

***

Irma set her fork on her empty plate and dabbed her lips with a napkin.

"It's rare to see you finish so robust a meal, my dear," Gerald said.

She arched her brow, trying to ignore the smile her mother was hiding behind the lip of her coffee cup. "Is it? It was a most delicious meal." She gave Gerald a slight pout. "Do you consider it unbecoming?"

"Not in the least. Your decorum remains intact."

"Thank you." She suddenly pressed a napkin to her mouth to stifle a burp, eyes widened. "Goodness. Please excuse me."

"Whatever for?" asked Gerald, lifting his own napkin.

Byrne set down his coffee cup. "Perhaps a glass of port and a cigar in the study will rightly polish the evening, Gerald." He looked sidelong at his daughter. "That is, if you've finished eating."

Irma smiled sweetly. "Need you ask?"

"Apparently."

She pursed her lips as her father set his linen on the table and rose. The rest of the family followed his lead.

Once in the study, the men selected cigars from a humidor. When they turned, Irma was peering through the doorway.

Her father frowned. "What is it?"

"Mother and I thought it might be nice to join you."

"That would be highly irregular," he huffed, rolling the cigar between his fingers.

"But so much more pleasant, don't you think?"

Gerald cleared his throat. "I don't mind, sir—that is, if the ladies' presence would not disturb you."

Byrne regarded him with a raised eyebrow.

Gerald tipped a shrug.

With a sigh, the patriarch nodded.

Irma flashed a smile at her fiancé and turned. "It's alright, Mother."

Kate's face appeared over her daughter's shoulder wearing a puzzled expression. "What is alright?"

"Why, our joining Father and Gerald in the study."

"What?"

Byrne narrowed his gaze. "So, your mother thought it might be nice, did she?"

Irma batted her eyes. "Well, she would have."

Her father sighed, dropped onto an easy chair, and waved them in.

As the women settled onto the settee, lightning flashed outside the window, followed closely by a clap of thunder. A single drop of rain splattered onto the glass, then more. Moments later, a solid sheet of water coated the window into translucence. Irma shivered and pulled a crocheted afghan from the back of the sofa onto her lap. Mrs. Callaghan entered, balancing a tray with a lead-crystal decanter of port wine and four small glasses. The libation poured and distributed, she exited the room. Seemingly oblivious of the storm outside, the men sniffed and inspected their cigars.

"I wonder what cigars taste like," whispered Irma.

"Ghastly, I'm sure," replied her mother.

"Their aroma is rather pleasant, actually."

"Until they're half burned. Then it resembles the dregs of a smelting factory, don't you think?"

Irma giggled. "Perhaps if we discontinue breathing at that point—"

"What are you two whispering about?" asked Byrne as he applied a cutter to the tip of his cigar, then offered the device to Gerald.

"We were simply admiring your choice of vices," Kate said.

"Cigars are not a vice, they are a necessity."

"A necessity?"

"Of course. Without quality tobacco to mellow a laborious day at the office, I should be quite intolerable."

"More so than you are now?"

He paused halfway through lighting his cigar and lowered his gaze at her. "Much more intolerable, I promise."

"Then by all means, continue."

Irma dipped her head to conceal her grin.

"Do you have such reservations concerning cigars, Irma?" asked Gerald, an unlit match poised to strike.

She cleared her throat. "Would it influence you one way or the other?"

"But of course."

Byrne snorted. "Grow a backbone, man."

Gerald stiffened and the women burst into laughter.

Kate reached for a glass. "You must give Irma something to complain about, Gerald, or she'll grow weary of you."

Her husband chuckled. "Then I need never fear that you'll weary of me, shall I, dear?"

"Never, my love," she replied, eyes sparkling.

Byrne lifted his glass. "A toast."

The others lifted their glasses.

He allowed a dramatic pause, eying his daughter, then his wife. "To complaining. May it never go out of style."

Irma giggled. "I assure you it won't in this household."

As they consummated the toast, Mrs. Callaghan entered the room. She sniffed. "An unannounced visitor is at the back door."

Irma and her mother exchanged knowing looks and set down their port. "I'll see to it," Kate said.

"Please let me, Mother." Irma rose from her chair, bringing Gerald to his feet.

"It's likely another beggar looking for a handout," Byrne groused. "Mrs. Callaghan can wrap up some morsels and send him on his way."

Irma demurred. "If that is the situation, I shall make quick work of it."

Gerald set aside his glass and unlit cigar. "Perhaps I can help."

"It's no trouble, really. I'll be right back." Irma hurried from the room.

Mrs. Callaghan continued drying the china as Irma swished through the kitchen toward the rear vestibule. She opened the door to Gabriel hunched on the stair with Isabelle clinging to his arm. A deluge of freezing rainwater drained over them from the roof. They all ducked their heads at a flash of lightning, followed by an immediate explosion of thunder.

"Gracious sakes, you'll catch your death. Come in." Irma stepped aside as the two huddled into the vestibule. She turned toward the cook, who kept her back to them. "Why didn't you let them in, Mrs. Callaghan?"

She did not turn around. " 'Tweren't my place, Miss."

Irma glared at the cook, then turned back to the shivering couple. "Here, let's get you out of those sopping wraps." She helped Isabelle loosen her coat.

"Sorry ta be a bother, Miz Kelly," Gabriel said.

"Bother?" Irma huffed as she hung Isabelle's coat onto a peg. "Let me never hear that word slip from your lips again."

Gabriel lowered his gaze when Irma gestured for him to remove his coat.

"We had no choice," continued Isabelle. "We got word the law was comin' an' lit out just 'fore they showed." She took Gideon's coat and hung it over her own, then turned back with apologetic eyes.

Irma grasped Isabelle's trembling hands. "Goodness gracious, it's warm baths and dry clothes or you'll both drop of fever."

Gabriel's eyes widened. "Oh, no. We'll be fine, Miz Kelly."

100

Irma poked a finger onto his chest. "Never argue with a proper Bostonian hostess."

Isabelle snorted a laugh. "Best do what she says, Gabriel. We both know once Miz Kelly's got her head set, ain't nothin' will turn her aside."

Irma peered around the corner toward the door to the parlor. None of the family was in view. "We must tread quietly," she said, turning back around. "Follow me."

She led them through the kitchen and into the hallway. They had mounted the first riser of the staircase when a voice brought them up short.

"Irma?" Her mother was standing in the doorway of the parlor, surveying Isabelle and Gabriel hunched against the wall.

Irma lifted a finger to her lips and looked toward her disheveled guests.

Her mother nodded. "I'll tend to you father and Gerald," she said quietly, then looked at Gabriel. "Get one of your father's nightshirts. He has several and will never miss it."

Irma smiled, eyes glistening. "I love you," she mouthed.

Her mother dipped her head. "And I you." She extended a smile toward Isabelle and Gabriel, then reentered the parlor.

-24-

Later that evening, Irma crept down the hallway carrying a covered basket from the kitchen. As she passed her parents' bedroom, her father's disgruntled voice drew her up short.

"Where is my nightshirt?" he grumped.

"Which one?" came her mother's reply.

"My favorite one."

A crash of either thunder or of a wardrobe coming apart rattled the walls, and her heart leapt into her throat.

"Perhaps it's in the laundry."

"It was here this morning." More rustling.

"Are you sure?"

"Of course I'm sure."

"Byrne?"

"Well, almost sure."

"I thought as much. You have plenty of nightshirts. Select another. I'm sure it will reappear with the next load of laundry."

A grumble followed another heavy sigh. "It better."

"There," her mother said. "That one's perfect."

"Not perfect, but it'll have to do."

Irma released her breath and tiptoed down the hallway. Turning a corner, she stopped at the door of a small guest room that hadn't seen use in years. Until now. She quietly knocked twice.

The latch clicked, and the door cracked ajar. Isabelle's anxious face appeared in the narrow opening.

Irma smiled and held up the basket. "Something from the kitchen."

Isabelle opened the door. "Miz Kelly, surely as the Lord saves, we're g'win ta get you into bad trouble."

"Nonsense." Irma thrust the hamper into the woman's hands. "You have to eat, don't you?"

Gabriel moved into view behind Isabelle. "She's right, Miz Kelly. We can't be stayin' here."

"You let me worry about that. Besides, where would you go if not here?" They flinched at a sudden flash of light bleaching the room through a window on the opposite wall. A deafening crack of thunder sounded an instant later. "You'd probably be struck dead before you were ten paces down the street."

"We seen worse than this comin' up from Carolina," he said.

"Then you don't need to see it again, do you?"

Isabelle looked back at Gabriel. "Tol' you it ain't worth the breath arguin'."

"I must go." Irma paused, cheeks warming as she looked at the only bed in the room. "I'm sorry we have the one room to spare. I set another pillow and blanket in the wardrobe."

Isabelle grinned. "Why Miz Kelly, ain't you figured out yet that Gabriel an' me is wedded?"

Irma's eyes widened. "It hadn't occurred to me, although I don't know why."

Gabriel laid his hands on his wife's shoulders and chuckled. "Ain't no man in his right mind could let a woman like this go 'round loose."

Isabelle smiled up at him. "G'won now."

Irma giggled. "Well, then. I'll leave you two alone until breakfast. Rest well."

***

After breakfast the next morning, Irma slipped into the kitchen and rummaged for leftovers. A small basket rested on the counter, soon filled with a small bowl of chutney and two warm rolls snuggled against chunks of hard cheese. She covered the basket with a cloth, turned, a drew up at her father's daunting figure filling the doorway.

He propped his hands on his hips. "A picnic so early in the day?"

Irma lowered her gaze. "Gerald and I thought to have lunch on the Commons."

"At nine o'clock in the morning."

"I ... well ... "

He chuckled. "Give my best to your guests."

She feigned a puzzled expression.

He cocked his head. "Dear child, please do me the courtesy of not thinking me a fool."

She swallowed. "Father?"

"You neglected to collect their sodden garments from the back vestibule. Neither did you wipe the drips of water from the staircase." His eyes twinkled. "I trust the east guest room meets with their satisfaction."

Irma tipped up her chin, but cast her gaze toward the floor. "How could it not, given the fate that awaits them should the scoundrels who attacked me discover their whereabouts?"

Her father stepped forward and stroked his fingertips along her cheek. "And for Gabriel's intervention I shall always be grateful. I was quite sincere when I asked you to convey my best to your guests."

Irma looked up, eyes moistening. "Thank you, Father. I shall do so."

"Very well." He donned his top hat and turned toward the cook, who had just entered from the larder. "Oh, and Mrs. Callaghan?"

"Sir?"

"I anticipate being particularly hungry this evening. Perhaps an additional measure of fried chicken and fixings would do."

The cook nodded.

He turned and strode down the hallway. "Enjoy your picnic, Irma," he called over his shoulder.

Irma smiled. "Thank you, Father."

***

After dinner that evening, Irma retired to her room amid conflicting emotions of excitement and anxiety. So much to be gained—or to be lost. *Am I doing the right thing or endangering us all?* She settled in front of her vanity, pulled the pins from her hair, and with a shake of her head, sent dark brown curls bouncing around her neck. Picking up her brush, she gazed thoughtfully into the mirror while attempting to tame the stubborn locks. Grimacing through a particularly difficult snag, she squinted down at a thick book next to her diary. She set down her brush, picked up the tome, and brushed her fingertips over its cloth cover. *Uncle Tom's Cabin; Life Among the Lowly.* It was a gift from her mother years earlier, but had only recently acquired some weight of purpose.

She flipped open to her silk-tasseled bookmark, and let her eyes wander. They widened when a snippet of text leapt from the page.

The slave Sam was crowing about his cleverness in aiding Eliza's escape from the slave trader Haley. *"…so yer see I's persistent either way, and sticks up to conscience, and holds on to principles …. what's principles good for, if we isn't persistent … ?"*

She closed her eyes and smiled. *What indeed?* She set the novel back onto the table, and picked up her diary. Opening to the last partial entry, she dipped her pen into the inkwell.

Of course, the call to arms must come, for the future of the slave is the future of the Union. Either we are a free country or we are not. I pray that very little blood will be shed in preserving the ideal that is America.

***

Gwen closed her grandmother's diary and hugged it close. *Oh, to have lived at such a time. And to have known such a woman. Could I ever have measured up to her?*

25

"Oh, c'mon, officer. Nobody stops at stop signs."

Brent looked at the address on the offender's Texas driver's license. "San Antonio, right?"

The driver straightened, his Stetson tilting askew against the car's roof. "Yep. We know how ta drive in the big city."

"Really?" Brent gestured toward a woman on the street corner who was hugging a young child against her coat and glaring at the driver of the rental SUV. "So, nearly running down pedestrians on a clearly marked crosswalk is the Texan way of knowing how to drive?"

A thickset woman in the passenger seat spoke up. "Admit it, Bubba. You weren't payin' attention."

He looked at her. "Whose side're you on?"

She jerked a thumb toward the woman on the corner. "Hers. This ain't the open range. Folks gotta be able to cross the street without gettin' run down."

Brent nodded. "The lady makes sense, sir."

Bubba drew a deep breath. "Sorry. Any chance of a warnin'?"

"If there had been no one at the intersection, no harm done. But you nearly cost us two innocent citizens, so I need to cite you." Brent reached for his ticket pad.

"Well, fer cryin' out loud! It ain't like—"

"Can it, Bubba," the woman said. "He's just doin' his job."

Bubba slouched in his seat and mumbled to himself.

Brent hid his grin and filled out the ticket. After handing the citation to Bubba, he tipped his hat. "Thanks for visiting Marble Falls, folks. Sorry this had to happen. Please drive carefully for your own sake as well as others."

The woman flashed a tight smile. "Thanks, officer. He's had it comin' fer a while. "

"Hey!" Bubba glowered at her.

"Well, ya have."

Brent chuckled and walked over to check on the woman and her child. After ensuring her peace of mind and informing her that justice had been done, he climbed back into his cruiser and cut the emergency lights. He was ready to pull back onto Main Street when his phone sounded.

"Hi, Gwen. I'm on Main Street, in case you're almost here."

Gwen's giggle tickled his ear. "You just don't quit, do you?"

"I'm parked across from the Sports Pub & Grill."

"I'm afraid I'm not—"

"And my shift is over, so it's no problem waiting."

"Brent!"

He laughed. "I get it. I don't like it, but I get it."

"You have no idea how much I hate disappointing you."

"So, what's new? Anything more on your father's estate, or from your grandmother's diaries?"

"Not so much on the former, a lot on the latter. I was hoping you might have some news."

"Not yet. Another stint on the computer is on the to-do list after I file my reports. What have you found out from the diary?"

"Oh Brent, I *so* wish I could have met her. She's incredible. I hope her journals tell more about the trunk, though."

"You can skip to the end, you know."

"Sure, but I need to make the journey if the destination is to mean anything."

"Smart girl."

"Not as smart as Grandmother Irma. I can't wait for you to read these."

"Maybe you can read them to me over cocoa in front of the fireplace."

"That sounds nice."

His tone took on a tease. "I'm thinking about that litho. What a hottie."

"Down, boy. She's way too old for you."

"Yeah, but still … "

"Careful, mister."

Brent laughed. "Do you remember what I said the first time I saw her image in the trunk?"

"Why, no. Remind me. And don't leave out any details."

"I commented how lovely she was, and how she looked a lot like you."

"Which Margie was quick to jump on. I never took her for the matchmaker she turned out to be."

He laughed again. "Neither did I. Sure glad she is, though."

"Me too."

"I need to go, but I promise I'll get back on the computer this evening."

"Thanks."

"You bet."

***

Gwen disconnected the call, finished loading darks into the washing machine, and unloaded a basket of whites from the dryer. She began folding pillowcases when a knock at the door startled her. Frowning, she looked at her watch and went to the foyer. She opened the door, and a large figure shifted in the shadows of the front porch.

"Oh!" Her heart shot to her throat, and she groped for the light switch. She exhaled when the porch lamp flooded the face of an equally startled Sgt. Ferguson, who stepped back and removed his hat.

"I'm sorry. I didn't mean to scare you."

Gwen clutched the collar of her blouse and willed her pounding heart to settle. "It's my fault. I should've turned on the light first."

"I tried to call you, but the line went straight to voicemail. Your place is on my way home, so I thought I'd take a chance and stop by."

"I was on the phone with Brent."

Sgt. Ferguson smiled. "So, how is Wild Bill doing?"

She stared at him. "Excuse me? 'Wild Bill'?"

"You need to ask him about that."

She broke a smile. "I certainly will." She stepped back. "Please come in. It's freezing out there."

"Thanks, I won't take up much of your time." He stepped across the threshold and brushed at a varnish of wet snow on his shoulders.

"Can I take your coat?"

"No need. I won't be here long."

Sandy RiverSandy RiverSandy River

Sandy River

"Nonsense, I have a fire going in the fireplace. You'll warm up much more quickly without that wet overcoat."

"Thank you." He shrugged out of the garment and handed her his hat.

Gwen forced herself not to gawk at his massive shoulders and thick neck as she hung his coat and hat on the hallway coat rack. Her forehead warmed as Brent's comment about the Incredible Hulk in a T-shirt resurfaced in her mind. She cleared her throat and led him into the family room. "Here, sit by the fire. I have some water heating for tea."

"That's not necessary."

"It wouldn't be a pleasure if it were necessary," she said and turned toward the kitchen.

A deep laugh erupted behind her. "Now Brent's description of you makes even more sense."

Gwen stopped in the doorway and turned back with a bemused smile. "What do you mean by that?"

"He mentioned a quick wit."

"Oh, he did, did he?" She tipped her head. "Well, I suppose that's alright."

She turned again, and another chuckle trailed her into the kitchen.

When Gwen returned with two cups of steeping Peking Oolong tea, a creamer, and a sugar bowl, Sgt. Ferguson was stooping by the fireplace, rubbing his hands near the flames. She placed the tray on the coffee table and went over to turn up the gas. "Sorry, I think this is actually more for ambiance than heat."

"It's great, ma'am. Thank you."

Her shoulders slumped. "This 'ma'am' thing is making me feel old. Please call me Gwen."

He laughed. "I mean it as a term of respect, not longevity. I guess I was raised that way. But, point taken." He smiled as he reached for the sugar bowl. "And 'Sergeant Ferguson' has to go too. It's Mark."

"Agreed."

They prepared their tea and settled onto opposite ends of the couch. Mark took a sip and set down his cup. "I wanted to talk to you about the housekeeper who reported your father's … situation."

"Please don't feel you have to walk on eggshells. I loved my father, but I've reconciled myself with his passing."

109

Mark dipped his head. "Yes, ma'am—er, Gwen." He leaned forward, elbows propped on his knees. "When you told me there was nothing in his financial records regarding a maid service, I checked into the housekeeper's statement. The contact information she left was bogus."

"Bogus?"

"The street address she left belongs to a vacant lot over by Mystic Lake."

Gwen frowned. "But, why would somebody do that?"

"I'm not sure." Mark paused. "I assume you haven't had any more strange occurrences, or you would've called, right?"

She lowered her teacup to the table, swallowing through a tight throat. "Why? Do you suspect something?"

He sat back. "I'm sorry, I've upset you."

She shook her head. "A couple of months ago I went through a difficult time. For some reason, it started coming back to me." She breathed deeply. "Please go on."

"I'm opening an investigation into your father's death. I'm not convinced it was accidental, like a drug overdose, though I'm not sure exactly what it was."

Gwen squeezed her eyes closed and struggled for breath. When she reopened them, Mark had blurred through a sheen that sent tears down her cheeks. "My father would *never* have abused drugs," she whispered, brushing the moisture away with the back of her hand.

He straightened. "I'm not saying he abused drugs. There's more than one way to fall victim to an overdose, and I haven't jumped to any conclusions."

She offered an apologetic smile. "I'm sorry. I didn't mean to imply … I know you're only trying to … " Her words caught, and she buried her face in her hands. Despite her strongest efforts, a deep sob convulsed her chest.

"Gwen?"

Mark's voice barely penetrated the buzzing in her ears as another choking sob robbed her lungs of air. She shook her head.

A moment later, large hands slid gently around her shoulders. Her forehead met a solid shoulder and she collapsed into him, weeping for what could have been seconds or could have been hours.

When she regained awareness, he was softly patting her back. She stiffened and drew back, glistening eyes widened at him.

He retreated to his side of the couch. "Are you okay?"

She managed a shallow nod and wiped the wetness from her cheeks on a sleeve.

"I wasn't taking advantage. I thought you might … well, you looked like you were going to faint."

She nodded. "I don't know what came over me."

He offered a tentative smile. "I don't mean to pry, but have you cried since you heard of your father's death? I mean, really cried?"

She dropped her gaze. "I think so … well, no, maybe I haven't." She looked back up. "I did love my father, but we weren't very close these past few years."

"Grief catches up with us at different times and in different ways."

"I guess I just didn't expect it to catch up at this particular moment."

He chuckled. "Good thing a friend was here."

She smiled, a surge of warmth returning to her cheeks. "Yes, it was."

"So, about the housekeeper. Is there any chance there's something in your father's records something you might have missed, something that might shed light on who she is?"

"I'll look again."

"Thanks." He checked his watch, and his eyes widened. "Oh, man. I am *so* late." He rose from the couch. "Thank you for the tea. I'll stay in touch."

She rose and escorted him to the hallway. "I hope I haven't kept you from anything."

"Not your fault. I promised Cassie I'd pick her up for dinner ten minutes ago."

"Brent mentioned a Cassie. Your girlfriend?"

He nodded with a broad smile as he shrugged on his overcoat and pulled his phone out. "You two would really get along. If we can get Wild Bill down here, maybe the four of us can catch a meal or something."

"That sounds like fun. By the way, he's researching my father's will. Maybe you can compare notes."

"I'll give him a call."

She opened the door, and Mark strode down the sidewalk, phone pressed to his ear. "I know, I know, I'm late. Sorry, I had to make a stop ... " His voice faded as he squeezed into a small lime-green Mazda 3.

Gwen giggled. *You've got to be kidding. He could probably pick that thing up under one arm and carry it home.*

26

Gwen pulled her phone from her purse on the way back to the family room and called Brent, barely suppressing a grin.

"Hey, Gwen."

"Hi, Wild Bill."

Brent's flattened voice dripped from the receiver. "Let me guess. You've been in touch with Mark again."

"Maybe."

He sighed. "I suppose he left the explanation to me."

"You're batting a thousand."

"Okay, I'll tell you. The only stipulation is that I tell you in person back here in Marble Falls."

"That's not fair."

"You'll have to deal with it."

She laughed. "You win. But don't you dare think I'll forget."

"I'm sure you won't."

Gwen settled back onto the couch. "So, were you able to find anything out about my brother?"

"Not so much about him, but a little about Teresa Hardy."

She leaned forward. "Really?"

"Hold on." The sound of shuffling papers rattled through the phone line. "Here it is. I found a Teresa Hardy whose last-known residence was Burlington, Vermont."

"Burlington? That's where Daddy amended his will—wait. What do you mean 'last-known' residence?"

"That's where it gets sticky. The house at that address burned down in 2012. There's no record of where she relocated after the fire. According to the Vermont Department of Motor Vehicles, she never renewed her driver's license."

"And there's no reference to a son?"

"Not yet. I'm checking into school records, but I'm not sure when Simon was born, whether he went to public or private schools, or even if he was homeschooled. A date of birth would sure be helpful."

"Wouldn't the birth certificate be registered with the county? How about local hospital records? Maybe he was in a day-care facility, or a Boy Scout troop. Maybe some civic organization—"

Brent laughed. "Ever consider going into law enforcement?"

"Sorry. I'm pushing your job down your throat."

"No, actually you're right on track. I'm checking into all of those possibilities. Simon Hardy is not that common of a name. It has to surface sooner or later. I'm running the same kinds of checks on his mother."

Gwen slumped against the back of the couch. "This is going to drag out forever."

"Doing the best I can."

"Sorry, I didn't mean to sound ungrateful. I really appreciate everything you're doing."

"I know. These things often take time, but then again, sometimes you get a break when you least expect it."

"Do you have a description of her?"

"According to her driver's license records, she was five-three, dark hair, brown eyes, 135 pounds—that is, if she was honest about the weight."

Gwen pursed her lips. "Not all women lie about their weight, Brent.

"Name one who doesn't."

"I don't."

"Oh? How much do you weigh?"

"None of your business."

"I can look it up with the Massachusetts DMV, you know."

"Don't you dare."

He laughed. "That's one way to keep from lying about it. But you have nothing to worry about, Gwen. You look incredible."

"Thank you, and we will never speak of this again."

"Got it."

"Back to Teresa Hardy. How old would she be now?"

Another rustle of papers. "Forty-six. If she told the truth about that too."

"Will you stop that? And quit laughing!"

"Just sayin'." He cleared his throat. "Why do you ask?"

"I don't know. I guess I wanted to get a mental image."

"I understand." He paused. "Chad's signaling to me from the Chief's office. I'm going to have to let you go."

"Thanks for all you're doing."

"Forever."

"Careful what you promise."

"Always am."

"I love you," she whispered. Gwen disconnected the call and laid the phone onto the end table.

***

After an impromptu meeting with Chad and the chief concerning the upcoming holiday schedule, Brent went back to the break room and dropped onto a chair at the computer. He placed a call on his cell phone, kicked off a boot, and propped an ankle across a knee. Wedging the phone between his shoulder and ear, he massaged his woolen-socked foot and waited. A half-dozen rings later, Mark Ferguson's booming voice exploded from the receiver. "Hey, Brent!"

Grimacing, Brent switched the device to the other ear. "Don't you have an inside voice?"

"Used to. Never did me any good, so I lost it. So, how are things in Sleepy Hollow?"

"Are you kidding? Marble Falls is hopping. Why, only today I issued a citation to a tourist for busting a stop sign. Still winded from all the excitement."

Mark laughed. "Pace yourself, bro. You have a really sweet catch of a girlfriend who doesn't need her main squeeze laid out from exhaustion."

Brent chuckled. "Thanks for the advice. Actually, Gwen is the reason I called. She said you stopped by, so I thought I'd see what you have so far on her father's death."

"Yeah, I was going to call you tomorrow." Mark paused. "Tell you what, Cassie and I are heading out to dinner in a minute. I have the investigation report and my notes in my phone. I'll email them to you, and we can talk later."

"Sounds like something's not quite right."

"It isn't. I'm not sure what to think yet, but something is screwy about the housekeeper who found her father's body."

"Really?"

"Yeah—oh, Cassie's ready to go. And you know what that means."

"Yeah, you better move."

"I'll send you the files from the restaurant. She always hits the ladies' room right after we order, so I'll have a couple of free moments."

"Thanks. Give her my best."

"Sure will. Oh, and I meant what I said about Gwen, Brent. You scored big time. She's a sweetheart."

"I know."

"Took you long enough."

"Mark—"

"Yeah, yeah, I know, none of my business. Still, Janet was great, but guys like you can't sacrifice girls like Gwen to the past. Four years was more than long enough, big guy. I'm glad she didn't happen by while you were still beating yourself up over Janet's death—which was zero fault of yours." He paused, and the cannon-like resonance of his voice softened. "I'm really happy for you. And Cassie is too."

"Got it, Mark. Thanks."

"You bet. You'll never hear another word about it from me, but from Cassie? Well, I make no promises."

Brent smiled. "I'll brace myself. Enjoy your date." He ended the call.

***

Gwen slid her phone onto the end table, where Grandmother Irma's diary caught her eye. There was nothing more to do this evening, so maybe an escape into the past with a little comfort food would settle her nerves.

Twenty minutes later, she settled back onto the sofa balancing a dish of fried diced potatoes with crumbled bacon and scrambled eggs topped with melted mozzarella cheese, and an oversized mug of non-fat artificially sweetened cocoa. Surely the lo-cal drink would offset any damage the comfort food might do.

After a brief word of thanks for the food and her safety, she downed a forkful of food, sipped her cocoa, and reached for the journal.

Friday, January 25, 1861

Joy! A letter from Mary Jane arrived today. It's so wonderful to hear from her after weeks of no news. But, I discern a note of solemnity, even fear, in her tone. Then again, perhaps it's my imagination. Still, I can't help but reflect back on our final conversation in Marble Falls.

27

Irma nudged a porcelain-handled letter opener beneath the flap, slit it open, and a single piece of paper slid onto her palm. She frowned. Mary Jane's previous correspondences had filled at least three pages, front and back. After the prolonged silence, it seemed she would have more to say. Indeed, Irma had written her three times since receiving her friend's most recent epistle, and she'd always enclosed trinkets or newspaper clippings of the latest doings in Boston.

But at least it was something, so she unfolded the leaf and read.

Dearest Irma,

Foremost, I'm sorry for taking so long to write. There are fewer chores during the winter months, but they take more time. That and the Yuletide holidays, and well, I'm afraid the time got away from me. A poor excuse, I know. You have been so faithful in writing—and so generous in the mementos you sent! I resolve to be a more worthy correspondent.

Winter settled in with a vengeance this year. The roads have been mostly closed since late November. Fortunately, Papa foresees the seasons astutely, and he laid in plenty of firewood and supplies. Mama canned and dried a supply of food, so we needn't worry about survival. Now there is only the isolation to deal with.

Marble Falls hosted a wonderful Christmas fete this year for sister settlements on the mountain. Families from all around came to join in the celebration. And yes, if you are wondering, Hiram's family was among them. He was as attentive to me as usual, even more so. Modesty prevents me from explaining, but we must speak. I am in need of counsel, and I do trust you in matters of the heart, despite your protestations. I hope you plan to travel to Marble Falls soon.

Regrettably, I must close. An unusual warm spell has settled over us, but it surely won't last, and if this letter is to make it off the mountain today, I must hurry it to the post.

Please respond with the promise that I will see you soonest, as I long sorely for your precious company.
Always and forever I remain your adoring friend,
Mary Jane

Irma slowly lowered the letter onto her dressing table. *My counsel? Hiram was "more attentive"? What are you trying to say, Mary Jane?*

She touched a fingertip tapping her chin, then reached for her pen and stationery. As she was about to dip the nib into the inkwell, a gentle knock came at her door.

"Come in."

The door opened to a maidservant. "Miss Kelly, you have a guest."

She turned toward the mantel clock over her bedroom fireplace. That would be Gerald arriving for dinner. She smiled at the girl. "Thank you, I'll be down shortly."

The maid quietly closed the door, and Irma leaned toward the mirror, brushed a curl back from her forehead, and rose.

Her journey downstairs passed amid pondering Mary Jane's puzzling words. Before she realized it, she was in the hallway, immobilized in Gerald's embrace. She turned her face slightly as he planted a soft kiss on her cheek.

"And how is Boston's loveliest young lady this evening?"

She lifted a light smile. "I am well, thank you." She permitted him to lead her into the sitting room where they settled onto the settee, she perched on the edge, he lounged back with a leg crossed over his knee. She lowered an awkward gaze and fidgeted with a blue-and-white bow on her evening dress, searching her beleaguered mind for conversation. *Any* conversation. Fortunately, Mrs. Callaghan rescued her by entering with a tea service.

"Thank you, Mrs. Callaghan." Gerald leaned forward and selected gingerbread from an orderly arrangement of biscuits, then lifted his teacup and settled back again. Irma did likewise.

"Of course, Mr. Fairchild. 'Tis a pleasure to serve you." The cook stepped back, hands clasped, fixed on Gerald, smiling a bit longer than social propriety might dictate.

Irma lifted a cool gaze up at her.

Mrs. Callaghan cleared her throat and turned back toward the kitchen.

"You have a gem of a cook in Mrs. Callaghan," Gerald said through a bite of biscuit.

"We do, don't we?" Irma was still frowning at the kitchen doorway.

Gerald pinched two sugars to his tea. "Have you heard of the latest developments in the South?"

Irma smoothed her skirts, making a mental note to keep a closer eye on the household staff.

At her pause, Gerald continued. "But of course you haven't. No need to fill your pretty head with the ugliness of current events."

She swiveled toward him, lips pursed. "Of course I've heard the news. I make a point of keeping abreast of what is happening both home and abroad."

His eyes widened halfway through another bite, and he lowered the gingerbread. "Indeed you do. I didn't mean to offend."

"No offense taken." She drew herself up and averted her gaze. "To which current events do you refer?"

"Why, Louisiana, of course. They joined the Southern rebellion yesterday. South Carolina, Mississippi, Florida, Alabama, Georgia, and Louisiana all have left the Union in the space of one month."

Irma's forehead heated in annoyance at her surprise, but she steadied her tone. "Indeed they have. One wonders where it will stop."

"It won't stop until all of the states south of the Mason-Dixon Line have bolted." Gerald laid the half-eaten morsel onto his tea saucer and set the refreshments back onto the tray. "This bodes ill for the Union. President Lincoln will not stand for its dissolution, nor should he." He shook his head. "I'm more convinced than ever war is inevitable."

A chill touched Irma's spine, and her saucer clinked onto the tray as she set it next to Gerald's. "But American against American? Family against family? I must believe that common sense will prevail."

Gerald shook his head. "Common sense is not common to all, and it suffocates beneath the weight of economics and nationalism at every contest." He reached for her hand. "There will be war. You may count on it."

They jolted as Mrs. Callaghan's voice interrupted them from the doorway. "Dinner is served. Mr. and Mrs. Kelly are in the dining room."

Irma and Gerald rose and joined their elders at the table. She scarcely heard the dinner conversation or tasted her food, her mind in a tizzy between disquieting news from Marble Falls and ominous tidings from Washington.

28

I cannot help but fear the worst. Where is the hope? What has become of the Lord's hand over the affairs of men?

Gwen replaced the diary on the end table and drew the afghan tightly around her shoulders. She stared into the fire. What would it have been like to sense the dread of war, one that would surely shake the foundations of family and country? She was not even a teenager when the attack on the World Trade Center prompted the longest war in the nation's history—and even that struggle was playing out in faraway lands, not a few hundred miles away on American soil. Could her grandmother have had any notion what the Civil War was going to do to the United States? Even now, over 150 years later, its effects still divided elements of society who could not reconcile themselves with its outcome. Yet, from what little she knew of Gabriel's and Isabelle's lot, and so many others like them, it was an eminently worthy cause. Costly, but worthy.

Her thoughts returned to Gabriel and Isabelle. Real people, flesh and bones, emotions and intelligence, not faceless statistics in some dusty history textbook on a library shelf. As she anticipated from the moment she found the diaries in the attic chest, Grandmother Irma's journal, although merely a sketch, had turned a distant reality into a vividly real and personal world. Gwen recalled Grandmother Irma's lithograph, those beguiling eyes, the vibrant personality evident behind them. She closed her eyes and tried to picture her grandmother's dear friends from the African Meeting House.

Gabriel, a big man with a big heart who had rushed into harm's way to defend Grandmother Irma, no matter that her race was so cruelly oppressing his. She was a friend and a woman of principle, which was enough for him to act without regard for his own safety.

That kind of selfless chivalry seemed so lacking in today's world. The thought took her back to the confrontation with Turk Sawyer in Corky Williams' root cellar, when Brent stepped between her and the psychopath's handgun. Her heart warmed. A foolish act on Brent's part? Perhaps. Could he have prevented either of their deaths if Turk had chosen to fire his weapon? Probably not. But Brent had also acted without consideration for his own safety. She smiled. Chivalry was not dead.

Then there was Isabelle, who had risked everything to protect the man she loved. Her example of selfless devotion stood in drastic contrast to today's social equality and the it's-all-about-me attitude. In response, Gwen's mind returned again to the root cellar, Brent lying unconscious in her arms, Sawyer's sneering threat to shatter Brent's kneecap with a 9mm slug. Her heart swelled remembering the fierceness that rose up in her, pulling close the man she loved, flinging defiance at their assailant. Could she have prevented Brent's maiming if Sawyer had fired his weapon? Probably not. But she had acted out of love and without consideration for herself, as she would surely have been next to receive a bullet. Perhaps real strength was not in the pursuit of self-actualization, but in willing self-sacrifice. It had certainly been a powerful force in Grandmother Irma's life, and Gwen liked to think it had traveled the years into her own as well.

She brushed her fingertips lightly across the journal. *I wonder how different Gabriel's and Isabelle's lives would be had they lived today.* Her fingertips paused over the faded initials "ILK" pressed into the diary's cover. *And mine, had I lived in their day.*

She drew the afghan over her shoulders and rested her head on the throw pillow. In the fireplace, a dancing blue-white gas flame tickling the underside of a decorative ceramic log. As she watched it, mesmerized, her eyelids grew heavy. Gradually, the flame blurred, stilled, then darkened.

*

Down a shadowed hallway, their feet trod quietly along an intricately patterned carpet runner. They stopped before a plain wooden door. A hand knocked.

The door cracked open, and Isabelle Jones' anxious eye peered through.

123

"All is well," Grandmother Irma whispered. "Gwendolyn is a friend—more than a friend."

The door opened further, revealing a lovely round face with deep-brown almond-shaped eyes and full lips, which spread into a tentative smile. "A pleasure, Miz Gwendolyn."

"The pleasure is mine, Isabelle. My friends call me Gwen." A pause. "And I would love for you to be my friend."

Grandmother Irma reached out, softly touched her wrist, sending a shiver up her arm, throughout her body. She peered into the young face of a time-distant grandmother and was rewarded with a nod of approval.

Her attention returned to the doorway. A tall broad-shouldered man with a serious expression stood behind Isabelle, hand resting on her shoulder.

Warmth flooded her body. "You must be Gabriel."

A bright-toothed smile softened his expression. "Yes'm. And you be Miz Kelly's family."

"How did you know?"

The smile broadened. "Y'all don't remember?"

A shiver chilled her spine. "What do you mean? Remember what?"

"Gwen?" A familiar voice behind her fluttered her heart, and the chill melted away. Masculine fingers brushed a wisp of hair behind her ear.

"Brent? What are you doing here?"

"You asked me to come."

"I did?"

Grandmother Irma laughed gently. "Come with me, child. There is much to discuss." The weight of Grandmother's touch on her arm turned to air, and the apparition's hand withered, gnarled, and purple veins snaked beneath cellophane skin.

"Grandmoth—"

"Hushhhh … "

Hazy air descended over the hallway, and breathing became a struggle. Door and wall shimmered, dissolved, and the fog retreated. She found herself alone beside a broken-down split-rail fence under a tufted charcoal-gray sky. Chilly wind swept over an endless field strewn with contorted bodies and rusty muskets, bayonets piercing veils of acrid smoke wafting from ranks of shattered cannon. A lone figure appeared from between tattered banners fluttering on broken staffs. Stumbling among the carnage, it paused, knelt beside a fallen blue-clad warrior. A trembling sob escaped the seeker's lips and he slowly lifted his head. "I'm so sorry, Gwen. So sorry."

"Daddy?"

***

"Daddy!"

Gwen awoke, chest heaving, her flailing arms sending the afghan to the floor. Rubbing her eyes, she blinked into a stream of sunlight flooding through the window next to the fireplace. Gas flames still flickered in the fireplace, and on the end table rested a half-full plate of congealed eggs and potatoes sitting beside an empty brown-smudged cocoa mug. She rose unsteadily and massaged an ache in her lower back. The dining room wall clock tolled the Westminster Chimes followed by nine beats in succession. *Nine o'clock? Already?*

Vivid remnants of last night's dream still clinging to her brain, Gwen began gathering the dirty dishes. When she lifted the mug, she froze. A piece of beige stationery, stained with a brown circle of chocolate, greeted her.

GOOD MORNING.
THANKS FOR THE HOT CHOCOLATE.

-29-

Gwen paced the driveway, hugging her waist, throwing terse looks back toward the house. The first few minutes of her frantic call to Mark Ferguson was spent with him calming her down. The next two minutes of her semi-coherent explanation was all he needed.

"Don't touch anything. I'm on my way. Is there a neighbor's house you can go to until I get there?"

"We didn't really socialize much with the neighbors …"

"Then I want you to go outside and stand at the end of your driveway until I get there. Understood?"

"I'm sure no one is still in the house."

"You're sure?"

"Well, as sure as I can be."

"That's not good enough. I want to see you outside when I get there. Leaving now."

She checked her watch for the umpteenth time and peered up the street as Mark's tiny Mazda spun around the corner and screeched to a halt at the curb. He shouldered open the door and heaved himself out. Five strides later his massive hands were grasping her by the shoulders. "Are you okay?"

Gwen hugged her arms tighter and nodded. "I … I—" Her throat clamped shut and eyes flooded. When she recovered, she found herself pressed against him, shuddering.

Vaguely, his voice filtered through. "Everything's going to be fine."

She blinked and drew a deep breath. *Get a grip, Gwen.* She pulled back, wiped her cheeks with her palms, and sputtered a short laugh. "You must think I'm an emotional mess."

He pulled a small packet of tissues from his pocket and offered it to her. "No, I think you're under a lot of pressure, and somebody is messing with you."

She dabbed her eyes and managed a nod.

Mark looked toward the house. "Is the front door unlocked?"

"Yes."

"Then stay here. I'll take a look around."

She shook her head. "I'm coming too."

"Gwen—"

"It's my house, and I might notice something that you wouldn't."

"All right, but stay close."

"Don't worry. I can handle the stress." She looked at him for a moment, then broke into shaking laughter. "That is, when I'm not choked up, bursting into tears, or looking like I'm about to faint."

Mark laughed. "Don't be too hard on yourself. It happens to the best of us."

"Somehow I can't see it happening to you."

His smile faded. "Never be too sure."

"I'm sorry. I didn't mean to presume."

He gestured toward the house. "Let's get to work."

Inside, Gwen led him to the back door. "I'm sure I locked the door last night, but this morning it was ajar."

He stooped and inspected the doorjamb. "Somebody masked the strike plate. The latch wasn't able to engage."

Gwen thinned her lips. "English, please."

"Somebody put clear tape over the hole in the frame. The doohickey that goes into it was blocked so the door wouldn't close right."

"Thanks."

Mark chuckled. "Glad to help."

He removed a pair of tweezers and an evidence bag from a small satchel he'd brought from the car, removed the tape and placed it in the bag. "There may be fingerprints on the tape," he explained. He performed a search of the back yard and garage, but had nothing to report when he returned. "Where is the note?"

She pointed toward the end table. "There."

When she reached for it, he stopped her. "Fingerprints."

"Oh, I didn't even think of that. I'm afraid I've already handled it."

"That's okay. There may still be something Forensics can find." He lifted the paper by a corner and slipped it into another evidence bag.

As Gwen told him about the dinner she'd prepared the evening before, a chill raced down her spine. *He was that close to me. What if . . .*

"Are you okay?" Mark was peering at her.

She nodded and gestured toward the end table. "I remember finishing half of my cocoa. I set the mug there beside my dinner plate."

"Where's the mug now?"

"In with the dirty dishes." She gasped. "Oh, no. I handled it too."

He chuckled. "Don't worry about it. We might still be able to pull something form it." He shrugged. "Besides, fingerprints are overrated."

She cocked her head. "With your bedside manner, you should have been a doctor."

"My mom told me the same thing when I went into police work."

He was about to place the stationery into the satchel when Gwen stopped him. "Wait a minute. I think I recognize that paper."

"You do?"

"Let's go upstairs." She led the way to her father's study. She opened the lap drawer and pointed to a pad of beige stationery. The top sheet was torn off beneath the flourish-scripted masthead, "From the Desk of James Byrne Kelly."

Mark aligned the intruder's note to the torn sheet. The ragged edges matched. He slipped the pad into the bag with the note.

Gwen's forehead heated. "That means … "

Mark nodded. "He did more than drink your cocoa. He came up here."

"So, how long was he in the house? Where else did he go? And what if he had … "

He patted her arm. "But he didn't, so apparently that's not on his mind."

"But why leave a note? He could've searched the house for whatever he wanted and left. Why deliberately leave evidence he was here?"

"A power trip? Intimidation? In any event, it shows a need for attention, and that may prove to be his downfall."

"Or mine."

"You're stronger than that."

She twitched her lips. "How would you know that?"

He jotted something in a small notebook. "Brent would settle for no one less."

Gwen's heart warmed. "Thank you."

He smiled at her and replaced the notebook in a hip pocket. "So, can you tell me if anything else has been disturbed?"

"Let me check." After a quick inspection of the desk drawers and the filing cabinet, she stepped back. "I don't see anything out of place."

"Good." He turned toward her. "I need to get this evidence to the station. Where will you be staying tonight?"

"Here, I suppose."

"Nope."

"I have nowhere else to go, and I can't afford a hotel for who-knows-how-long this will take."

"Let me make a call." He pulled his phone from his pocket.

"I don't want to inconvenience anyone."

He lifted a finger. "Hey, Lover. How are you doin'?"

Gwen stared at him. *Lover?*

Mark laughed. "You know, I've stopped counting the number of answers you have for that question ... Okay, so I'll stop asking. I need a favor." He rolled his eyes. "Yes, another one. So, you remember Gwen Kelly? ... Right, the one who busted open Wild Bill's concrete shell."

Gwen smiled in spite of herself.

"She needs a place to stay."

Gwen's eyes widened. "Mark, no. I'm not going to impose on—"

He turned away and covered his free ear. "I'll explain later, but you'll get it, trust me ... Yeah, I know you know that." He looked back over his shoulder at Gwen, whose arms were crossed over her chest and eyes narrowed at him. A grin broke out. "Uh huh. No question you'll get along. So, how about forty-five minutes? ... You're the best." He laughed again. "Yeah, I know you know that too."

He disconnected the call and turned toward Gwen. "Better get packed. We don't want to keep Cassie waiting."

She tapped a forefinger on her arm. "And I have nothing to say about this?"

"Before I called Cassie, you might have. But now?" He shook his head. "No ma'am."

30

Gwen leaned against the passenger door of the Mazda, Mark's bulk taking up the rest of the front seat area. He offered her an apologetic smile. "Sorry. It's a little cozy in here."

She grinned. "That's like saying it's comfy in a can of sardines."

He laughed. "Yeah, I guess so."

"Whatever possessed you to buy such a small car?"

"Gas mileage and city driving."

"Seriously?"

"Yeah, Cassie wanted me to try out a Mazda 2, but it wasn't going to happen."

Gwen laughed. "A Mazda 2? Has she looked at you lately?"

"More than you might know."

Her forehead warmed. "Wow, I really stepped into that one."

Mark laughed. "That's not what I meant. Cassie is the most observant person I know. She never ceases to amaze me."

"How so?"

"Well, let's use my car as an example. She suggested I look at the Mazda 2, knowing it would be inadequate and aware I'd appreciate the Mazda 3 in comparison."

"It's still so small."

"But it's all I need. More would be excess, and there are other things I'd rather spend my money on."

"Like what?"

"Like Cassie."

Gwen laughed. "She must be something special."

"You're about to find out." He pulled into the driveway of a single-story red-brick house.

Mark retrieved her bags from the back seat and walked her to the front door. He tucked her large suitcase and carry-on bag under one arm and knocked.

"It's open," called a faint voice from within.

Mark pushed on the door, and they stepped inside.

A modest living room with a dark hardwood floor softened with area rugs spread beyond the foyer. On the walls was an eclectic array of two- and three-dimensional artwork beneath a ceiling framed by scrolled crown molding. On the far wall, fully loaded bookcases framed a brick fireplace where a crackling log fire radiated warmth and a cheery glow.

Gwen unbuttoned her coat. "This is beautiful."

"Company!" he called as he closed the door behind them.

"Be right there," came the response from an arched doorway leading into a narrow hallway.

"I'll take your bags to the guest room," Mark said, and moved toward the archway.

"Wait. Aren't you going to introduce us?"

"You'll do fine."

When he had disappeared around the corner, Gwen walked into the room to savor the fire and study the decor. She was leaning toward an absorbing oil painting of a stormy-skied mountain landscape, when a woman's voice floated over her shoulder.

"Do you like it?"

Gwen nodded. "It's absolutely beautiful, but also … I don't know, haunting. I so wish I could—" She turned around and went still.

A trim brunette in a teal short-sleeved sweater was regarding her evenly from the doorway. On her left arm, she balanced a small tray of snacks. Her right arm was missing below the elbow. She stepped forward, and the firelight glinted from a metal prosthetic limb protruding from the right leg of a pair of navy-blue capris. A creamy complexion scattered with freckles covered the left side of her face, feathering down into a mottled layer of red and gray wrinkles that covered the right side of her neck. "Could what?"

Gwen swallowed. "Create something so lovely."

Cassie set the tray on a sofa table and limped to Gwen's side. She peered at the picture. "It was my first attempt to paint with my left hand. It's passable, I guess."

" 'Passable'? It's entrancing."

"Thank you." Cassie extended her left hand. "I'm Cassie. You must be Gwen."

Gwen grasped it, slightly wincing at the firmness of her hostess' grip. "It's wonderful to meet you. Mark speaks so lovingly of you."

Cassie looked back at the painting. "He's sweet."

Mark's booming voice interrupted them from the archway. "So what are you two colluding about?" He moved up behind Cassie and rested his hands on her shoulders.

"Gwen was explaining how my painting was—what word did you use?—haunting."

"Yes." Gwen turned back to the landscape.

"How so?" he asked.

"Well, look at the sky. It looks so threatening, but the landscape is so serene. It's as though something dreadful is about to happen, but the mountains and meadow don't seem to care."

"Maybe the mountains and the meadow don't know what's about to happen to them," Cassie said quietly.

Gwen's forehead warmed at Cassie's thickened tone. She turned and was about to apologize for ... anything, when Mark spoke first. "Or maybe they do know, but they also know they can handle whatever the storm dishes out."

Cassie kept her gaze on the painting. "How can they know that?"

"Because they've been through storms before, and they come out strong and even more beautiful."

Cassie's chin twitched, and she kept her gaze on the painting.

Gwen swallowed. "Well in any event, I love it."

"Why do you love it?" Cassie persisted.

"Because I love pictures that make me wish I were there."

"Great answer," Mark said.

Gwen looked back at him. "I liked yours better."

He gave a light shrug.

Gwen readdressed Cassie. "Where is this place? Have you been there?"

"Only in my mind."

"Really? You imagined this? I thought for sure you copied it from a photograph, or maybe painted it *en plein aire.*"

Cassie lifted a brow. "Are you a painter? Few non-artists know what *en plein aire* is."

"I have a friend who taught me about art. She said it's when the artist goes to the site and paints the scene 'in plain air' as it appears at the moment."

"That's right. Sometimes the site is in my mind, as I imagine it. Or maybe as I want it to be."

"It must be really hard to paint something from the imagination."

"Less and less as time goes by."

Mark turned Cassie around by the shoulders and pressed a kiss to her forehead. "Next summer we take a trip to the Appalachians. There you can get all the inspiration you want."

"If—"

"If nothing. We'll plan on it." He brushed a finger across her cheek. "Enough melancholy. You have a guest."

Cassie turned back toward Gwen and cleared her throat. "Sorry. Sometimes I get lost in myself."

"Don't we all?" asked Gwen.

Cassie gestured toward the sofa. "Have a seat. Dinner will be ready soon." She picked up the tray of hors d'oeuvres and laid it on a coffee table in front of the sofa.

Gwen surveyed the array of cheese and crackers. "It looks wonderful, but I wish you hadn't gone to such trouble."

Cassie shrugged. "If it was no trouble, it wouldn't be worth it."

Gwen giggled and looked at Mark. "So that's where your appreciation of wit comes from."

"She never fails to impress."

Cassie rounded the sofa toward the doorway. "I have to check on dinner."

"Can I help?" asked Gwen.

Mark shook his head and lifted a finger.

"I can manage," Cassie said over her shoulder.

When she'd gone, Gwen leveled a terse expression at Mark. "You could have told me."

"Told you what?"

She lifted an eyebrow at him.

He shook his head. "I wanted you to meet her on her terms." He smiled. "And you couldn't have been more perfect."

"May I ask what happened?"

Mark reached toward the snack tray. "Afghanistan. She was riding shotgun with me in the lead vehicle of an ammunition convoy, and an IED detonated beside the road. The blast caved in the side of the Humvee, burning her neck and shattering her arm and leg."

Gwen cupped her hands to her cheeks. "Oh, how awful."

He drew a deep breath. "I was driving. If she hadn't absorbed the explosion, it would've taken me out instead."

"Oh, Mark—"

He leveled his gaze at her. "Cassie and I were seeing each other before the attack. I was in love with her before it happened and am as much in love with her now."

"I'm sure of that." Gwen paused. "Brent mentioned Cassie when I told him you and I had met. Did he know her in Afghanistan too?"

"He was in the second vehicle. He saved both of our lives in the firefight that broke out after the convoy was halted. So much of it is a blur now, but I remember him crouching beside my door, directing a counterattack and returning fire at the insurgents while I tended to Cassie's wounds. He took a couple of rounds that were meant for us. That's where he earned his Purple Heart."

Gwen's eyes rounded. "Purple Heart? I never knew ... " She closed her eyes, chest tightening.

"You have a heckuva guy in Brent, Gwen. Never let him go."

She nodded. "I don't intend to."

"Dinner's in ten minutes," Cassie's announced from the archway. "Who's hungry?"

"I am," Gwen and Mark chorused.

Ten minutes later they were into a hearty meal of Caesar salad, homemade lasagna, and garlic bread. Conversation was stilted at first, but had relaxed by the end of the meal. After dinner, Gwen excused herself to unpack while Mark cleared the dishes and Cassie put finishing touches on three helpings of crème brûlée for dessert. Exiting the guest room, Gwen slowed as Cassie's voice floated down the hallway. "I'm glad you're in a position to help, Mark."

"So am I."

"She's beautiful, isn't she?"

"Yes, she is. Brent's a lucky guy."

Cassie's voice faltered. "Very beautiful."

A pause followed, and his softened words barely made their way down the hall. "And maybe someday she'll be almost as beautiful as you are."

Gwen smiled and slipped into the bathroom. Coming in second place never felt so good.

31

"Why didn't you call me?" Brent scolded.

"Because you can't do anything from Marble Falls," Gwen replied. "And you told me to call Mark if I needed anything. Besides, it's not that big of a deal."

"You keep saying that, but the deal keeps getting bigger and bigger. I want you back in Marble Falls."

"That's the other reason I didn't call you. You know I can't come back until Daddy's estate is settled. I'll be fine now that I'm at Cassie's, so you can stop worrying."

"Promise me you won't go back to your house without someone with you, preferably Mark."

"Brent—"

"Promise."

She sighed. "Okay."

"I hate this separation."

"So do I, for a lot of reasons—oh, Cassie just signaled that breakfast is ready." She frowned. "I sure wish she'd let me help out. I keep offering, but she waves me off."

"She's always been like that. More so after Afghanistan."

"Well, something is going to have to give. I'm not going to sit around and mooch off of her."

"Good luck with that."

"Thanks. Talk to you later." She disconnected the call and walked to the kitchen. Eggs Benedict with hashed brown potatoes, fresh grapefruit sections, and hot coffee were already on the table. Cassie was seated, so Gwen settled onto a chair across from her.

"Dig in." Cassie said, and she picked up her fork.

"Can I say a quick blessing?" asked Gwen.

Cassie straightened, fork poised over her plate. "Um, sure."

"We don't have to."

"It's fine. I guess I got away from that sort of thing." She set down her fork.

After Gwen offered a brief word of thanks, they started eating.

"This is incredible," Gwen said, dabbing her mouth with a napkin. "But you can't keep cooking like this, or I'm going to gain a ton."

"Somehow I don't think you have too much of a problem in the weight department."

"Don't kid yourself. I can put it on with the best of them." Gwen sipped her coffee. "And another thing. I don't know how long I'll be here, but I want to chip in for groceries and help with chores for however long it might be."

"That's not necessary."

"Maybe not, but I want to."

Cassie's tone took on an edge. "I said that's not necessary."

"But—"

She dropped her fork onto her plate and stared down Gwen. "I'm perfectly capable of taking care of this house."

Gwen set down her coffee mug and met Cassie's eye. "Of course you are," she said evenly. "That's obvious. But because you *can* doesn't mean you should have to. I would expect to help out no matter who I was staying with."

"Would you?"

"Yes." Gwen folded her hands on the table. "You've been kind enough to take me into your home, and I want to show my appreciation by helping out. Unless I'm totally off the mark, you would feel exactly the same way if our roles were reversed." She chanced a smile. "Am I right?"

Cassie blinked, then looked down at the table.

"It's settled then." Gwen rose from her chair. "I'm out of coffee. Can I top yours off?"

Cassie lifted her gaze, expression even.

Gwen maintained her smile and extended her hand.

Cassie pulled in a deep breath and handed Gwen her mug. "Thanks."

"You're welcome." Gwen walked over to the counter and replenished their coffee from a carafe. "So, how long have you known Mark?"

"A little over five years."

"Did you meet when you were overseas?"

"Yes."

She returned to the table and set down their coffee. "He told me you also knew Brent over there."

Cassie nodded and lifted her mug to her lips.

Gwen smiled and tipped up her own cup.

Cassie paused. "What's so funny?"

"Tell me what he was like when you met him."

She lowered her mug abruptly. "Who, Mark?"

Gwen giggled. "No, silly. Brent."

"Oh." Cassie set down her mug, her cheeks tinging pink.

"Brent and I have only known each other for a few months. There's still so much I don't know about him."

"Have you asked him?"

"Sure, but there are things he doesn't seem to want to talk about."

Cassie sighed. "There are things none of us want to talk about."

Gwen creased her brow. "What do you mean?"

Cassie turned her right shoulder toward Gwen and lifted her upper arm, tone flattening. "If you came back home like this, would you want to talk about it?"

A wave of heat enveloped Gwen's head. "Of course not. I'm sorry, I didn't mean to be insensitive."

Cassie leaned back and stared into her coffee. "Brent was there when it happened. If not for him, I'd have come home in a box. Probably Mark too."

Gwen quieted. "Yes, Mark shared that with me."

Cassie looked up, and the edge returned to her voice. "Seems Mark shares a lot of things with you."

Gwen straightened and met Cassie's eye. "Actually, would you like to know the most intimate thing he's shared with me?"

Cassie went rigid and fire sparked in her eyes, but Gwen continued. "How much he loves you, and how much you mean to him." She reached across for Cassie's hand, but she pulled back.

"Look at me," Cassie said hoarsely. "He puts up with me now, but how will I ever keep him?" Her chest convulsed and she dropped her gaze.

Gwen rounded the table and knelt at Cassie's side. "Brent loves me, but the day I see in his eyes what I see in Mark's when he looks at you, I'll know I have arrived. Honestly, I can't imagine you ever losing him."

***

Gwen sat near the fire, nursing a cup of decaf French roast. She warmed to the yellow flames and glowing embers, keenly aware of her hostess' singular attention to Mark, who rested his head onto the back of the sofa, eyes closed, his cup resting on his lap.

"Tough day? she asked.

He cracked open an eyelid and smiled at her. "Not anymore."

"The coffee helps?"

"I was thinking of you."

Cassie shifted in her chair, but said nothing.

Mark closed his eyes again and drew a deep breath. "There's nothing better than a quiet evening, warm fire, and the woman I love."

Gwen drained the last ounce from her cup and rose. "If you'll excuse me, I've got some things to do before bed."

Mark leaned forward. "I hope you're not leaving on my account."

"Not at all." She moved toward the hallway. "It's been a tiring day, and I'm bushed. Goodnight."

After depositing the coffee cup in the dishwasher, Gwen crept down the hallway past a very quiet living room to the guest room. She prepared herself for the night, but when she slipped under the bedcovers, sleep eluded her. She stared at the ceiling, looked over at the bedside table, then reached for Grandmother Irma's diary.

Monday, March 18, 1861

Boston is disquieted, one can easily discern it. Whispers on street corners, innuendoes in the newspapers, once talkative neighbors hurrying past with downcast eyes. How much longer can the life we know endure so dark a cloud of impending war?

32

It was well after six o'clock before the creak of the front door carried up the stairwell from the foyer, breaking Irma's concentration on her journal. Her father's tired voice trailed it. "My dear Kate. You look lovely, as always."

"And you as handsome."

"Perhaps in a previous lifetime," he grumbled.

Irma closed her journal and hurried from her bedroom to the top of the staircase. "Good evening, Father. How was your day?"

He handed his hat and overcoat to a servant, and looked up at her. "It was long. But nothing for you to worry about."

"Did you stop at the club after leaving the office?"

"For a few moments, yes."

"What news is there from—"

Her mother stepped in front of him and tipped her head up. "Heavens, Irma, let your father breathe. He just walked in the door."

Irma dropped her gaze. "I'm sorry, Father."

Kate turned toward her husband and straightened his collar. "There's a glass of sherry awaiting you in the sitting room. And dinner will be served shortly."

He kissed her cheek. "Ah, Kate. You know me so well."

"What, sherry and dinner?" She brushed a bit of lint from his shoulder. "Goodness, Byrne, you're not that difficult to keep up with."

He tipped back his head and laughed. "I suppose not. But then, you have forgotten one thing."

"And that might be … "

"My pipe, of course."

"It's with your tobacco pouch by the armchair."

"I might have known." He kissed her forehead, then tipped up her chin and tenderly kissed her lips. Irma's eyes widened, and she looked away, cheeks warming and heart throbbing. *Oh, to be in love.*

When she returned her attention to the foyer, her parents were walking the hallway arm in arm, her mother gesturing for Irma to follow.

Settled on the sofa, her father took a sip of his sherry and reached for his pipe and tobacco. Irma took her place on an overstuffed chair. She shifted on the edge of her seat. "Was there any news at the club then, Father?"

He tamped tobacco into the pipe's bowl. "I assume you refer to the secessionist movement?"

"I do."

"Much opinion, little substance."

"Then tell me of the opinion. It often leads to substance."

"Not with this crowd," her father muttered as he struck a match. "I sometimes wonder why I waste my time there."

Irma leaned forward. "Surely there's something of value you've gleaned."

She fidgeted while he painstakingly lit his pipe, puffing purplish gray clouds of smoke into the shadowed room. He shook out the match and dropped it into a shallow ashtray. "Why does this interest you?"

"Because it may bode tidings for the future."

"Any particular tidings?"

She swallowed back her impatience. A plea of simply keeping abreast with current events would likely fall on unsympathetic ears. But another approach might garner a more receptive response. "You heard Gerald vow to enlist in the Union cause should hostilities with the South arise. If we are to be wed—I mean, *when* we are to be wed, the state of the Union figures very strongly in my—in *our* future."

She stole a quick look toward her mother, who wore a discomfiting expression. Irma returned her attention toward her father.

He prolonged her agony by taking a measured sip of sherry. "Very well, the prevailing opinion is that we shall find ourselves at war in two months."

"Do you share this opinion?"

He pulled a deep draft from his pipe and released another stream of smoke toward the ceiling. "I do not."

"What do you believe?"

"I believe we will be at war in one month."

Irma straightened. "One month? Why?"

He lowered the pipe and set his jaw. "It's merely a feeling, but it rises from deep in my gut. Not only will it begin within the month, but it will not be as swift in its conclusion as many opine."

"But surely the Union will prevail and do so quickly."

"Why do you believe that?"

"Because our cause is just. Slavery is an affront to God and to man, and it will be crushed swiftly and decisively. Why, look at Wilbur Wilberforce's victory over slavery in England."

"Indeed his cause was just, but Wilberforce employed patient stealth and guile in dealing with Parliament to attain his victory. It was not a change in the nation's heart, it was political maneuvering." He shook his head. "Your reasoning fails you at the point where you limit the cause to be one of slavery alone. The South will fight to preserve its culture, its way of life, its economy, and its honor. Political guile is no longer an option in the American scenario." He matched his daughter's intensity. "I deal regularly with the Southern states in procuring cotton for my mills. I know them, understand them ... perhaps even sympathize with them to an extent."

Irma's forehead heated. "Sympathize with them?"

"They are men who have been born, reared, and are wholly assimilated into a culture whose economy cannot flourish without forced labor ... at least not yet. Is this wrong? In my heart, I believe so, but my heart is constrained by reason. Which is the more fruitful approach, to evolve our Southern brotherhood's economic and social culture into a more humane model, or brashly impose one upon them at the point of a bayonet?"

"Do you really believe it can evolve?"

"Given time, industrialization will render forced manual labor less and less relevant."

"But how many negroes must suffer and die in agony until industrialization wins the day?"

"How many men—white and black—will die in bloody conflict to usher that day in prematurely. And what of the residual effects of such a conflict over years to come? A military defeat may dampen a man's spirit, but it will not change his heart. The aura of a war like this will linger for God knows how long." He pulled another draw from his pipe and released it. "Also, men will always find ways to exploit other men. A single war will not put an end to that human failing. It will simply redirect it."

"Father, I'm truly shocked. You sound so … so defeatist."

Byrne swirled his sherry. "Not defeatist, my dear, pragmatic. Every day, I evaluate return on investment, assess the near-term and long-term impacts of the decisions I make." He paused and stared into the amber liquid settling in his glass. "I recently made a long-term decision to stockpile cotton in the face of what I considered to be imminent disruption to my supply lines. I did this despite the short-term risk of alienating my board of directors."

Irma smiled. "I overheard your discussion with Mr. Wilkinson. You were masterful."

Her father leveled a weary gaze at her. "If you had lived my day today, your smile would have disappeared before your breakfast had settled. That decision may have saved the company, but the culture I violated will not so quickly recover." He lowered his pipe. "Likewise, war may save the principles upon which our Union was founded, but the culture it violates will be less resilient."

Irma set her jaw. "Then war it must be, if it leads to emancipation."

He leaned forward. "An easy declaration for one who will not carry a musket into battle."

"I would be willing."

"Another easy declaration."

"Father!"

Kate's calming voice interrupted their verbal joust. "I suspect we are in violent agreement here. Please allow the agreement to override the violence."

Irma and her father relaxed, but held each other's eye.

At that moment, Mrs. Callaghan appeared in the doorway and announced dinner was served. Her father drained his sherry and rose. He extended a hand toward Irma.

She looked at it, then lifted her eyes toward his.

"Civility, Irma," cautioned her mother.

Irma sighed, accepted her father's hand, and rose. Her mother slipped her hand under his other arm, and they walked to the dining room.

***

After dinner, Irma grumbled as she ascended the stairs behind her mother. "I don't know why he does that."

"Does what?"

"Goads me so. I *would* carry a musket into battle if society would allow it."

Her mother turned at the top of the stairs, a smile softening her features. "I fully expect you would."

"Thank you."

"And your father believes you would as well."

Irma snorted.

Her mother lifted a brow. "Hardly a ladylike response, Irma."

"Forgive me, Mother, but yours was hardly a believable assertion."

"Not at all. Try to step out of yourself for a moment."

Irma frowned. "What do you mean by that?"

"If you truly want to understand someone, you need to step out of your own shoes and walk a few paces in theirs. Your father is a pragmatist, a realist. As such, he has little patience for grandiose declarations that have little chance of engaging with reality. To him, saying you're willing to march off to war is like a crippled man boldly alleging that in an earlier day he could have bettered a hale man in a race. A grand pronouncement perhaps, but in reality toothless, without risk. Simply put, neither your battle nor the crippled man's race will ever come to pass, and so assertions are easy to make."

"But—"

"Self-righteously declaring that war may be necessary to assuage your own sensibilities, knowing you will never undertake the risk of facing its horrors, sorely disregards the lives and fortunes of those who will inevitably face those horrors. Your father simply wants you to fully appreciate your sentiment, to realize what war may bring to families you will never have to console and necessitate graves you will never have to dig." Her mother searched Irma's eyes. "You may take exception to his rhetoric, but you cannot fault his logic … can you?"

Irma lowered her gaze. "I cannot, Mother." She looked back up. "And having learned of his own father's fate and its effect on grandmother's mental welfare, I understand his vehemence."

"Exactly." Her mother reached out and lovingly squeezed Irma's wrist. "I knew you had at least a modicum of perceptiveness in you."

"Mother!"

Her mother laughed. "I'm teasing you. Work a little harder on that perceptiveness."

Irma's lip quivered, and she broke into a smile as well. "As Father would say, point taken."

"Goodnight, dear."

"Goodnight, Mother."

Irma stared at a blank page of the journal, the fountain pen twitching between her whitened fingertips. Finally, she lowered it into the inkwell and poised it above the fresh page, still dithering on an opening sentence. A single drop fell from the nib and stained the paper, penetrating its fibers like the dread permeating her mind. She touched a corner of her hankie to the blotch, aware it would have no cleansing effect, but still disappointed when it didn't. She swirled an exaggerated serif around the violation in an attempt to transfigure it into something beautiful, or at least acceptable.

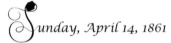

unday, April 14, 1861

There, that should help. She continued writing.

The day that for months some have fretted, some have ignored or even denied, and still others embraced, has finally arrived. Yesterday, Fort Sumter fell to rebel cannon. And so the bloodshed begins.

Irma paused, irresistibly drawn back to the ink blot. She set the pen down. The flourish had not graced the blemish, the blemish had sullied the flourish. She re-read her opening lines. As the ink smear had stained the paper, American blood had stained the soil of Fort Sumter Island. No imagined glory of battle could grace the carnage, the carnage would sully the glory. Equally, the new war would defile this great nation's heritage. Past blessings would not purify it nor heal the gaping wound now inflicted between brothers. And the more bloodshed, the greater the defilement, the deeper the wound, the more sullying the blemish.

She cupped her hands over her face, and drew a deep breath. *Oh, dear Lord, what have we wrought?*

"Irma?" Her mother's voice floated up the stairway from the foyer.

She lowered her hands. "I'm here, Mother."

"Gerald has arrived."

"I'll be right down." She replaced the stopper on the inkwell, permitted herself a cursory self-inspection in the dressing table mirror, then rose on unsteady legs.

Her fiancé beamed at her from the foot of the stairs as she descended, but his expression sobered when she reached the landing. "You're pale, my dear. Are you ill?"

She forced a smile. "I am well. Though I must confess the news from South Carolina distresses me."

He touched her cheek. "You mustn't worry yourself over such things."

She stepped back, eyes lit with indignation. "Of course I must. Every patriot must, I no less than any other."

His eyes widened. "I did not mean—"

"Irma?"

Irma pivoted. "What, Mother?"

Her mother stood at the doorway to the sitting room, face tipped upward.

Irma tightened her lips. After a moment, her chin quivered, and she broke eye contact.

Her mother's voice softened. "Invite Gerald in, dear."

Gerald fidgeted with his hat. "Perhaps I've come at an inopportune time."

"Please forgive me," Irma said, reaching for his arm. "I'm not myself today."

He offered a tentative smile. "You're as beautiful I've always known you to be."

She cocked her head. "Oh Gerald, how do you always know the perfect thing to say?"

"Because he makes the effort," interjected her mother.

Irma threw an annoyed glance over her shoulder, and her mother responded with a gesture toward the sitting room. Irma slipped her arm under Gerald's. "Won't you please come in?"

He covered her hand with his. "I would love to."

"Dinner will not be long," Kate said as the couple passed through the doorway. "Meantime, I'll arrange an aperitif."

He smiled at her. "Thank you, Mrs. Kelly. That sounds wonderful."

Gerald stood while Irma lowered herself onto the settee. She folded her hands on her lap, gaze lowered toward the floor. He settled down beside her, his soft voice barely penetrating her heavy thoughts. "You are deeply moved."

She looked up. "How can I not be?"

"The Union will surely prevail."

"But at what cost?"

"At any cost."

She straightened. "Any cost?"

"What will become of us if it does not?"

"What will become of us regardless?" She tilted her head, then shuddered. "You've enlisted in the army, haven't you?"

He reached for her hand. "The 11th Massachusetts Infantry will soon be mustering. A friend is to command Company A of the 1st Brigade, 3rd Division. He has promised me—"

"Stop!" Irma clapped her hands over her ears and turned away. "All these numbers, these titles. They sound so ... so deathly."

Gerald slipped a hand over her wrist. "They mean salvation for our country's future."

"Or condemnation for our own."

He smiled and touched her cheek. "I will return to you. The war— should it even come to full-scale war—will end quickly. The rural South hasn't the resources to sustain hostilities against an industrialized North."

"But they have shed the first blood on their soil, which means the Union armies must aggress and march southward. The secessionist states will be defending their families, their land, and all of their worldly goods." She shook her head. "It will not end so quickly if our leadership should plan campaigns in the belief that it will."

Gerald chuckled. "Look who has become the political military strategist."

Irma pulled back her wrist and glared at him. "Do not patronize me. It takes neither a commission from West Point nor a degree from Harvard to understand what such a war means. All else is empty bravado."

A burly voice startled them from the doorway. "What's this I hear?"

Gerald rose from the settee. "Good evening, sir."

Irma rose as well, hands propped on her hips. "Father, Gerald has enlisted in the Army."

"Well, not quite yet," he interjected. "You see, sir, the 11th—"

"I heard that part." Byrne strode into the room and lifted a third glass from the aperitif tray. "Let's sit." He dropped onto an overstuffed chair, seemingly absorbed with swirling the tawny liquid around his crystal glass. When Irma and Gerald had resumed their seats, he continued without looking up. "In what capacity do you intend to serve?"

"I have some assurances from a well-placed friend—"

"I heard that part too. What assurances?" He lifted an even gaze. "What kind of position?"

Gerald straightened his shoulders. "I'm hoping for a commission as an officer in the infantry."

"The infantry."

Gerald nodded.

Byrne tipped back his sherry and rose. "Then I would like you to have something."

"Sir?"

He left the room, and the sound of heavy footsteps plodded up the hallway staircase. A few minutes later, equally heavy footfalls descended, and he came through the doorway holding a folded strip of white cloth. He extended it to Gerald.

With a puzzled look, Gerald accepted it.

Byrne cleared his throat. "This was my father's uniform sash. He wore it at New Orleans. I would like you to have it."

Irma smiled at him. "Why, Father. It must mean everything to you. What a noble gesture."

Gerald admired the piece." I don't know what to say, sir. I will cherish it always."

Her father remained silent.

Gerald unfolded it gently to its full length, then stiffened.

Irma gasped.

The sash, yellowing and frayed along the edges, hung limply from his fingers. Marring the heirloom at chest level was a ragged musket-ball hole framed in a dark reddish-black stain.

Irma's eyes brimmed.

Gerald lifted a questioning gaze toward his future father-in-law.

Byrne turned and strode into the hallway.

34

Two weeks passed, uneventful but for growing tension that gripped the Kelly household as it had the entire city. No further words concerning Gerald's enlistment were exchanged. Nonetheless, its pending reality draped the air like an invisible shroud.

The evening of April 25 found Irma in her room, oblivious of the deepening twilight. Elbows propped her on the vanity, she fingered her fountain pen, blank gaze fixed on the unopened journal. She absently brushed a fingertip over the cover. Time spent with the diary had dwindled over the past several days, much like her time with Gerald. There was no doubting his devotion to her, but something new preoccupied his thoughts. And darkened hers. Fort Sumter had indeed served as a call to arms, and men from all walks of life in nearly every state heeded it. Massachusetts was not only caught up in the patriotic fervor, in many ways she led it. Closer to home, the handwritten note lying at Irma's side confirmed her fear had been realized.

Today Company A, 1st Brigade, 3rd Division, 11th Massachusetts infantry mobilized in Boston under the command of Captain Maclelland Moore for a term of three years. True to his word, Gerald had appealed to his friend for a position. The promise of a commission laid beyond the captain's sphere of influence, so all he could offer was the rank of a non-commissioned officer. So Gerald became a sergeant in charge of an infantry section of twenty-five men.

Pleased, honored, and humbled at the responsibility over the lives of so many brave souls, Gerald threw himself into the task of preparing his troops for battle. The precious sash his prospective father-in-law had bequeathed him lay secreted in his breast pocket, and, far from the ominous message his benefactor had clearly intended, Gerald drew strength from its glory and its reminder of a beloved fiancée.

On the evening of April 27, Gerald appeared at the Kelly doorstep in full uniform. A servant answered his firm knock, bade him entrance, and summoned Mrs. Kelly. Overhearing the commotion,

Irma stepped from her bedroom to the top of the stairs. She halted at the sight of her betrothed in such unfamiliar garb.

Her mother was greeting him. "My, Gerald, don't you look dashing."

He bowed. "Thank you, Mrs. Kelly."

"But I understood our colors were to be blue."

He brushed his hands down his gray tunic. "There seems to be some confusion over that. The state committee sent us these, even charged us for their cost." He looked back up with a slight frown. "I confess I was unprepared for both the color selected and the payment assessed." Then his tone brightened. "But, to be fair, there is no prescribed standard for Union colors. Actually, there is quite a variety, I hear, depending upon the unit's heritage. Brilliant reds, deep blues, and yes, even gray."

Irma shifted her stance, drawing an upward glance from Gerald. "Irma, my dear. I've come to see you."

She descended the stairs. "I'm glad you have. Will you be staying for dinner?"

"Not this evening, I'm afraid. I'm bivouacking with my men tonight. We begin training maneuvers early tomorrow morning."

She slowed her steps. "Bivouacking, maneuvers. It all sounds so ... so martial."

He laughed. "Perhaps that's because it *is* martial."

Irma forced a smile, but her drawn expression robbed it of any mirth.

An awkward moment later, her mother stepped forward. "If you change your mind about dinner, Gerald, please let me know. We would love to have you stay."

"Thank you again, Mrs. Kelly, but I must depart soon. I hope you understand."

"Of course." She hesitated, then looked at her daughter. "I'll leave you two alone."

Irma glanced at her mother anxiously.

Kate touched her daughter's arm. "I'll be in the sitting room."

When her mother left, Irma turned back.

Gerald pulled her hands into his. "I don't know when we will be called upon to march south. We will likely deploy from Fort Warren, but after that, who knows?"

"Indeed, who knows?" she murmured.

He drew her into his arms. "Despite your fears, I know this conflict will soon be over, my love. I will return and our life together can begin in earnest."

She lifted her gaze, eyes glistening. "But—"

He touched a finger to her lips. "No buts. In fact, there is another reason I came here this evening."

She tilted her head.

"Might you be willing to gift me something as a reminder of what I'll be fighting for."

"You want something of mine?"

"Yes. Perhaps a handkerchief or a scarf?" He searched her puzzled expression, then eased back. "But, then I'm being presumptuous."

Irma shook her head, cheeks warming. "Of course you're not. I would be honored for you to take something of mine with you."

He smiled. "Only honored?"

A genuine smile broke the surface. "And pleased. Very pleased." She pulled back. "Please wait here."

She bustled upstairs and rummaged through her Jenny Lind hope chest, where she drew out a lily-white handkerchief with dainty tatting along the edges and embroidered with her initials in deep scarlet thread. A gift from Grandmother McCann on her mother's side, the treasured piece had lain in her top dresser drawer among a collection of favorites until Irma transferred it to her hope chest. Too precious for common use, but perfect for this most gallant of occasions.

After smoothing it gently against the surface of the dresser with her palm, she hurried downstairs where Gerald waited in the foyer, ramrod stiff. She stepped close and offered him the silken treasure. He draped it across his hand and smiled at its inspection.

"No man will carry a more cherished relic into battle."

Irma's chest seized at the word, and she grasped his wrist. "Oh Gerald, are you sure this is the path you must take? There is still time to heed my father's advice. "

"No, my dear, there is not." He tipped up her chin with his finger and peered into her eyes. "Please don't be distressed. I will return with this precious gift, its noble purpose fulfilled. Count on that."

She nodded, vision blurring.

Gerald leaned forward, kissed her lightly, then passionately. When he stepped back, a loving smile softened his lips. "If that doesn't bring me home, nothing will." He bowed, the door clicked shut, and he was gone.

Irma remained still, a blank stare leveled at the door, until a soft touch on her shoulder startled her. She turned.

Her mother beckoned toward the sitting room. "Shall we?"

Irma nodded dumbly and followed. She settled onto the sofa, her mother resting easily beside her. Kate grasped her daughter's hand. "He is an honorable man, as good as men come."

Irma nodded, eyes cast downward.

"You have his heart."

Irma nodded again.

"But he does not have yours."

Irma looked up, eyes widened. "What do you mean?"

Her mother tilted her head.

Irma shifted on the cushion. "I love Gerald."

"As he loves you?"

"How could I know the answer to that?"

"You're evading the question."

Irma frowned, but couldn't hold her mother's eye. "I don't know what you're implying."

"I think you do." Her mother sat back. "There is loving someone, and there is being in love with someone. You love Gerald. Gerald is in love with you."

"Mother—"

"It's alright, Irma. There is no dishonor in that. It simply is as it is."

Irma fought for an even breath under her mother's penetrating gaze. "I want him to live … to come home."

"Of course you do. We all do. But what then?"

Irma studied her left hand, a gold ring with a large emerald surrounded by a cluster of brilliant diamonds flashing in the candlelight. "I have pledged myself to him," she said quietly.

"And you have done well."

Irma looked up, perplexed. "Then why do we speak of this? What point are you making?"

"Simply this. You are a vibrant and ardent young woman, two traits that I admire so deeply in you. I can see them in the fire in your eyes and the fervency in your voice when discussions arise concerning your deepest convictions and commitments." She slipped her hand over Irma's. "Marriage is the deepest and dearest of commitments. If it is not, it is not marriage, rather an empty arrangement that will teeter on the precipice of dissolution for the entirety of one's life, nudged continuously nearer to the edge by a longing—imagined or otherwise—for what else might have been."

Irma crossed her arms. "I still don't understand your point."

"Can you picture yourself sitting on the periphery of the emancipation movement or women's rights, cheering them on, but holding back, not fully engaged?"

"Certainly not. Slavery and inequality ache my heart. You know that."

"I do know that. I also know you must allow the same measure of heartache to influence your union with your husband. To love, yes. But more so, to be in love—heart, soul and mind—with a man who extends the same love toward you."

"You refer to Gerald's love."

"Do you return it?"

"I do." She looked down. "It's that ... "

"That what, dear?"

"My mind is at peace, but my emotions languish." She looked back up. "I don't know why, but I have yet to sense any ... any ... " She averted her gaze.

"You mean your body does not respond to his words, his gaze ... his touch. There is no flutter of the heart at his appearance."

Warmth flooded Irma's cheeks, then fanned into flame. "There is not."

Her mother leaned forward. "How important is that to you?"

Irma's chest heaved. "I don't know, as I have no experience with it. I pray it will come, that I will grow into it with time."

"And until it does?"

She swallowed and drew a deep breath. "Until it does, I choose to return his love." She met her mother's eye. "It is the right thing to do."

"And ... if it does not?"

Irma quieted, still gazing at the ring. "It is still the right thing to do."

Her mother sat back with a gentle smile, but glistening eyes. "I believe today you have become an adult."

... and so I await his promised return. For I resolve to honor his devotion and pray that someday the fervor of my heart will match his. And so it must. Gerald is a wonderful man. He deserves nothing less than my all.

***

Gwen reluctantly closed the journal, massaging her gritty eyes. The time gaps between entries had increased, but when Grandmother Irma did commit her thoughts to paper, their eloquence betrayed such incredibly deep and intimate feelings. Writers of that age expressed themselves in so carefully considered terms that stirred the heart and soul, such a contrast to the hastily thumbed-in texting of her fast-paced generation.

She nestled her head into the plush pillow, her grandmother's dilemma turning her thoughts to Brent. Here, Gwen had an advantage. Brent very much owned her heart, she was very much in love. She turned onto her side, hugging the pillow as she closed her eyes. But it would be so wonderful to be able to express that love as beautifully as her grandmother did. What if she could reach back through the ages, sit at Grandmother Irma's side, learn to craft such language. She reflected on the final words of the diary entry and drew a deep breath. *Brent also deserves nothing less than my all.*

She clicked off the lamp amid a yawn, and her eyelids sagged, settled.

Deep sleep was quick in coming, as were dreams.

*

A tastefully ornate bedroom faded into view. Floral wallpaper, wooden floors with embroidered throw rugs, a four-poster bed.

Ethereal light penetrated curtains over a high window, illuminating a translucent figure bent over a dressing table.

"Grandmother Irma?"

The figure straightened. "Gwendolyn, dear."

"I'm reading of you and Gerald."

"And so you are."

"I want you to know that I, too, love a man. His name is Brent. I am in love with him. Deeply. Completely."

"And for that you should be grateful."

"Can you teach me how to tell him, to express my feelings as beautifully as you express yours?"

"You need me to teach you how to tell Brent of your love?"

"No, but I would like you to."

The figure smiled. "Well spoken."

"I am so inspired by your journal." A pause. "I hope it doesn't bother you that I am delving into your thoughts."

"It is why I wrote them."

"Yet, there is so much to your life I fear I'll never know, and I want to know everything."

"What I do not write, you will perceive."

"How?"

"You are a Kelly. And so you will understand. Just read. And ponder. And love."

"I would so love to have met you."

"You have, dearest child. You have."

*

Gwen jolted from sleep and sat up, her breath short. Darkness still shrouded the guest room, the only light seeping under the bedroom door. Lying back against the pillow, she pressed hands against her eyes. *Only a dream, but so real.*

She jumped, when the alarm clock began beeping. 6:00 a.m. Fumbling, she silenced it and threw off the bedcovers. On her feet, she pulled on her robe and quietly opened the door.

A bright glow spilled down the hallway from the kitchen as she padded forward, stopping in the doorway. Cassie was laboring at the stove.

"Good morning."

Cassie spun around and dropped to a crouch. After a moment, she pulled up.

Gwen stepped back, eyes widened. "I'm so sorry. I didn't mean to startle you."

Cassie managed a shallow laugh. "Sorry." She drew a deep breath and turned back toward the stove. "I tried to be quiet. I didn't know how early you're used to getting up."

"The alarm clock got me up."

"Oh, sorry. I forgot to check the setting. The last person who slept there was an early riser."

"I was awake anyway." Gwen stepped into the kitchen and inhaled the aroma of fresh coffee. "So, who was your last guest?"

"Mark. He crashed here after a long day."

Gwen settled onto a chair at the table. "You're a very fortunate woman."

Cassie turned around, but avoided eye contact. "Mark and you will be spending time together on this case."

"He told you about my father's estate and the break-in at the house?"

She ignored the question. "Mark is the most desirable man I've ever met."

"He's quite the catch."

"Tell me you haven't noticed him."

Gwen knit her brow. "What do you mean?"

"You're evading the question."

"I am not."

"Have you touched him?"

The memory of her tearful collapse into Mark's arms resurged, and Gwen hesitated for a moment. "We haven't—"

"Too late." Cassie flipped the spatula into the sink and strode toward the doorway.

Gwen rose and grasped her arm as she passed. "Cassie, stop."

Cassie pulled loose, eyes aflame. "You're an attractive woman and … whole." Her voice quavered. "I cannot compete with you."

"Compete? I have no desire to compete with you. We've discussed this. Didn't you listen to a word I said?"

"Words." Cassie spat.

Gwen propped her hands on her hips. "What else can I give you?"

"More."

Gwen glared at her. "Like what? What have I done to earn so much distrust?"

Cassie's jaw worked and eyes glistened. A tear snaked down her cheek. The stump of her right arm jerked forward. She glanced down, then wiped her face with her left hand.

Gwen stepped forward. "Oh, Cassie."

"Don't." She moved back.

Gwen pressed forward and grasped Cassie's shoulders. "Listen, because this is the last time I'm going to tell you this. I have absolutely no interest in Mark and he has *never* even remotely come on to me." She searched Cassie's eyes. "I love Brent, and Mark loves you. I would *never* do anything to harm your relationship with Mark."

Cassie shook her head, eyes glistening. "Don't you see? I'll never be able to keep him from someone like you."

Gwen released her and huffed. "Boy, for a woman in love, you sure sell your man short."

"What?"

"You heard me. You must not think very much of him."

The fire returned to Cassie's eyes. "I would give my life for him."

Gwen leaned forward, hands on her hips. "Of course you would. You nearly did, and he for you."

Cassie faltered. "He told you about the ambush?"

"Yes, and someday I'll tell you about the ambush Brent and I survived."

The furrows on Cassie's brow deepened. "The what?"

"You share a bond with Mark like the one I share with Brent. You could never break ours, and I would never try to break yours."

Cassie slowly relaxed her stance.

Gwen grasped Cassie's hand. "Cassie, I'm your biggest cheering section for a 'happily ever after' with Mark. And I sure hope you feel the same way about Brent and me."

Cassie's expression flattened. "Cheering section? Seriously?"

Gwen shrugged. "Well, don't expect pompoms for Christmas, but yeah. Cheering section."

Cassie's chin quivered, and she sputtered a laugh. "I guess I never thought of it that way."

"Well, start thinking of it that way, will you please?" Gwen paused. "Hey, do you have a sister?"

"A what?"

Gwen rolled her eyes. "A sister. C'mon, work with me here."

"No. Why?"

"Because I don't either. But I've always wanted one."

Cassie cocked her head.

Gwen smiled. "We're not blood relatives, but can't we be something like sisters anyway? Maybe seeing me in that light will help."

Cassie shifted her weight, then tipped up her shoulders. "I don't see why not."

Gwen's smile broadened. "Of course, sisters get to rag on each other's boyfriend, right? Do I get to poke fun at Mark?"

"If I can poke fun at Brent."

Gwen gave her a mock frown. "Point taken. Boyfriends are off limits."

"You have a deal."

36

That evening, Mark came over for dinner. Gwen took his coat in the foyer and told him Cassie was in the kitchen. He smiled and stepped past cradling a bottle of Cabernet. Gwen slipped into the hallway and peeked through the kitchen doorway. All that was visible of Cassie beneath Mark's stooping bear hug was her face squeezed between his neck and his shoulder and her arm stretched to the side. An oven mitt occupied her hand, a patient smile her face.

"Hey, pretty lady. You've been on my mind all day."

Gwen caught Cassie's eye. *So, remind me again. You were worried about what?*

Cassie rolled her eyes, but the smile lingered.

Mark released her and held her at arm's length. His voice quieted. "Your eyes are teary. Is something wrong?"

"Nothing a stiff drink can't fix."

"How about a kiss instead?" He pulled her in, and Gwen quietly returned to the living room, warmth pulsing through her body. Inspired, she dug through her purse for her phone.

"Hi, Brent."

"Hey, pretty lady."

She laughed. "You have no idea how well timed that was."

"Why? I've called you 'pretty lady' before."

She looked back toward the hallway, smile deepening. "We'll talk later."

"You're being cryptic. What's going on?"

"Nothing really. I'm at Cassie's. Mark came over for the evening, and they're in the kitchen. Together."

Brent's tone smiled. "Oh."

She lowered her voice. "Brent, why hasn't Mark asked Cassie to marry him? It's obvious he loves her and she loves him."

"Are you sure he hasn't?"

Gwen hesitated. "No. I guess I just assumed. I haven't asked him."

"It's probably a good idea not to."

"Oh?"

"There are some issues they're sorting out."

"Okay, I'll let it go then."

"Good."

"For now."

"Gwen … "

She laughed. "I'm kidding. You know me well enough to know I won't butt in."

"Yup. I also know you well enough to know you'll be dying slowly inside until you get the whole story."

"Brent!"

He laughed. "Admit it."

"Never."

"Oh c'mon—wait, the chief's here. I need to go. I've got a few things to discuss with him."

"You're still at the office?"

"Yes, doing more research on your dad's case. I'm chasing a rabbit, and it might be a fat one. Call me back later?"

"You call me."

"Will do." He paused. "Love you, pretty lady."

"Now you're just saying that."

"Maybe. Maybe not."

***

After polishing off hearty plates of Beef Stroganoff and a salad of crisp field greens, cranberries, and feta cheese, Gwen, Cassie, and Mark went to the living room. Cassie balanced a tray with dessert bowls of mandarin oranges dusted with cinnamon, and crystal aperitif glasses of Grand Marnier.

Gwen accepted her dessert and eased into an easy chair, sighing appreciatively. "Dinner was fantastic. I only hope I can finish this dessert without exploding."

Mark sat down beside Cassie on the sofa with a proud smile. "Stroganoff is one of Cassie's specialties. It's one of the reasons I have so much trouble keeping in shape."

Both women stared at him, simultaneously lifting eyebrows.

He looked back and forth at them. "What?"

"Never mind," Cassie said.

Gwen grinned and sipped her drink.

"So, Brent told me a little bit about your adventure with the old steamer trunk," Mark said as he forked an orange section from his bowl. "He mentioned something about a diary and a family connection."

Gwen nodded. "It's a long story. I'm not sure how much of it will interest you."

Cassie set down her fork. "I haven't heard anything about it."

Mark picked up his glass. "Fill us in."

"Okay, but promise you'll let me know if it gets boring."

"You'll be able to tell," Cassie said. "Mark snores."

Gwen laughed. "I'll be careful to listen." For the next thirty minutes, she shared the experience of last October's drama in Marble Falls surrounding the old steamer trunk. She told them of her dear friend Margie, owner of the antique shop where the trunk mysteriously showed up, described the eccentric Corky Williams whose cabin at Quimby Pond held the secret of the trunk, and about the good-natured seaplane pilot, Skeeter, who had been so instrumental in her rescue from her abductor, John Smith. She reserved most of the story to talk about Brent, their start-again stop-again relationship, and the danger they faced together.

Mark and Cassie interjected occasional questions, smiled at Gwen's descriptions of her quirky friends, and laughed over Margie's matchmaking efforts to bring Brent and Gwen together.

"Margie sounds awesome," Cassie said.

Gwen nodded. "She is. You two would so get along."

"I kind of got a kick out of Corky and Skeeter," Mark commented.

"That's because you have so much in common," Gwen teased. She stopped and cast a worried glance at Cassie over violating the boyfriend pact. Cassie was too busy laughing to notice.

"I'm fine with that," Mark said wryly. "They may be eccentric, but they're both responsible for you being alive today."

"They sure are." She continued the story with the discovery of her grandmother's lithograph matching the one in the trunk and the discovery of the old journals that had so captured her heart. "On one hand, I can't wait to finish reading them. On the other hand, I don't want them to end."

"I get that," Cassie said.

"Hopefully, they'll shed some light on how her trunk ended up in Marble Falls."

"What a coincidence, your ancestor being associated with a trunk you were restoring over a hundred years later." Cassie leaned forward. "Do you believe in fate?"

"What do you mean?"

"You know, that some things are meant to happen."

"Well, I guess I believe things are meant to happen, but I've come to understand them more in the light of God's design."

Cassie sat back. "Oh. A different perspective, I suppose."

"Part of the story I didn't mention was a prayer I said right before I went into the cemetery. It made all the difference when Turk Sawyer abducted me. As I look back on it, I believe God answered it." She tipped her shoulders. "I've tried luck, and it has never given me the sense of peace that prayer did."

Cassie sipped her drink. "Or maybe it was a psychological crutch, some kind of spiritual sedative."

Gwen shrugged. "I thought of that. My childhood experiences with prayer were pretty bland." She paused. "I once asked Brent about it after noticing he'd prayed during a particularly trying time."

Mark paused, a forkful of dessert halfway to his mouth. "What did he say?"

"He's more comfortable with it than I am, although he admitted not praying as often as he should." She drew a deep breath. "In any event, I'd never experienced the peace I did in the cemetery— especially under so much stress." She reached for her dessert bowl. "If it was psychological, it will probably fade. Feelings usually do. But if it was God, maybe not so much. Only time will tell, I suppose." She speared an orange section. "But I think I owe God as much of a chance as I do fate. Dismissing him out of hand wouldn't be very intellectually honest, would it?"

Mark set down his fork. "But then God doesn't seem very consistent in answering prayer." He looked over at Cassie, who was quietly swirling her drink. "Or manipulating fate."

Gwen nodded. "It sure seems that way sometimes. I don't have all the answers, and I probably never will. But if you're looking for 'scientific proof' between fate and God, I think you're going to be disappointed."

Cassie cleared her throat and set down her glass. "So, when is Brent going to get his tail end down here?"

Gwen sighed. "I wish I knew. We're in peak ski season, and the Marble Falls police department is so small he can't leave. I hope I can settle Daddy's estate soon and get back to Maine."

Mark shook his head. "With all the weird stuff floating around this case, I'm not sure how soon you'll be able to leave."

Cassie threw him a terse look, and Gwen jumped in. "But I wouldn't have to stay in Medford the whole time. I could keep in touch from Marble Falls and come back down if I'm needed."

He nodded. "I suppose so, although that wouldn't be very convenient for you."

"Being home with Brent would be worth any inconvenience."

Mark smiled. "Well spoken." He reached for Cassie's hand. "I'd feel exactly the same way."

Cassie briefly met Gwen's eye, then looked down.

37

An hour later, Mark said goodnight and departed. Gwen helped Cassie with the dishes, then excused herself for the night. She had changed for bed and was brushing her hair when her phone chimed.

"Howdy, Wild Bill."

"That does it. Time to get you out of there. Mark and Cassie are obviously having a bad influence on you."

"Oh, I don't know. We're really starting to bond."

"That's what I'm afraid of."

She lowered herself onto the edge of the bed. "So, what's this fat rabbit you're chasing?"

"It's about Teresa Hardy's disappearing act. I checked each of the surrounding states, and her name popped up on Maine's Bureau of Motor Vehicles. Believe it or not, she has a Farmington address."

"You're kidding. That's only an hour down the road."

"I know."

"From where you are … "

"Yes."

" … right now."

"Gwen."

"When do you get off shift?"

He laughed. "I don't know how the weather is in Boston, but we've had eight inches of snow in the past three hours, and there's no sign of it stopping."

"Your truck has four-wheel drive, right?"

"Gwen!"

"I know, I know. You can't go right now." She heaved a sigh. "It's frustrating knowing she's that close."

"*Thinking* she's that close. The license was issued four years ago, so we can't be sure the BMV address is current. Unless she gets a citation pinpointing where she is now, well … "

"Spoilsport."

Brent laughed. "Reality sucks, huh? I'll call the Farmington PD to see if they have any information on her. Unfortunately, I have no basis to involve them officially. It'll have to wait until I can get there myself and approach her informally."

"Fine then," she grumped. "I guess I'll wait to hear back."

"Did Mark have anything to report?"

"He's going over to the house tomorrow for another look around. He'll probably come over this evening. I'll ask him."

"All right, I won't bug him. Let me know what he says."

Gwen's voice quieted. "I sure miss you."

"Don't stop."

"Why?"

"Because misery loves company, and I'm miserable without you."

"Aw, that's sweet … I think."

***

After breakfast the next morning, a knock sounded on the guest room door as Gwen was making her bed.

"I'm up," she called.

The door opened and Cassie's head poked through the opening. "I've got a couple of errands to run. It's freezing out, so I lit a fire if you want to sit in the living room. Throw a log on every now and then to keep it going. Mark will be over later this afternoon, and he likes a good fire."

"So does Brent. Is there anything I can do to help around the house?"

"Can't think of anything. I'll only be an hour or two."

"Take your time. I have some reading to do."

"Cool. See you later."

The door closed, and by the time Gwen finished tidying up, collected Grandmother Irma's diary, and walked the hallway to the living room, Cassie had left. The fire was crackling over the hearth, bathing the room in a natural warmth and flickering glow, relaxing her mind. After a detour into the kitchen to heat a cup of Constant Comment tea, she settled onto the couch and opened the journal. She stopped and blinked at the wavering script, so out of character from Grandmother Irma's usual flourished penmanship. After reading the first line, she understood.

Tuesday, May 7, 1861
Today, Gerald marched off to war.

***

Irma laid a hand on her quivering wrist, but it would not steady. The writing on the page, a scribble compared to her normal pristine writing, had blurred.

True to Gerald's word, Company A had deployed to Fort Warren on Boston Harbor's Georges Island at four o'clock that afternoon. His most recent letter, lying on the side of her dressing table, carried an upbeat tone. His cohort of soldiers had bonded through disciplined training, fair treatment, and mutual respect. If any unit would survive the ordeal to come, it would be his. And if he was not mistaken, his efforts had been recognized by his superiors. A unit vote was impending, and perhaps his coveted commission would be soon in coming.

In the Kelly household, life carried on with faint regard to the travails southward. None of the family was ignorant of the disruption the war had introduced into the city, but each kept pace to survive the present and keep alive hope for the future.

The future.

She laid the pen on the table and turned toward her hope chest, mind at war with heart. Last evening's conversation with her mother rose again in the back of her mind. There could be no finer man under God's heaven than Gerald Fairchild. So then, why did her heart neither lurch at the mention of his name, nor stir while basking in his sparkling green eyes, warm smile, loving words? Where was the delicious shudder a loved one's touch should bring? She closed her eyes. Strange, how the thought of him being in harm's way weighted down her mind, but left her more visceral emotions at rest.

Irma had just lowered the pen when a resounding knock on the front door reverberated up the stairs. She jerked up her head at the high-pitched nasal voice that followed.

"I require the presence of Mr. Byrne Kelly, posthaste."

The calm voice of Gibbons, their senior manservant responded. "Mr. Kelly is not yet at home, sir. May I be of some assistance?"

"No, you may not. This is an issue for the head of the house."

"Very well, perhaps I can suggest you return when the Master does. Would six o'clock be convenient?"

"Again, it would not. Matters of the law cannot be delayed for the sake of convenience."

Fear pricked Irma's brow. *The law?*

Gibbons' tone remained even. "Then let me rephrase, sir. I cannot conjure up Mr. Kelly where he does not exist. If you wish to speak with him, you must return when he is here."

"Watch your insolence, man. I am an officer of the law."

"I gathered that, sir. I do not intend insolence, rather merely to state fact. Mr. Kelly will be available after six this evening. No sooner."

"Very well," the officer groused. "I shall return this evening. And he had better be here."

"I shall do everything in my power to ensure he is," responded the servant, his glib tone barely suppressed.

The door closed and Irma hurried to the top of the stairs. "Gibbons."

He looked up the stairway. "Miss Kelly?"

She offered him a smile. "My compliments. You were masterful."

A smile tugged at the corners of his mouth, and he dipped his head. "Thank you, Miss, although I am not certain to what you are referring." Then he looked back up. "Perhaps a word of warning is in order for your ... guests?"

"Very much so." Irma turned down the hallway.

Since their arrival, Isabelle and Gabriel had thrown themselves into serving the household in whatever capacity and as inconspicuously as they could. Mindful not to step on the toes of the hired help, Isabelle cleaned and Gabriel took on heavier chores, both disappearing upstairs whenever a knock came at the door. Irma's parents pretended the negro couple did not exist, except to ensure adequate food and laundry were prepared for their accommodation. When the occasional conversation did arise as to long-term plans regarding them, Irma quickly changed the subject. But it appeared now that the issue could no longer be avoided.

Isabelle's smiling face appeared at Irma's anxious knock on the door. "Miz Kelly. You're just in time. I got somethin' for you." She opened the door wider and gestured her hostess to enter. Irma hesitated, then stepped into the guest room.

Gabriel rose from a chair by the window at her entrance. Isabelle lifted a folded cloth from the bed and offered it to Irma. Surprised, Irma unfolded it and draped the fabric over her arm. Her eyes immediately welled up. Beautifully hand-stitched on the white linen was a scene from *Uncle Tom's Cabin*, that of Eliza and her son, Henry, reunited with her husband, George, after their harrowing escape from Kentucky into free Ohio. Captured in the glow of a roaring fire in the great room of the Quaker family with whom they had taken refuge, the joyful expression on their faces was unmistakable.

Irma's breathing became difficult when, after further inspection of the portrayal, it became evident Isabelle had overlaid her own visage onto Eliza, Gabriel's onto George, and Irma's onto the Quaker matron. She closed her eyes and held the precious artifact to her chest. "Oh, Isabelle. This is so beautiful."

Isabelle beamed.

Irma opened her eyes. "And it breaks my heart."

Isabelle's smile faltered. "Lawd, Miss Kelly. I meant for it ta make you happy."

Irma nodded. "I will treasure it forever." She swallowed through a thick throat. "But you must gather your things. It's time for you to go."

38

At 6:05 that evening, the Kelly family had just sat down to dinner when a persistent knock sounded at the front door. Gibbons left to answer it, then returned shortly to announce the local constabulary was waiting impatiently in the foyer for an audience with the master of the house.

"You could have invited them into the sitting room," Irma's father said as he rose.

Gibbons nodded. "Indeed, sir. I could have."

Irma pressed hands to her mouth too late to stifle a giggle.

"Do not forget your position, Gibbons," Byrne admonished.

The servant lowered his gaze. "My sincerest apologies, sir."

"Accepted." Byrne tugged at the hem of his vest and strode into the hallway, giving Gibbons an affirming slap on the shoulder as he passed.

When the servant looked back up, Irma smiled her thanks.

"Gibbons, perhaps you should linger near the sitting room doorway, lest Mr. Kelly require anything further from you," Kate said quietly.

"As you wish, madam." He bowed and departed the room.

Ten minutes passed amid the rising and lowering of heated voices echoing down the hallway. Irma clutched her water goblet, struggling to catch the men's conversation. Several times she looked over at her mother, who, much to Irma's frustration, seemed completely detached from the moment. "How can you sit there so quietly, Mother? I'm dying to know what's happening!"

Her mother dabbed a napkin to her lips. "The night is young."

"What is *that* supposed to mean?"

"Patience, Irma. All will be revealed in time."

"I hate patience."

"How often you make that clear."

Irma pulled her napkin from her lap and laid it on the table. "I can't endure this. I'm going to find out—"

"Sit still, Irma."

Her mother's sharp tone drew Irma up. "But what if the police force Father's hand, and there's no time to warn Gabriel and Isabelle?"

"That's why I sent Gibbons."

"What?"

Her mother took an excruciatingly long sip from her goblet before answering. "Your father will know Gibbons is monitoring their conversation and, if urgency is required, he will stall the inspector until we have time to act."

"But how—"

At that moment, Gibbons reappeared in the doorway, expression terse. "Madam, I recommend hasty action."

Before Irma could react, her mother was on her feet. "Thank you, Gibbons. Irma, escort Gabriel and Isabelle to the cellar niche."

Irma leapt up. "Of course." She rushed into the hall toward the stairs. As she passed the sitting room, the men's voices grew stronger.

"I assure you there is no basis for whatever preposterous rumors you have heard regarding escaped slaves and this household, Inspector. I'm sure my good friend the Chief Inspector can vouch for my strict adherence to the law."

The inspector's tone raised in pitch. "The Chief Inspector is in Lexington for the week and is therefore unable to corroborate your character, sir. Therefore, I must insist upon your cooperation. Surely a cursory inspection of the premises should be of no concern, if you have nothing to hide."

"Nothing to hide?" blustered her father. "I resent your implication, sir."

"I'm implying nothing, Mr. Kelly—"

"You most certainly *are* implying something. I shall not stand for it!"

The tirade faded as Irma hurried upstairs and turned the corner toward the guest room. She rapped on the door.

It opened immediately, and Gabriel's face appeared.

"There's no time to talk, Gabriel. You must hurry to the cellar."

"We heard the row, Miz Kelly. We done got everything together."

"Follow me, then. Quietly as you can."

The trio hurried to the top of the stairs and paused. The altercation in the sitting room continued unabated, so they slipped down to the hall and into the kitchen to the steps leading to the cellar. Once in the basement, Irma turned to the couple. "I'm so sorry. Mother and I cleaned it as much as we could, but—"

"Lawd, Miz Kelly," interrupted Isabelle. "This ain't nuthin' compared to places Gabriel an' me have hid in since Carolina. We'll be fine. Now you better git back upstairs 'fore somebody suspects somethin'. And … " her voice rasped, "… no matter what happens, we owe you everything."

Irma touched Isabelle's cheek. "Nothing is going to happen. Just remain quiet, and we'll take care of the rest." She hurried upstairs, locking the cellar door behind her.

Her father stepped into the hallway with the inspector and a constable as she entered from the kitchen. She halted, hands clasped at her waist. "Father, dinner is getting cold." She turned a puzzled look toward the policemen.

The inspector's eyes widened for a moment, and he offered her a genteel bow. "My apologies for the disruption, Miss. I will try not to delay your meal beyond reason."

Irma subdued a smile and stepped forward, offering her hand to the inspector. He paused, then raised it to his lips. When he lifted his head, his cheeks had tinged red.

She donned a charming smile. "Why, thank you, sir. But, whatever could be the matter?" She glanced at her father, whose expression delivered a warning, then turned back toward the fidgeting officer.

The inspector cleared his throat. "A report has been lodged at the station that asserts a runaway slave guilty of assaulting two of our fine citizens has sought this household for refuge. I am obligated under the Fugitive Slave Act of—"

Irma stepped back, eyes widened. "Fugitive slaves? Here?" She pressed a hand to her chest. "Gracious, how dreadful a thought."

The inspector's face blanched. "I'm sure there is no basis to the allegation. Still, I'm afraid I must investigate."

Irma looked again at her father. "Father? Surely there couldn't be … oh dear." She raised the other hand to her cheek and lowered her eyes. "I feel faint."

Her mother moved to Irma's side and grasped her arm, leveling a narrow look at the officer. "I hope this intrusion has been worth risking my daughter's fragile health, Inspector. Honestly, a runaway slave? You cannot be serious."

The inspector turned a pinched look toward the constable, who avoided eye contact. He looked back, face growing scarlet. "Madam, please believe that in no way would I wish to injure your daughter's health."

Irma moaned, teetered, and leaned into her mother.

Kate wrapped an arm around her daughter's waist. "A noble sentiment, but one rather late in coming." She turned toward her husband. "Byrne, your assistance, please?"

"Of course, dear." He reached for Irma as she rolled her eyes back and went limp. Lifting her into his arms, he pivoted back toward the peace officer, voice lowering to a growl. "This nonsense has gone far enough, don't you think, Inspector?"

"I'm sorry, sir. I never intended—"

"Perhaps when the Chief Inspector returns, we can revisit this issue with some measure of decorum," Kate said as she held Irma's limp hand and patted her wrist.

"Certainly, madam," the inspector squeaked. "Please forgive me."

Irma lolled her head onto her father's shoulder, lest the quivering at the corners of her mouth give her away. Hasty footsteps retreated down the hallway amid more profuse apologies, and when the door closed, she snorted a laugh into her father's lapel. When she opened her eyes, he was glaring at her.

"Thank you, Father. You rescued me not a moment too soon." She planted a kiss on his cheek and hugged his neck.

"Irma Louise Kelly," he groused. "One day you are going to be the death of me."

She giggled. "Oh, but what fun we shall have until then." He lowered her to the floor, and she smoothed her dress and hair. "Well, then. That should have bought us some time."

Her father folded his arms across his chest. "What concerns me, young lady, is how quickly and convincingly you are able to so easily contrive feminine wiles to beguile a man."

She smiled. "I'll accept that as a compliment, Father." Then her eyes narrowed. "Except for the 'contrive' part."

"Irma—"

"Don't start, you two," Kate said, gesturing toward the dining room. "Mrs. Callaghan will never let us hear the last of it if dinner cools beyond redemption. We can continue our discussion at the table." She looked pointedly at Irma. "After you resettle our guests back upstairs."

39

Irma delivered a full tray to the guest room before joining her parents at the supper table. Their meal passed with much discussion, but few decisions. Where could the fugitive couple possibly go? How widely were they being sought, given the assault charge? Was their own house being watched, and if so, how difficult would it be to spirit Isabelle and Gabriel away undetected?

Her most recent exchange with her father did little to assuage her fears.

"*Surely you have friends who could help us, don't you Father?*"

"*None comes to mind, I'm afraid. Harboring fugitives of any color is risky business.*"

"*Well, we simply must do something.*"

"*On that point we agree. Give me a day, and we shall see.*"

Dessert arrived almost unnoticed, so conflicted was Irma in spirit and mind. She had just pushed away the remnants of her blueberry pie, when Gibbons appeared at the doorway with the evening post. Her father shuffled through the few envelopes, then pulled one from the stack. "Irma?"

She was staring into her coffee cup, absently stirring in two lumps of sugar and dollop of cream.

She jolted when her mother touched her wrist. "Irma?"

"Mother?"

"Your father is speaking to you."

She looked at him. "I'm sorry—oh! Is that for me?"

He nodded. "It appears to be from your friend in Marble Falls."

"Mary Jane?" She smiled. "How wonderful." She accepted the letter and slit the open envelope with her butter knife.

Kate sighed. "Irma, we do have proper letter openers ... "

178

Extracting the letter, Irma absentmindedly dropped the envelope onto her dessert plate.

" ... and proper refuse receptacles."

"Yes, Mother," Irma murmured as she scanned the news from Maine. "Things are fine in Marble Falls ... the Toothakers are doing well ... the lakes are nearly clear of ice and snow ... there are—oh my! She's getting married." Irma looked up at her parents, face aglow.

"How lovely for her," Kate said.

Irma resumed reading. "Hiram proposed and ... " She stopped.

"Is something wrong?" asked her father.

"It appears the wedding is next month." She looked up again. "Yet this is the first she's mentioned it, and I received her previous letter only a few weeks ago."

"Perhaps they saw no need to wait," Byrne interjected. "Long engagements are often needless ... and can be detrimental." He lifted his coffee cup as Irma lowered the letter and met his gaze.

"Meaning ... ?"

He shrugged. "Meaning nothing. I was merely thinking of you and Gerald, wondering if things might be different if a full year's engagement had not been decided upon."

"Different how?"

He eased his cup onto the saucer and dabbed his mouth with a napkin. "Different in that he may not have been so hasty to engage with this war if he had a wife, perhaps even a family, to consider."

"Surely you do not blame me for Gerald's decision to enlist." Irma's tone cut the air like a saber.

He shook his head while swirling his coffee. "I do not. However, it is lost neither on your mother nor myself that your ardor for marriage is less than equal to his. Is it unreasonable to assume that the term of engagement was more your idea than his?"

She frowned. "I will have you know we reached that decision mutually."

"I see." He cast a nonchalant look at the table and wiped his lips with his napkin. "And this evening's display of manipulative feminine wiles had no role in those negotiations?"

Kate leaned forward, a serious gaze leveled at her husband. "I must take Irma's side in this. Your assertion is neither with proof nor in any way helpful. It is unkind conjecture, and it casts your daughter in a most dishonorable light." She paused. "Surely that is not what you intend."

Irma's lip trembled. "I do believe you hold higher regard for Gerald than you do for me, Father."

He clasped his hands on the table, switching his gaze from his wife to his daughter. "First, it will never be true that I hold anyone on earth in higher regard or with greater love than I do the two women in this room."

"Then why—"

Kate lifted a hand but kept her gaze on her husband. "Let your father finish."

Byrne resumed. "Second, it will never be true that I know anyone on earth better than I do the two women in this room."

"Apparently, that is not the case," Irma muttered.

"Irma!"

Irma sat back and crossed her arms, glaring straight ahead.

"Perhaps I can offer evidence for that assertion." Her father's tone lightened. "I cannot fault your heart, Irma, but I do not see Gerald as having captured it as fully as you have captured his. Am I wrong?"

Her throat tightened and she glanced at her mother. Kate cocked her head. When she looked back at her father, an unusually gentle smile had smoothed the wrinkles in his face, and her heart lurched. "You are not wrong, Father." She looked down. "But to be fair, I have tried. I really have."

"I know you have. And in counterpoint to my unduly harsh words a moment ago, negotiating a lengthy engagement perhaps reveals a mercy on your part, as it would grant you time to better understand your heart, and for him to better understand you. For that, I commend you."

Irma's reply came in a whisper. "Thank you."

He lifted his cup again. "Despite the feminine wiles most likely employed in exercising that mercy."

Her eyes narrowed. "How are you so sure I was manipulative? "

"Irma?" Kate's tone betrayed a smile.

She looked at her mother, then back at her father. "But ... I really didn't ... " Her shoulders drooped and gaze lowered. "Well, perhaps a little bit."

Kate laughed. "You really shouldn't try to hide things from your father, you know."

"Oh, shouldn't she now?" Byrne turned a smile toward his wife. "Such as you hiding your distaste for the sport of fishing?"

Kate's jaw slackened. "I beg your pardon. When have I ever objected to accompanying you on your fishing trips?"

Irma's giggle earned a reproachful glare from her mother.

Byrne laughed. "Never. But it's clearly a matter of debate as to who enjoys those excursions less, you or the fish."

Her cheeks reddened. "How can you possibly know such a thing?"

He leaned back, an amused expression lighting up his face. "Come now, dearest Kate. Why do women assume men lack even a modicum of intuition? It's really quite demeaning, you know."

She pursed her lips. "Perhaps because you so rarely display one?"

Byrne grinned. "Touché, my dear. But in this case ... ?"

Kate released a grudging smile. "And touché to you, my love." She shook her head. "To think after all these years, I thought I had you fooled."

He sipped his coffee through a victorious smile. "You have been the model of devotion in supporting my avocation. But the look on your face when I reel in a prize trout, the way you tuck away from a large-mouth bass flopping in my net." His eyes sparkled. "I must confess, that sight has provided far greater amusement than any fish I've ever fought onto the deck of a boat."

"Byrne Kelly! Why I should—"

Irma interrupted. "Fishing."

Her mother stared at her daughter. "Irma?"

"Mary Jane said the lakes have cleared. Mightn't it be time for a fishing trip to your new property on Quimby Lake, Father?"

"Now?"

"Especially now." She looked toward the ceiling. "In fact, we may need help to transport all of your fishing gear along with our luggage."

Her father stroked his chin. "Indeed we might."

Irma hunched her shoulders. "Canada is not far from Marble Falls, true?"

"Very true."

Kate reached for her coffee, a light smile curving her lips. "And Canada is a safe haven from slavery."

***

... and so two days' hence, we depart for Maine. But the question remains, how do we secretly convey Gabriel and Isabelle with us? And once we do, how will I ever be able to say goodbye?

40

In Farmington, Brent eased his black Ford F-150 to the curb in front of Java Joe's and cut the engine. Leaning back, he heaved a sigh and rubbed his aching eyes. The drive from Marble Falls had taken more than twice as long as it normally did, creeping behind snowplows clearing the aftermath of the heavy snowstorm that had socked the mountain in for two days. A godsend for Saddleback's ski slopes, but a bane for transportation and commerce, its residents doggedly braved the billowy mounds of white that had nearly buried the small town.

Still others capitalized on it. The Lodge, a quaint inn on the eastern shore of Marble Lake, laid large wooden planks on the wide staircase leading up from the shoreline up to their back lawn. Loyal patrons snowmobiled across the lake's frozen surface and up the makeshift ramp into the warm glow of the inn's gourmet restaurant and pub, combining a classy evening with the rugged exhilaration of a favorite winter sport.

Tucked into a valley further south, Farmington was spared the worst of the winter onslaught, a mercy Brent appreciated as he stepped from his truck onto a thin layer of icy slush. Ten minutes later, a steaming cup of robust Back Draft coffee and a bagel slathered with cream cheese in hand, he climbed back into the truck and checked the BMV printout for Teresa Hardy's last known address: 118 Academy Street.

He continued down Main Street, turned left on Academy, and pulled into the narrow driveway of an old multi-story white structure at the corner of High street. His shoulders slumped at the sign announcing the property to be the Farmington Historical Society.

Gritting his teeth, he punched the steering wheel. *Fake address. Big mistake, Teresa. Now the spotlight is really on you.*

He was jotting a note on his pad when a knock at the window startled him. A smiling blonde's red-cheeked face was peering at him through the glass. He lowered the window.

"Something I can help you with, sir? We normally open by appointment, but I can make an exception. Are you researching something?"

Despite his frustration, Brent mustered a return smile. "Nothing historical. I was given this address as someone's current residence."

"I'm afraid the Titcomb House hasn't been a current residence for quite some time."

"Do you have a Teresa Hardy working here, or anyone by that name ever associated with the Historical Society?"

"Not that I'm aware of."

"That's what I figured." He sighed. "Thanks for your time."

"Are you sure I can't interest you in a tour? We have some wonderfully unique displays."

Brent shook his head. "I'm sure you do, but it'll have to be another time."

"Very well." She handed him a card and stepped back. "I'm Emily Davis, the curator. Feel free to call anytime."

He smiled. "Thanks."

"We do group tours as well," she called as Brent slipped the truck into reverse and rolled up the window. As he backed onto Academy, a final peering through the windshield caught the curator waving, smile undiminished.

He shook his head with a smile as he returned a wave. *Now there's a lady who loves her job.*

***

Back in Marble Falls, Brent tossed the notepad onto his desk and reached for his phone.

Gwen picked up on the first ring. "Hi. I was thinking about you."

"Right. What were you really doing?"

She laughed. "I was reading Grandmother Irma's diary. But if I hadn't been doing that, I'd have been thinking of you."

"She's the only competition I'll accept." He slung his coat over the back of a chair.

"Are you calling with news?"

"I just got back from Farmington."

"Already? From the weather reports, I didn't think you'd be able to get through for another day or two. Did you find Teresa Hardy?"

"Sorry to say, I didn't."

Gwen groaned. "She's moved on then?"

"I'm not sure. The address the BMV had for her was phony."

"Why would she—wait a minute."

"What?"

"This may be a coincidence, but Mark said the housekeeper who found Daddy gave a fake address for the police report. I wonder if it's the same person."

"Could be coincidence, or there may be a connection. Somebody's obviously trying to cover their tracks though."

"Maybe the officer who interviewed the housekeeper can verify whether or not they're the same woman."

Brent chuckled. "I tell you, you missed your calling."

"Uh oh. I'm doing your job for you again, aren't I?"

"Don't stop. In the business, that's called collaboration."

She giggled. "Be careful what you ask for. You might get it."

"I'm counting on that."

***

Gwen disconnected the call and checked her watch. Cassie had said she'd be gone a couple of hours, and it was coming up on that now. Maybe a hot cup of cocoa would be appreciated after a morning out in the cold.

Setting aside the journal, she replenished the wood on the fire and went into the kitchen. When the hum of the garage-door opener vibrated through the wall, she poured two big mugs of cocoa. A moment later, the door leading out to the garage opened and Cassie stepped through with a plastic shopping bag looped over her arm. She set it on the table, leaned her crutch against the wall, and unwrapped a heavy woolen scarf from her neck. "I can't believe how cold it is out there."

Gwen smiled and extended one of the mugs. "I poured some hot chocolate."

"Sounds great. Thanks." Cassie laid her coat over a chair and accepted the steaming mug.

"And I stoked the fire. C'mon into the living room."

"Nice. I could get used to having you around."

"It's the least I can do." Cassie followed and Gwen resumed her place on the couch. "I really owe you for your kindness."

Cassie shook her head. "Friends don't keep score." She eased into an armchair near the fire and took another sip of cocoa. "So, what did you do all morning?"

"Read and spoke with Brent on the phone."

"So, have you and he moved in together yet?"

Gwen coughed and nearly dropped her hot chocolate. "Um, no."

"Why not? Brent's a hunk, and you two are obviously into each other."

Heat crept over Gwen's forehead, and she set down her mug. "I suppose our relationship isn't there yet."

"Where does it have to be?"

Gwen gave her a pointed look. "It has to be when we're wearing each other's wedding rings."

Cassie laughed. "Wow, that's kind of old-fashioned, isn't it?"

"Maybe that's a point it its favor, given the mortality rate of relationships today."

The laugh died, and Cassie sat back. "Sorry. Didn't mean to rile you."

Gwen leaned forward. "What about you? I didn't notice Mark having a key to the house."

Cassie's eyes flashed. "Whether Mark has a key to my house is none of your business."

"Neither was Brent's and my living arrangements any of yours. But, here we are."

Cassie looked at the floor. "Okay, I deserved that."

Gwen softened her tone. "Sorry if I snapped. I guess I wasn't prepared for this conversation."

"Touchy one, huh?"

"Maybe." Gwen lowered her voice and clasped her hands on her lap. "I was engaged once. To a guy in college. He pressured me to move in with him, but it didn't feel right."

"Why not?"

"I'm not sure. Something inside."

"Was it a God thing?"

Gwen blinked. "God thing?"

"Yeah, you said prayers at breakfast. I wondered if you're religious and that was stopping you."

Gwen shook her head. "Not back in college. I was nowhere near being religious then." She looked back up. "But the cemetery experience I told you about woke me up to a notion of God that was totally different from what I had during my growing-up years. You can say what you want about spiritual crutches, but to go through what I did without completely falling part, something I'd normally have done, made me wonder if God was in it."

"Huh." Cassie took another sip. "So, what about Brent? Hasn't he asked you to move in?"

Gwen sputtered a laugh. "Boy, you don't varnish your questions, do you?"

A rare blush tinged Cassie's cheeks, and a smile escaped. "I guess I never saw much point in it."

"To answer your question, no. He's never suggested it. Frankly, I'd be shocked if he did."

A corner of Cassie's mouth wrinkled. "Don't tell me Brent found God too."

"Would that surprise you?"

"Yeah. War doesn't always bring out the best in a person, and he was no exception."

Gwen nodded thoughtfully. "I don't know what happened, or when it happened, but Brent's an elder in his church now. He's the most respectful guy I've ever met."

"Hmm." Cassie shook her head and reached for her mug again. "Well, I don't know where the respect thing comes in, but you're a babe and he's still a guy. I can't believe he hasn't thought about it."

Gwen giggled. "Thanks for the compliment ... I think." She paused. "So, if Mark asked for a key, would you give him one?"

Cassie hesitated for a moment, then tipped up her chin and looked away. "Of course."

Gwen cocked her head. "You don't sound very convincing."

A slow breath escaped, and Cassie's voice dropped to a whisper. "He won't ask." She lowered her gaze to the titanium cylinder protruding from her jeans. "Maybe once. But not now."

Gwen moved to Cassie's side. "May I share a story with you?"

Cassie shrugged.

"A friend of mine who was coping with a life-changing disease once told me something her doctor said, 'You can never go back to your old life, but you're in a really good place in your new life'." She laid a hand on Cassie's arm. "Mark is so utterly devoted to you. What better place could you ask for in your new life?"

Cassie closed her eyes. "I want my old life back."

"I don't blame you. But Mark is here in the new one. Maybe he needs some help in figuring out where he belongs in it."

41

That evening, dinner passed with little more conversation than a few benign 'how was your day' niceties. After several failed attempts to stimulate conversation, Mark attempted a joke. Cassie seemed not to hear, and Gwen responded with a polite smile. Finally, he set down his fork. "Okay, what's going on?"

Cassie didn't respond, so Gwen dabbed her mouth with her napkin and turned toward him. "Going on?"

He twitched his lips. "C'mon, give me a little credit."

Cassie continued to stare at her spaghetti, and Gwen said, "It's not really my place to—"

Cassie turned toward Mark. "Why do you love me?"

Gwen's eyes widened, and she looked down.

Mark stared at Cassie. "Why do you think?"

"That's a lousy answer."

"It's no worse than the question."

Cassie's jaw tightened. "It's a perfectly valid question."

"Really? After all this time and after all we've been through, you still don't get it?" He leaned back. "The Cassie I know is a lot smarter than that."

"Brains don't trump matters of the heart."

"Life would sure be easier if they did."

"Sorry, philosophy won't get you off the hook. Answer the question."

He leaned back forward and propped his arms on the table. "Fine, but first let's be fair. I feel like I've walked into an ambush here. You've clearly had a conversation about whatever this is, and now I'm on the spot to answer an unanswerable question."

"Why is it unanswerable?"

"Because there is no reason why I love you. It has nothing to do with your intelligence, your personality, the color of your hair, the shape of your face, the curves of your body, the way you smile at me, or the fact that you love me too. And yet it has everything to do with all of those things." Cassie stiffened when he reached for her hand. "So, let me ask you the same thing. Why do you love me?"

She swallowed. "Because you're ... it's ... oh, I don't know."

Mark grinned. "I rest my case." He glanced at Gwen, who was fingering her napkin. "Maybe we can pick this up later? We're making Gwen uncomfortable."

Gwen stopped fidgeting, eyes rounding. "Um, that's okay. I can leave."

"Mark's right," Cassie said. "I'm not being fair."

Gwen gave a slight shrug and smiled, then reached for Mark's plate. "Here, let me clear the table. Maybe we can have dessert in the living room." She set about arranging a tray with coffee and small bowls of gelato noticing that Mark quietly studied Cassie, who stared at the table, shoulders hunched.

As Gwen picked up the tray and moved into the hallway, Cassie murmured, "I want us to be like we were before."

"We weren't perfect before either." he responded quietly. "When you're ready to start looking forward rather than backward, maybe we can discuss this again."

***

Over dessert, Cassie seemed to make an effort to lighten the mood. She talked about pulling her oil paints back out and reminded Mark about that trip to the Appalachians he'd promised her. He told her to name the date and they'd be off, but preferably when the temperatures were tolerable. She laughed, countering that it would definitely be during the autumn for the tree colors.

At 8:30, Gwen drained the remainder of her coffee and rose from her chair. "I'll take care of the dishes. Then I think I'm going to head back to the bedroom."

"Already?"

"I've intruded on your couple time enough. Besides, I have some reading to do."

Mark flashed her a grateful smile.

"Leave the dishes in the sink," Cassie said. "I'm a night owl, and they'll give me something to do while I unwind."

"Alright." Gwen stacked the tray full and bade them goodnight.

A half hour later, Gwen crawled between the sheets, fluffed the pillow, and reached for Grandmother Irma's diary. The bookmark protruded nearly three quarters of the way through the volume. She surveyed volumes two and three on the dresser across the room. So much history to cover in such little books. She frowned. *You better not leave me hanging after all of this, Grandmother Irma.*

She flipped open the book and melted into the past.

Saturday, May 11, 1861

How glorious to be back in Maine! And all the more glorious, given our extraordinary trip from Boston. Yet, despite the excitement of seeing Mary Jane again, my heart aches.

42

Mind racing, Irma scurried about her room collecting whatever she thought she might require for their trip to Maine. How long would she be there, and what could she expect of the weather? Even more unsettling was how to explain Isabelle and Gabriel? Would they be household servants accompanying the family on vacation? Surely that excuse had been worn thin by so many others aiding slaves escaping to the north. And with Gabriel being accused of assault, would the authorities be even more vigilant? The silver lining in her cloud of doubt was that she would see Mary Jane again, renew a prized friendship that had been stretched thin by the miles.

So much to think about, so much to do. Immobilized with worry, she finally dropped her armload of folded undergarments onto the floor and plopped onto the edge of the bed, head in her hands.

A knock at the door startled her.

"Irma?"

"I'm here, Mother."

The door opened, and Kate stood in the entranceway. She surveyed the disheveled room. "I see there is still progress to be made."

Irma shifted a sidelong gaze toward her mother. "You are very quick on the uptake."

"You provide me considerable opportunity to exercise it."

A pause, and both women burst into laughter.

Irma wiped a tear from her cheek. "Will I never get the upper hand in a match of wits with you?"

"Only if you stop trying, dear." Kate propped her hands on her waist. "How can I help?"

Irma gestured toward the open travel kits and pile of clothing on the floor. "You can finish for me."

"Short of that."

"You can pray for me."

"Always. But I fear even that may not be sufficient in this case."

"Probably not." Irma sighed. "How long do you think we will be in Maine?"

"I have planned for a week."

"You must have a mountain of luggage."

"Two bags."

Irma rolled her eyes. "I will *never* understand you."

"Again, only if you stop trying."

Irma laughed, then sobered. "What about Isabelle and Gabriel? How will we ever get them away undetected?"

"Your father will handle that."

"And if he fails?"

"When was the last time your father failed us?"

Irma shook her head. "I don't know of a time."

"Then take heart, and leave the worrying to him."

"I don't know of a time he worried either."

"Then take even more heart."

Irma tipped her head. "Very well. I will do my part and leave the rest to you and Father."

"A wise decision." Kate paused. "Isabelle and Gabriel are relying on you for peace of mind, Irma. Do not wear your heart on your sleeve, lest your worries incite theirs."

Irma's shoulders sagged. "I know, but it's so difficult. I should never have dragged them into this."

"Why?"

"Because I fear I'm not up to seeing the task through."

"I couldn't disagree with you more."

Irma looked up.

Her mother smiled. "I will trade banal security for fiery passion any day of the week in seeing tasks through. In that respect, you have no equal."

Irma's eyes filmed over. "Thank you."

Kate smiled and turned away.

The door closed, and Irma gathered her clothing from the floor, spirit renewed.

***

Before dawn the next morning, Irma rapped quietly on the guest room door. The door creaked open to Gabriel's weary face.

"How soon can you be ready to leave?"

"We been ready since yesterday," he responded as Isabelle appeared at his side. "Ain't neither of us slept a wink."

"Maybe you can rest on the train."

He nodded through a yawn.

She looked over her shoulder. "Now all that remains is to get you to the station."

"That'll just be the start of it, I 'spect."

Irma swallowed. "Perhaps."

Isabelle offered her a warm smile. "There ain't enough years in a lifetime to repay you for what you done for us, whether we get caught or not."

Irma frowned. "There will be no talk of getting caught, hear me? Father knows what he's doing. If you're safe with anyone, you're safe with him."

"Yes'm."

Irma stepped back as Gabriel opened the door and ushered his wife through. He slung two bags over his shoulder and followed the women along the hallway.

In the downstairs foyer, a small mound of baggage lay piled near the hall tree. Irma's father was peering through the window next to the doorway while her mother whispered something to Gibbons. When Byrne turned from the window and gave a nod, the servant pulled his collar up and slipped out the front door.

Byrne quietly addressed the small group. "In a moment, we will load the carriage and climb aboard. After that, watch me and listen carefully." He leveled a serious look at his daughter. "And obey instantly without question."

Irma eye's rounded. "But of course, Father."

Her mother reached over and squeezed her hand.

When her father returned to the window, she leaned toward her mother and whispered, "What did he mean by that?"

"Shh."

"Let's go." Byrne reached for the door handle. "Gabriel, assist with the baggage, please."

"Yessir."

When he looked back toward the group, the big man had already hefted all of the parcels but one.

"Good heavens, man," muttered Byrne. "I've never seen such a thing."

Gabriel lowered his head. "Sorry, sir. I tried ta grab the last one but didn't have no hands left."

Irma giggled softly, then sobered at a tighter squeeze from her mother's hand.

Isabelle lifted the remaining bag. "Ready to go."

Byrne opened the door, and the entourage hurried to where Gibbons was waiting with a carriage on the cobblestone entryway next to the gate. The family's luggage went onto the back of the carriage, but as Gabriel began to hoist his two bags, Byrne laid a hand on his arm. "Keep them with you."

Gabriel nodded.

They piled into the carriage, and Gibbons eased the two-horse team through the wrought-iron gateway and down Mt. Vernon Street. Squeezed between her parents, Irma looked up at her father. He was staring back toward the house. Her gaze traced his, and she squinted at a pinpoint of candlelight wavering from an upper window. Suddenly, the curtains dropped back into place and the light disappeared.

"Now, Gibbons," her father said.

The carriage stopped. Byrne thrust open his door. "Quickly. Everyone out and follow me."

Irma frowned. "What on earth—"

"Irma." hissed her mother. "Obey. Now."

Irma scrambled down from the carriage and joined the others as her father met Gibbons' eye. "There will be a hefty raise in your salary for this, my good man."

"No need, sir. The thrill of the chase is payment enough."

"We will revisit that sentiment after the authorities get through with you." The servant chuckled as Byrne slapped him on the shoulder. "Go."

Gibbons slapped the reins against the horses' rumps, and the carriage clattered off down the cobblestones. Byrne signaled to the group, and they hurried along a dark side street.

Irma looked over her shoulder at her mother. "What about our baggage?"

"Trust and obey, dear," came the breathy response.

"I hate answers like that."

"Of course you do."

Her father halted at the entrance to a gated home. In the dim light of a street lamp, a figure stepped into view through the gateway.

"Henry?" asked her father.

"Indeed, Byrne. Who else?"

Irma's eyes widened at the voice of Henry Wilkinson, the man with whom her father had argued about the stockpiling of cotton.

"A silly question, but can you fault me, considering the circumstances?"

Henry chuckled as he unlatched the gate. "I suppose not. Come through."

The group stepped into a large courtyard. Against the stone wall stood a team of horses hitched to a black carriage. To Irma's surprise, her mother moved forward and reached out to Henry. "How can we ever repay you for your kindness?"

Henry tipped his head. "My dear Katherine, if my wife should discover I'd entertained such a question from the lady who has been so stalwart a supporter of the children's hospital, she would have my head. Therefore, I beg you to withdraw it."

Kate laughed softly. "Although I question such severity could come from a heart as soft as Anabelle's, I shall respect your wishes."

Henry lifted her hand and kissed it. "Thank you." Then he looked over at Byrne. "If only you were as diplomatic as your wife ... "

Byrne huffed. "If I were, why would I need her?"

Kate turned on him. "Byrne!"

The men laughed, and Henry stepped back. "Quickly now. You must be off."

Byrne grasped Henry's hand, then hustled his group onto the waiting carriage, himself taking the reins. Irma scanned the rear of the cart where several familiar-looking pieces of luggage were neatly stacked. When they settled onto the rear seat, she gripped her mother's arm. "I saw my hope chest in with the baggage."

Her mother nodded. "Your father had your belongings transferred last night. The only container you hadn't packed was the chest."

Irma frowned. "Transferred by whom?"

"Gibbons is the only one we can truly trust."

Irma blanched. "Gibbons? My private garments were in the valise."

Her mother smiled. "I believe we can count on his discretion."

"Then, if my clothing is here in my hope chest, what is in the carriage with Gibbons?"

"Baggage loaded with dead weight."

Irma's shoulder sagged. "I don't understand."

Her father leaned toward her. "I suspected our movements were being watched, so I dropped hints that we would be departing from Boston harbor to Portland, Maine via steamship. Instead, we are going to the train station in Haymarket Square and traveling north through Nashua to Farmington. We'll proceed via carriage from there to Marble Falls. A circuitous route, but one that should confound attempts to track us down."

Irma shook her head. "Dropped hints where and to whom?"

"Near the kitchen, as well as leaving an annotated maritime timetable left on the sideboard. All left where I knew Mrs. Callaghan would notice."

"Mrs. Callaghan?"

Her mother touched her arm. "You really must learn to read people, Irma."

"So, she was the one with the candle in the upstairs window? Sending a signal?"

Her father nodded. "Very perceptive, young lady. Gibbons will proceed to the harbor where he will certainly be intercepted by the inspector's men. Meanwhile, we shall be on the morning's first train out of Boston."

Irma shuddered. "Poor Gibbons."

"At least he'll still have a position when we return. Mrs. Callaghan will not be so fortunate."

Isabelle's worried voice crept forward from the back of the carriage. "A man in jail an' a woman losin' her situation because of us?"

Byrne turned toward the back. "He won't go to jail, he'll simply be questioned and released under suspicion." He chuckled. "And knowing Gibbons, he will revel in the experience. Mrs. Callaghan, on the other hand, will be dismissed forthwith. I cannot abide help whom I cannot trust, and tonight she confirmed I cannot trust her. You simply brought an issue to the forefront that needed to be addressed."

He turned back toward the front and clicked his teeth at the horses, who picked up their pace. "All is as it should be."

Irma smiled at Isabelle. "In any event, you and Gabriel are well worth whatever may befall us."

Isabelle offered a weak smile, then sat back. A hushed whisper came from her husband, and he drew her close.

43

Irma peered out as her father pulled the carriage to a halt in front of the Haymarket Square train station. A timid dawn had barely lightened the sky's hue to pewter, but sufficiently to give form to billowing clouds that appeared overly anxious to empty themselves onto the city. As if in reply to her thoughts, a roll of thunder shook the heavy air. She stepped down to the pavement and set off toward the station when a sudden flash of lightning startled her, pulling her gaze upward toward the building's edifice. A large clock that was centered over the words "Boston & Maine Railroad" read 6:50. She tightened the bonnet ribbon beneath her chin and set off toward the station.

"Irma!"

Startled, she turned back toward her mother's voice.

"Perhaps you can help with your smaller bag? Gabriel is but one person, and your father must tend to the carriage."

"Of course." She gathered up her skirts and hurried back, grimacing at the first large raindrop splattering off the brim of her hat.

Byrne led to an arched entrance and ushered everyone inside as the cloudburst began an earnest assault on the pavement. He turned to the group. "Henry has a man waiting to receive the carriage. I'll be right back." He looked at Gabriel and Isabelle. "Maintain a respectful distance and subservient attitude. If you were traveling alone, your status as freemen could be assumed, although still challenged. But appearing in the company of an upper-class family of whites, it could beg questions."

Irma's forehead warmed, and she turned a defiant eye toward the couple. "I'll lag behind with you."

"Begorra, cailín, you will not!" Her father drew a deep breath. "Will you never learn to think beyond the moment?"

199

Irma drew up. "I am not a girl, I am a woman."

"Then behave as one."

Her mother stepped between them and straightened his collar. "Best hurry, or we'll miss our train."

He kissed her on the cheek. "Try to keep everyone out of trouble, will you, Kate?"

"Of course, dear."

After another sidelong look at his daughter, he strode out into the gathering storm.

***

Perched on the edge of a wooden bench, Irma stared at the floor and fidgeted with the strap of a travel bag lying next to her. Isabelle and Gabriel huddled a short distance away against the wall with the baggage piled near them. Finally, she heaved a sigh and released the strap. *Shouldn't Father have returned by now? I so dislike waiting!*

She looked over at her mother, who sat erect with a small purse clutched on her lap. A chill traveled Irma's spine when her mother glanced at the pendant watch pinned to her coat lapel and frowned toward the door. Anxiety was a rare emotion for her mother, and her pinched expression was disquieting.

Irma slid closer. "Mother? Is everything alright?"

"I hope so, dear." Kate gave her a tight smile, then froze, gaze fixed beyond Irma. She quickly rose.

Irma looked toward the door and bolted up from the bench. Her father had reentered, soaking wet and glowering. Two men followed directly behind him, one of whom was the constable who had accompanied the inspector to their home. She sought her mother's hand, but Kate had stepped out of reach.

"Byrne?" she said in an even tone as the trio arrived at the bench.

"Nothing to be alarmed about. A simple misunderstanding."

The constable touched the brim of his hat. "Mrs. Kelly."

"Constable." Kate dipped her head, but her gaze never left her husband.

The constable scanned the parcels on the bench. "Your family travels light, Mr. Kelly. What brings you to the train station so early and on such a dismal day?"

"When have the travel habits of law-abiding citizens become of concern to the constabulary?" Byrne retorted.

200

"They haven't."

Byrne pivoted toward the officer and stared him down. "I resent the implication, sir. My family has never run afoul of the law, and we have no intention of starting now. You'd better have just cause for detaining us, or I'll have your badge."

The constable met Byrne's eye. "Bluster has less effect on me than it does on my superior, sir. I repeat my question. If you intend to travel, where is your baggage?"

Byrne's stare lit the air between the men. "Right there." Without looking, he pointed toward the wall behind the constable.

Irma's heart leapt to her throat.

All eyes but Irma's followed her father's gesture toward a stack of luggage against the wall. She held her breath and cringed at the inevitable.

"Does that satisfy you?" her father growled.

Irma slowly turned toward the wall. Gabriel and Isabel were nowhere in sight. She shuddered, quelling the urge to exhale all at once. A quick survey of the station revealed no evidence of the fugitive pair.

The constable turned back toward Byrne. "Not quite, sir. Why the sudden plans to travel, when you agreed to wait for the Chief Inspector's return from Concord and settle the matter of the escaped slaves."

Byrne rolled his eyes. "Blast it, man. Are we back to that?" He arced his arm across the cavernous train station. "Do you see any escaped slaves here?"

"Well, I—"

"And I did not agree to wait for the Chief Inspector's return. My wife merely suggested that we could revisit the issue at some point after his return."

"That hardly—"

"In the meantime, my daughter has received a letter from dear friends in Maine announcing their daughter's impending nuptials, and we were loath to miss the blessed event. Surely even the Boston constabulary harbors some sense of loyalty between friends."

The constable's jaw twitched. "An impending wedding in Maine."

Irma stepped forward, fishing Mary Jane's most recent letter from her handbag. "It's right here. You can read it for yourself." She raised a silent prayer the bluff would work, as the letter had specified the wedding would not take place until the following month.

The constable looked at the letter, then at Irma, then back at Byrne. "Why are you taking the train when your stated plans involved steaming to Portland?"

Byrne stiffened and stared down the constable. "How do you know of my 'stated plans'?"

The officer stepped back, cheeks tinging scarlet. "It had come to our attention—"

"What had come to your attention? And by whose mouth?" Byrne closed the gap and leaned forward, bending the officer backward. "Is there no confidence, no privacy to be enjoyed by the citizens of Boston? Have we returned to the days of Redcoat occupation, of nefarious spies and dastardly intrigue?"

The constable swallowed. "Of course not, Mr. Kelly."

Byrne's tone lowered to barely above a whisper. "Bluster aside, I intend to revisit this encounter with the Chief Inspector. And I couldn't care less now about your badge."

The constable's tacit appeal to his companion met with avoided eye contact. He swallowed. "I'm sure my superior's concerns are unfounded, Mr. Kelly. My sincerest apologies for detaining you. I was merely obeying orders."

A piercing whistle split the air, and Kate touched her husband's arm. "Byrne, our train."

The Kelly patriarch stepped back, but kept his gaze fixed on the hapless constable's. "You have delayed us beyond the point of securing assistance with our luggage." He glanced at the second officer. "I'm sure I can rely upon both of you to remedy that."

The officers hurried to the wall to collect the luggage. Irma hid a grin when the senior constable hefted Gabriel's and Isabelle's bags and trudged toward the train platform.

Their baggage stowed, Byrne thanked the officers and dismissed them with a casual comment that perhaps he would soften his account to the Chief Inspector. The lead constable tipped his hat, and the men set a quick pace to the entrance of the train station.

When they were out of sight, Irma wrapped her arms around her father's neck. "Will I never learn to trust you with all of my heart?" she whispered into his ear.

202

"I've often wondered the same thing."

She pecked him on the cheek and loosened her embrace as a burst of steam from the locomotive's pistons engulfed them.

The whistle sounded again, and her mother took her by the arm. "We'd best get aboard."

Irma hesitated. "But Gabriel and Isabelle. We can't leave without them."

"Don' worry, Miz Kelly. We ain't lost."

She spun around at Gabriel's deep voice and gaped at the couple appearing beside them out of the dissipating steam cloud.

"How on earth ... ?"

Isabelle gave her a broad smile. "When you live like we do, you learn how to lose yerself quick. Just needed a minute or two." She turned an eye toward Irma's father. "Thank you for distractin' the police, sir."

Byrne handed Gabriel two tickets. "We transfer to a connecting train in Nashua, so stay close when we disembark. We'll be in first class. You're in the back of coach. Try to remain unnoticed."

Irma looked at her father's even expression, then at Gabriel's and Isabelle's grateful smiles.

Perhaps it's best not to argue this time.

Late that evening, three weary upper-class Bostonians debarked at the Boston & Maine Railroad terminal in Farmington, shadowed at a distance by two cautious negro passengers. Porters transferred their baggage to a covered carriage, bowed gratefully at the sizable tip bestowed upon them by the obviously rich gentleman, then hurried back into the station before the gentleman realized how generous his tip had been.

The young carriage driver doffed his hat and offered a hand to the two ladies as they climbed into the carriage. He was less cordial to the dark couple approaching the carriage behind them. However, a reassuring nod from the white gentleman—undergirded by a discreetly transferred measure of silver—seemed to allay the driver's concern, so he turned his back while the colored pair slipped onto the back seat and huddled low beneath the fringed cloth canopy. The driver climbed up to his bench, slapped the reins, and the buggy jolted out onto Bridge Street for the short journey across the Sandy River bridge and into Farmington Village.

"I trust ye're comfortable," he called over his shoulder to his passengers. "Farmington's known fer buildin' the finest carriages in New England," he boasted.

Byrne tossed a sideways glance at his smiling wife and responded, "Quite comfortable, thank you."

"Aye-uh," the driver continued. "Ye'll not find a finer rig this side of New York, I promise ye that. What with the war an' all, 'twouldn't surprise me if the village grew by bounds. There's a call fer this kind 'o craftsmanship, there is."

"I'm sure there is." Byrne cast a sidelong look at Irma who thought she'd muffled a giggle more effectively than she actually had.

"Why, 'twas only yesterday—"

"Are you familiar with the Stoddard House, sir?" interrupted Byrne.

"O' course. 'Tis a short way up Main Street, then 'round the corner on Broadway."

"We'll be staying there for the night."

The driver hesitated. "Will ... all of ye be stayin', sir?"

Byrne leaned forward and gripped the man on the shoulder. "Never you mind, lad. Take us to the hotel."

"Aye-uh." The driver hunched and urged the team forward.

***

As the last remnants of twilight dissolved into blackness, the carriage veered off Main Street onto a side avenue, muddy and rutted from a recent rain, and pulled up in front of a grand building. A wooden sign suspended from the second-story balcony announced they'd arrived at the Stoddard House hotel. Irma leaned out and peered up into the welcoming glow of kerosene lanterns and candlelight emanating from windows on all four stories, as well as twin dormers clinging to the sloped roof. Above them, two chimneys wafted lazy gray-white ribbons of smoke into the still air. She closed her eyes and drew in a deep breath, savoring the fragrance of pine mingling with the aroma of a cook stove.

When the carriage shuddered to a halt, her father leaned toward the driver's back. "Continue around to the side of the building," he instructed, voice lowered.

The young Mainer looked over his shoulder. "Sir?"

"I trust you heard me the first time."

The driver shrugged, then urged the team off the street onto a side yard, where they halted, engulfed in the inkiness of the hotel's eastern shadow.

The cushioned bench seat creaked as Byrne turned, laid a restraining hand on his daughter's arm, them said, "Gabriel, your assistance, please."

Irma frowned. "Father?"

Her mother patted Irma's other hand.

The axles groaned under the men's shifting weight as they disembarked and unloaded the baggage. They helped the women down from the seats and escorted them to the side wall. Gabriel remained with them while Byrne dismissed the driver.

Irma leaned toward her mother. "I don't understand."

"Hush."

"That'd be good advice, young lady," came a man's deep voice from out of the darkness. "Best heed it."

Irma grasped her mother's arm and stared in the direction of the voice.

Her father spoke up quietly. "Captain Childs?"

" 'Tis indeed," replied the voice. "Mr. Byrne Kelly, I'll wager."

"You would win the wager, sir. Thank you for meeting us in such an inauspicious setting."

"The setting's ideal, and the pleasure mine, though I must insist our association be brief."

"Of course."

"Where be my guests?"

"Gabriel. Isabelle. Do you have your bags?"

"Yessir," Gabriel responded.

"Off you go, then. Godspeed to you both."

A wave of heat surged through Irma's head. "Wait. Where are they going?" she cried.

"Irma, keep your voice down." her mother hissed.

A large hand patted Irma's shoulder, and a smaller one squeezed her arm as the couple slipped past her. A moment later, three faint silhouettes rounded the corner at the back of the hotel, leaving behind nothing but silence.

Irma's chest seized and tears flooded her eyes. "But I didn't have a chance to say goodbye."

Her father's arms encircled her shoulders, drawing her to his chest. "It was the only way," he whispered. "Not everyone in Maine sympathizes with the abolitionist movement, and people like Captain Childs take great risks to see escaped slaves through to Canada where they will truly be free."

"But I thought they were coming to Marble Falls with us."

"That would strand them in the wilderness, leaving them to find safe passage on their own. Captain Childs will house them tonight, then escort them to another safe house on the road north." He released her. "Don't you worry. They'll be well taken care of."

Irma sniffled. "You could have at least told me we would be separating here."

Her mother's hushed voice carried a smile, but one softened with sympathy. "It was difficult enough getting them this far with you, dear. Imagine how you'd have behaved if you knew this was the end."

206

A half-smile forced its way to Irma's lips despite her sorrow. "I suppose so." She drew a quavering breath and peered toward the back of the hotel. "It's just that they've become so important to me. After all, Gabriel did save my life."

"That he did," her father said. "And now you've saved his."

***

Later, after bidding her parents goodnight, Irma snuggled away from the chilly Maine air beneath a thick feather comforter and padded cotton quilt, head propped on a tufted goose-down pillow. A single taper glowed on the bedside stand, casting flickering shadows on the flowered wallpaper of her third-floor room. A yawn threatened, but the insistent mental image of Gabriel's and Isabelle's figures disappearing forever into the night denied her any hope of sleep. She released a weary sigh, then looked over at the nightstand, where her journal lay. Stowing it with the pen and inkwell into her travel bag had been a last-minute whim, one to which she'd succumbed despite the risk of ruining her belongings should the inkwell's cap become dislodged. Mercifully, it had not, so she intended to record the day's harrowing—and sorrowful—events even while they still pierced her soul.

Arching her knees beneath the covers, she reached for the writing implements and nestled them carefully on the comforter at her side. She rested the diary against her tented legs and opened it to the next blank page. After documenting the day's events, she gazed out at the darkened window, recalling her dear friends vanishing into the night like shadows.

Dipping her pen into the inkwell, she added one more note.

Gabriel and Isabelle are on their way to freedom, yet I cannot help but lament my own loss. Is that selfish? Perhaps. But then, my heart takes solace in that I would have it no other way.

***

Gwen laid the diary aside and yawned. A flicker from the alarm clock changing minutes startled her. 2:37 a.m. *Great. I'm going to be a zombie tomorrow.*

She clicked off the lamp and curled onto her side. Snuggling into a fluffy woolen blanket against a New England winter chill, she turned half-closed eyes toward the far wall. Lazy shafts of moonlight seeped through lace scrims over the bedroom window, gradually lulling her into slumber.

But not one without dreams.

*

The hotel room laid in twilight stillness, silent but for the scratching of a pen nib over manila paper. Against the far wall, faint candlelight cast the blurry shadow of an elegant figure in repose. The scene came into focus, the pen stilled, and the figure's head tipped up. "You think me silly to make such a fuss."

"Not at all, Grandmother. It's endearing."

" 'Endearing' you say? Why?"

"It betrays a tender heart, one I would so love to have inherited."

"But you have. And more so."

"I think not."

"Thinking has little to do with matters of the heart."

"How strange. A friend said something similar not long ago."

"Indeed she did."

"You know of my conversation with Cassie?"

A sigh. "Such an odd name, Cassie."

"But how could you know?"

"How could it be that you are here speaking with me now?"

"I ... I don't know. A dream?"

A breathy laugh tilted Grandmother Irma's head. "Perhaps someday we shall learn the secret of dreams. What they might actually be."

45

At the breakfast table the next morning, Cassie leveled an amused gaze over the rim of her coffee cup. "Rough night?"

Gwen nodded as she brushed a tousled strand of hair from her brow. She groped for her mug, eyelids half-opened. "Late one. Did some reading. Dreamt a lot once I did fall asleep."

"Really?" Cassie set down the cup. "About what?"

Gwen took a sip of coffee, chin propped on one hand. "About my grandmother."

Cassie's shoulders slumped. "Oh. I was hoping for something a little juicier."

Gwen giggled. "Sorry." She sat back, hands cupped around the warm mug. "What are your dreams like, Cassie?"

"Depends. Usually they're all over the map." She paused, absently reaching for her missing arm. "Sometimes, though, they're way too vivid."

Gwen shifted in her seat. "I'm sorry."

Cassie lifted a dismissive hand.

Gwen leaned forward. "Do you ever carry on conversations in them? I mean, conversations that seem to make sense?"

"You're leading up to something."

"I told you about my grandmother's diaries, right?"

"Yes."

"Well, when I read them late at night, I often dream about her."

"And?"

"At first, the dreams were fragmented, like—how did you put it?—all over the map. I was an observer. But they've become progressively more coherent. I actually have conversations with my Grandmother Irma, and she ... "

"She what?"

"Well, she's said some really cryptic things, like what she had written was specifically for me."

"That's a little creepy."

"Last night she knew what you said about matters of the heart."

"More creepy."

"She even knew your name."

Cassie sat back. "Okay, now I'm getting weirded out."

"I know, right?"

"But then, doesn't it make sense? Dreams are just figments of our own imaginations. You're just dreaming about what you know."

"Maybe, but I've never dreamt like this before."

"You've probably never read a diary like this before."

Gwen laughed. "Good point. I'm probably being silly."

Cassie leaned back. "Not silly. Sensitive. The mind's a funny thing. It's amazing what comes to us in the middle of the night that would never occur to us during the day. There's got to be some rhyme or reason to where our brains go when we're asleep."

Gwen tipped her head. "I can't help but feel my brain is trying to tell me something."

"Or your grandmother is."

"Okay, now you're weirding *me* out."

As Cassie laughed, her phone chirped from the kitchen counter.

"I'll get it," Gwen said rising.

Cassie's smile thinned. "You don't need to. I'm perfectly able—"

Gwen lifted a hand. "I'm getting more coffee anyway." She grabbed the phone on the way to the coffee maker and tossed it to Cassie, who snatched it deftly from the air.

"Was that supposed to be a test?"

Gwen turned and met her gaze. "We've had this conversation, and I'm not going there again." She turned back toward the counter.

When Cassie answered the call, her voice immediately lightened. "Hey, big guy ... No, we've finished breakfast ... I got up at five for PT ... No big deal. Some days are easier than others." She laughed, then paused, face clouding. "Um, sure. Hold on." She turned toward Gwen. "He wants to talk to you."

"Me?"

Cassie gave a slight shrug, tossed the phone to Gwen, and turned back to her coffee. Gwen nearly fumbled the device to the floor, but managed to hold on. She shot a look at Cassie before answering. "Hello?"

"Morning, Gwen. I want to take another look at your house this morning. Can I swing by and pick you up?"

"Sure, I suppose."

"You sound hesitant. Did you have other plans?"

Gwen threw a quick look back at Cassie. "Umm, it's just that Cassie and I were going to go to the mall and do some window shopping."

Cassie pivoted in her chair and stared at her.

"Wow. Cassie window shopping in a mall? This is huge. Snap a photo for me, would you?"

Gwen's cheeks warmed, and she averted her gaze. "Well, I hadn't actually asked her yet. I thought it might be nice to get out a little." Another glance toward Cassie revealed an arched eyebrow, and the heat spread to Gwen's forehead.

"But I was hoping to close the loop on a couple of things at the house."

"Maybe Cassie can come along."

"That would be great," Mark said.

Cassie's other eyebrow arched, and Gwen turned away, clutching the phone with both hands. "She's never been to my place, and she might have some new insights. Afterward, maybe we can grab some lunch ... you know, the three of us ... or the two of you, and I can go somewhere else ... whatever."

"Gwen, is something wrong?"

"Of course not. Why do you ask?"

"You're rambling."

"Am I?"

"Never mind. I'll be there at 10:30. Doing lunch sounds good." He chuckled. "And you don't have to go somewhere else."

"Good. It's a date." She cringed inwardly at her choice of words, and glanced back at Cassie who was still staring at her. She disconnected the call, grabbed their mugs, and returned to the table with the phone.

"The mall? Seriously?" Cassie shook her head.

"Spur of the moment idea."

Cassie set the phone on the table. "Why didn't he call your cell? I'm sure he has your number."

"Two thoughts come to mind."

Cassie cocked her head.

Gwen sipped her coffee, then set down the mug. "First, maybe he wanted to talk to you more than he wanted to talk to me."

Cassie drummed a slow cadence on the table with a forefinger.

Gwen folded her arms. "Second, transparency."

"Transparency?"

"He wanted you to know he was calling me."

"Why would he care?"

"The tension in this conversation suggests he should care, and maybe he's more perceptive than you give him credit for."

"Tension?"

Gwen cocked her head. "C'mon, Cassie. You're way more genuine than that."

The twitching moved to Cassie's lower lip, and she looked away.

Gwen leaned forward. "When are you going to accept the fact that Mark only has eyes for you?"

Cassie's tone dropped to a whisper. "When my arm and leg grow back."

"Then you're dooming him to the impossible. If Mark steps away, it won't be because of your body. It'll be because of your mind."

"Easy for you to say."

"Maybe. But no less true."

46

Brent propped his elbow on the desk and rested his forehead on the palm of his hand. His other hand held a telephone to his ear. "Howard, I really don't have time for this."

"How can you not have time for a law-abiding citizen's complaint?"

"I have plenty of time for those."

"Why, Officer Newcomb, I resent your implication. Do you have some basis for questioning my strict adherence to and heartfelt admiration for the law?"

"Not yet, but it's only a matter of time."

"Well, I'll have you know I'm both shocked and dismayed. And until you do discover some basis for this inexplicable distrust, I demand you take action on my call."

Brent suddenly smiled. "Very well, but I'll need to gather some details. Why don't I drop by after my shift this evening at, oh, say around seven, and you can file a formal report."

"Today?"

"Today."

"But it's Thursday."

"Yes, it is."

"Um, I'm sort of busy this evening."

"But your complaint sounds urgent, and I won't have spare time again until after the weekend."

"It can wait."

"If you say so. But, for the record, I'm more than willing to meet with you on my own time."

"Right. Thanks." Howard hung up.

As Brent replaced the telephone receiver in its cradle, Chad Tucker, fellow officer and close friend, looked up from his computer. "Dobbs again?"

Brent nodded. "He doesn't give up."

"Yep, he's a pest—but truth be told, I was too, not all that long ago."

"You still are."

Chad laughed. "Yeah, well you're no saint either. How did you shut him down?"

"I offered to follow up on his complaint this evening."

Chad paused, searching Brent's face. "You know tonight's his poker night, right?"

"Yep. And the last thing he wants is me showing up."

"It's not illegal."

"I know, but rumor has it that some of the late-night pots have gotten pretty hefty, enough so that he gets a little skittish when the subject comes up outside his in-crowd." Brent smiled. "And I am nowhere near his in-crowd. So it seemed like a good way to put him off." He grinned. "And maybe rattle him a little, just for fun."

Chad shook his head with a smile as he turned his attention to the monitor.

Brent reached for his coat, stopping when his cell rang. "Hey, Gwen. What're you up to?"

"My ears in curiosity."

Brent laughed. "Curiosity? About what?"

"Cassie and Mark."

"What about them?"

"You said they have some issues to work through, but I feel like I'm walking on eggshells here."

"How so?"

"Cassie and I seem to go around in circles whenever Mark's name comes up. On one hand, she's super jealous over him, and on the other hand, she holds him at arm's length."

"I get that."

"Mark seems pretty balanced about everything. I can't help but wonder why he sticks around, honestly."

"Before you're tempted to take sides, be aware that Mark doesn't wear a pure-white hat in the relationship either."

"Really? Everything I've seen so far makes him a candidate for sainthood and her for the loony bin."

"That's not fair, Gwen." He winced at the sharpness in his rebuke.

Her voice thinned. "Sorry. I probably didn't word that very well."

"I didn't mean to jump on you. There's some history you're not privy to. I can understand why you feel this way, but Mark has made his share of mistakes, and frankly, Cassie's hypersensitivity is understandable."

"Can you enlighten me?"

"I'd love to, but I'm on my way out to my rounds, and it will to take more time than I have right now."

"So, what do I do, keep stepping around emotional landmines?"

"You might have to for now."

"Any suggestions as to how?"

His tone lightened. "You could use that 'women's intuition' thing."

"Oh, don't you *even*—"

Brent laughed. "Sorry, sweetheart. Gotta go. Duty calls."

"Don't you dare hang up on me ... Brent?"

He ended the call before his laugh broke loose.

***

Gwen glared at the silent phone. *He's lucky I'm not back in Marble Falls right now.*

"Gwen?" Cassie's voice echoed down the hallway. "Mark's pulling into the driveway."

"Coming." She tucked the phone into her purse and hurried out to the foyer.

Bundled against the cold, the women opened the door just as Mark touched the doorbell. He grinned. "That was fast. I must have the touch."

Cassie deadpanned him. "Don't flatter yourself, bud. Anyone can spot that florescent Mazda a mile away."

He laughed and pulled her into his arms. "Admit it. It's my aura."

"Right. It's your—"

The remainder of her words suffocated under a kiss.

Gwen looked away, as a memory of Brent's lips pressed against hers erased everything else in her mind. Even the biting winter gusts and tiny ice crystals pricking her skin failed to cool her cheeks. She drew a deep breath. *I need to get back home before I explode.*

"I bet you're about ready to get back home, aren't you?"

Her eyes widened, and she turned. Mark was smiling back at her as he steadied Cassie's descent down the short flight of ice-crusted steps to the driveway. She laughed. "Great minds."

"What?"

"Never mind." She followed them to the car and climbed into the back seat.

After settling Cassie onto the passenger seat and propping her crutch onto the floor behind her, Mark wedged himself behind the steering wheel.

Gwen stifled a giggle at the site of Mark hunched over in the small sedan, the top of his head brushing the ceiling. At least she thought she'd stifled it.

"What's so funny?" He was looking at her through the rearview mirror.

"I still can't get over the sight of you crammed into this car."

"I like this car."

"You must."

"It keeps him humble," Cassie said.

Mark turned toward her. "Humble? I'm the most humble person in the world."

The women laughed, and Gwen said, "It makes me anxious to get my own car back. I love my little Corolla."

Mark returned his attention to the road. "It's probably a good thing we left it at the house. It gives the impression someone is home."

They turned onto Gwen's street, then slowed as they approached the driveway.

Gwen straightened, stared through the windshield, and gasped.

"What?" asked Cassie.

"My car. Someone slashed my tires."

***

Gwen pressed the phone to her cheek while Mark inspected the vehicle. "I have no idea, Brent, but it's infuriating. I haven't done anything to deserve all of this."

"Of course you haven't. And I'm going to say again that you need to come back home. It's obviously not safe there."

"I'm comfortable at Cassie's, for as long as she'll have me." She glanced over at the Mazda, where Cassie remained huddled inside.

"Where's Mark?"

"He's looking over the car."

"Let me talk to him."

Gwen walked over to where Mark was leaning close to the driver's door. "Mark, can you talk to Brent?"

"Sure." He accepted the phone. "Hey ... Yeah, I know. It sucks ... There are fresh scratches on the top of the driver's door, probably from a slim jim. Looks like the guy couldn't get the door open, so he slashed the tires instead ... Of course Gwen can stay with Cassie. She likes the company." He looked up. "No, Gwen's a tough lady, bro. You done good." He grinned. "Why, only this morning she told me she'd never dreamed she'd land a guy like you, and that she can't live without you."

"Hey!" Gwen grabbed for the phone, but Mark laughed and stepped back.

"You bet I will ... Sure, here she is." Grin widening, he handed back the phone.

She lifted the phone to her cheek, narrowing her eyes at him. "So what was that all about?"

"Guy talk."

She refused to speak.

"Uh oh."

" 'Uh oh' is right." She broke a smile, her gaze still skewering Mark. "It's getting colder, so we're going inside. I'll call you this evening."

"Promise?"

"Do I need to?"

47

In the house, Gwen hung up their coats and ushered Cassie into the family room while Mark went to take a quick look around the house.

"Have a seat. I'll start a fire." Cassie sat down and laid her crutch against the sofa while Gwen pulled a long wooden match from a box on the fireplace mantel and reached for the gas cock. "It won't be nearly as cozy as your place, but at least it'll make you think you should be warm."

"Gwen?" Mark's voice boomed from the top of the stairs.

"Yes?"

"Is this your bedroom to the right of the bathroom?"

"Yes."

"Can you come up here for a minute?"

Cassie stiffened and lowered her gaze to the floor. Gwen forced a light tone. "I'll be right back, Cassie." She hurried up to her room, where Mark was looking out the window. He turned. "Take a look here."

Cassie's reaction still vivid in her mind, Gwen avoided walking near the bed as she crossed the room. Mark pointed through the swirling snow toward a set of shallow footprints crossing the backyard. "With the wind we've been having, those prints can't be that old. They seem to come from the one-story over there." He turned toward her, and she involuntarily shifted away. "Do you know who lives there?"

Gwen shook her head. "We didn't socialize much with the neighbors, I'm afraid." She leaned toward the window and gestured toward rooftops a couple of blocks away. "Wright's Park is beyond that row of houses. If somebody is sneaking around, it would be a good place to hide."

Mark bent down and squinted the direction she was pointing.

"What's so interesting?" came Cassie's voice from behind them.

They jumped, colliding shoulders as they pivoted. Mark bumped his head on the top of the window frame.

"Ouch!" He rubbed his head. "Don't do that. I nearly jumped out the window."

Gwen quickly stepped away from the window, heat coursing through her head despite her best efforts to subdue it. "Mark spotted some tracks in the snow. We were trying to figure out where they were leading." Her words tumbled over each other.

Cassie gave her a blank look, and the temperature notched up, burning Gwen's cheeks. She mentally kicked herself. *Get a grip. You didn't do anything wrong, and you're acting like an escaped convict.*

"And where *were* they leading?" asked Cassie, tone quieted, eyes flicking for an instant toward the bed.

Mark stepped forward. "Nowhere, Cassie. Nothing was leading anywhere." He took her gently by the arm. "Let's go back downstairs."

He ushered her into the hallway, and Gwen followed behind, forehead heating now from frustration. So much drama. Maybe it would be best to pack up and move out of Cassie's house. Even the cost of a hotel room would be preferable to this emotional roller coaster ride.

When they reached the top of the staircase, Cassie looked at Mark. "Don't you think you should turn off the lights?"

"What lights?"

She nodded toward the study. Through the half-closed doorway, a low-watt bulb glowed from a desk lamp.

He frowned. "I didn't turn that on."

"Neither did I," Gwen said. "And I'm sure I turned it off the last time we were here."

They backtracked around the railing, and Mark pushed open the door. An overstuffed chair with a reading table and lamp next to it sat between a wooden filing cabinet and an oak roll top desk. The room appeared undisturbed, but for the desk lamp being on. He turned toward Gwen. "Did your father keep a spare set of house keys in here?"

"He used to. Check the top right drawer of the desk."

He opened the drawer. It was empty. He turned back toward Gwen. "The last time we were here it didn't appear anything was missing either, but did you check this drawer?"

"No, I didn't think to."

"I wonder if—"

The creak of a floorboard cut him off, and they swiveled in unison toward the hallway door. Running footfalls echoed up from the first floor, followed by a door slamming shut.

Mark ran downstairs, followed closely by Gwen. She suddenly remembered Cassie and turned back. Cassie was halfway down the stairs, bracing her descent against the railing. "Go!" she yelled. "I'll catch up."

Gwen continued her pursuit. Mark had reached the foyer and was grasping the front doorknob.

"That was the back door slamming," she called. "I know the sound."

He rushed back to the family room, wrenched open the door to the back porch, and raced out into the gusting wind. The snowfall had picked up in intensity, swirling large flakes into Gwen's face as she skidded to a halt just short of running into Mark's back. He was scanning the yard, shielding his eyes against the wind. She joined his search, but even the neighbor's house across the street had all but disappeared into the growing storm.

They rounded the side of the garage, gazes raking the ground for fresh footprints. Finally, Mark straightened and turned around. "This is hopeless," he hollered against the wind. "I can't see a thing."

Gwen agreed, and they retreated to the house.

When they stumbled into the family room, brushing snowflakes from their hair and shoulders, Cassie was sitting on the sofa across from the fire, rubbing her good thigh.

Mark sat down beside her. "You okay?"

"Yeah. Stretched a muscle coming down the stairs, that's all."

He squeezed her arm, then looked up at Gwen. "Sorry. Lousy luck, the weather."

She nodded, then shuddered. "How creepy, that the guy was in here the whole time."

"Apparently."

She rubbed her arms. "I feel so ... violated."

"I get that," Cassie said quietly.

"That's long past, Cassie," countered Mark.

They locked gazes for a moment, and Cassie murmured, "Not so long for me."

Gwen sighed inwardly. Then her mind flashed back to the missteps she and Brent had experienced in the days following their first meeting. The awkward history she shared with the man she now loved so deeply awakened a sense of empathy. If she and Brent had weathered their storm into such a wonderful calm, surely there was hope for Cassie and Mark. She drew a resolute breath. *Maybe a little more grace on your part, Gwen?* She cleared her throat. "Can I get us something hot to drink?"

Cassie kept her gaze on the floor, but Mark stood. "That would be great, thanks. I'm going to look around a little more."

When Mark set off for the hallway, she turned toward Cassie. "Cocoa sound good?"

"Sure."

Gwen hesitated. "Cassie, would it be better if I found another place to stay?"

Cassie looked up abruptly. "Why?"

"I can't help but feel I'm intruding."

"How so?"

"Do you want an honest answer?"

"Of course."

"You and Mark seem to be working through some things, and you don't need me around."

"Working through what?"

Gwen slumped her shoulders. "You have an annoying habit of asking questions you already know the answers to."

Cassie's frown wavered, and a smile broke through. "Mark tells me the same thing."

Gwen returned a smile. "Does he?"

"I don't want you to leave. It's nice having someone around." She tipped an apologetic shrug. "Even though I don't always show it."

"I don't want to be a speed bump for you guys."

"You aren't. It's me. I need to get over it."

"Over what, may I ask?"

That moment, Mark came back downstairs. He put on a mock pout, hands propped on his hips. "What, no hot chocolate yet?"

Cassie looked at him, then back at Gwen. "Have you ever seen anything more pitiful?"

Gwen shook her head.

They laughed, the women exchanged glances that promise a continued conversation, and Gwen excused herself to the kitchen.

48

Mark finished noting the incident for his report and suggested having the locks on the exterior doors replaced.

"That's going to be expensive," Gwen said with a sigh.

"You might also have an alarm system put in," Mark said, helping Cassie on with her coat.

"I guess I should, although I hate to spend the money this close to selling the house."

"I get that, but at least consider it." He finished tucking Cassie's scarf beneath her collar, then pulled Gwen's coat from its hanger.

She slipped her arms into the sleeves and buttoned up. "Thank you."

Mark looked back at Gwen. "You'll also need to call someone about your tires."

"I called while I was making the cocoa. Daddy knows ... " she blinked and swallowed, "Daddy knew a man who owns a garage, and we have good credit there. He's sending someone over." She glanced at her watch. "In fact, he should be here any time now. Sorry to mess up our lunch plans."

"No problem. I'll wait for him," Mark said. "You two head on back to the house. I don't want you staying here alone."

She offered a grateful smile, retrieved her keys from the hall table and gave them to him. "I don't know any locksmiths, though, and I'm not sure I have the money on hand. "

"Let me take care of that."

"Thank you. Unfortunately, all of Daddy's assets are tied up until I find Simon."

"Any more news on that?"

She shook her head. "Brent's had a couple of leads, but he hit a dead end."

"If anyone can find his way out of a dead end, it's Wild Bill," Cassie said.

Mark handed his car keys to Cassie. "Be careful with my car."

She sniffed. "Seriously?"

"I've seen you behind the wheel of a Humvee."

She punched his arm, and Gwen giggled.

Cassie looked back as she reached for the door. "Baked chicken tonight?"

He flashed a broad grin. "Need you ask?"

***

Brent tapped a pencil on the desktop and frowned at the computer monitor. How could someone disappear so completely? All he had was a trail littered with false addresses, lapsed driver's licenses, and a house fire in Burlington. But now that Farmington had entered the equation, things were hitting too close to home.

He stared glumly at a notepad lying beside the keyboard. On the top margin, the title "Simon Hardy" was double underlined. The remainder of the page was blank.

The phone rang, and he absently reached for the receiver.

"Marble Falls Police Department."

"I want to report an incident."

Brent's head dropped, chin hitting his chest. "I'm really not in the mood for this right now, Dobbs."

"I'm serious."

"Sure you are."

"Really, this is legit."

Brent glanced at his watch. "You have thirty seconds to convince me."

"Thirty seconds? Do you impose limitations on other upright citizens — "

"That's it. Have a nice day."

"No, wait. You really want to hear this."

Brent's voice tightened. "I don't know what I've done to earn this much attention from you, Howard, but there are people who actually need ... friends who have ... " He rubbed his forehead and sighed.

A moment of silence, and Howard's quieted voice broke through. "Friends? What's up, Officer Newcomb?"

"Why would you care?"

"Because friends are everything."

"Even a cop's?"

"Even a cop's."

Brent tightened his jaw. "This friend means everything to me. She's not to be messed with."

"I don't mess with friends." A smile overtook Howard's tone. "Especially 'she' friends."

Brent chuckled in spite of himself. "So, why should I share my problem with you?"

"Maybe you shouldn't. Maybe I'll throw it back in your face."

Brent paused. "And maybe you won't."

"Pretty sure I won't."

Brent summarized the issues with Gwen's estate and her enigmatic half-brother. He related his own efforts to track down Teresa and Simon Hardy and confessed frustration at the blank notepad sitting in front of him.

"Farmington, huh?" Howard asked.

"Teresa Hardy's last known address."

"Maybe I can help."

"How?"

"My Thursday evening ... social event draws folks from as far away as Augusta and most places in between."

Brent leaned forward. "Like Farmington."

"Especially Farmington."

"Influential folks?"

"Okay, we'll call them 'influential'."

"Are you saying you might be able to shed some light on Teresa Hardy?"

"Put a capital letter on the word 'might'."

"That's good enough for me."

"Let's do it, then."

Brent paused again. "Why would you do this, Howard? You're not exactly a candidate for Police Auxiliary Member of the Year."

"And I never will be. But I like you."

"You like me? Why?"

"Don't push it."

"Right."

The phone clicked dead, and Brent slowly set the handset onto its cradle.

***

Following a dinner of fall-off-the-bone baked chicken breasts coated with a crispy seasoned batter of "Special K" cereal, a rice pilaf, sautéed vegetables, and salad, Mark embraced Cassie and punctuated it with a lingering kiss. "You are *so* best."

"That's your stomach speaking."

"My stomach and I are one."

Cassie gave him a sardonic look as he resumed his seat. "That's an understatement if there ever was one." She laid her silverware on her plate. "You can take the leftover chicken with you for lunch tomorrow."

He reached for the serving platter. "What leftover chicken?"

Gwen giggled. "I wonder who would win an eating contest between you and Brent."

Cassie shook her head. "Brent made the mistake of challenging Mark to a pizza snarf-off a couple of years ago. Mark almost put him into the hospital."

"Seriously?"

"Then he took me out for a pie-and-ice-cream dessert."

Gwen laughed. "I'll never understand how guys can pack it in without packing it on."

"Fast metabolism," mumbled Mark through a mouthful.

"A couple of hours at the gym almost every day doesn't hurt," Cassie said.

Gwen gathered her dishes and took them to the sink. "If you don't mind, I'm going to go to bed early this evening. For some reason, I'm exhausted."

"I wondered," Cassie said. "You didn't eat much."

Mark looked up. "Too much excitement this morning?"

Gwen shook her head. "I feel a little tired and achy." She turned around, rubbing her shoulder. "I hope I'm not coming down with something."

226

"You need a good night's sleep," Cassie said as she brought her own plate to the sink.

"Probably. G'night you guys. Thanks for dinner, Cassie. As usual, it was incredible." She gave her friend a pointed look. "You haven't cooked for Brent, have you?"

"Once or twice."

"Great," Gwen muttered on her way out of the kitchen. "Another high bar to clear."

***

Back in the guest room, Gwen crawled into her nightgown and trudged to the bathroom, every step seeming more laborious than the last. When she finally collapsed into bed, she heaved a sigh and closed her eyes. But despite the weighty fatigue, sleep proved elusive. After a half hour of tossing side to side, she turned on the nightstand lamp and reached for the diary. She thumbed through the few remaining pages to the back cover. So little room and so much of the story yet to be told.

She opened to the marked page. At first, the writing refused to focus. Gwen rubbed her eyes and squinted, then turned back to a page she'd already read. It also looked strange. *What's going on?* Her hand slipped to her forehead. Warm. She kicked off the heavy quilt, despite the chill of the room.

Leafing forward again, she squinted at the text.

Sunday, May 12, 1861.

So much has happened these past few days, I scarcely know where to begin.

Frowning, she lowered the book closer to her face.

It was so shocking to discover

A sizzling hiss rose from the back of her head, and her ears began to ring. Her vision tunneled, and everything went dark.

49

"Are you all right, Gwendolyn?"

The vaguely familiar voice poked Gwen's sluggish mind. She drew a shuddering breath and swallowed through a dry throat, head lolling on her shoulder, body jerking and swaying as though the earth pitched beneath her.

"You appear ill."

Her eyelids parted and the back of a man's top-hatted head came gradually into focus. On one side, trees passed by slowly against the expanse of a clear blue sky, and the sound of rushing water caught her ear. A snort perked her ear. Was that a horse? She straightened and rubbed the back of her neck. "Where am I?"

"With me, of course."

She turned toward the quiet voice and froze wide-eyed at the curly-headed young woman sitting beside her, smiling. Grandmother Irma laid her hand on Gwen's arm and smiled. "I think it's time we became better acquainted."

Gwen's eyes rolled back, and she passed out.

***

The murmur of women's voices filtered through complete darkness. Slowly, the words gathered themselves into a semblance of order, and Gwen fought through a stupor to catch them.

"Your father will want to get an early start in the morning."

"Yes, Mother."

"Do you intend to join his expedition?"

"I think so."

"You must decide quickly. Quimby Lake beckons, and he is not one to dither when angling is at stake."

"I know. There's something I'd like to attend to first."

"You refer to Mary Jane."

"I do."

"I understand. However, do not supplant your desire to draw nearer to your father with reacquainting with a friend. As lovely a girl as Mary Jane is, family comes first."

"I will never forsake family."

"I know you won't." Hinges creaked and the voice dropped. "Your father and I will be back from the main house before dinner to prepare. We are to dine with our hosts this evening."

"Enjoy your visit."

A door closed, and Gwen rolled onto her side. She groaned.

"So, you've awakened."

Gwen opened her eyes to the foggy image of a rough-hewn wooden wall. Gradually, shadows undulating over its knotty contours in flickering candlelight came into focus. She propped herself up onto her elbow and stared into the duskiness of a small room. "Where am I?"

"You are in Marble Falls, Maine."

"Marble Falls? I live here."

"In another time, perhaps."

"What other time?"

A smile tickled the voice. "You ask many questions. Such behavior is not becoming in young ladies of our day."

Gwen sat up, willing the grogginess from her mind, and peered up at the young woman standing before her. "How can I not ask?"

Her young grandmother laughed softly. "We are so alike. Still, if you are to learn of me, you must come to terms with my day. Such learning does not come without concessions."

"Concessions?"

"Try to arise."

Gwen pivoted awkwardly to the side of the bed and settled her feet onto the floor. Her eyes widened as a billowing brown skirt cascaded over her legs. Matching high-laced brown shoes disappeared beneath the dress's hem as it settled over her ankles. Thin strips of material brushed the sides of her face, prompting her hands to her head where they encountered a bonnet. Her attempt to draw a full breath met with resistance, and her hands dropped to explore her waist, fingertips pressing against a firm sheath buried beneath the folds of her dress.

"Be grateful it's a nonchalante, a travel corset," her grandmother said. "They are much more forgiving than the whalebone prisons in which we are normally confined."

"Corset? Where on earth did I get a corset—and this dress, for that matter?"

Her grandmother smiled. "Where indeed," she murmured. "Oh, and as for the undergarments, you may keep them. I shan't be wanting them back."

"Undergarments?" Gwen pulled her skirt up to her thighs, revealing a white cotton chemise with drawers extending below her knees.

"Gwendolyn Kelly, what *are* you doing?"

She jolted and released her skirts. "What?"

"Heavens, such a shocking display of immodesty."

Gwen's cheeks warmed. "I'm sorry. It didn't occur to me."

"Concessions, child."

Gwen crossed her arms. " 'Child'? I'm older than you are ... well, sort of."

A pause, and both women burst out laughing.

"I sense this is going to be quite an adventure," Grandmother Irma said, wiping her eyes.

Gwen nodded, struggling against more giggles. "I'm twenty-six and you're, what, eighteen? How is *that* supposed to work?"

"Not without a concerted effort on both of our parts, I suspect."

"As do I." Gwen pressed a hand to her mouth. "Good heavens, I'm even beginning to sound like you."

"Really? I hadn't noticed." Her grandmother's eyes twinkled in the candlelight.

A knock on the door widened Irma's eyes. "That will be Mary Jane. She said she'd visit after her chores."

As Gwen turned toward the door, her throat inexplicably tightened.

Mary Jane Toothaker. In Gwen's world, a bygone name penned in an ancient journal, and now undoubtedly inscribed on a cold headstone in a country cemetery somewhere. A young woman who a century-and-a-half ago experienced the totality of her life, now resting in eternity with her loved ones. But she was here, alive, knocking on a door not ten feet away. Gwen clasped the frills of her unfamiliar clothing and stared at the door her teenaged grandmother had risen to open. Would Mary Jane appear as she imagined her from the journal? But, most importantly, how would Grandmother Irma explain who Gwen was?

"Mary Jane!"

When the door opened, there stood the Mary Jane Toothaker of her imagination. Flowing brown hair, high forehead, gray homespun dress, just as she remembered from the dream.

Except for one thing.

"How lovely to—" Grandmother Irma paused, then stepped back from the doorway, staring at her friend's swollen midriff. Mary Jane dropped her gaze and fidgeted, clutching her skirts at her side.

"Oh, Mary Jane."

Mary Jane's cheeks turned crimson. "I wanted ta tell ye, but ... " She drew a deep breath and threw a furtive glance over her shoulder. "I shouldn't've come."

She began to turn, but Irma reached out and grasped her hand. "No, wait. Please forgive me. I didn't ... well, I suppose it startled me."

Mary Jane nodded, head lowered.

Grandmother Irma's hands moved slowly to her friend's waist and traced the bulge with tender fingertips. Mary Jane stiffened and lifted her gaze. Grandmother Irma smiled. "I believe it suits you. You were far too thin the last time I saw you."

They sputtered laughs, then embraced.

"Oh, Irma how I've missed ye!" Mary Jane said as they parted. "Thank ye for writing."

"I've missed you, too, although I wasn't nearly as faithful a writer as you. But where are my manners? Come in and sit down." She giggled. "After all, it *is* your cabin."

Gwen pivoted on the bed and smiled as Mary Jane entered and settled into a rough wooden chair in the corner. Grandmother Irma scooted a similar chair closer from the opposite wall and sat knee-to-knee with her friend.

"I received your letter regarding your wedding next month," she said, holding Mary Jane's folded hands.

"Yes. Hiram's an honorable man."

"And he loves you?"

She smiled. "I truly believe he does. He's building our cabin near his parents' homestead in Strong, else we'd have married before this." She looked down again. "Ye don't think poorly of me, do ye?"

"We've discussed that, and I don't want to hear such nonsense again."

Mary Jane's grateful nod carried a note of relief.

From the bed, Gwen cleared her throat and looked expectantly at her grandmother, but neither she nor Mary Jane acknowledged the overture.

Grandmother Irma continued. "And when is the blessed event to occur?"

"The middle of September, best figurin'. Everyone thinks it's a boy, but I think it's a girl."

"Then a girl it will be."

"My mother insists I return ta Marble Falls for the birth, but we'll have ta see about that."

Gwen frowned and shifted as nosily as she could on the straw mattress.

Her grandmother glanced at the floor in her direction and briefly lifted a forefinger.

"And what've yer engagement, Irma? How is Gerald?"

"Off to war, I'm afraid."

"Oh, dear."

"He enlisted in April. We pray for him daily."

"As will I."

"Thank you."

A woman's voice in the distance called Mary Jane's name, and she quickly rose. "I must go. Time ta begin supper fixin's. Ye're dining with us this evening, aren't ye?"

"I understand we are."

"Wonderful. I'll see ye then."

They embraced, and Mary Jane departed.

Gwen stood and faced her grandmother as she closed the door. "Why didn't you introduce me?"

"She was unaware of your presence."

"How do you know?"

"I became aware when my parents showed no mindfulness of you in the carriage. I helped you to the cabin while they were greeting the Toothakers."

Gwen shook her head. "How can you see me when no one else can?"

"I'm not sure." Grandmother Irma cocked her head with a smile. "This is rather a new experience for me as well."

50

Gwen drew her knees to her chest and leaned against the back of the wagon as it creaked along the road westward from Marble Falls. Grandmother Irma sat stiffly on the driver's bench beside her father who remained silent, but for an occasional click of the tongue to urge the horse onward. A wicker tackle box with a matching creel and two wooden poles disassembled into sections and bundled in cloth sheathes rested behind the bench, as did a linen-covered basket from which the faint aroma of a fried chicken rose into the morning air.

When her gaze fell on the picnic basket, the thought occurred that she'd not eaten since this otherworldly experience began, surprised even more so that she wasn't hungry. What other strange things would happen before this … whatever it was, ended?

The cart trundled down the dirt road, and she surveyed the passing landscape. In her day, this would be two-lane asphalt-paved Route 4. But today, it was a rutted pathway barely wide enough to accommodate the wagon in which she rode. The weather was a perfect, mild temperature, the sky a translucent azure, morning sunlight slicing through the boughs of hardwoods and firs lining the road. Another less-pleasant familiarity was the cloud of black flies buzzing around the two figures on the driver's seat. None of the pests seemed to notice Gwen. She smiled. *Perhaps being a ghost has its advantages after all.*

Grandmother Irma finally broke the silence. "Oh, this is intolerable!" She swiped at a fly darting past her face. "How can you stand it, Father?"

"Sit still. They'll ignore you."

"I've tried ignoring them, and I have two welts on my neck to show for it."

"Perhaps you should have foregone the toilet water this morning. The flies seem as intensely attracted to you as Gerald is."

Gwen muffled a laugh, and Irma tossed a narrow frown over her shoulder.

"I folded some silk netting onto the brim of your sunhat," her father continued. "Lower it to your shoulders."

"I wondered what that was for." She unfurled the mesh around her face and neck, then breathed a sigh of relief. "This is perfect. Why didn't you tell me about it sooner?"

"I waited until your inclination to argue would be at its lowest."

At this, Gwen laughed aloud, drawing another more extended glare from her young grandmother.

"What do you keep looking at?" her father asked, peering over his shoulder.

Grandmother Irma resumed her attention forward. "Nothing. Absolutely nothing."

Presently, her father veered the cart off the main road onto a smaller byway. "This is the road to Quimby Lake. The scenery is quite beautiful if you take a moment to enjoy it."

They passed a farmhouse on their right. "That's Daniel Quimby's homestead. He is the gentleman from whom I purchased our property."

Gwen stared at the wooden structure. *This is where Howard Dobbs lives now. How strange to see it in the past.* She shaded her eyes from the sun, and after a moment shook her head. *Then again, I don't see that he's made all that much improvement.*

A short distance up the road, they passed a small building to their right. Children's voices filtered through the open front door.

"What is that?" Grandmother Irma asked her father.

"A local schoolhouse. District Number Two, if I recall correctly."

Gwen's eyes widened. *District Number Two Schoolhouse? "D2SH" on the smuggler's map.* In her day, little more than a hollow depression with a few scattered foundation stones and the remnants of a drinking well remained. Her chest constricted. It was here her abductor, John Smith, drove her to her knees, his pistol pressed to her head.

Instinctively, she scanned the left side of the road for the overgrown pathway to Corky Williams' cabin. But of course it wasn't there.

She looked back at the schoolhouse as the wagon continued along what would become Quimby Pond Road, until the structure disappeared behind the trees. Soon, the cart was crossing a rushing creek. She closed her eyes and pictured the location from her present time. *This must be Quimby Brook. But it's so much larger here than it is in my day.* When she opened them again, the cart had turned off the road into the trees.

Byrne halted the horse and tied off the reins. He stretched, clambered down from the cart, and assisted his daughter to the ground. "Our nearest neighbor is Nicholas Kimball." He pointed toward the south, then turned around. "The Ellis property abuts ours to the north. And we have access to the lake through these trees."

Grandmother Irma surveyed the densely forested surroundings. "So remote. In Boston, I can almost converse with the neighbors from my bedroom window."

Her father drew a deep breath and spread his arms with a great smile. "But is this not so much better?" He reached into the cart for the fishing gear. "You may convey our foodstuffs. I shall handle the tackle."

Gwen climbed down from the back of the cart, gathered together her skirt, and hurried to keep up with her ancestors' pace toward Quimby Pond ... rather, Quimby Lake.

***

Two hours and seven fish later, Grandmother Irma and her father paused for lunch.

Byrne's impatience was palpable. "This is insufferable!"

Grandmother Irma regarded him with an even expression. "What is, Father? Do the black flies vex you as well?"

"You know very well what vexes me."

She innocently adjusted the brim of her bonnet. "Could it be that six of our fish found their way to my lure instead of yours?"

He glared at her from the corner of his eye as he tore a piece of bread from its crust. "Gloating does not become you, young lady."

"I owe everything I know of fishing to you, Father."

"Indeed." His face softened into a grudging smile. "And the student has surpassed the teacher."

At her distant grandfather's words, Gwen's mind flew back to a moment at her own father's pistol range.

"You only do this to annoy me, don't you Gwen?"

"What do you mean, Daddy?"

"Your bullseye is completely obliterated, while mine looks like a poorly endowed slice of Swiss cheese."

"You taught me everything I know about shooting."

A rare smile. "Yes, and the student has surpassed the teacher."

Quimby Lake lost focus through a sheen of tears, and Gwen rubbed her eyes. Her throat tightened, and a choked sob erupted.

Irma looked over at her, concerned.

Gwen forced a smile and shook her head. *Sorry, it's nothing.*

***

Early the next morning, Gwen settled onto the rear seat of the carriage and watched the Kellys prepare to depart Marble Falls for Boston. Byrne and Kate were bidding a fond and grateful farewell to Abner and Phoebe Toothaker. Grandmother Irma and Mary Jane were walking arm in arm toward the road, hugging close as though they would never see one another again.

When they reached the carriage, Mary Jane grasped Irma's hands. "Is there any chance ye can return for the weddin' next month?"

Grandmother Irma smiled. "If there is, I shall certainly be here."

"Then I shall cling ta that hope."

Grandmother Irma held Mary Jane at arm's length. "But if I cannot be here, you have a mother who loves you dearly and who may be even a better confidant than I, given the chance."

Mary Jane looked down. "Oh, I don't know. My condition's burdened our relationship."

"But you will never truly know her heart until you seek her out, will you?"

Mary Jane cast a sorrowful look toward her parents and shrugged.

"What can be lost in trying?"

She looked back, smiled, and kissed her friend on the cheek. "Nothin' at all."

"If I cannot return this summer, you must promise to write me after the birth."

"It'll be my first joyful chore."

They hugged again, and Grandmother Irma accepted the coachman's hand to climb aboard while her parents concluded their goodbyes.

236

Despite their lack of awareness of her presence, Gwen shrank against the rear seatback as her ancestors settled themselves onto the bench in front of her. Byrne looked over his shoulder, and at his daughter's nod signaled the driver.

They'd only traveled a short distance when Gwen's vision began to darken, and a woozy numbness slid over her brain. She shook her head and rubbed her eyes.

Irma leaned forward and peered into her face, touching her forehead with a cool hand. "Gwendolyn? Are you well?"

***

"Gwen? Are you okay?"

She jerked, and her eyelids cracked open. *Cassie?*

A cool damp cloth pressed against her forehead. She blinked, and the guest room ceiling slowly came into focus, followed by Cassie's concerned face.

"I think she's coming around."

The bedsprings creaked, as someone sat down at her side. She turned her head to a smiling face, and the cobwebs enshrouding her brain vanished.

"Brent!"

51

Brent bent down, and Gwen hugged his neck. He returned the hug, but when he began to pull back, she tightened her hold.

"I refuse to let you go," she whispered.

"I can't breathe," he muffled into the pillow.

"Oh. Sorry." She released him, and he pressed a tender kiss to her forehead.

"You had me scared to death, kiddo." He brushed a strand of hair from her forehead.

"What are you doing here?"

"I'm here because you're here."

Gwen tried to sit up, but the room began to spin and a dull ache snaked through her head, forcing her back onto her pillow.

Brent touched her shoulder. "Take it easy. You just woke up."

She pressed a hand to her forehead. "What happened?"

Cassie spoke up. "You've been down with a fever for two days. When I couldn't rouse you yesterday morning, I got Doc Andrews from next door. It looks like you picked up a nasty virus. She gave me care and feeding instructions to help you ride it out, and said she'd check back in a day or two."

Gwen smiled weakly. "Thanks, Cassie. I'll reimburse you for any medical fees."

"No you won't."

Gwen reached out and grasped her hand, then squinted up at Brent. "When did you get here?"

"Around noon. Cassie called me early this morning when you didn't seem to be getting any better." He looked at Cassie, thin lipped. "She should've called sooner."

"Yeah, isn't hindsight peachy?"

He chuckled. "Sure, but how can I let an opportunity to give you a hard time pass by?"

"With a little more effort."

He grinned and turned back to Gwen. "I explained the situation to Chief Lawson and told him he was going to have to get along without me for a while."

"What did he say to that?"

"He asked why I was still standing there and not already on my way to Boston."

"That sounds like the chief." She reached up and touched his cheek. "I'm so glad you're here."

"Me too."

She closed her eyes against a blossoming headache. "I had the strangest dream."

"Not surprised," Cassie said. "You were delirious most of the time." She lifted the damp cloth and laid the back of her fingers against Gwen's forehead. "Fever's broken. You were really burning up. I was half afraid you might spontaneously combust."

Gwen tried to laugh, but it spiked the headache, and she moaned and laid her head back onto the pillow.

"Sorry," Cassie said.

"Not your fault ... maybe a nap ... " Gwen slurred.

Brent planted another kiss on her forehead. "I'll be here when you wake up."

She groped for his hand and drifted off as his fingers closed around hers.

***

Brent cupped his hands around a mug of fresh coffee and looked across the kitchen table at Cassie. "You don't know how much I appreciate what you and Mark are doing for Gwen."

She tipped a shrug. "It's what you do for friends."

"And you guys are the best. When does Mark get here?"

She checked her watch. "Any minute. I told him I was ready for a break from kitchen duty, so he's stopping for pizza on the way."

"He knows I'm here?"

"Yup. I told him to come on in when he gets here."

Brent lowered his gaze to the mug. "So, how are you guys doing?"

She looked away. "Fine."

"That's like the all-time worst noncommittal answer in the world."

"It'll have to do."

He looked back up. "Didn't mean to be nosy."

"You aren't. It's just the best I can do. Two steps forward, one step back. Sucky progress, but still progress."

"In short, fine."

"Yeah."

"Anybody home?" came Mark's booming voice, followed closely by the slamming of the front door.

"In the kitchen," called Cassie.

She and Brent rose from the table as Mark barged through the doorway balancing three large pizza boxes.

"Three pizzas?" asked Cassie. "For just us?"

"Right." He grinned. "One for Wild Bill, one for me, and one for you."

"I'm supposed to eat a whole pizza?"

Brent and Mark looked at each other, then back at Cassie. "No," they deadpanned, then broke into laughter while Cassie rolled her eyes.

Mark set down the food and gave Brent a bear hug, slapping him on the back. "Too long, bro."

"Sure has been—ouch! Man, this is the second hug today that has nearly killed me."

Mark stepped back and gave Cassie a quizzical look. "Really? You've never been that much of a hugger."

"Not me, Gwen. The fever broke an hour ago. She's asleep now, but I think we're past the worst of it."

"Good." He pulled a bottle of red wine from his coat pocket, set it on the table, and distributed the pizza boxes. "C'mon, dinner won't eat itself."

Forty-five minutes later, the empty boxes were crammed into the pantry wastebasket, and the three friends retired to the living room. Mark nursed a stack of kindling into a roaring blaze, laid on a couple of logs of split oak, and then dropped into an easy chair with the remnants of his wine.

Brent smiled and took a sip from his glass. "Nothing like a fire." He leaned back. "So, now that we've caught up with each other, what's the latest with Gwen's case?"

Mark fingered the stem of his glass. "Not much to tell. Whoever broke in has done a good job of covering his tracks. We're keeping an eye on the residence."

"This makes no sense. What do you think our guy is up to?"

"Are you so sure the intruder is a man?" Cassie interjected.

Mark and Brent looked at each other.

"You have a good point," Mark said. "Maybe I've biased my thoughts toward a male perp."

Brent nodded. "Me too. In fact, the only person of interest we have is Teresa Hardy."

"So how would we approach the investigation differently if our bad guy is actually a bad gal?" asked Mark.

Cassie winced. "You know I hate that word."

"Gal?" Mark grinned. "Oh yeah, I forgot."

"Sure you did."

"It could be Simon," Brent said. "If he's in Mr. Kelly's will, he could be involved in all of this. What I want to know is why he's so blasted difficult to track down? If he stands to gain part of an estate, why not come forward?"

"Fake identity?" suggested Cassie. "Or maybe Teresa tricked Gwen's dad into thinking she had a son by him. If they were involved at one time and broke it off, he may have trusted her word that there was a child."

"What would she gain by doing that? Why not just have him include her in the will?"

Cassie shrugged. "Maybe she figured she could leverage his sentiments for a blood heir better than for a love interest that didn't last."

"Teresa's done a pretty good job of disappearing too," Mark said.

"Yeah, but she's left a trail on a couple of driver's license records. Burlington and Farmington."

Brent nodded. "You might be onto something." He tipped back the last of his wine. "I have someone checking out the Farmington connection, such as he is. I have no idea if it'll pan out, but at least something's in motion."

Cassie frowned. " 'Such as he is'?"

Brent smiled. "Yeah, someday I'll have to tell you about Howard Dobbs."

"Let's focus on Teresa Hardy, then, rather than Simon," Mark said. "If we find her, we should find him."

"Agreed."

A scream from down the hallway jolted them, and Brent leapt to his feet. He ran to the guest room and flipped on the light to find Gwen sitting up, staring at the window, covers pulled to her chin. Mark and Cassie pressed into the room behind him.

Brent hurried to the bedside. "What's wrong?"

"S-someone was looking in the window," she gasped, shuddering.

Mark crossed to the window and peered through. He looked back, shook his head, and headed for the door. "I'll take a look outside."

"You're sure you saw someone?" asked Cassie.

Gwen closed her eyes and nodded.

"I'll get you some water, or I can put on some tea or coffee."

"Tea sounds good, thanks."

When Cassie left, Brent urged Gwen back onto her pillow, but she resisted. "No, I want to get out of this bed."

"You sure you're up to it?"

"I have to be. Can you get my robe, please?"

Brent retrieved the garment from a chair near the bed and helped Gwen sit on the edge of the bed. She shrugged into the robe while he knelt and eased a pair of slippers onto her feet. She managed a weak smile. "Hmm, I kind of I like this. Maybe I should get sick more often."

He smiled as he rose to his feet. "Yeah, you're definitely feeling better. There's a fire on in the living room. How about we move you to the couch?"

"That sounds great."

He helped Gwen to the living room sofa and was tucking an afghan around her when Mark returned. "Too dark to see much, even with a flashlight. The guest room window is out of the wind, and the snow has drifted too far away from the house to see any footprints. I want to wait for daylight to look closer so I don't trample over anything." He removed his overcoat and looked at Gwen. "You're sure you saw someone?"

She looked up sharply. "People keep asking me that. I'm not delirious anymore. Somebody was outside that window."

"Mark's on our side," Brent said quietly.

Her shoulders drooped. "I know. I'm sorry, Mark. I didn't mean to snap at you."

"Well, you have a great excuse," he said with a smile. "Heck, if I were as sick as you've been, I'd be the world's worst grouch."

"You can bet on that," Cassie said, coming into the living room with a steaming cup of tea.

Gwen accepted the cup. "Thank you, Cassie. You've been so great."

"You sure have," Brent said. "I don't know how to repay you guys."

His phone beeped, and he pulled it from his pocket, frowning at the Caller ID. "Looks vaguely familiar." He punched the Accept button. "This is Brent."

" 'Brent'? Gee, I was looking for an Officer Newcomb."

"Hello, Howard."

"Hello ... Brent."

"Stick with 'Officer Newcomb', and we'll be good."

"What if I told you I found who you were looking for?"

"Then it's 'Brent'."

"Got a pencil?"

"Wait a second." He looked at Cassie. "I need something to write with."

She handed him a pen and notepad from the end-table drawer.

"Go ahead." Brent scribbled on the pad. At one point, he abruptly stopped. "You're kidding." A moment later, he shook his head and continued writing. "Got it. Thanks, Howard. I owe you."

"You sure do."

"Don't take that too literally."

"Define 'too literally'."

"It means 'no promises'."

"Well, *that* favor sure went bust in a hurry."

"Let's just say you have my undying gratitude."

"Great. That and a buck seventy-five will get me a cup of coffee at a really cheap joint."

Brent laughed. "You know something, Howard? You're still a pain in the neck."

"It's a talent I've worked hard to perfect. See you later ... Brent."

"You too." He disconnected the call.

"Howard?" Gwen asked. "Howard Dobbs?"

He nodded, as he jotted on the pad. "One and the same."

"Why in the world would Howard Dobbs be calling your cell?"

He tore off the sheet of notepaper. "Because he found Teresa Hardy."

52

Gwen creased her brow. "How did Howard even know about this?"

Brent pocketed his phone and sat down beside her. "A weak moment on my part."

"Sounds like a lucky weak moment," Mark interjected. "Spill it."

"Who is Howard Dobbs?" asked Cassie.

Brent briefly described the Nuisance of Marble Falls Law Enforcement. When he mentioned Howard saying he liked Brent, he almost choked. "That one still mystifies me."

Gwen huffed. "What mystifies me more is how someone like Howard was able to track down in less than two days someone we've been floundering to find for nearly two weeks."

Brent shrugged with a smile. "It appears we owe this all to a poker game."

"A poker game would certainly tie Howard in, but I still don't get it." She looked at Mark and Cassie. "Every Thursday evening Howard hosts a poker game that has grown into something of an institution over the years. People come from all over for the silly thing—what are you grinning at, Mark?"

Mark widened innocent eyes. "Nothing. Go on."

Cassie narrowed her gaze at him. "Huh uh, I know that look. Spill it."

His cheeks reddened. "I've been to one of Howard's poker nights."

"What?" asked Gwen and Cassie in unison, while Brent burst into laughter.

"A couple of years ago, Brent invited me up to do some fishing. He got a late call for a domestic disturbance, so I ducked out to catch a hand or two."

Cassie stared at him.

He straightened. "Don't look at me like that. I broke even."

She rolled her eyes.

Mark cleared his throat. "Anyway, you were saying?"

Brent consulted his notes. "It's a little sketchy, but here's what we have so far. One of Howard's regulars works in the Farmington municipal offices. The last address we had on Teresa was in Farmington, so Howard put a bug in the clerk's ear."

Gwen sniffed. "I can't imagine what Howard promised in return for the 'favor'."

"I didn't ask," Brent said, smiling down at his notepad. "Anyway, the clerk contacted him with some interesting information. A month ago, a woman matching the description on Teresa Hardy's BMV records made an inquiry at the municipal office. The clerk remembered her because she seemed nervous, and when he asked her for her contact information, she left."

"What was she asking about?"

"She was interested in deed information on a real estate holding. Problem is, when he asked for the identification, she balked and left without completing her inquiry."

"Where did she go?"

"He didn't' know. But at least we know now that Teresa Hardy is interested in real estate in Farmington."

Gwen sighed. "What good does that do?"

"It gives us one more piece of information than we had before."

***

Gwen relaxed under the bedcovers with a deep yawn. "I'm so sorry. I must be horrible company."

"You have a good excuse," Brent said as he tucked the quilted bedspread under her chin.

She aimed a mock pout at him. "Oh, then you're saying I *am* horrible company."

He thinned his lips. "In law enforcement, we call that entrapment."

She laughed. "Well, I can't think of anyone I'd rather be entrapped with than you."

He smiled. "In law enforcement … well, we don't have a term for that in law enforcement, but I'll come up with one." He kissed her on the forehead.

"Stay for a few minutes? I'm tired, but not very sleepy."

"Sure." He reached toward the nightstand and picked up the journal. "Is this your Grandmother Irma's diary?"

Gwen nodded. "The first of three volumes. I'm close to the end."

"I see that," he said, opening to the bookmarked page. "What if I were to read to you? Would that help?"

"I don't know if it would help with sleepiness, but it would be really nice."

"Let's see ... " He scanned the page, then began reading about the carriage trip from Farmington to Marble Falls.

"Wait," Gwen interrupted. "I already read that part."

"Are you sure? It's past the bookmark."

"Maybe I slipped it into the wrong spot."

He flipped to the next page and continued reading about Irma's fishing excursion with her father.

"Oh, dear," Gwen said. "Still not far enough. I know she caught six fish while her father caught one."

Brent frowned and moved to the next page. "This says she caught more fish than her father did, but it doesn't mention any numbers."

"It has to. The memory is as clear as day. Keep reading."

He held up the journal open to the page he'd just read. "I can't. We're at the back cover."

Gwen creased her brow. "That's impossible. I also remember her saying goodbye to Mary Jane and asking her to write after she had her baby."

"Hold on a second." Brent grabbed the second volume from the dresser and scanned the first page. "There's a continuation here where she writes about a farewell, but nothing about a baby. There is mention of encouraging Mary Jane to draw closer to her mother."

Gwen pushed herself to a sitting position and stared at the book. "I remember that conversation too, but ... "

"But what?"

"How can I know what she wrote in the second journal when I haven't finished the first one yet?"

53

The next morning, Gwen and Cassie were loading the dishwasher when the doorbell rang. Cassie looked through the kitchen window toward the front porch. "Oh, it's Doc Andrews." She dried her hand and went to the foyer while Gwen wiped down the counter.

A moment later, Cassie called from the front room. "Gwen, got a minute?"

"Sure." Gwen hurried to the front room where a slender red-haired woman in a teal blouse with beige slacks was handing her coat to Cassie. The woman looked at Gwen and beamed a warm smile. "Well, you look considerably better than the last time I saw you."

Gwen approached the doctor and extended her hand. "I am, thanks to you."

Dr. Andrews grasped her hand firmly. "You did all the work. I only made grand pronouncements over what I thought was wrong with you and went on my merry way."

Gwen laughed. "Somehow I think you did more than that."

"Not much."

At Cassie's suggestion, the two women made themselves comfortable in the living room while she went to the kitchen for coffee.

Dr. Andrews folded her hands on her lap. "I stopped in to see how you were getting along. You took a major hit from that virus."

Gwen reflected on the dream she'd had during her delirium and nodded. "It was ... well, something of a journey."

The doctor lifted an amused brow. "That's an interesting way to put it." Gwen only smiled, so the doctor continued. "You're feeling well enough now, then."

"Absolutely." Gwen paused and looked down.

"But ... ?" When she looked back up, the doctor had cocked her head.

"I hate to take advantage of your professional time, but could I ask you a medical question that has been bothering me? It's not about my illness."

"I'm not on the clock for another half hour, so ask away."

"It has to do with my father. He recently passed."

"Oh. I'm sorry."

"Thank you. He fell and hit his head. The medical examiner said the blow by itself wasn't terribly serious, but there was an unusual amount of cranial hemorrhaging that killed him. We don't know why he bled so much."

The doctor sat back. "I see. Was your father on any medications?"

"I found one prescription for cholesterol. He'd been on it for years."

"Anything nonprescription?"

"There was a bottle of low-dose aspirin in his medicine cabinet. I remember him taking one a day as a precaution against stroke. Other than that, just vitamins and some herbal supplements in the pantry."

"What supplements?"

"Some kind of ginseng. I think it began with a 'P'."

"Panax Ginseng."

"That's it. I hadn't heard of it before."

"It's an Asian root extract, a wonder tonic to some people. Although it does have some positive qualities, it's been hyped so much, folks buy it to cure everything from baldness to excessive navel lint." She rolled her eyes.

Gwen giggled. "Seriously?"

Dr. Andrews laughed. "Maybe I'm exaggerating a little bit, but not much. Herbal supplements have their place, and I have nothing against them, but they're not benign. They do have side effects, and when combined with other medications, the effects can be serious. Do you know why your father was taking ginseng or how much of it he was ingesting?"

"No, although he did have a lot of it. I found a carton in the pantry with several more bottles."

"How was his demeanor? Did he seem remote or easily distracted?"

The doctor's unexpected question misted Gwen's eyes, and her throat tightened.

Dr. Andrews touched her hand. "Forgive me. I'm sure the emotions surrounding your dad's memory are still very tender."

Gwen shook her head and managed a weak smile. "Please don't apologize. You described him exactly, and it kind of set me back. My mother died when I was twelve, and Daddy never really recovered. He seemed to lose focus on life—if that doesn't sound too melodramatic."

"It doesn't sound melodramatic at all. I asked because ginseng is often used as a treatment for depression." She tilted her head and held Gwen's gaze. "And dementia."

Gwen's jaw slackened. "The depression fits, but dementia never crossed my mind. Looking back, though, it makes sense."

Dr. Andrews offered a sympathetic nod. "If he was self-treating against depression, and if he suspected he was slipping into dementia, he could have relied too heavily on the ginseng." She paused. "Tests have shown that large amounts can inhibit blood clotting. If he was already taking aspirin as a blood thinner against stroke, and he ingested heavy doses of ginseng over an extended period of time, the combination could have contributed to the abnormal bleeding. And as far as the fall goes ... "

"What?"

"Another side effect of ginseng is dizziness."

Gwen covered her face and stared at the floor. "Oh, dear Lord, don't tell me ... "

The doctor softened her voice. "I'm not making a diagnosis here, Gwen. It's just a possibility."

Gwen cleared her throat. "But wouldn't that much ginseng show up in an autopsy?"

"I'm not sure. If it were detectable, though, it would likely depend upon the actual dosage and the time elapsed since he last took it."

Gwen wiped moistness from her cheek and regained the doctor's eye. "It ... it doesn't seem like a natural supplement like that would be so dangerous."

"Taken wisely, with a physician's knowledge, and cognizant of potential side effects mixed with other medications, it isn't dangerous. It's actually a pretty good supplement." She shook her head. "It's the 'natural' part that trips people up, thanks largely to popular advertising. Just because something is natural doesn't mean it's harmless—or even necessarily good for you. I mean, arsenic is natural, but I don't recommend stirring it into your coffee."

"Did someone say coffee?" Cassie was standing in the doorway, a tray balanced on her forearm.

Gwen shook back her hair and drew a breath, then turned the brightest smile she could muster toward Cassie. "We did. That smells good."

Dr. Andrews squeezed Gwen's hand and echoed the sentiment.

The remainder of the visit passed with Gwen only half engaged.

***

Brent and Gwen sat on the living room couch, knees brushing. He held her hands and gazed into her hazel eyes, heart at the bursting point. "I have bad news."

"Oh?"

"Chief Lawson texted with a none-too-subtle hint that I'm needed back in Marble Falls."

Gwen frowned. "Oh."

"I head back this afternoon."

"Oh."

"You already said that."

"Oh."

"Stop it!"

She giggled. "I'm stalling. Anything to keep you here, even if it means annoying you.

"Oh."

She laughed. "Now *you* stop it."

"One good annoyance deserves another."

"The stuff relationships are made of."

She touched a finger to his lips. Smiled. Replaced her finger with her lips. Lingered. Repeated.

Cassie's flat voice wedged its way between them from the hall doorway. "Should I have a fire extinguisher standing by?"

"Doubt it'll help," Brent mumbled against Gwen's cheek.

Gwen whispered a laugh and pushed him back. "Maybe she has a point."

"So do I." He leaned back in.

"Brent!" She tucked back her hair, cheeks flushed, smiling at the floor.

"Oh, alright." He threw a mock glare at Cassie. "Your timing sucks."

"I'm always here for you."

"Thanks."

Cassie limped around the sofa and lowered herself onto the easy chair. "I heard you say you're driving back to Marble Falls this afternoon. Did Gwen tell you about her conversation with Dr. Andrews?"

"No." He looked at Gwen and cocked his head. "You're okay, aren't you?"

"Yes. It was about Daddy." She related the discussion earlier that day, adding that, although the doctor's comment regarding the aspirin and ginseng was not a formal diagnosis, it made enough sense to feel closure on her father's death. It was reasonable to assume there was no foul play, that he had died innocently by his own hand. The truth hurt, but it also healed.

When she finished, Brent took her hands into his. "I'm glad at least that part of the story has been resolved. Now to clear up the rest of it. I promise to turn the heat up under my research tomorrow."

"Thanks."

"Selfish reasons. I want you back home as soon as possible."

"Even better."

Cassie looked at her watch and rose. "I'll fix an early dinner early so you can get on the road. Mark should be here anytime now." She tipped a half-smile. "And I'll leave the fire extinguisher by the door."

-54-

After dinner and mutual promises they'd be reunited as soon as possible, Gwen buried herself in Brent's embrace amid the frigid wind hurling icy snow across Cassie's driveway. She kissed him as though she'd never see him again, then glumly watched him climb into his truck and drive away. Back in the living room, Cassie gave Gwen her space, quietly depositing a half-glass of Merlot on the end table so as not to disturb her friend's contemplation as she stare into the crackling fireplace. Only once did Cassie attempt to offer solace.

"You really love him, don't you?"

No reply.

"That says it all."

And she quietly slipped from the room.

To ward off despondency, Gwen went about the remainder of the day with Cassie's laptop researching more firms that managed estate sales and adding to her list of promising real estate agents. At eight o'clock, still dragging from her recent illness, she excused herself and went to bed early. But despite her physical weariness, her mind refused to release her into sleep.

Huffing a frustrated sigh, she shifted onto her side and fluffed the pillow beneath her head for the umpteenth time. The alarm clock clicked from 10:34 p.m. over to the next minute. Her gaze settled on the old journal, the clock's yellow display casting a jaundiced pallor on it. A nagging feeling stopped Gwen from turning on the light and opening the diary. How could she have read into the second volume without realizing it? Yet the accounts of the events in Marble Falls that Brent had read to her were so familiar, so ... personal.

She fisted the pillow again. *That's silly. Cassie said I was delirious. Who knows, I could've done anything, even read more of the journal ... somehow. And I*

253

could have imagined the details about the number of fish Grandmother Irma caught and the fact of Mary Jane's pregnancy ... right?

Groaning, she flipped onto her back, flopping her arms out to the side. Her right hand slapped the top of the second journal. She puffed a curl off her face and brushed reluctant fingertips across the book cover. Heaved another sigh.

Elbowing herself up to a sitting position, she tugged the switch chain on the lamp and drew the diary onto the quilt over her stomach. The first page confirmed her prior knowledge of the carriage departing Marble Falls for Farmington. She turned to the second page, picking up the narrative where her memory left off.

So much has happened the past few days, I can scarcely take it all in. Eluding the authorities at the train station, losing Isabelle and Gabriel to their freedom, Mary Jane's impending wedding. Yet, perhaps the sweetest memory of all will be the fishing trip with Father. Despite the annoying bugs and slimy fish, the day could not have been more perfect, for I've never felt closer to him. I've always known he loves me, but yesterday there was something different in the way he treated me. Or was it simply joy at being immersed in his beloved outdoors? I don't know for certain, but I choose to believe he looked at me through different eyes, and, truth be told, I beheld him in a similar fashion.

***

Irma jolted at her mother's touch. "We're arriving in Boston, dear. Best put away your things."

"Already?"

"Already, indeed. When you haven't been writing, you've been dozing. It's not surprising the trip from Nashua passed so quickly for you."

Irma peered through the window at the city's murky outskirts. The vista of gray clouds hugging the tops of high buildings shimmered through streaks of rainwater on the smudgy glass. The day of her return was as dreary as the day of her departure had been. "Strange," she said, capping the inkwell, "in some ways, it seems we've just left Boston. Yet in other ways, it seems a lifetime ago."

"The older you become, the more often that conundrum addles you," her father said as he stood and slipped on his coat.

She offered him a coy smile. "You're not old, Father. You're mightily experienced."

He chuckled, retrieving his umbrella from the overhead baggage rack. "And with mighty experience comes great age. There's no escaping it."

The smile widened as she stowed her writing material into her bag. "Could you not just once grant me the last word?"

"You had the final word yesterday with your fishing rod. That should suffice for quite some time."

She giggled. "Beginner's luck. Although I must confess the fish dinner we shared with the Toothakers last evening seemed tastier than others I can recall."

"Hmm," he muttered with a grudging smile as the train slowed, then came to a hissing rest at the platform.

Irma half expected to see the inspector and a contingent of policemen awaiting them when they transited the Haymarket Square station, but the journey home passed uneventfully. She soon found herself stretched across her cozy quilted bedspread, tempted to remain there until morning. The summons to a late dinner burst that wish, though, and she trudged downstairs to the dining room, bags left unpacked.

"My, this is delicious," she exclaimed, scooping up a second spoonful of creamy clam chowder. "Mrs. Callaghan has outdone herself."

"Mrs. Callaghan is no longer in our employ," responded her father. "I remind you of her subterfuge at our departure."

Irma looked up. "If not her, then who?"

Gibbons appeared in the kitchen doorway, an apron tied to his waist. "Will there be anything more you require, Mr. or Mrs. Kelly?"

Byrne gave the manservant a broad smile. "This is more than adequate. Superb chowder, my man."

"Thank you, sir. However, I'm afraid you've now experienced the extent of my culinary skills. The dinner rolls that were to accompany the chowder met their demise in an overheated oven. My sincerest apologies."

Irma beamed at him with a teasing smile. "Have you become our new cook, Gibbons?"

His eyes widened. "Dear heavens, no, Miss Kelly. I merely filled the role until tomorrow morning when Mrs. Kelly will interview candidates for the position."

Her father lifted a napkin to his mouth. "While we were in Farmington, I wired Gibbons the empowerment to dismiss Mrs. Callaghan and seek fresh help for the kitchen. Once again, he has not disappointed."

"Disappointed?" Irma exclaimed after savoring another spoonful of chowder. "I would suggest he has excelled."

Irma's mother smiled at the servant. "Thank you for arranging the interviews, Gibbons. I'll make every effort to ensure the duration of your kitchen duty is as brief as possible."

"And for that, I believe we shall all be most grateful, madam."

He bowed and retreated to the kitchen amid the Kellys' laughter.

The remainder of their dinner passed with each family member stifling yawns. The physically and emotionally draining journey had exacted its final toll, and Irma was first to surrender to it. She dabbed her lips and dropped her napkin onto the table. "I simply must retire, lest I collapse in my chair. Goodnight, Father, Mother."

They bade her a good rest, and Irma mounted the stairs to her room. She surveyed the unpacked bags once again, then shook her head and began to undress. Twenty minutes later she was fast asleep beneath the covers.

***

Irma awoke abruptly at a bright light flooding her face. She sat up and shielded her eyes against the morning sunlight streaming through the window. The dresser clock scolded her with an announcement that the morning was already half spent. She sat up and rubbed her eyes. *Why did no one awaken me for breakfast?*

As though in response, a gentle knock sounded on her bedroom door.

She stretched. "Come in, Mother."

The door opened, and a deep voice filled the room. "This is the second time you've confused my knock with your mother's."

Irma smiled through a yawn. "My apologies, Father. I'm not accustomed to such a gentle summons from you."

"And with which kind of summons do you most often associate me?" He cocked his head.

256

Irma sat up and evened her gaze at him. "One of strength."

He broke eye contact, then regained it with a dip of the head. "And I of you, daughter."

She blinked, cheeks warming at the unexpected sentiment.

He cleared his throat. "Your mother requests your presence in the dining room. She has interviewed candidates for Mrs. Callaghan's replacement, but she would appreciate your assessment of those who have survived the initial evaluation."

Irma smoothed the bed covers over her lap, still reveling in her father's unexpected affirmation. "Of course. I'll be there shortly. I'm honored she values my opinion in these matters."

"As well you should be." Her father offered a brief smile and began to exit the room.

"Father?"

He turned back.

"I've never known you to play the messenger."

"And for good reason."

"But now?"

He tipped his head. "Your absence at the breakfast table was sorely noted."

"To such a degree as to warrant your personal attention?"

"I've come, haven't I?"

"But—"

He lifted a finger. "Do not dawdle. Your mother awaits." He stepped back through the doorway.

Irma hugged her knees to her chest and stared at his figure retreating down the hallway. *Will I ever truly understand you, Father?*

55

Irma folded her hands on her lap and looked at her mother. "My vote belongs to Miss Doyle."

"Her credentials are impressive, but she is rather young."

"I believe that to be a strong point."

"Of course you do," her mother said with a smile.

"And consider the fact that she alone thought to bring samples of her baking." Irma eyed the dessert dish where the few remaining flakes of a scrumptious raspberry scone dared her to ignore them. She forfeited the contest, pressed her fingertip onto a morsel and brushed it onto the tip of the tongue.

Her mother frowned. "Where are the table manners I've labored so hard to instill in you?"

Irma bit her lip and returned an impish smile. "There's one crumb remaining."

"I see it," her mother replied with a hint of annoyance.

"Well then ... ?"

Kate's countenance wavered, broke, and with as close to a giggle as Irma had ever heard from her, dabbed the tidbit onto her fingertip and slipped it between her lips. "Heavenly," she pronounced, eyes closed.

Irma laughed.

Her mother opened her eyes. "Very well, Miss Doyle it is."

Irma clapped her hands. "Wonderful."

"But never let me see you breach table manners in such a way again," her mother admonished, smile barely submerged.

"You have my pledge."

They exchanged laughs, then jumped at a deep voice coming from the doorway. "Such mirth this early in the day?"

Kate smiled at him. "We've settled on a new cook, Byrne. You will be pleased."

"I'm sure I shall," he murmured, looking down while buttoning his coat. "Meantime, there is a matter of some urgency that requires my presence at the office."

Kate's smile faded. "On a Saturday? Surely it can wait until Monday."

"I fear not." He pulled his top hat from under his arm and fingered the brim, looking from one woman to the other. "If I'm detained ... er, unduly delayed, do not hold dinner for me."

"It's not even noontime. Do you anticipate such an extended delay?"

His fingers stilled on the hat, and he stared at the floor.

"Byrne?"

After a pause, he looked up, as though seeing her for the first time. "I'm sorry, what did you say?"

"What aren't you telling us?" she asked, voice quieting.

"Nothing, my dear. It's nothing."

Irma rose from her chair. "We know you far too well to believe it's nothing, Father. You appear distracted, and you're never distracted."

He drew himself up with a frown. "So, I'm to face an inquiry in my own home as well?"

"Is that where you're going?" Kate asked. "To face some sort of inquiry?"

"You're putting words in my mouth."

"Only because you refuse to do so yourself."

His chest deflated. "Very well." He laid his hat on the table. "Here's the short of it. You recall my decision to stockpile cotton against the advisement of my board of directors?"

"Is that what this is about?" Irma asked.

Her father nodded. "The board is threatening action to the point of accusing me of speculation before the law courts."

"But that was months ago, and your decision saved them from ruin."

"Perhaps. But to torture The Bard's famous adage, Hell knows no fury like the bruised ego of a board of directors."

Kate's face darkened. "I cannot believe Henry Wilkinson would turn on you like this. Why, I've a mind to—"

Byrne lifted a hand. "Henry is my sole advocate. Despite his initial misgivings, he saw wisdom in my foresight, if not in my disregard for protocol. It's because of his argument on my behalf that I've not already been formally censured." He sighed. "Alas, time has withered his influence, and it is now up to me to mount my own defense before the self-righteous mob of prigs."

"Byrne, your language!" Kate turned toward her daughter, who was struggling to maintain a straight face. "This is not funny."

Irma cleared her throat. "Of course not, Mother."

Byrne retrieved his hat. "I'm running late, and if I hope to regain the favor of any of my board members, I best not keep them waiting."

Kate rose and rounded the table to her husband's side. "Irma and I will pray they appreciate their continued prosperity more than they lament their bruised egos."

He kissed her cheek. "Please do."

With that, he turned and strode down the hallway toward the front door.

***

Irma paced her bedroom, pausing for what was certainly the hundredth time to consult the dresser clock. 6:05 p.m. Normally, dinner would be underway, but her mother had ordered the repast delayed until Mr. Kelly's return, whenever that might be. Miss Doyle had nodded dutifully, wringing her hands, eyes downcast, until her mistress softened her tone.

"Forgive me, Miss Doyle. It's been a trying day. Please preserve dinner as best you can. I'll not hold you accountable for our exigencies."

Miss Doyle lifted rounded eyes at the unexpected kindness from her new employer. She glanced at Irma, who was standing in the doorway nodding affirmation, then curtsied and slipped back out of the room.

That exchange had taken place shortly before 5:00 p.m., after which Irma took to her bedroom. Instinct urged her to remain downstairs and commiserate with her mother, but sore experience with her mother's preference for solitude during times of burdened thought overrode it. And so Irma paced alone, equally burdened, but aching for the solace of companionship.

After what seemed like hours, a creak at the front door caught her ear. She rushed to the top of the staircase as her mother was dismissing Gibbons from receiving her husband's hat and coat, taking them herself. Wordlessly, they walked arm in arm slowly into the study. Irma hurried down the stairs and burst into the room, drawing up short at the sight of her parents embracing. "Father? What has happened?"

He turned tired eyes toward her and gestured for her to sit. She eased onto the edge of a chair, while her parents moved to the sofa, hands still intertwined.

He drew a deep breath. "All is not lost ... at least yet."

Irma relaxed the tension in her shoulders, but retained her posture. "Yet?"

"The board is split on its decision to move forward with the censure. Henry was persuasive in my defense, and I suspect the sustained prosperity they enjoy at my 'speculation' mitigates their indignation."

"As well it should," Irma muttered.

Her father tipped a thin smile. "But for how long? That is the question. Once prosperity is secured, its source is often conveniently forgotten. Then ego will once again hold sway."

Irma sputtered her contempt, earning a chastising look from her mother. "I know, I know." She raised her hands. "Decorum. Still, I refuse to apologize. How much decorum does such spinelessness from the board of directors deserve?"

"You are responsible for your own demeanor, dear. Don't let others drag you down to a level you clearly detest in them."

Irma dipped her head, but not convincingly.

Her father reached for a glass of sherry Miss Doyle had thoughtfully prepositioned on the parlor table. "For once, I share Irma's sentiment."

Kate frowned at him. "Your complicity in her delinquent attitude is unhelpful."

He smiled and squeezed her hand. "Our current circumstances would indicate she inherited her delinquency from me, so how severe can I be?"

"When will you learn of the board's final decision?" Irma asked.

"Within the week, I suspect."

"What can they do? What power do they hold? It is your company, after all."

"It is, but their interests in the firm extend beyond a meeting or two each month. They have invested significant portions of their wealth in its success. So, to be fair, they have a right to influence its operation."

"I suppose."

Byrne suddenly lifted his head toward the dining room and sniffed. "Is that pork pie I smell?"

As if on cue, Miss Doyle appeared in the doorway, blanching at her first sight of the master of the house. She dipped a quick curtsey and averted her gaze. "Dinner is ... " she cleared her throat.

Irma smiled. " ... served?"

The cook looked up, cheeks tinging pink. "Indeed, miss."

Byrne rose and strode toward the new cook, who stepped back, eyes wide. He halted three paces away and regarded her, hands on hips. She cringed under his scrutiny, and Irma took a step forward, watchful should the young cook faint.

"Miss Doyle, is it?" Byrne asked.

She nodded, eyes still downcast.

"My wife speaks very favorably of your culinary skill."

Miss Doyle tentatively lifted her head. "Thank you, sir."

"And if the aroma wafting through the doorway is any evidence, then her usual impeccable judgment has again served us well. I trust you will be as comfortable in our employ as we are pleased to have you."

She straightened and met his eye, venturing a cautious smile. "I'm sure I shall, sir."

"If you find yourself in need of anything, inform Gibbons. If he is unavailable," he threw a look over his shoulder at Irma, "I fully suspect my daughter will be pleased to accommodate you. As drawn as she is to your prowess in the kitchen, I suspect she is equally drawn to your youth as a welcomed respite in a household of oldsters."

Kate frowned at him. "I'll thank you to speak for yourself, Byrne."

Irma giggled, and even Miss Doyle barely suppressed a laugh, clamping both hands to her mouth. Irma sent her a warm smile. "Yes, I expect we shall get along nicely."

Miss Doyle curtsied again and backed through the doorway.

Irma joined her mother, who took her husband's arm as they retired to the dining room. She looked up at him. "Regarding the board's action, 'expect the best, but prepare for the worst'?"

He nodded, patting her arm.

Irma lowered her head, eyes absently tracing the intricate pattern of the oriental rug as it passed beneath her steps, a strange uneasiness gripping her mind. *Surely not the worst ...*

56

Brent's ringtone was the first thing to jolt Gwen from her thoughts the next day, his words pulling her to the edge of her seat.

"There's been a break in the case." His excitement reverberated through the phone.

"What break? What do you mean?"

"Teresa Hardy. I think we found her."

"Where? When?"

"She showed up in the Farmington town office again. This time, Howard's poker-playing clerk recognized her and positioned himself to assist her."

"And?"

"And he bluffed her into revealing some details about herself."

"A true poker player."

He chuckled. "Yeah, according to Howard, this guy wins more than he loses. Anyway, it seems Teresa was interested in deed information for Franklin County. He offered to help her search, but told her he'd need identification before he could continue. She balked at first, but then produced her driver's license. He pretended to be entering the information into a form on the computer, but was actually typing the details into a blank file. When he finished, he told her there must be some mistake, because he knew that address to belong to the Historical Society. He offered to submit a correction to the BMV for her, but she became flustered, muttered something about being late for an appointment and left. She even forgot to take her license.

"So, how is this a break in the case? We already have her driver's license information with the fake address."

"The clerk tailed her to where she'd parked her car. Before she drove off, he snapped a picture of the car and license plate with his phone."

"Did you look up the plate numbers?"

"Yes, and you'll never guess where they trace to."

"Where?"

"Right there in Medford. I've already emailed the information to Mark. Oh, and one more thing. The clerk was smart enough to handle the license by its edges, so I have the Farmington PD pulling fingerprints from it. We'll see if she's anywhere in the system."

Gwen gripped the phone with both hands. "Oh, I so hope this turns out to be a solid lead. It's been driving me crazy to know I have a brother somewhere, but have no idea how to find him."

"Hang in there. We're getting closer."

At that moment, Cassie came into the room and signaled to Gwen, her phone in hand. Gwen nodded. "Can you hold a sec? Cassie needs something."

"I've got to go now anyway. I'll be in touch."

She smiled. "You'd better."

They signed off and Cassie handed Gwen her phone. "It's Mark."

"Oh. Thanks." She accepted the device. "Hi, Mark."

"Hi, Gwen. Have you heard from Brent?"

"Yes, just now."

"Good. Can you meet me at your house? I need to check out a final couple of things in your dad's paperwork, and I'd like you there. Besides, the locksmith should be finishing up, and he'll have your new keys."

"Um, sure. Right now?"

"Soon as you can."

She disconnected and handed the phone back to Cassie. "Mark wants to meet at the house." She paused. "Do you want to ride along?"

"Not necessary."

"Are you sure?"

Cassie tipped a smile. "It's pretty clear you're a one-guy girl. Either that, or you're an incredible actress."

Gwen laughed. "I stink on stage. My high school drama teacher wouldn't even let me stand near the prop table without being supervised. I think it would be more fun if you were to come along, though."

Cassie shrugged. "Why not?"

***

When the women arrived at the house, Mark's car was parked at the curb next to a panel truck with *Medford Locksmith* emblazoned on the side. Mark was conversing with the technician through the driver's window. They shook hands, and the locksmith backed out of the driveway just as Gwen's Corolla pulled in.

Mark squinted in through the windshield and flashed a surprised smile at Cassie. He opened her door. "Didn't expect to see you," he said, helping her out of the car. He kissed her on the forehead.

"I felt like getting out a little."

"Glad you did." He turned toward Gwen, who was closing her door. "Hope I didn't interrupt anything."

"You didn't." She looked at the panel truck. "I thought the locks would've been changed by now."

He handed her the new house keys. "They would've been, but there was a communications glitch, and the station didn't put in the request until this morning."

"The police station put in the request?"

"We get a good rate due to all the business we send their way, so I put the request in through channels and had them forward the bill to me. I thought you might appreciate the discount."

"Very much so. Thanks."

He leveled a grim expression at the front porch. "I don't like that the house sat all this time with the old locks. That's the other reason I asked you to come over, to make sure nothing else is out of order."

"Okay."

Mark steadied Cassie with her crutch as Gwen followed them up the icy porch steps. Once inside, they stowed their coats while Gwen tested each of the new keys in the locks. Task completed, she entered the family room and dropped the keys onto the end table. "What are you looking for in Daddy's paperwork?"

"The information Brent sent me on Teresa Hardy included an address here in Medford. It looked familiar, so I cross-referenced it to the false address the housekeeper gave the investigating officer after your father's death."

266

"And they matched?"

He nodded. "I'm thinking the housekeeper was Teresa. Since you found nothing in your father's financial records indicating he had secured a housekeeping service, I wanted to do a more thorough check for anything that might indicate a personal employment, maybe someone not associated with a legitimate house-cleaning outfit."

Gwen went silent at the flurry of possibilities Mark's comment evoked, some of them disquieting. Her father's slow withdrawal following her mother's death was one thing, but the thought of an unknown woman having independent access to his home was too much. Was she Simon's mother, and had her father remained in touch with his former lover over the years? Gwen's forehead heated. No, there was no way he could have kept such a liaison secret for so long. Perhaps they reconnected after her mother's death.

"Gwen?"

She opened her eyes to Mark and Cassie studying her. "Sorry, it's a lot to take in."

"Understandably," Mark said.

She turned toward the stairway. "Well, let's get to it."

"Mind if I stay down here and light a fire?" asked Cassie, glancing at the fireplace.

"Sure. Matches are on the mantle."

Gwen and Mark went upstairs to her father's study. She flipped up the light switch and propped her hands on her hips, surveying his desk. "So, where do we start?"

He moved across the room to a four-drawer file cabinet. "Let's look—"

Something bumped in the hallway, and they turned in time to see someone rushing toward the stairs. Mark bolted toward the door. "Oh, no you don't. Not this time." He careened through the doorway with Gwen close behind.

A figure in a hooded sweatshirt had passed the midway landing and was halfway down the lower staircase.

"Stop! Police!" Mark lunged forward, taking the steps three at a time. He hit the landing, vaulted the banister, and crashed onto the lower staircase four steps behind the intruder.

The stranger spun, pulling out a revolver and leveling it at Mark's chest. He grabbed the railing and pulled up short.

Gwen halted on the landing, heart in her throat.

"Stay back!" Mark stiff-armed a restraining hand behind him, but kept his focus on the interloper. His voice lowered. "Put down the gun. You have nowhere to go."

The gunman said nothing, but began to back down the remaining two stairs, the pistol leveled. As the intruder came abreast of the archway into the family room, an aluminum rod flashed downward, crashing onto the extended arms. The stranger screamed, and the pistol clattered to the floor.

Cassie leaned through the archway and rammed the tip of her crutch into the prowler's rib cage. The hooded figure doubled over and crumpled to the floor.

Mark leapt forward, kicked the gun aside, and drove his knee down into the middle of the person's back. He looked up at Cassie. "You haven't lost your touch."

She shrugged, a satisfied smile curving her lips.

Gwen stepped forward. "Mark, be careful with your knee."

"Why should I?"

"That didn't sound like a man's scream."

He yanked back the parka hood, and dark hair spilled out, framing the face of a pale woman, cheek pressed against the floor.

Gwen laid a hand on his shoulder. "Maybe you can ease up a little. She's in pain."

"Don't be fooled." He pointed to the revolver lying against the wall. "A woman will pull a trigger as quickly as a man will." He pulled out his handcuffs and pulled her arms to her back.

"He's right," echoed Cassie. "No mercy for gender."

Gwen stepped to his side. "Can you wait a second?"

He glared up at her. "You're interfering, Gwen."

The woman spoke, her raspy voice quavering. "I wouldn't ... the gun's not real."

Cassie crossed the hall and picked up the revolver. "It's a starter's pistol. Takes blanks, and this one's empty."

Mark glared down at the woman. "I'm armed. One wrong move, and I would've shot you."

She lowered her face against the floor and closed her eyes. "I almost hoped you would," she murmured.

Gwen knelt onto the floor in front of the woman. "Are you the same person we chased from the house a couple of days ago?"

The woman nodded briefly, then looked up.

Gwen sat back on her heels. "Wait. I've seen you someplace before."

Mark pulled the woman to her feet and led her into the family room. At Gwen's request, and after his search yielded nothing more than a cell phone and a set of car keys, he reluctantly put away the handcuffs and led her to a chair. She sat and rubbed her bruised wrist. Gwen perched on the corner of the hearth, peering intently at the woman. She broke the silence. "Can I get you some tea or coffee?"

The woman lifted a puzzled look.

Cassie groaned. "Oh, for the love of—this isn't a social call, Gwen."

"I know, but look at her. I doubt she's a serious threat."

"Sweeter faces than hers have detonated suicide vests."

"I understand your point, but we're not in Afghanistan."

"Maybe." Cassie sat back, expression stony.

Gwen returned her attention to the stranger. "So, about that tea?"

The woman frowned. "You're serious."

"Of course."

She shrugged. "Sure."

"Where do you keep it?" asked Cassie as she rose from the sofa, shaking her head. "I'll only be a distraction here. May as well make myself useful."

Gwen told her where to find the tea, and Cassie left the room. Gwen returned her attention to the intruder, struggling to place where she'd seen her before.

"I should be taking you to the station in cuffs right now," Mark said. "You're lucky Gwen is as persuasive and compassionate as she is. Even so, I need to tell you that whatever you say here can and will be used against you in a court of law."

She rolled her eyes. "Thanks, but I'm familiar with Miranda."

"I'm not surprised. Still ... " Mark recited the remainder of the advisement.

"So, I'm under arrest?"

"I've got you breaking and entering, and resisting arrest. What do you think?"

Mark pulled the woman to her feet and led her into the family room. At Gwen's request, and after his search yielded nothing more than a cell phone and a set of car keys, he reluctantly put away the handcuffs and led her to a chair. She sat and rubbed her bruised wrist. Gwen perched on the corner of the hearth, peering intently at the woman. She broke the silence. "Can I get you some tea or coffee?"

The woman lifted a puzzled look.

Cassie groaned. "Oh, for the love of—this isn't a social call, Gwen."

"I know, but look at her. I doubt she's a serious threat."

"Sweeter faces than hers have detonated suicide vests."

"I understand your point, but we're not in Afghanistan."

"Maybe." Cassie sat back, expression stony.

Gwen returned her attention to the stranger. "So, about that tea?"

The woman frowned. "You're serious."

"Of course."

She shrugged. "Sure."

"Where do you keep it?" asked Cassie as she rose from the sofa, shaking her head. "I'll only be a distraction here. May as well make myself useful."

Gwen told her where to find the tea, and Cassie left the room. Gwen returned her attention to the intruder, struggling to place where she'd seen her before.

"I should be taking you to the station in cuffs right now," Mark said. "You're lucky Gwen is as persuasive and compassionate as she is. Even so, I need to tell you that whatever you say here can and will be used against you in a court of law."

She rolled her eyes. "Thanks, but I'm familiar with Miranda."

"I'm not surprised. Still ... " Mark recited the remainder of the advisement.

"So, I'm under arrest?"

"I've got you breaking and entering, and resisting arrest. What do you think?"

Gwen knelt onto the floor in front of the woman. "Are you the same person we chased from the house a couple of days ago?"

The woman nodded briefly, then looked up.

Gwen sat back on her heels. "Wait. I've seen you someplace before."

Gwen halted on the landing, heart in her throat.

"Stay back!" Mark stiff-armed a restraining hand behind him, but kept his focus on the interloper. His voice lowered. "Put down the gun. You have nowhere to go."

The gunman said nothing, but began to back down the remaining two stairs, the pistol leveled. As the intruder came abreast of the archway into the family room, an aluminum rod flashed downward, crashing onto the extended arms. The stranger screamed, and the pistol clattered to the floor.

Cassie leaned through the archway and rammed the tip of her crutch into the prowler's rib cage. The hooded figure doubled over and crumpled to the floor.

Mark leapt forward, kicked the gun aside, and drove his knee down into the middle of the person's back. He looked up at Cassie. "You haven't lost your touch."

She shrugged, a satisfied smile curving her lips.

Gwen stepped forward. "Mark, be careful with your knee."

"Why should I?"

"That didn't sound like a man's scream."

He yanked back the parka hood, and dark hair spilled out, framing the face of a pale woman, cheek pressed against the floor.

Gwen laid a hand on his shoulder. "Maybe you can ease up a little. She's in pain."

"Don't be fooled." He pointed to the revolver lying against the wall. "A woman will pull a trigger as quickly as a man will." He pulled out his handcuffs and pulled her arms to her back.

"He's right," echoed Cassie. "No mercy for gender."

Gwen stepped to his side. "Can you wait a second?"

He glared up at her. "You're interfering, Gwen."

The woman spoke, her raspy voice quavering. "I wouldn't ... the gun's not real."

Cassie crossed the hall and picked up the revolver. "It's a starter's pistol. Takes blanks, and this one's empty."

Mark glared down at the woman. "I'm armed. One wrong move, and I would've shot you."

She lowered her face against the floor and closed her eyes. "I almost hoped you would," she murmured.

"And they matched?"

He nodded. "I'm thinking the housekeeper was Teresa. Since you found nothing in your father's financial records indicating he had secured a housekeeping service, I wanted to do a more thorough check for anything that might indicate a personal employment, maybe someone not associated with a legitimate house-cleaning outfit."

Gwen went silent at the flurry of possibilities Mark's comment evoked, some of them disquieting. Her father's slow withdrawal following her mother's death was one thing, but the thought of an unknown woman having independent access to his home was too much. Was she Simon's mother, and had her father remained in touch with his former lover over the years? Gwen's forehead heated. No, there was no way he could have kept such a liaison secret for so long. Perhaps they reconnected after her mother's death.

"Gwen?"

She opened her eyes to Mark and Cassie studying her. "Sorry, it's a lot to take in."

"Understandably," Mark said.

She turned toward the stairway. "Well, let's get to it."

"Mind if I stay down here and light a fire?" asked Cassie, glancing at the fireplace.

"Sure. Matches are on the mantle."

Gwen and Mark went upstairs to her father's study. She flipped up the light switch and propped her hands on her hips, surveying his desk. "So, where do we start?"

He moved across the room to a four-drawer file cabinet. "Let's look—"

Something bumped in the hallway, and they turned in time to see someone rushing toward the stairs. Mark bolted toward the door. "Oh, no you don't. Not this time." He careened through the doorway with Gwen close behind.

A figure in a hooded sweatshirt had passed the midway landing and was halfway down the lower staircase.

"Stop! Police!" Mark lunged forward, taking the steps three at a time. He hit the landing, vaulted the banister, and crashed onto the lower staircase four steps behind the intruder.

The stranger spun, pulling out a revolver and leveling it at Mark's chest. He grabbed the railing and pulled up short.

supervised. I think it would be more fun if you were to come along, though."

Cassie shrugged. "Why not?"

***

When the women arrived at the house, Mark's car was parked at the curb next to a panel truck with *Medford Locksmith* emblazoned on the side. Mark was conversing with the technician through the driver's window. They shook hands, and the locksmith backed out of the driveway just as Gwen's Corolla pulled in.

Mark squinted in through the windshield and flashed a surprised smile at Cassie. He opened her door. "Didn't expect to see you," he said, helping her out of the car. He kissed her on the forehead.

"I felt like getting out a little."

"Glad you did." He turned toward Gwen, who was closing her door. "Hope I didn't interrupt anything."

"You didn't." She looked at the panel truck. "I thought the locks would've been changed by now."

He handed her the new house keys. "They would've been, but there was a communications glitch, and the station didn't put in the request until this morning."

"The police station put in the request?"

"We get a good rate due to all the business we send their way, so I put the request in through channels and had them forward the bill to me. I thought you might appreciate the discount."

"Very much so. Thanks."

He leveled a grim expression at the front porch. "I don't like that the house sat all this time with the old locks. That's the other reason I asked you to come over, to make sure nothing else is out of order."

"Okay."

Mark steadied Cassie with her crutch as Gwen followed them up the icy porch steps. Once inside, they stowed their coats while Gwen tested each of the new keys in the locks. Task completed, she entered the family room and dropped the keys onto the end table. "What are you looking for in Daddy's paperwork?"

"The information Brent sent me on Teresa Hardy included an address here in Medford. It looked familiar, so I cross-referenced it to the false address the housekeeper gave the investigating officer after your father's death."

266

"The clerk tailed her to where she'd parked her car. Before she drove off, he snapped a picture of the car and license plate with his phone."

"Did you look up the plate numbers?"

"Yes, and you'll never guess where they trace to."

"Where?"

"Right there in Medford. I've already emailed the information to Mark. Oh, and one more thing. The clerk was smart enough to handle the license by its edges, so I have the Farmington PD pulling fingerprints from it. We'll see if she's anywhere in the system."

Gwen gripped the phone with both hands. "Oh, I so hope this turns out to be a solid lead. It's been driving me crazy to know I have a brother somewhere, but have no idea how to find him."

"Hang in there. We're getting closer."

At that moment, Cassie came into the room and signaled to Gwen, her phone in hand. Gwen nodded. "Can you hold a sec? Cassie needs something."

"I've got to go now anyway. I'll be in touch."

She smiled. "You'd better."

They signed off and Cassie handed Gwen her phone. "It's Mark."

"Oh. Thanks." She accepted the device. "Hi, Mark."

"Hi, Gwen. Have you heard from Brent?"

"Yes, just now."

"Good. Can you meet me at your house? I need to check out a final couple of things in your dad's paperwork, and I'd like you there. Besides, the locksmith should be finishing up, and he'll have your new keys."

"Um, sure. Right now?"

"Soon as you can."

She disconnected and handed the phone back to Cassie. "Mark wants to meet at the house." She paused. "Do you want to ride along?"

"Not necessary."

"Are you sure?"

Cassie tipped a smile. "It's pretty clear you're a one-guy girl. Either that, or you're an incredible actress."

Gwen laughed. "I stink on stage. My high school drama teacher wouldn't even let me stand near the prop table without being

· "Sure. Kick me to the curb."

Brent chuckled in spite of himself. "You have a point. I can't go into detail, but as soon as I'm free to release anything about our person of interest, you'll be the first to know."

"Fair enough. Oh, and Merry Christmas."

"You too, Howard." Brent cut over to the incoming call. "What's up, Mark?"

"You can stop searching for Teresa Hardy."

"Really? You've located her?"

"Yup. We caught her in Gwen's house."

"What? Is Gwen all right?"

"Sort of."

Brent stiffened. "What do you mean 'sort of?'"

"Physically, she's fine. Emotionally, not so much."

"What do you mean?"

"It looks like 'Teresa Hardy' is an alias, and she denies any knowledge of a Simon Hardy. The news has hit Gwen hard."

"Oh, man." Brent scraped fingernails through his hair. "Can I speak to her?"

"I think she needs to collect herself first, but I expect you'll be the first person she calls after that. Not sure how soon that will be, though."

"Thanks for the update."

"You bet."

Brent ended the call and tossed the phone onto the table. He stretched back in the chair, palms pressed to his forehead.

"Problem?" asked a gruff voice.

Brent lowered his hands. Chief Lawson was standing in the doorway brushing snow from his shoulders. "It's not good news."

The Chief tossed his hat onto the table and unzipped his coat. "Go on."

Brent recapped the situation regarding Gwen's struggles with her father's estate, ending with the distressing news over the truth about Teresa and Simon Hardy. "We still don't know the whole story, but apparently it's got Gwen on the verge of a breakdown."

The Chief folded his arms. "So, what're you still doin' here?"

Brent creased his brow. "What do you mean?"

"I'd be in Boston by now."

272

Gwen leaned forward. "I'm sorry, but I need to know something. What's your name? Is it Teresa Hardy?"

"Sometimes."

"What do you mean 'sometimes'?"

The woman flipped back her hair. "It means what it means."

"You're one more wisecrack away from those cuffs," warned Mark. "No tea or sympathetic faces downtown."

She locked eyes with him, then faltered and lowered her gaze. "My name is Sally Finn. Teresa Hardy is an alias."

Gwen frowned. "An alias? Then ... there's no real Teresa Hardy?"

Sally shook her head.

"But ... " She cast a beseeching look at Mark.

He leaned forward. "What about Simon?"

"Who?"

Gwen slumped and buried her face in her hands.

Cassie came through the doorway with a tray. She drew up at the sight of Gwen's bent figure and Sally's drawn face. "I'm guessing we're past the point of tea," she said to Mark.

He nodded.

***

Brent glanced at his beeping phone lying on the table next to the breakroom computer, then fingered a few more keystrokes and reached for it.

"Brent Newcomb here."

"Of course it is. I dialed your number."

Brent smiled. "What is it, Howard?"

"So, whad'ya find out about this Teresa person?"

"How do you know we found out anything?"

Howard laughed. "Do you think the police are the only ones who get intel? It was my contact who ratted her out, remember?"

"He didn't rat anybody out. This is a legitimate search in an ongoing investigation—which, by the way, is why I can't answer your question."

"That's gratitude for you."

"You have my gratitude, just not my information."

"Which is more than you'll ever get from me again."

"Look—" Brent's cell phone buzzed. "Sorry, Howard. I've got to take a call."

He sat up. "You're kidding."

"I never kid. You'll owe Chad your firstborn for this, but he and I can pick up the slack." The chief strode to the coffee bar and yanked the carafe from the hot plate, sloshing black fluid over the glass rim. "Besides, it's not like you'll be any good here with your head in Massachusetts." He poured a mugful and leaned against the counter. "Just don't turn this into a vacation." He tipped the coffee to his lips.

Brent pulled on his coat. "No chance of that, Chief. I really appreciate this."

"Ugh!" Chief Lawson grimaced into his mug. "Who in the—"

"Chad made it," Brent offered in the way of an excuse.

The Chief coughed into his sleeve. "What, last week?"

"About fifteen minutes ago, before he left on patrol. He goes a little heavy on the grounds."

"A little?" the chief grumbled. He began to dump the coffee into the sink, then paused, scowling. "There's a crack in the parking lot this could seal." He rumbled through the doorway into the hall.

Brent reached for his own mug of coffee before grabbing his hat and coat. Downing it in one gulp, he rinsed out the mug and set it on the counter. *It's not that bad, once you get used to it.*

He drove to his house, threw some clothes into a gym bag, punched out a text message to Mark, and was back on the road south within a half hour.

58

Awkward silence followed Teresa's—Sally's—stark admission that she knew nothing of a Simon Hardy. Gwen stared absently at the braided throw rug beneath her feet, fingers interlocked so tightly her knuckles shone white. If Teresa Hardy didn't exist, and the imposter had no knowledge of Simon, what was all of this about? A look upward caught Sally also staring blankly at the throw rug.

Mark sat beside Cassie with a wary eye on Sally. His hand rested lightly near the holster clipped to his belt, expression betraying conflict between respect for Gwen's wishes and suspicion over Sally's intent.

Finally, Gwen spoke. "So, how do you figure into my father's will—wait, it's coming back to me." She leaned forward. "You were at my lawyer's office. You came in while I was waiting to see him."

Sally averted her gaze.

Gwen rose from her seat and took a step forward. "If you're supposed to be Teresa Hardy, and you know Henry Forbson … " She tightened her hands into fists. "Is he in on this? "

Mark came to his feet, and she faced him, forehead heating. "This whole thing is a farce. No Teresa, no Simon, a fake codicil—and it's all leading back to my lawyer." She turned back toward Sally. "Did Henry Forbson put you up to this?"

Sally hunched in her chair.

Gwen propped her hands on her hips. "Answer me! I've agonized for weeks over having a brother, my father dying unexpectedly, his estate locked in probate." She raised her arms. "You owe me an explanation."

"I don't know what to tell you."

She took another step forward. "Well, you better come up with *something!*"

274

"Gwen, relax—"

She spun on him. "Relax? Would *you* be able to relax?"

He held up his hands. "I'm saying we need to calm down if we're going to get to the bottom of this. Take a breath."

She shot an angry glance at him. Sucked in a deep breath. Slowly released it. Tapped her foot. Then she rounded on Sally again. "Well, *that* sure didn't help. You better have some answers—whoever the heck you are!"

Mark took her by the arm. "Let's sit down."

Gwen reluctantly sat down next to Cassie. Mark turned back toward Sally. "Start from the beginning."

"I don't know how much I can tell you that'll make any difference."

"We'll decide what makes a difference," Gwen interjected. "Just don't leave anything out. For instance, are you the person who left the note about drinking the hot chocolate and slashed my tires?"

Sally shrugged. "I had to scare you out of the house."

Gwen's voice lowered. "Wait. Are you also the one who looked at me through the bedroom window over at Cassie's?"

Sally looked away.

Gwen came to her feet. "What kind of stupid stunt was *that* supposed to be?" she shouted. "You almost gave me a heart attack!"

Mark moved close again, but she stepped away from him, still glaring at Sally. "How did you even know I was there?"

"I was driving here," she glanced at Mark, "when I saw you and him put your suitcases in a car and drive off, so I followed. I wanted to know if you were staying close by. I noticed he didn't stay the night, so later I decided to check out the house to see who else was in the mix. I didn't know that was a bedroom window."

"Good thing you didn't look in *my* window," Cassie muttered. "You wouldn't be around to talk about it."

Gwen shook her head. "I sank a pile of money I don't have into new locks and new tires. Couldn't you have found a cheaper way to get my attention?"

"It worked, didn't it?"

Gwen bristled. "Given where we are now, apparently not very well."

The women glared at each other, and Mark spoke up. "Let's back up. What's your association with Henry Forbson?"

"A little over a year ago, his office got me off the hook on a DUI charge. I didn't have the money the fee, so I got a chance to work off the debt. So, I've done a few … errands for him."

"What kind of errands?" asked Mark.

"Various things, like picking up packages at the post office and dropping them off at different places."

"What was in the packages?"

"Didn't know, didn't care."

Gwen interrupted. "All of this is really interesting, but what does it have to do with how you became my father's housekeeper?"

"Little over a month ago, I was told to get a key to this house."

"That should've raised a red flag," Mark said.

Sally looked down. "Yeah, but it was too late by then."

"How so?"

"I figured after all the errands I'd run that I'd paid off my debt, so I tried to cut ties. He said I was in too deep now, that he had evidence I'd been involved in illegal activity, and that he'd give me up to the cops if I didn't cooperate."

"What illegal activity?"

"I don't know, but the packages I'd handled had no markings saying they belonged to Forbson, and my fingerprints were all over them. The expense money he gave me was always in cash with printed instructions in a post office box, so there was nothing linking me to him. If the packages did hold anything illegal, I was the only one who could be tied to them."

Mark shook his head. "So much for 'didn't know, didn't care'."

She huffed. "Easy for you, cop. You don't have a sick kid to feed and no marketable skills. I take what I can get."

Gwen interrupted. "I still don't understand how you came to be my father's housekeeper."

"I pretended I was starting a housecleaning business. I gave your father a hard-luck story and promised him a no-risk guarantee if he'd take me on trial."

"But why did Forbson want a key to my father's house?" Gwen asked.

"No idea. I only know I was to make a copy of the key."

Cassie spoke up. "It's kind of obvious, isn't it?"

The other three looked at her.

"Forbson goes to great lengths to secure a house key and to tie your dad's estate up in probate with a fake codicil. Clearly he's looking for something and is buying time to get to it. We need to figure out what it is."

59

"So, what do we do now?" Gwen asked. "Arrest Mr. Forbson?"

Mark shook his head. "On what charge? There's nothing but Sally's word to tie him to any of this. We need to let him think everything is normal until we find out what he was searching for."

"How do we do that?"

"Did your father have any other association with Forbson besides being his lawyer?"

"They were members of the same shooting club. My parents had dinner with him and his wife a couple of times. Other than that, I don't know."

Mark frowned and scratched his neck. "Not much to go on."

"What about me?" Sally asked.

"You go downtown," Mark replied. "Remember, I've got you on breaking and entering, not to mention aggravated assault, even though the weapon turned out to be harmless."

Gwen touched his arm. "As upset as I am, I'm not sure I want to press charges. If it's true she has a child to care for, it would only make the situation worse. And if that turns out to be a lie—"

Sally straightened, eyes glistening. "It's not a lie. His name is Cameron."

"Where is he now?"

"With a friend."

Gwen turned back to Mark. "I doubt she can post bail, and her freedom might be of more value to us in bringing Forbson to account."

He turned toward Sally. "Where do you live? And this time, how about a real address?"

She averted her gaze. "I got a place through the Somerville Homeless Coalition. I can give you the address."

Mark picked up her car keys and dangled them from his fingers. "The Coalition is for the needy. These belong to a late-model Nissan." He cocked his head.

"Forbson provided it. I doubt you'll be able to trace it to him, though."

He handed her his notepad and a pen. "How do we know you won't run?"

"I have nowhere to go. Cameron has special needs, and I won't take any risks with his medical attention." Sally scribbled a couple of lines in the pad, returned it and the pen, and leaned back in the chair with a sigh. "Besides, I'm tired of running. Sure, I've been on the receiving end of Miranda a few times, but it's never been because I had much of a choice."

"We all have a choice."

Sally lowered her hands a tossed Mark a sarcastic look. "Well, some people get better choices than others."

"Like me?" asked Cassie, pushing herself up from the sofa with her crutch. "Say the word, and I'll trade places with you."

Sally's jaw tightened. "That's not what I meant."

"Then what did you mean? That life dealt you a tough hand, so you get to whimper your way out of trouble when you get yourself into it? Is this the life you want for your son? There's more to taking care of a kid than getting him medicine."

Sally reddened, and her chest heaved. "Oh, I suppose you've got it all figured out, right? You have no idea what I have to do every day to keep us out of the system."

"Like you did today? If Mark had played it by the book, you'd be downtown right now, and Cameron would be with a social worker. I think that's referred to as 'the system'."

Sally's fists clenched, and a vein on her forehead bulged. "I will never let ... *anyone* take ... " Her voice seized, and she began hyperventilating.

Mark leaned forward and caught her as her eyes rolled back and she teetered forward.

Gwen rushed to her side and they eased her back into the chair. He lowered her head between her knees to flow blood back to her brain and massaged her back. Gwen looked over her shoulder at Cassie. "That was a little harsh, don't you think?"

"No, I don't." Cassie was glaring at Sally. "I hate whiners. She needs to get a grip, or she's going to lose everything she's screwing up her life to save."

Gwen rose and moved to her friend's side. "We aren't all as strong as you are, Cassie."

Cassie flinched, and she turned her head. Gwen's eyes widened at the moisture brimming in Cassie's eyes. "Strong? I'm a disaster."

Gwen shook her head. "You're the strongest woman I've ever met."

"An act," Cassie muttered. "I have no idea what I'm doing, where I'm going, or why I even try. I only know that if I cave in, I'll die." She returned her gaze to Sally's hunched form. "She's caving in, she'll die, and she'll take her son with her."

Gwen looked at Sally, whose breathing had evened. Mark eased her up against the back of the chair. Gwen looked back at Cassie. "So, what are you going to do about it?"

"What *can* I do?"

"Don't let her cave in."

Cassie looked back at Sally, who was staring blankly at the ceiling. She tightened her jaw and stepped forward.

"So, what happens now?" she asked.

Sally looked at her. "What do you mean?"

"Do you want out of this, or don't you?"

"Sure, if there's any way I can get out from under Forbson—"

"That's not what I'm asking. Do you want to fix your life or don't you?"

Sally creased her brow.

"C'mon." Cassie gazed at her flatly. "Forbson is a symptom. Your life is the disease. Do you want a treatment or a cure?"

"I don't know what you mean."

"You said Cameron is your motivation, right? The reason you do what you do."

"Yes."

"So how do you offer him a decent life?"

Sally sputtered a laugh. "By winning the lottery."

"Another shortcut. That would kill him faster than running away would. Try again."

Sally's shoulders drooped. "I—I don't know."

"C'mon, think!"

Mark and Gwen studied Cassie, but she kept her focus on Sally. "You've got a freakin' brain. Use it. What do you really want for your son?"

"I—I want him to have what I never had."

"A platitude. Try again."

"What do you want from me?" Sally choked. "I love my son. I want him to have a chance to succeed, to … "

Cassie leaned forward. "To *what*?"

Sally buried her face in her hands. "To never become what I've become."

Cassie lifted her eyes toward the ceiling. "Thank God, we're finally getting somewhere." She looked back down. "Then change what you've become."

"How?" Sally cried. "It's too late for me."

Cassie straightened, voice even. "Okay, then I guess it's too late for him, too, right?"

"No … I don't know … I don't want it to be."

Cassie rolled her eyes. "Geeze, woman, grow a backbone and be a mother."

Sally jerked up her head and launched to her feet, face inches away from Cassie's. "You have *no* right to say that to me," she hissed.

Cassie held her gaze. "Tell me why."

Sally thrust a forefinger toward Cassie's face. "I have done more for my son in five years than you'll do for a child in a lifetime."

Cassie stiffened, eyes taking on a glisten, then leaned back forward, jaw clenched. "Really? How's that working out for you? I see you facing jail time and your kid dumped into foster care."

The air between them sizzled.

Gwen threw a nervous glance at Mark, who kept his focus on Cassie.

Interminable moments later, Sally's jaw trembled. Her chest heaved, and she broke eye contact.

Cassie leaned closer. "Don't you dare look away from me."

Sally jolted and reengaged Cassie with rounded eyes.

"It's now or never, *Mom*," Cassie said. "What's it going to be, more excuses, or change your kid's future?"

Sally's eyes brimmed. "How do you expect me to *do* that? Show me a way, and I'm on it."

Cassie leaned back and cocked her head. "You mean that?"

Sally turned toward Mark and Gwen, eyes overflowing. "I don't know what she wants. It's not like I haven't tried."

Cassie lowered herself onto the edge of the sofa, voice calming. "I get it that you've tried. Like I've tried to recover from being blown up in Afghanistan."

Sally stiffened, and her gaze flicked to Cassie's prosthetic leg. "I'm sorry. I didn't know."

"Of course you didn't," Cassie huffed. "That doesn't matter. What matters is that you don't give up, that you don't cave in to this 'victim' crap." She lifted the stub of her right arm. "I'm right-handed. But two months ago, I painted a picture."

Gwen spoke up. "And it's gorgeous."

Cassie glanced at Gwen, then returned her focus to Sally. "The point is, I painted a picture. The first one in my life with my left hand. I didn't collapse into excuses, as much as I sometimes wanted to."

Sally's voice quavered. "How did you do it?"

"Guts and the grace of God."

Gwen perked. The 'guts' part made sense, but the grace of God? Where did *that* come from? "What are you saying, Cassie?" she asked.

"That there's more to our circumstances than we can blame on chance," she replied. "You showed me that." She returned her focus to Sally. "And what we do with circumstances makes us what we are." She sat back. "So, what's it going to be? Status quo, or something better?"

Sally snorted. "I'm stuck in a homeless system with a special-needs son. Thanks for the pep talk, but give me a road map. Where do I start?"

Cassie leaned back. "Move in with me."

"What?"

"You heard me."

Sally's tone flattened. "What's the catch?"

"There is no catch."

"There's always a catch."

"Okay, if you want one, here's a catch. Unscrew your life and do something constructive for your son."

"Just like that."

Cassie rolled her eyes. "Of course not just like that. I'm offering you a start. You have to figure it out from there. School. A real job. Something more than Band-Aids on your hard luck." She sat back. "If you really care about your son, put your money where your mouth is."

Sally cocked her head. "You're serious, aren't you?"

"No, I joke about stuff like this all the time. It's a hobby."

"Please don't." Sally's eyes watered. "This is too important. I need to know if you're really serious."

"Never more serious in my life."

Gwen's vision blurred and throat tightened. Mark sat back and pulled a deep breath.

Sally's voice broke. "Then I accept."

Cassie looked over at Gwen. "You need to move out."

Gwen smiled. "Consider me gone."

Sally shook her head. "I still don't understand why you're doing this for me after everything I've done."

Cassie tipped her head, voice quieting. "I'm not sure either. But maybe your son can have the second chance I won't have."

"Don't be too certain about that," Mark said, moving to her side.

60

Later that evening, Brent steered the F150 into Cassie's driveway, rubbing grittiness from his eyes. A light snow had begun to fall, small flakes flickering in the truck's headlights. He shut off the engine and looked through the windshield at the darkened house. *So, where is everybody?*

As if to answer, a small green car pulled into the driveway behind him, followed by a blue Corolla. His pulse quickened when the Corolla's dome light flashed on, and the most desirable blonde in New England smiled at him through the windshield.

He shouldered open the door and stepped out, eyes fixed on her.

Gwen bolted from her car and ran to him. In the late afternoon dimness, their shadowed forms melded into one. "What are you doing back in Medford?" she asked after the first kiss. "I thought the chief needed you in Marble Falls."

"He's on board with me being here, but I'm going to owe him and Chad big time."

She kissed him again. "Then so will I."

"I cannot live a second longer without you," he whispered into her ear.

She pulled back and smiled into his face. "That's what I've been wanting to hear."

"Really? I haven't been clear about my feelings?"

"Feelings are only a part of it." She stroked his cheek. "I need you so much, now more than ever."

He searched her eyes. "We need to talk."

"Yes, we do."

"Break it up, you two," Mark said coming up behind them with Cassie.

Brent laughed. "You're just jealous."

Mark shook his head and tucked Cassie closer to his side. "Not even remotely."

"Well spoken, sir." Brent winked at Cassie, then looked past her at a hunched figure.

Mark followed his gaze. "Meet Sally Finn, alias Teresa Hardy."

Sally took a tentative step forward. Brent threw a terse look at Mark. "I don't see any cuffs, and this isn't the police station."

"True on both counts."

Brent cocked his head, and Mark returned an expression that suggested patience. "C'mon, it's freezing out here. Let's go inside."

Cassie turned toward Sally, nodded toward the house, and the five of them trooped up to the porch.

Once inside, Cassie went into the kitchen to prepare hot drinks and order pizza while Mark kindled a blaze in the fireplace. Gwen excused herself to use the bathroom, which left Brent and Sally standing in the living room studying each other. Finally, he gestured toward the sofa.

Sally eased down onto the cushion, back straight, face pinched.

He sat in an easy chair facing her and leaned forward, elbows on his knees. "I've driven over half the state of Maine looking for you, Ms. ... Finn. Forgive me if I'm at a loss for words."

Sally attempted a half-smile, but it quickly faltered.

"She's going to help us nail Henry Forbson," Mark said from across the room. He closed the metal screen and turned around. "Aren't you, Sally?"

She lowered her gaze.

Brent looked at him. "Gwen's lawyer?"

"It looks like he's been scamming her the whole time. The codicil to her dad's will was a fake." He gestured toward Sally. "There is no Teresa Hardy, and there's no Simon Hardy."

"Why would he scam Gwen?"

"We don't have all of the details, but over the past year, Forbson has been blackmailing Sally to do his dirty work, the most recent scheme being getting access to Gwen's house. By appearances, the fake codicil was designed to tie up the estate in probate in order to find something belonging to Mr. Kelly. Trouble is, we don't know what that is."

"Can't you bring him in?"

Mark shook his head. "He's covered his tracks too well. The word of a respected lawyer against that of a homeless single mom who's got a rap sheet. If he holes up, we may never get to the bottom of this."

"So what's the plan?"

He grinned. "That's what you're here for, Sarge."

Brent rubbed his jaw. "So, we need to flush Forbson out."

"Yeah."

"Like we did Hassan."

"Yeah, like—what?"

Brent looked up at him with a flat smile. "Wait for it … wait for it …"

Mark's eyes widened and he slapped his forehead. "Exactly! Hassan!"

"Bingo."

"Why didn't I think of that?"

"Because apparently that's what I'm here for."

At that moment, Cassie and Gwen came through the doorway with mugs, a teapot, and a tray of fruit. Cassie pulled up. "Hassan? Ahmad al-Hassan?"

Brent grinned at her. "Yup."

"You're planning a flush, aren't you?"

Brent laughed and looked back at Mark. "She always did catch on quick."

"Who is Ahmad al-Hassan?" asked Gwen.

"Afghani. Northern Province warlord," Cassie said as she rounded the sofa. "We duped him into an ambush."

"How?"

"Played on his ego." She glanced over at the men. "Works every time."

"But how does that help us with Forbson?"

"He's a guy, right?"

"Yes."

"And a lawyer."

"Uh huh."

"The perfect ego storm."

Gwen laughed. "You're a hoot."

"Enough with the guy jokes," Brent said, casting a narrow look at Cassie.

She returned an even expression. "Someone was joking?"

He began to retort, when Mark interrupted. "So, what do you have in mind?"

"I'm guessing Sally isn't Forbson's first patsy. Jerks like him get lax over time. We hit him where he's most likely to slip up."

"Where would that be?"

"Hassan tried to push his influence one village too far, and it came back to bite him. So, who would Forbson likely consider to be a good soft target? Who can we make his 'bridge too far'?"

"How can we know something like that?" Gwen asked.

Brent looked at her.

Then Cassie did.

Then Mark.

She straightened. "What?"

Brent moved to the sofa and took her hands in his. "Sweetie, you're about to become Sally's best friend."

***

Over pizza, the three veterans grilled Sally over every detail of her dealings with Henry Forbson. When did he first contact her? How did he prefer to communicate, transfer resources, avoid anything being traceable to him? Most of all, how could Gwen get herself into an exploitable position, maybe something related to her father's estate?

Gwen's face paled as the conversation progressed. The horrifying events she'd endured a couple of months prior resurged, sending a trickle of sweat down her spine.

Brent held up his hand, halting the conversation. "Gwen? Are you all right?"

She could only shake her head. He put his arm around her shoulder. "I would never put you in harm's way. You know that, right?"

She nodded dumbly.

He took her hand into his. "Cowards like Forbson let other people take their falls. He won't risk doing anything that could get him on the wrong side of the defendant's table in a courtroom." He paused. "And I'll be beside you every step of the way."

The cloud dissipated from her face, and she smiled. "Then I'm good with whatever."

He looked at Sally. "This will involve you too."
Her eyes widened. "How?"

61

The next afternoon, Gwen entered Henry Forbson's waiting room and crossed to the reception desk. The receptionist was staring intently at her computer monitor. She cleared her throat. "Ms. Stilwell?"

The office worker jerked her head up. "Oh! You startled me." She threw another glance at the monitor, clicked the mouse, and looked back up. "May I help you?"

"I have a 2:30 appointment with Mr. Forbson."

"He's at the courthouse, but should be returning shortly."

"Thank you. I'll wait."

Gwen took a seat on the couch, hugging her purse to her stomach. Five minutes later, she relaxed when the door from the outer hallway opened and Brent sauntered in. He plopped onto a chair across the room, grabbed a *Sports Illustrated* magazine from the end table and opened it.

She cleared her throat.

He looked up, then turned back to the front cover.

It was the swimsuit edition.

With a sly grin, he slowly opened the magazine again.

She cleared her throat louder.

He heaved an exaggerated sigh, flipped it aside, and picked up a copy of *Good Housekeeping.*

She rolled her eyes.

"Can I help you, sir?" The receptionist was standing behind her desk and looking toward Brent.

"No, thanks. Waiting for a friend."

She sat and returned her attention to the computer.

A few minutes later, Sally entered the waiting room and took a chair near Brent. Slouching in the seat, she crossed her legs and fixed a dull stare at the TV monitor where Dr. Oz was promoting a special blend of probiotics.

A slight movement across the room caught Gwen's eye. Mona had leaned forward and was staring at Sally. Her eyes met Gwen's, and she sat back.

The hallway door opened abruptly, and Henry Forbson entered. Frowning at a sheaf of papers in his hand, he strode through the room without acknowledging anyone's presence.

Ms. Stilwell rose. "Mr. Forbson—"

"Not now, Mona." He continued into his office and sharply closed the door.

She pursed her lips and sat back down. Almost immediately, her desk phone buzzed, and she reached for the handset. "Yes, sir … no, there have been no calls from the police." Her head remained bent, but eyes flicked up toward Gwen. "Yes, I have the file. I'll bring it in." Her voice lowered. "You know she's here in the waiting room, don't you, sir? … I understand." She replaced the handset and stood with a manila folder tucked under her arm, then turned and disappeared through a rear doorway.

Gwen looked at Brent, rounded her eyes and swallowed. He returned a reassuring smile.

She forced a smile.

"Ms. Kelly?"

Gwen jumped and turned toward the reception desk.

Mona had returned and was standing behind her desk. "You can go in now."

Gwen rose and headed across the room.

Brent laid the magazine aside, pulled out his cell phone, and began poking the screen with his thumbs.

Sally looked up at Gwen, lips pressed thin.

The door to Forbson's office opened as she approached it, and the lawyer stood in the entryway, his expression troubled. He gestured for her to enter. Gwen slipped a hand into her purse as she walked toward a visitor's chair and tapped the Record button on her cell phone app. She took a seat and laid the partially opened purse on her lap.

Forbson sat behind his desk and leaned forward, fingertips tented against his chin. He lost no time getting to the point. "What is this I hear regarding your father's estate?"

She willed her breathing to steady, praying the attorney wouldn't hear her heart pounding against her ribcage. "I was hoping you could tell *me* that, Mr. Forbson."

"Clarify, please. I have a brief note that the police are interested in the matter, that's all. Something about fraud. How else could they have become involved if not on your behalf?"

Gwen met his eye. "Since my father's death, our house has been broken into, vandalized, and his belongings rummaged through. My property has also been targeted. Add to that the suspicious circumstances of his death, and—"

Forbson interrupted her. "What suspicious circumstances?"

"The autopsy revealed excessive hemorrhaging, possibly caused by overmedicating."

He sat back. "Overmedicating? Jim? Impossible."

Gwen paused at Forbson's familiar use of her father's name, then continued. "And finally there's the apparent existence of a half-brother delaying the settlement of the estate."

" 'Apparent' existence?" He leaned forward again. "Do you doubt the legitimacy of the codicil to your father's will?"

"In a word, yes. It's been over two weeks, and we've found no trace of a Simon Hardy."

"Who is 'we'?"

The intercom on his phone buzzed, and he jabbed a button on it. "I'm with a client, Mona. You know better than to disturb me. "

"I'm sorry, sir, but a policeman is here. He wants to speak with you immediately."

"He can wait."

"He ... he has a warrant, sir."

"A warrant? Whatever for?"

The office door suddenly opened, and Mark's imposing bulk filled the doorway, followed closely by Brent. He flipped open his ID wallet as he stepped in and flashed a shield. "Mr. Henry Forbson?"

Mona appeared in the doorway behind him. "I'm sorry, sir. I tried to stop him."

Forbson jerked up from his chair, face red. "What do you think you're doing? You have no right to—"

"This gives me the right." He pulled a folded paper from his inside coat pocket. "It's a search warrant for this premises. We have reason to believe you're holding material evidence relevant to an ongoing investigation."

"What investigation? Here, let me see that." Forbson extended his hand for the warrant, but Mark had already turned around. "Detective Newcomb, secure the premises."

Brent stepped Mona backward with a glare and closed the door. Mark turned back, tucking the paper back into his pocket.

Forbson rose from his chair. "I demand to know what's going on."

"You can make this easy, or you can make it difficult." Mark took another step forward, fists propped on his hips. His massive frame towered over Gwen, and the rock-hard look on his face caused even her to flinch. A quick look back at Forbson revealed the intimidation tactic had achieved an effect.

Mark suggested Forbson return to his seat, then looked down at Gwen. "Apologies for the disruption, ma'am, but we'll need some alone time here."

As she rose from the chair, Forbson made a flustered attempt to regain control. "I'm sure this is all a mistake, Ms. Kelly. Please remain in the waiting room."

"Ms. Gwen Kelly?" asked Mark.

"Yes, officer?"

"The daughter of James Byrne Kelly?"

"Yes."

"Then perhaps you'd like to stay. This warrant pertains to your father's case."

"I suppose—"

"Wait a minute," Forbson interrupted, frowning. "There's something wrong here. If you intend to execute a search warrant, where is the forensics team? And it would be highly inappropriate for a civilian to remain at an investigation scene." He looked at the three of them in turn, then held out his hand. "I want to see that warrant."

"It may not need to come to that," Mark said. "We can clear this up with a few questions."

Forbson propped his arms on his desktop. "Now I know you're bluffing. There is no warrant, is there?"

Gwen suddenly spoke up. "Mr. Forbson, I'm sorry for all the drama, but we need your help."

Mark stared at her. "Gwen?"

"My help?" Forbson sputtered. "You must be joking." He looked back at Mark. "And I assume by the familiarity that you're acquainted with Ms. Kelly." Then he looked over at Brent. "And who are you, a hired thug?"

Brent looked at Gwen, then back. He sighed. "I'm the boyfriend."

"You've got to be kidding," Forbson muttered. He dropped back into his chair and laced his fingers across his stomach, glowering at them. "I doubt you have any idea how poorly this will go for you in court."

Gwen leaned forward. "Please listen for a moment, sir."

"Oh, it's 'sir' now, is it? Apparently at least you grasp the gravity of what you've done."

"I do, but I think you'll understand once you've heard me out."

Brent stepped forward. "Gwen, what are you doing?"

Forbson reached for the phone. "I'm going to call the real police."

"I am the real police," Mark said. "I'm just not acting in that capacity at the moment."

"Nor will you ever do so again, if I have anything to say about it."

"Please Mr. Forbson," Gwen pleaded. "If you're not satisfied with what I have to say, go ahead and report us."

He stared at her, jaw clenched, then replaced the handset. "I'll do it for your father."

"That's why I want to explain. A few moments ago, you seemed genuinely concerned about him."

Forbson lifted his hands, palms up. "Of course I'm concerned. He was a dear friend. My wife and I were devastated at his passing." His gaze swept the three of them. "What are you not telling me?"

"We found Teresa Hardy, one of the signatories on the codicil."

"You did?"

"The name is an alias. And there is no Simon Hardy." She paused, voice quieting. "I have no brother."

Forbson shook his head. "I don't understand."

"The codicil was a fake, a ruse to buy time."

"Time for what?"

"To search my father's house."

"Again, for what?"

"We don't know yet."

Brent moved forward. "Mr. Forbson, are you saying you had no knowledge of this?"

"None whatsoever. I accepted the codicil as valid." He opened the manila folder and pulled out a sheet of paper. "It has the required signatures and notary validation," he said, scanning it. "There was no reason to challenge it, even though I was puzzled why Jim had not involved me in its preparation. It even ... wait a minute." He pulled the document closer. "This is odd."

"What?" Gwen asked.

"I don't know why I didn't notice it before, but this is a standard form. It was updated a few years ago."

"Is that a problem?"

"It is if the codicil was prepared in 2004. This format didn't exist then."

"Who else would have been aware of Mr. Kelly's legal affairs enough that they could insert a false document into his file?" Brent asked.

"No one. Well, except for Mona. As my legal assistant, she has complete access to my records."

"I thought she was just your receptionist," Gwen said.

"We're a small office. She performs a broad range of legal and administrative functions."

Mark and Brent exchanged looks.

Forbson stiffened. "Surely you don't suspect her."

Brent glanced at Mark, then back at Forbson.

The lawyer punched a button on the intercom. "Mona, could you come in here, please? ... Mona?" He looked up.

Brent opened the door and shot into the waiting room. He returned in a moment, jaw clenched. "She's gone. And so is Sally."

62

"What?" cried Gwen. "So Sally was in on it the whole time?"

Forbson sat back in his chair and massaged his forehead. "I can't believe this."

Brent moved to Gwen's side and gently squeezed her shoulder. She stared forward, shaking her head.

Mark pulled out his cell phone and punched a button. "Cassie?"

Her terse voice scraped through the speaker. "I'm on it. They came out a few minutes ago and got into a black Chrysler. I'm two cars back and we're heading east on Salem—wait, they exited the roundabout toward Fountain … now they're turning onto the ramp to I-93 north."

"Don't lose them, babe."

"Lose them? You forget who you're talking to—and you know I hate 'babe' even more than I do 'gal.' "

Mark grinned. "Make sure they don't see you following them."

"Right. Be inconspicuous in a neon-green Mazda. I'll do my best."

"Let me know when they go to ground. And you know better than to engage, right?"

Silence.

"Cassie?"

"That little tramp played me with a fake sob story."

Mark's grin dissolved. "I don't care."

"I do."

"Cassie, I want to hear you say you won't engage."

"Sorry, you're breaking up."

Cassie? … *Cassie!*"

The call dropped. Mark glared at it.

Gwen stood. "Cassie was outside? How did you know Mona and Sally would run? "

"I didn't. Cassie suggested taking flank in case things didn't go as planned."

"Always the tactician," Brent said.

"Yeah, but she also always stretches herself too far. If Mona and Sally turn on her, it won't be a fair fight."

Brent laid a hand on his friend's shoulder. "So, let's be there when it goes down. You don't have her phone tagged on GPS by any chance, do you?"

"She'd kill me if she knew this, but yes."

"Then let's go." He turned toward Gwen. "You and Mr. Forbson stay here. You have some things to settle regarding your dad's estate now that there's no Simon Hardy." He looked at Mr. Forbson. "And if Mona and Sally manage to lose Cassie, they may contact you to make a deal. They can't stay on the run forever."

The lawyer nodded.

Brent gave Gwen a kiss. "We'll be back in no time."

She touched his cheek. "I'll hold you to that."

As he and Mark bolted from the room, Forbson's amused voice trailed behind. "So, he really is the boyfriend."

Brent's heart squeezed when she replied, "Oh, he's so much more than that."

***

Brent careened off the roundabout onto the I-93 north ramp. The truck's engine whined as he shot onto the northbound lane, cutting off a Walmart eighteen wheeler. "Sorry," he muttered at the blast of the semi's air horn.

Mark didn't appear to notice as he stared at the "Find My Phone" app on his cell. "She cut off onto I-95. They're about twelve miles ahead."

"Where in the blazes are they going?"

"No idea, but if I know Cassie, they won't get there alone."

The next half hour passed with no change in their relative positions.

"I'm doing 75," Brent said. "They're pushing it. With any luck, they'll get stopped by a state trooper."

"Like that one?" Mark was looking over his shoulder. Brent caught the red-and-blue flash of a Massachusetts state patrolman's lights in his rearview mirror. He rolled his eyes, and pulled onto the shoulder of the highway.

Negotiations with the trooper went swiftly, aided by Mark's badge, and they were back on the road in ten minutes. He shook his head. "They're at the state line. My badge won't do a whole lot of good in Maine if we get stopped again."

"Mine will," Brent said, and he accelerated to 80 miles per hour. Crossing the state line at Portsmouth, he flicked on the emergency flashers embedded in the grill and framing the rear window.

"Nice touch," Mark commented.

Forty-five minutes later, they had closed the gap to fifteen miles.

Suddenly Mark tensed. "She's exiting the freeway."

"Where?"

"Route 202." He looked over at Brent. "It's your state. Where in the heck does 202 go?"

"Unless I miss my guess, she's headed to Farmington."

"Isn't that where Sally was researching real estate deeds?"

"Yup."

Mark shook his head. "This is bizarre." Fifteen minutes later, he again broke the strained silence. "We should be closing in on them pretty soon. They're slowing down ten miles ahead."

"Crap!"

"What?"

Brent was frowning at his dashboard display. "Fuel."

"Oh, you've got be joking."

"I didn't get a chance to gas up before we drove to Forbson's office. I didn't think we'd be taking a road trip." He looked sidelong at Mark, who was shaking his head. "It's not like this was planned."

Mark slouched back and stared at the roof.

"Like you could do better," Brent muttered as he pulled off at the next exit advertising a gas station. When he jumped back into the truck after refueling, Mark was staring at his cell phone, tight-lipped.

"Where is she?" Brent asked as he started the engine.

"I have no idea. She's dropped off."

"What?"

Mark glowered at him. "Let me guess. You guys have crappy cell coverage too."

Brent threw the truck into gear and peeled out of the gas station. "Well, maybe it's not the best."

"It's barely qualifies as the worst."

A sudden thought occurred, and Brent grabbed his phone off the dashboard. Two bars of signal strength. He smirked at Mark. "Maybe it's your carrier."

"That's right, blame 'the system'."

Keeping one eye on the road, he punched in a number. "C'mon Howard, pick up—Howard. This is Brent."

Howard Dobbs' slick voice filtered through the phone's speaker. "Well, well, Officer Newcomb. What a surprise."

"I need your help."

"Always here for the police."

"Right."

"This being Thursday, though, I'm a little busy."

"Is the Farmington clerk there?"

"Maybe."

"It's important."

Howard allowed a dramatic moment to pass. "Hold on." Shortly, a nasally male voice squeaked through the speaker. "Hello?"

"This is the Marble Falls Police Department."

"Oh, dear. It's about that parking ticket, isn't it?"

Brent almost laughed. "All is forgiven, if you'll answer a question for me."

"In that case, I'll certainly try."

"A couple of days ago, Howard asked you about a Teresa Hardy who visited the Farmington municipal offices about a real estate inquiry."

"I remember."

"Do you have any idea where the property is that she was interested in?"

"We never progressed to the formal inquiry, but ... "

"But what?"

"I saw a town map sticking out of her purse that had pencil markings on it. It looked like she'd circled the Octagon House."

"What's that?"

"A historic landmark on High and Pernham. It's part of the Farmington Historical Society's holdings."

Brent rubbed his jaw. Sally had used the Farmington Historical Society's address as point of reference, whether intentionally or not. Was the Octagon House the object of her inquiry? And was that where she and Mona were heading now? Another question occurred to him. Why leave a trail of breadcrumbs like this? Did Sally set the whole thing up?

The clerk's tentative voice interrupted his thoughts. "Excuse me, but does that answer your question? Do I still owe you for the parking violation?"

"No, sir. I'll take care of the ticket."

"Oh, thank you so much. I really can't afford it, you know."

Brent shook his head. *But you can afford to play poker.* "Enjoy your game." He ended the call and looked over at Mark. "Farmington it is."

"You're sure?"

"Not absolutely, but it's all we have."

Mark slouched and crossed his arms. "How reassuring."

***

Halfway between Portland and Farmington, twilight descended, and a wash of snow flurries enveloped the truck, worsening visibility. Brent turned on the windshield wipers and looked at the dashboard clock. 6:43 p.m. "I saw a Weather Channel advisory on the TV in Forbson's waiting room. There's a nor'easter moving in, but it wasn't supposed to hit until later tonight."

"Could be the leading edge," responded Mark, as he leaned forward and stared into the gathering darkness. "How far to Farmington?"

"About forty minutes. Any hits on GPS?"

"A couple, but they died." He looked at Brent. "So, when do Maine telecommunications intend to join the twenty-first century?"

"Never. It's part of our charm."

"How quaint."

"Yeah." His phone rang. He connected hands-free and Gwen's voice filled the cab. "Hey, Brent."

"Hi, Gwen. Is everything all right?"

"I'm good. Where are you?"

"Almost to Farmington."

"Farmington? What in the world are you doing up there?"

"I'll tell you as soon as I figure it out. What's up?"

"We've gone back through my father's will. Except for the fake codicil, everything is in order. I can proceed with the settlement."

"Excellent. Thank him for me—oh, and you can include an apology in there somewhere."

"I already have, from both of us. He was very gracious and offered to take me back to the house since you and Cassie have the cars."

"Then thank him again for me. We'll call as soon as we have something to report."

"I'll keep the home fires burning."

"Sounds cozy." He smiled and glance at Mark.

Mark's mouth twitched. "Seriously?"

"Oh, hi Mark," Gwen said.

"Hi, Gwen."

"I hope you—"

"Hope I what?"

Brent stared at the screen, which displayed a dropped call. "Nuts."

Mark offered a sardonic chuckle. "Charm strikes again."

Fifteen minutes later, complete darkness hid the landscape and the flurries swelled into a thick curtain of large wet snowflakes that spattered onto the windshield and caked the wiper blades. A gust churned the thickening blizzard and shuddered the truck cab.

"How much farther?" asked Mark.

"We should be at the Sandy River bridge any time now. That'll put us into town. When was the last hit you had on Cassie's phone?"

"I have her now. She's stopped at the corner of Academy and High Street."

"That's the Historical Society."

"Wait, she turned onto High Street ... stopped again."

They jolted when Mark's phone suddenly chirped. He punched the screen and Cassie's voice crept from the speaker. "I assume you're about here, right?"

Mark frowned. "How did you know we were following you?"

"Why else would you have our phones put on the same plan? I've been tracking you too."

Despite the tension, Brent laughed aloud at Mark's flustered expression.

Mark cocked his head. "What's that noise?"

"Probably the wind. It's getting nasty out here."

He leaned forward. "What are you doing out of the car? There's a nor'easter blowing in."

"I know. It should work to my advantage."

"Get back in the car. You don't know what you're walking into. We'll be there in a couple of minutes."

"The Chrysler pulled over a block ahead. I saw the taillights go off, but the weather's turning into a whiteout. I should be able to get close without being seen."

"You're not listening."

"I'll let you know when I have something if you don't get here first."

"Cassie, get back to the car ... *Cassie!*"

The call ended.

Mark tossed the phone onto the floor and slammed his hammy fist onto the dashboard.

Brent flinched. "Go easy on my truck. It's only made of steel."

"If she gets herself hurt, I'm going to kill her," Mark fumed.

"That makes sense." Brent veered onto the Sandy River bridge, squinting into the snowy blast coming straight at the windshield. "We should be there in a minute. There's a flashlight in the glove compartment. Be ready to move."

"I've been ready to move since we left Afghanistan," muttered Mark.

Brent glanced at him. "You mean Medford."

"No, I mean Afghanistan." Mark returned Brent's look. "I don't know what my problem has been, or why I've been such a jerk. I thought I was giving her space to recover, but it was more my tail between my legs at the thought of asking her."

"Asking her what?"

"To marry me." He looked at Brent. "Seeing you and Gwen together has been an eye-opener for me." He turned forward, jaw muscles knotting. "Man, how I love that woman. If I lose her now ... "

"We're not going to lose anyone," Brent replied as he turned off Main Street onto Academy. "Her car's around the corner."

Mark retrieved his phone from the floorboard, then pulled his service weapon from inside his coat, checked the safety, and tucked it into an outer pocket. He opened the passenger door and jumped out before the truck came to a stop behind the Mazda.

A few seconds later, Brent caught up with him on the sidewalk. He zipped his coat tight and shone his flashlight into the blizzard. "She's right that the storm should work in her favor," he offered, looking up at his friend, who was hunched forward, staring straight ahead. "I can't see ten feet in front of me."

Mark shook his head. "She doesn't do well on ice and snow without her crutch, and I don't remember whether she had it in the car."

As if on cue, Brent slipped on a patch of ice, and he grabbed Mark's arm. "Sorry."

Mark didn't seem to notice. He was staring at his cell phone, cupping his other hand around the screen against the snow. "She's across the next intersection." He pressed forward, jamming the phone into his pocket, his hand reemerging with the pistol.

"Ease up," Brent said. "We have no reason to believe Mona or Sally are violent. Remember, Sally's last choice of weapons was a fake gun."

"Pretend it's Gwen up ahead. Now what's your advice?"

"Okay, I'll give you that one." Brent had already moved his own Glock into his coat pocket, but Mark needed to calm down before they stepped into whatever laid ahead. High emotions and firearms made a dangerous combination, no matter how proficient the marksman.

They barged across the next intersection and drew up as the blurry form of a black sedan in the driveway of a tall house to their right took shape. Exchanging quick looks, they skirted the car, and climbed a low staircase. The door on the landing had been forced open.

Brent turned and put a hand on Mark's chest. "I'm going in first."

"Nope."

"Yup. First, I want you covering my back, like you did in the desert. Second, you have too big of an emotional investment in this, and nobody needs to get shot."

Mark glared at him.

Brent held his ground. "We're wasting time."

Mark's mouth tightened, but he nodded.

Brent turned back toward the door and pushed it open.

They stepped inside, and a gunshot sounded.

63

Gwen studied the floor of the family room while she paced, arms folded across her stomach. She looked at her phone lying on the end table and checked her watch yet again. It had been nearly an hour since her previous contact with Brent. The last two times she'd tried to call, his phone went to voicemail. Was he in cellular dead spots, or had something happened? Mental images of a truck's twisted wreckage on a snowy roadside crowded her mind, but she forced them away. Brent knew how to handle snowy conditions, but that didn't mean other drivers silly enough to be on the road during a nor'easter were. She groaned inwardly.

In the background, her father's legacy continued to churn through her mind. If he had no relationship with a Teresa Hardy, if there was no Simon, why all the intrigue? He wasn't wealthy, hardly a prime target for extortion. Why would Mona and Sally go to the trouble of tying up his estate? She dropped onto the sofa, head in her hands. Last October's harrowing events in Marble Falls piled onto the current drama unfolding in Medford, and she scrunched tufts of blond hair in her fists. Was everybody's life this chaotic? Surely not.

The afternoon's tension planted a numbing fatigue in her sluggish mind, and to her surprise, Gwen found herself stifling a yawn. She settled onto her back, arm draped across her eyes, succumbing to a mind-dulling weariness. Making sense of the past twenty-four hours was like rowing a boat through a quagmire. She rubbed her eyes, tried to shake away the encroaching stupor, but instead slipped further into its grip. How could she even remotely consider resting? Everyone else was out solving her problems, and there she lay, drained and impotent.

Think, Gwen. Think.

"Dream, Gwendolyn. Dream."

The nearly audible words stiffened her back, and a chill tickled her spine. She drew a heavy breath. Her eyelids quivered, then closed. After a moment, her breath evened and the present fell away.

*

In the void between consciousness and sleep, inky darkness and silence ungrounded her, and she began to squirm. Suddenly, a single candle flame crackled to life, illuminating a solitary figure in a rocking chair, fingers entwined on a lap covered by a flowing dark dress with a lacy white collar. The apparition regarded her with a serene, but slightly amused, expression.

Gwen squinted at her. "Grandmother Irma?"

"Gwendolyn."

"Did ... did I hear you call my name?"

"I sensed you needed me."

"What how can you possibly help?"

"Perhaps in no way, perhaps in much."

"What do you mean?"

"Search your mind, your memory."

"For what?"

"You recall Isabel and Gabriel?"

"Yes."

"Where we released them to their freedom?"

"It was in Farmington."

Grandmother Irma nodded.

"Brent is in Farmington right now. Mona and Sally led him there."

The rocking chair squeaked, and her grandmother smiled. "Think, Gwendolyn. We discussed this."

"Discussed what?"

"Matters of the heart."

"Matters of—"

*

The grandfather clock in the hallway chimed, and Gwen's eyelids fluttered open, dissolving the vision. She sat up, heart lodged in her throat, her grandmother's final words echoing through her mind. Discussed what? When? She fought to remember the dreams she'd had of her grandmother.

Grandmother Irma and Mary Jane by the shore of Marble Lake, her presence noticed as she lurked behind the sumac bush.

Her encounter in the hallway near Gabriel's and Isabelle's door that had morphed into the eerie battlefield scene.

The hotel room in Farmington when her grandmother spoke of dreams.

The journey she shared so vividly with her ancestor's family to Marble Falls where—wait, go back!

Farmington. The hotel room after her grandmother parted with Gabriel and Isabel. What was it she said? *"Thinking has little to do with matters of the heart."*

The phrase nipped at her mind like a pesky insect. *Matters of the heart … matters of …*

Gwen lurched to her feet and hurried upstairs to her father's study. She pulled open the bottom drawer of the filing cabinet and lifted out the antique jewel box. The faded gold letters *MOTH* gleamed from the velvet. When she opened it, an embossed logo *"Matters of the Heart"* gleamed at her from the silk lining on the inside of the lid. Resting on a tufted base of the box laid a diamond pendant on a thin sterling silver chain. The gem flashed in the brightness of the desk lamp as she lifted it from its mounting. She examined the setting for an inscription, unusual marking, any clue as to how the relic might relate to her father's legacy or Brent's situation in Farmington. Nothing came to light but the diamond flashing its brilliance.

She heaved a frustrated sigh and began to return it to the box, when a tiny tab protruding from a depression in the silk caught her eye. Gwen tugged on the tab, and the mounting pulled loose. Beneath it, a flat brass key rested on the bottom of the box, with it a USB flash drive. Fingers trembling, she drew them out and set the box and necklace on the desk.

The notched key had a local bank's logo and a number etched into the grip. The flash drive's label had one word written on it.

Gwen.

She set the key beside the pendant and slipped the drive into a port on the side of her father's computer. When the machine awoke, she clicked the drive's icon. A few image files, a spreadsheet, and a couple of text documents appeared on the screen. She selected a text document with the filename "Gwen."

A document flashed onto the screen, but as she stared to read, the first line set her back in her chair.

Dearest Gwen, if you are reading this alone, I am most likely no longer alive.

-64-

Brent and Mark edged into the house, weapons drawn. Brent played the flashlight beam around the room. He looked back at Mark and gestured toward a door in a slanted wall to his right.

Mark took position. Brent grasped the doorknob, pulled it open, and they stepped through.

The adjoining room was dark and empty. Brent's sweeping flashlight beam revealed angular contours to the walls, similar to the one they'd just left. He looked for a good defensive position, but the strange architecture stymied him.

"What's up with this place?" he muttered. "I feel like I'm in a carnival fun house."

Mark pointed toward a dim glow seeping under a door to their left. "There's a light on in the next room."

Brent nodded. "Let's move."

They approached the door, and on Brent's signal, burst through the doorway.

Sally was doubled over against the far wall, gripping and arm dripping with blood. She straightened at their entrance, eyes widened.

Her stare shifted past him, and a chill raced up Brent's spine.

He spun around to the sight of a revolver pointed into his face.

***

Gwen swallowed and leaned back toward the monitor.

Try as I have to put myself together after your mother's death, I've failed. All that remains is you, my precious daughter.

"Precious daughter." She swallowed past a lump in her throat. Where was the preciousness in his voice, his actions, his demeanor

307

toward her during the years she needed him the most? She drew a deep breath and read on.

The necklace in this box has been in the Kelly family for over a hundred years, originally belonging to your distant Grandmother Irma Kelly. If you look in the attic, you'll find a trunk containing her diaries and an album with her photograph.

Grandmother Irma? Could this be a coincidence? But then, her dreams, their conversations, the intuition they had shared over the ages flashed back, and any notion of coincidence fell apart. Was there a reason she had been led here?

She shook her hair back and picked back up reading her father's note.

Oddly, she specified in her will that this pendant was to be held in trust for her fifth-generation granddaughter, as though she were able to look ahead over time. You are that granddaughter, Gwen.

Gwen shot to her feet. "It can't be." Scrambled images of the past few months flew past. The "bridal" trunk with Grandmother Irma's image sewn into its lining, the photo album and diaries that had sent her on this journey, Grandmother Irma's words only minutes ago, and now this necklace.

She lowered herself unsteadily back onto the chair and stared at the screen.

I should've given it to you sooner, but I didn't have the heart to part with it after photographing your mother modeling it. She was so excited to present you the necklace when you came of age. It was among her happiest expectations, and my heart aches that she never had the opportunity to realize it.

Snippets of her mother's face and personality buried in Gwen's mind had blurred into vague memories. But her father's words brought them back into sharp focus. Her heart nearly burst at the mental clarity of her mother's deep blue eyes, flowing red hair, and impish smile. Her soft alto voice whispering lullabies rose in Gwen's heart.

She wiped a tear from her cheek and turned back to her father's message.

But, there is more to this legacy. It holds the key to another inheritance held in trust for you. It's a historic landmark in the town of Farmington, Maine called the Octagon House.

Farmington? Gwen pinched the edges of the paper with whitened fingertips. Was this the connection to Brent?

I don't have all of the information regarding the property yet, so I've petitioned my lawyer, Henry Forbson, to research the legal implications of your grandmother's will and the bill of sale for the property. You'll find an image of it on this flash drive, and the authentic document in a safety deposit box at my bank. There's also a print of it in a file folder in this drawer. When I hear back from Henry's office, I'll finalize this note, and you can claim your inheritance. Until then, I will keep this to myself until I'm sure your future is assured by this inheritance.

One more thing, dear daughter. If you are reading this alone, please forgive me for withholding my condition from you. I have not been well, and I've taken a rare moment of lucidity to write to you this note. I pray the matter will be resolved before I succumb.

His words stopped abruptly.

Gwen scrolled to the end of the file, but there was nothing more. She sat back. What condition? If he was ill, why didn't he tell her? Could it have been—as Dr. Andrews had mentioned—dementia? Alzheimer's?

Despite the angst over her father's words, the urgency of the present broke through. Her father's contact with Forbson's office would have gone through Mona, who now appeared to be a guilty party. Had Forbson even known about the property, or had Mona kept the information to herself and enlisted Sally to do the research on it? That would explain both Sally's deed inquiry in Farmington and her soliciting a job as a housekeeper for Gwen's father. Could the bill of sale be what she was looking for?

Gwen rubbed her temples. Still too many loose threads. She reached for her phone. Maybe Brent had discovered something in Farmington by now that could shed more light on this. Or maybe her new discoveries could somehow help him.

If he would only answer her calls ...

65

Brent glared at Mona over the barrel of her revolver.

"Guns on the floor. Now." She stepped away from the wall.

Mark pivoted, raising his handgun.

Her eyes flicked toward him and cocked her pistol. "Go ahead." She jerked her head toward Sally. "She didn't think I'd pull the trigger either."

"Don't get excited." Mark raised his left hand, stooped, and laid his weapon on the floor. Brent did the same.

Mona gestured toward Mona. "Over there. Hands where I can see them."

The men backed across the room toward Sally, who was cringing against the wall, blood seeping between fingers clasped over a wound in her upper right arm. Mark reached for her, but Mona intervened.

"Leave her alone." She kicked the men's guns into the corner behind her. "She'll live. And if not, so what?"

"What now?" asked Brent, assessing their captor. Was she was faking the bravado, or was she experienced at this? So far, her demeanor favored the latter.

"First, you all strip down."

"What?" they all chimed in unison.

"Aside from the distraction, you won't be able to hide anything."

Mark shook his head. "That's not—"

"And then you tie each other up until I've had a chance to get what I came for."

Brent scanned the room. "Tie each other up with what?"

"With your clothing, moron." She gave him a condescending headshake. "Don't worry, I'll talk you through it."

Brent tightened his jaw.

"One at a time, and I want to see the palms of your hands every step of the way." She turned toward Mark and smirked. "You first, big boy."

"And if I don't?" Mark asked.

310

"Easy." She brandished the pistol. "If you're dead, there's also no distraction, and you still can't hide anything. Which is it going to be?"

He glowered at her, then began unbuttoning his overcoat.

"Remember, palms outward where—"

"What's going on in here?"

They jumped at a voice coming from behind Mona. Emily Davis, the Historical Society curator, was standing in the doorway with a flashlight. She crossed her arms and surveyed the trespassers. "What are you people doing here?"

Mona swung the pistol toward her. Emily stared it for a moment, then glowered at Mona.

At that moment, Cassie's voice came from across the room. "Drop the gun!" She was leaning against the wall of the entryway, a long-barreled weapon raised to her shoulder and pointed at Mona.

Mona faltered, and in an instant, Emily slashed her flashlight down across Mona's wrist. She screamed, and the gun dropped from her hand.

Emily stepped forward and slapped Mona across the face, toppling her backward onto the floor. "How *dare* you point that thing at me," she huffed, hands propped on her hips.

Brent and Mark pounced on Mona. They yanked her to her feet, and Mark drew a pair of handcuffs from his belt. He offered them to Brent. "Care to do the honors? It's your turf."

"Glad to."

As Brent was cuffing Mona, Cassie lowered her aluminum crutch and limped into the room.

Mona stared at her. "That was what you pointed at me?"

"Yeah. You're kind of new at this, aren't you?"

Mark hugged her. "Perfect timing."

"Maybe, although I admit I was tempted to see how far down you'd strip down."

He narrowed his eyes at her, then laughed. "How long were you there in the next room?"

"I turned left coming in from the porch and waited for you to break in. After the gunshot, I decided to pinch her between us."

"How were you so sure we'd come in that door?"

"You always turn right."

"I do?"

"We've kicked down too many doors not to notice."

She looked over when Sally moaned and slid to the floor, face ashen, a widening pool of blood forming at her side. Cassie walked over and inspected the wound. "Not good." She held her hand out toward Brent. "Toss me your belt."

He complied.

Sally grimaced as Cassie cinched a makeshift tourniquet above the wound and drew it tight with her teeth.

"We're not done here, Brent," Mark said as he hustled Mona against the wall and sat her down. "Keep an eye on her."

He picked up Mona's revolver and retrieved their service weapons from the corner.

"I still don't know what's going on," Emily said, eyeing the room. Her gaze stopped on Brent. "You look familiar."

"We met a couple of weeks ago."

"Oh, that's right. You were the guy in the truck."

"Yup." He gave her a slight smile. "And, to be fair, you did invite me to come back."

Her mouth twitched. "I sort of meant during normal hours. And without guns."

Brent chuckled. "Sorry. I'm with the Marble Falls Police Department. This is Sgt. Mark Ferguson out of Boston."

Mark tipped his head.

"We followed a suspect to this house," Brent continued, gesturing toward Mona. "But that's about all we're certain of at this point."

"Except that we're losing Sally," Cassie interjected from across the room. "We need to get her to a hospital."

Emily cast a terse look at Sally's arm. "I'll call an ambulance. Meantime, there's a first aid kit in the kitchen." She hurried through the doorway, raising a phone to her ear.

As Brent hovered over Mona, his phone vibrated. He pulled it out, glanced at the screen, and turned away from the group. "Hey, Gwen."

"Don't you 'hey Gwen' me. Where are you, and why haven't you answered my calls? I've been worried sick."

"Sorry, it's been a little busy here. I'll fill you in as soon as I can, but it'll have to wait until after the ambulance leaves."

"Ambulance? What happened? Are you hurt?"

"I'm fine. It's Sally. She's been shot."

"*Shot?* Brent, you're not making things better."

He chuckled. "Don't worry. Everything's under control. I'll call you back within a half hour."

"Be sure you do. I have some information for you too."

"Good. Love you."

"You'd better after all of this."

66

Fifteen minutes later, the ambulance arrived. After inserting an IV and lifting Sally onto a stretcher, one of the EMTs turned to the group. "Nice job, whoever applied the tourniquet. It saved her life."

"That would be this lady," Mark said proudly, putting his arm around Cassie's shoulders. The EMT's mouth twitched at the sight of Cassie's missing arm, and he tipped his hat. "Really nice job."

"Mind if I ride along to the hospital?" she asked.

"Not at all."

She turned to Mark. "Someone should stay with her. We still don't know what her part is in all this."

He nodded. "I'll help clean up here."

She handed Mark the keys to the Mazda, and followed Emily and the ambulance crew out. Brent and Mark returned their attention to Mona, who was sitting against the wall with her cuffed hands tucked beneath her knees. "I think she broke my arm," she said through gritted teeth.

Brent regarded her with a stony expression. "You'll live. And if not, so what?"

She glared up at him as Mark laid a hand on his shoulder. "Not helpful, bro. She's clean, right?"

"Yeah."

"We should check her arm."

Brent pulled out the handcuff key and flipped it to Mark. "Here. I'm not feeling the love right now."

Mark removed the cuffs and examined a livid purple bump on her wrist. "Nice welt, but it's not broken."

"We're on Farmington PD's turf," Brent noted. "We owe them a call."

Mark nodded, then paused. "Or we can beg forgiveness. "

"What do you mean?"

He faced Mona. "The hospital will notify the police that they have a gunshot victim. It won't take long for them to find out where it happened. So, if we're going to make any deals, it'll have to be quick. They don't know what's going on, and frankly I don't expect them to care."

"What kind of deal?" she asked.

"You tell us everything, and we'll put a good word in that you cooperated."

"What does that get me?"

"I don't know yet, but it sure can't get you any worse than what you're facing now."

She hesitated, then looked down.

Brent crossed his arms. "You seriously want to play the odds on this? You're already nailed for breaking and entering, assault and battery, attempted murder, and kidnapping, assuming you coerced Sally to come with you. By the time you become eligible for parole—*if* you become eligible for parole—middle age will be a distant memory."

She looked up sharply. "I didn't coerce Sally to come with me."

"Right. She came along voluntarily so you could shoot her."

Mona's shoulders sagged, and she heaved a sigh.

"Start from the beginning," Mark said. "And if we find out you lied or withheld anything, all bets are off."

Brent's phone rang again, and he pulled it out, signaling Mark to hold on for a second.

"Hi, Gwen."

"You were going to call me in a half hour. I gave you a five-minute grace period. What's going on up there?"

"Sorry. Let me put you on speaker. We're getting Mona's story. Maybe you should hear it." He punched a button and held the phone out. "Listen closely. We don't have much time."

Mark turned toward Mona. "Were you involved in James Kelly's death? Oh, and you are aware that his daughter is listening in, right?"

She paled. "I didn't have anything to do with his death. You have to believe me. I was only interested in the land bill of sale he was researching through our office."

"So you prepared the fake codicil?"

She nodded. "I couldn't allow the estate to be liquidated before I figured out how to get to the bill of sale, so I contrived a second heir to tie it up in probate."

"How did Sally fit into this?"

"I had her over a barrel financially, so I used her."

"Did Forbson know about this?"

"No. I communicated through typewritten notes and non-attributable emails. Over time, it became evident she thought Forbson was the one manipulating her, and I let her believe that."

"You had her get a foot in the door with Mr. Kelly so she could search for more information on the property?"

"Yes."

"What property?" asked Brent.

"I don't know all the particulars, only that it seemed to be a hot prospect. He was going to send more information the day he died."

"I can answer that," interjected Gwen's voice.

Brent stared at the phone. "What?"

"The property is in Farmington. Something called the Octagon House."

Brent and Mark traded puzzled looks. "I think that might be where we are now," Brent said.

A voice from behind interrupted them. "That's exactly where you are now." They turned. Emily was standing in the doorway after having seen off the ambulance. "What's this about a deed?"

Gwen continued. "Apparently there's a connection to a distant grandmother of mine who came through Farmington in the 1860s, but I haven't discovered what that connection is yet."

Emily frowned. "The Historical Society purchased this property five years ago from the family who's owned it for years. I don't see how there could be another deed."

"Maybe that's the snag Mr. Kelly was trying to research," Brent said.

"From what I saw," interjected Mona, "his claim could have merit. There are a few gaps that need to be filled in from a legal standpoint."

Emily shook her head. "The Octagon's ownership lineage is pretty straightforward."

"But if—"

She rounded on them, eyes flashing. "The rights to this house are not going anywhere!"

Brent stepped back and lifted his hands. "We understand, ma'am. We're not trying to solve that problem here." He looked at Mark, widening his eyes for an instant. "Let's stick to the matter at hand."

A pounding on the outside door interrupted them. Blue and red lights flashed through the windows, and a voice called for entrance.

Brent grimaced. "Farmington PD is here, Gwen. I'll have to call you back."

"Again?"

"Sorry." He disconnected the call and pocketed the phone.

Mark glanced at him. "Ready to grovel?"

Emily looked over her shoulder. "That's Fred Wilson's voice. Don't worry, he owes me a favor." She turned and marched off to the front room. "Hold your horses, Fred," she shouted. "I'm coming."

Brent and Mark exchanged relieved looks, hauled Mona to her feet, and palmed their badges.

-67-

When Brent and Mark arrived at the Franklin Memorial Emergency Department, Cassie was lounging in the waiting room. She flipped aside her magazine the moment they came through the door.

"It's about time," she said, rising. "I hate hospitals. Let's get out of here."

"Let me check on Sally's status first," Mark replied. He walked toward a sliding-glass window beneath an Emergency Check In sign, leaving Brent to help Cassie on with her coat.

"Mona began to cooperate before the police arrived, so we tried to put some perspective on the situation with the arresting officer," he told her.

"Was he peeved you didn't notify them sooner?"

"A bit, but the curator smoothed things over."

"Lucky for you."

"I'd really like to get Sally's side of the story," he said, glancing at his watch.

"So would he." She gestured toward a uniformed officer slouched in a corner chair. "I overheard the nurse tell him he'd have to wait until Sally was out of surgery and stabilized to get a statement."

"Which probably won't be until tomorrow morning," Mark said as he walked up. "I hate to leave before talking to Sally, too, but spending the night in this waiting room isn't a very attractive prospect."

"We won't be," Cassie said. "There's a Comfort Inn less than a mile from here. I booked us in."

Mark smiled and shook his head. "Always one step ahead."

"Somebody has to be," she replied. "Besides, there's no way I'd be driving back to Boston in this weather, Sally or no Sally."

***

Gwen stopped pacing when Brent's call finally came in. "If you tell me you're going to have to call me back one more time, I'm coming up there."

318

"Really? Do you promise?"

"Yes I do, and don't you dare."

He laughed. "I wouldn't want you driving into this snowstorm anyway. We're holed up in a Comfort Inn until tomorrow morning when we can question Sally."

"So catch me up."

He filled her in on everything that had happened since leaving Medford.

"So Sally really was a victim. What about Mona?"

"We'll inform the Farmington police of her activities in Boston. I think we can talk the Historical Society out of pressing breaking-and-entering charges once they know the whole story. And if Sally chooses to do likewise regarding the shooting, maybe we can get them to release Mona into our custody. There will still be some clean-up to do, but Farmington PD is a good outfit. I think they'll work with us."

"Do you know why Mona and Sally drove to Maine in the first place?"

"We don't know everything yet, but the information you gave on the deed of sale seems to fit in." Brent chuckled. "Although I won't be bringing *that* up in front of the curator again anytime soon."

"I heard her over the phone. Wow."

"She's passionate, you've got to hand her that."

"A thumb drive with a copy of the bill of sale was tucked away with a family heirloom—a diamond necklace. Guess who the original owner was."

"No idea."

"Grandmother Irma."

"You're kidding."

"Nope. And there's an even freakier part to this, but it'll have to wait until you get back. Which needs to be soon."

"A minute from now is not soon enough for me."

Gwen smiled. "Sleep well, and come back to me."

She disconnected the call and dropped onto the couch. Frozen rain pellets shot downward past the window, an occasional gust of wind pinging them against the pane. She drew her sweater up to her neck and hugged her waist. With Cassie in Maine, she'd be spending the night in her father's house. Alone. Again.

The depressing thought threatened to smother her heart, but she shook it away. *Snap out of it, Gwen. You don't go to pity parties, so no sense in hosting one of your own.*

After a light dinner of scrambled eggs and toast, she curled up on the sofa with a cup of hot oolong tea. Draping the afghan over her shoulders, she sipped and stared into the fire. Her most recent exchange with Grandmother Irma fueled the desire to resume reading the diary, but the book was back at Cassie's house, so her mind roamed back through what she'd already learned.

The clock sounded the three-quarter hour, and her eyelids drooped to half-mast. The fireplace glow gradually softened. Twice she caught herself nodding off, nearly spilling the remnants of her tea onto her lap. She set the cup on the end table, pulled the afghan up to her chin, and snuggled her head against the throw pillow. The last thing she remembered before drifting off was the clock striking eleven o'clock.

*

Grandmother Irma drew up as the clock on her dresser chimed the eleventh hour. She laid down her fountain pen, blew gently on the fresh ink, and closed the journal. The house lay quiet, her parents having already retired.

The evening post had brought a surprise, a diamond-heart necklace in a sterling silver setting on a delicate twisted-link chain. Beside the polished mahogany box, silk-lined and embossed in gold with the jeweler's insignia, *Matters of the Heart*, laid a carefully penned note.

My Dearest Irma,

Tomorrow we deploy to Fort Warren on Georges Island. We will continue training until we march south. So begins our unhappy separation. I pray it will be a brief one, that our country's differences will be settled quickly. This I leave in God's hands.

Until then, please accept this token of my love and my commitment to return to you. You never leave my thoughts, and now I leave you my heart. Perhaps in that, we shall feel close.

Always and forever, I remain,

Your loving Gerald

She lifted the necklace, twirling the pendant in the soft glow of her reading candle. Its faceted gemstones sent tiny pinpoints of light chasing each other around the walls and across her ruffled-lace nightgown.

"It's beautiful."

She focused past the necklace into the mirror. "Someday it will be yours, Gwendolyn."

"I would be honored to receive such a treasure."

Grandmother Irma replaced the pendant in its box. "I shan't wear it until Gerald places it around my neck."

"I—I'm sure that will be soon."

A pause. "Your tone belies your words."

An awkward shifting of weight.

"As does your silence. This conflict will not be a short one, will it?"

"It will not be our nation's longest war."

Grandmother Irma smiled. "A compassionate response."

"The North will win."

"Then all will be well."

"However—"

Grandmother Irma lifted a hand. "That suffices."

"You can see into my time, but you don't know what happens in the interval between us, do you."

"I see only you."

"I wonder how."

"Perhaps we shall discover that together."

68

Brent, Mark, and Cassie arrived at the Franklin Memorial early the next day, Cassie with a small bundle under her arm. The nor'easter had abated during the night, leaving behind elongated drifts across the parking lot and a coating of ice-crusted snow plastered against the building. The sun had not yet crested the horizon, but a soft yellow aura crowning the trees to the east promised a clear morning.

When they entered the Emergency Department, Mark went to the reception window while Brent and Cassie scanned the room. The chair the Farmington officer had occupied the evening before was empty. In fact, the entire waiting room was vacant.

She sniffed. "Amazing how therapeutic a little bad weather can be on hypochondria."

Brent chuckled. "Your compassion is showing again, Cassie."

"I'll try to hold back the tears."

Mark returned, unbuttoning his coat. "We can see Sally in a few minutes. Farmington PD is in with her now."

"Nuts," Brent muttered. "I hoped we could get to her first."

No sooner had he spoken, than the officer exited the ED and crossed the waiting room to the outside door. When he'd gone, the trio were given permission to see Sally.

She was sitting up in bed, bandaged arm in a sling. She stiffened against the mattress when they came into the room. "I just gave my statement to a local cop."

"We know," Brent said. "Can you fill us in on what you told him, so we know what we're up against with Mona?"

"After this." Cassie stepped around the men and tossed the bundle onto the bed. "Here. Not the trendiest, but it'll get you home."

Sally unfolded the package to find a set of clothing. Relief flooded her face, and she smiled up at Cassie. "Thanks. They cut away my blouse in surgery, and my jeans are pretty blood-stained. I wasn't sure what I was going to wear out of here. Where did you get the clothes?"

"I keep an R-O-N kit in the trunk. You never know when you'll get caught out late." She jerked her head toward the men. "Or who you'll get stuck with."

"R-O-N kit?"

"Yeah, 'Remain Over Night'. I'd give you my toiletries, too, but you probably don't want a used toothbrush and deodorant stick."

"Right, thanks. This'll do."

"Okay," Mark said. "If the sorority party is over, maybe we can get back to business." He flinched at Cassie's narrowed expression. "Just kidding."

Brent took the lead. "We'd like to take Mona back to Boston, but that'll depend on what you told the police officer, Sally."

"If it helps, I didn't tell them I was brought here against my will, and I minimalized the shooting as more accidental than intentional, although I must admit that part took some fast thinking. I'm not sure he believed me."

Brent breathed a sigh of relief. "Good."

"When you've been questioned by the police as much as I have, you learn what to say."

"So you don't plan to press charges against Mona?"

"I figured that would screw up the big picture."

"Speaking of which," Mark said. "What is the big picture? How did you get tangled up with Mona, and how did you both end up here in Farmington?"

"I didn't know I was tangled up with Mona. I thought Forbson was pulling the strings until she hustled me out of the office at gunpoint when you all were in his office."

"What about Farmington, especially the Octagon House?"

"Mona made me drive when we left Forbson's office. She was dithering as to where to go, so I took a chance and suggested we come here. I told her it would get us out of Massachusetts, and that it was the end of the trail on what I had discovered about the Kelly inheritance. That last part was a stretch, but she wouldn't know that.

What I didn't tell her was that it would also buy time for you to track us down, which I assumed you would."

"More quick thinking," Brent said.

"More experience," Sally replied.

"How much did you know about the Kelly inheritance?"

"Not as much as I led Mona to believe. I came across a copy of an old document in the filing cabinet and snapped a photo of it. I barely managed to put it back before you came upstairs and chased me out."

"What document?"

"A bill of sale. I thought I might get something over on Forbson, so I came up to Farmington to see what I could find out about the property. I got nervous when the clerk asked for identification. So I left."

"Do you still have the photo?"

"No, it was on my phone. Mona grabbed it from my purse and threw it out the window on our way here. It's probably in pieces somewhere along I-95."

"But you know where the document is."

"Yes."

Brent reached for his phone. "Tell me. I'll let Gwen know."

After Sally had related the document's location, a nurse entered to prepare her for discharge. Brent, Mark, and Cassie went back to the waiting room to wait, and he placed the call to Gwen. Then they worked on a plan for approaching the Farmington PD regarding Mona's case.

***

Gwen opened the bottom drawer of the filing cabinet in her father's study and drew out a manila folder. Settling at his desk, she snapped on the lamp and opened the folder. A Xerox copy of an old document slid onto the blotter. The ink on the original had faded, making it difficult to read.

The large title, handwritten with a flourish, declared its purpose. "Sale Bill of" followed by "Ino. Mr. Ramsdell's Property."

She squinted at the smaller cursive text, but the fuzzy reproduction made the details difficult to make out. Sitting back and rubbing her eyes, she scanned the desk for anything that might help. Tucked into a cubbyhole was a mahogany-handled magnifying glass with a matching fountain pen. She reached for the magnifier.

True to Sally's word, the bill of sale was for a property in Farmington, Maine, naming "F.X. Jones" as the recipient. It specified a location at the corner of High Street and Perham Street, along with the terms of the sale. At the bottom, it was signed "Hiram Ramsdell," followed by the date "3 February 1868," and annotated "To be recorded."

Gwen's pulse quickened. *Francis Jones?* If Grandmother Irma had met up with him, as the caption on her lithograph suggested, the property would belong to them and their estate.

Setting down the document, she leaned against the back of the chair and rubbed her temples with her fingertips. The legal status of the property would have been what her father was trying to consult with Henry Forbson about, had Mona not intercepted the inquiry. But the annotation "to be recorded" was puzzling. Did that mean the bill of sale had never been completed? What were the rules about finalizing land purchases in Maine during the nineteenth century? Only one person she could think might have an answer, although it may be difficult to solicit her help, given what she might have to lose.

She turned to her father's computer, searched for the contact information for the Farmington Historical Society, and began typing an email.

Dear Ms. Davis,
I have something of interest to you...

69

Negotiations with the Farmington PD progressed better than expected. Brent had convinced Emily Davis that it would serve the larger interest if she would refrain from pressing charges against Mona for breaking and entering. She responded with a tongue-in-cheek reminder that he had also broken and entered, and that she hadn't decided what to do about him yet. When she finally conceded with the proviso that he repair the bullet hole in the parlor wall and help clean the blood stains off the floorboards, he agreed, offering to sweeten the deal with coffee and donuts.

"Sure. And when you finish in the library, there's a floorboard loose upstairs— "

"You're pushing."

"Sorry."

Mark's and Brent's explanation of the investigation into Mona's activities in Medford, paired with Sally's watered-down statement and reticence to press charges, persuaded the Farmington Police Chief's cooperation to release Mona into their custody with the understanding that she could be recalled. They agreed, and they were on the road back to Boston by early afternoon. Brent transported the handcuffed Mona in his truck while Mark rode with Cassie and Sally in the Mazda. Attempted conversation was spotty, but Brent sensed a defeated attitude in her, so he pressed for more details about her scheme concerning the Kelly estate, as well as others she'd concocted.

They arrived in Medford around 5:10 p.m. and drove directly to the Kelly home.

Mona peered through the window. "Aren't we going to the police station?"

"In time," Brent replied as he came to a stop behind Mark's car. "I told the others when we stopped for gas that it might be good to have an informal chat before processing you."

She laid her head back on the headrest and sighed. " 'Processing me'. I feel like canned meat."

"You don't know how lucky you are. Sally could have turned you over to the feds for aggravated kidnapping across state lines and attempted murder. She did you a huge favor by fudging on her statement."

Mark opened the passenger door and took charge of Mona. "There's someone waiting for you." He poked his thumb over his shoulder toward the house. Gwen was standing on the porch, hugging her waist against the cold.

Brent ran up the sidewalk and engulfed her in a hug. When he released her, she punched his arm. "You worried me to death! Don't you ever do that again."

"It's what you get for falling in love with a cop."

"Oh, you're *that* sure I've fallen in love with you."

"Uh huh." He leaned in and pulled her into a kiss. She pushed against his chest, relaxed, then melted into him. When they finally separated, he grinned. "See?"

Mark's voice boomed from the sidewalk. "Okay, break it up you two. You're the only ones out here who aren't freezing to death."

Brent looked over his shoulder. "Spoilsport." He turned and led the way indoors, hugging Gwen to his side.

Once inside, Mark removed Mona's handcuffs and reexamined her wrist. The bruising had spread, yellowing along the brownish-purple edges. "Sit," he told her, and she lowered herself onto the sofa, cupping her forearm. "We've got some holes in the story that need filling in."

As Brent and Mark questioned Mona, the story unfolded of her illegal activities which began two-and-a-half years earlier. A dubious liability claim came across her desk that reeked of fraud. After some research, she manipulated the paperwork and killed the case before money had been paid out. She felt justified in tampering with the falsified claim, enjoying the sense of self-righteous gratification it gave her. That led to more opportunities, until an estate settlement of a shady client came along from which she could also divert some profit to herself with little chance of being caught. Why not? She was doing society a favor by sticking it to the fraudsters. Why not reward herself for the time and effort? The skills she gleaned from that endeavor opened other doors, and over time rationalization became easier.

Gwen interrupted her. "My father was not a crook. He was an honest man, so why did you target him?"

"By the time your father's inquiry crossed my desk, it was all about the money. I like the horses and had gotten myself into trouble with a bookie." Mona shrugged. "I saw an opportunity to get out of it."

Gwen glared at Mona.

"Do you have anyone other than Sally on the hook?" Mark asked.

Mona shook her head. "I worked alone until I saw a chance to leverage her."

"You did a great job making me think it was Forbson," Sally said flatly.

"Thanks."

"That wasn't a compliment."

The women exchanged narrowed looks.

Mark rose and gestured to Mona. "Time to go." He looked at Sally. "I'll drop you off at home on the way. If you can be ready tomorrow afternoon, I'll pick you and Cameron up, and bring you to Cassie's."

She nodded and flashed another grateful smile at Cassie.

Mark turned toward Cassie. "If you can catch a ride with Brent and Gwen, I'll stop by before I head home for the night."

"Don't get lost."

"Unlikely." He smiled and kissed her on the cheek.

***

Back at Cassie's house, Brent tended to the fireplace while Cassie went into the kitchen to scrounge remnants of leftover tiramisu and brew coffee. Gwen took a seat, and her cell phone beeped. The number was unfamiliar, but it displayed a Maine area code. She answered and put it on speaker.

"Hello?"

"Hello, is this Gwen Kelly?"

"Yes, it is."

"This is Emily Davis with the Farmington Historical Society. I'm responding to your email."

Brent looked up with a smile. "Hey, Emily!" he called.

Her tone flattened. "Oh, it's you."

He laughed. "Miss me already?"

"Only until my property is repaired." She cleared her throat. "Ms. Kelly—"

"Call me Gwen, please."

"Very well, Gwen. I understand you're trying to take away our Octagon House."

"Um, no, I wouldn't put it like that."

"How would you put it?"

Gwen's voice tightened. "I'd put it this way. I'm trying to tie up a loose thread in my recently deceased father's estate."

Emily's voice softened. "Oh, I'm sorry. I didn't know."

"Look, the last thing I want is a fight. I'm sure the house is wonderful, but I have no interest in owning a historical landmark, so frankly, if it did turn out to be a legitimate part of my father's estate, I'd donate it back to you anyway."

"You would?"

"Trust me."

Emily assumed a lighter tone. "Well, thank you. We had a community fund-raising effort to purchase the property a few years ago, and it was the wish of the seller that it would remain open to the public. We've invested a lot of money in renovation, and I'm afraid the idea of suddenly losing it got under my skin. I apologize if I came across harshly."

"It's completely understandable."

"I do have a question, though. The bill of sale you attached to your email was too grainy to make out most of the details. Can you give me the date on the document?"

"I think it was February 3, 1868."

"And it was signed by Hiram Ramsdell?"

"Yes."

A deep sigh of relief spilled from the receiver. "Then it's a fake."

"What?"

"Cryus Ramsdell built the Octagon in 1858. He sold it to his brother, Hiram, in 1868."

"Yes?"

"*August* 1868."

"Then ... "

"Right. Hiram didn't own the house in February, so he couldn't have sold it."

"Then where on earth did the bill of sale come from?"

"I have no idea, but it can't be genuine."

Gwen looked at Brent, who shrugged.

"I don't know what to say, Emily. This catches me as much by surprise as it did you. I'm so sorry for all the unnecessary drama."

"Please don't apologize. You did what anyone would do. I'm glad we got it resolved so quickly. Things like this can get bogged down in the legal system forever, and we would have had to put a hold on restorations."

"I'm glad too. Actually, I look forward to seeing it someday."

"You're welcome anytime. Maybe you can help Officer Newcomb clean up the mess he left in the library."

"Nope. He's on his own with the housecleaning."

"Hey!" yelled Brent from across the room.

The women laughed, bade farewell, and ended the call.

70

Gwen set down the phone and stared into the fireplace. "So, all of this was for nothing."

"What do you mean?" asked Brent.

"I wasted almost three weeks of my life searching for a missing brother I don't have and chasing down a piece of property I don't own." She gave him a blank look. "Not to mention running Mark and you all over the place, and imposing on Cassie's hospitality."

"You were no imposition," Cassie said.

"You rescued me from a boring desk job," added Mark. "This was the most action I've seen since South Boston."

"And you made some cool friends." Brent lifted his coffee mug to the room with a smile.

"Hear, hear!" Mark said with a grin, and tipped back his mug.

Cassie glanced at him from the corner of her eye. "You're not *that* cool."

"Maybe not, but together we're that cool."

"Really?"

"Really." He looked at her for a moment, and his expression grew serious. "In fact ... "

"What?"

Mark set down his coffee, rose, and crossed the room to the foyer. He dug through the inside of his overcoat for a moment, then returned and stood looking down at Cassie.

She frowned. "What are you up to?"

"This." He took her mug and set it on the end table, lowered himself to a knee, and slipped his hand beneath hers.

Cassie's eyes widened when Mark opened his other hand to reveal a black velvet box. Her voice dropped to a hoarse whisper. "Mark?"

"I've been carrying this around with me for too long, waiting for the right moment." He looked over at Brent, who was wearing a big grin, and Gwen, who was tearing up. "I don't think there could be a better time than now." He opened the box, and the firelight flashed on a brilliant pear-shaped diamond in a white gold setting.

Cassie's chest heaved and her eyes filled as he reached up and brushed her cheek with the back of his fingers. "Cassandra Lynn Hastings, would you do me the honor of becoming my wife?"

She stared at the ring, looked up and him, then pressed against the back of the chair. "I ... I can't."

He shook his head. "You've proven to me time and time again that there's nothing you can't do. So either you will or you won't, but I'm not going to let you hide behind 'I can't'."

She closed her eyes. "Mark. Look at me," she whispered.

"I never stop looking at you. And I see everything I've ever wanted." He lifted the ring from the box. "Please say yes, Cassie."

Her eyes opened, releasing a trickle of tears down both cheeks. She threw a panicked look toward the sofa.

Brent arched his eyebrows, and Gwen nodded vigorously.

Cassie looked down at the ring.

Mark reached for her hand.

She swallowed, then slowly extended her fingers.

He smiled. "I'll take that as a 'yes'."

He slipped the ring onto her trembling finger, and kissed her hand. "Here's to the rest of our lives."

Gwen wiped her moist cheek with her sleeve and reached for Brent.

***

The following morning, Brent and Mark returned to Cassie's house for breakfast. Gwen met them at the door, eyes dancing.

"What are you all giddy about?" Brent asked, hanging up his coat.

"Cassie. You should see her." She glanced toward the archway. "She hasn't taken her eyes off of that ring all morning. I had to take over cooking the bacon for fear she'd burn either it or herself. And I won't even think about letting her anywhere near a knife." Gwen giggled. "She's even been singing."

Mark winced. "Singing isn't one of her strengths."

"Don't try to tell *her* that."

They went into the kitchen where Cassie was wiping up a spill on the floor next to an overturned carton of orange juice. She looked up. "I don't know what happened. One second it was on the counter, then it was on the floor."

Gwen hurried over. "Let me finish making breakfast. You go sit down."

Cassie turned toward the men, face flushed, making a very poor job of subduing a smile. Her eyes locked onto Mark, and the flush deepened. "Um, grab a seat. I'll get some hot coffee—"

"No." Brent lifted his hands. "I'll get it. You do as Gwen says."

Ten minutes into breakfast Cassie didn't even touch, Brent's phone sounded. "That's Chief Lawson's ringtone." He pulled out his phone. "Yes, sir ... Yes, I remember what you said about not turning this into a vacation. We're wrapping things up ... I'll be back in Marble Falls this afternoon ... Absolutely, Chief, thanks ... Right, I'll tell her." He disconnected the call.

"Tell who what?" asked Gwen.

Brent gave her a sidelong look. "He said to bring that cute blonde back with me, because I'm completely useless without her."

They laughed.

He reached for her hand. "I wish you could come back with me this afternoon."

"I can."

"What?"

"Mr. Forbson called this morning. The police notified him regarding Mona's case, since he's also a potential plaintiff. Now that the deed to Daddy's house is clear, he said he'd be happy to arrange for a realtor and set up an estate sale. It was the least he could do for all the trouble his office had caused me." She flashed a wide smile. "I'm free to go back to Marble Falls."

"Perfect."

"All I have to do is pack and stop by the house to pick up a few things."

"Like what?"

"My car, for instance."

"We'll be towing that back home."

She gave him a puzzled look. "Why? It's perfectly drivable."

"I'm not about to look at you in my rearview mirror when you could be sitting beside me in the truck. You're riding with me."

She leaned over and kissed hm. "I was hoping you'd say that."

***

Gwen hugged Cassie while Brent took her suitcases out to the truck. "Brent and I better be at the top of your wedding guest list."

"You are."

Mark stared at her. "You've already made a list?"

She tinged pink. "Maybe."

Gwen laughed as Brent came back through the doorway. "Ready to go?"

"More than ready." She turned back to Mark and Cassie. "How can I ever thank you enough? Your hard work, Mark, and your wonderful hospitality, Cassie. I have no idea what I'd have done without you."

Cassie looked up at Mark. "I think we all got something out of it."

He kissed her forehead. "We sure did." He gave Gwen a hug, then gripped hands with Brent. "Drive safe, Wild Bill."

"Hey, that's right," Gwen said, turning toward Brent. "You can tell me about that 'Wild Bill' thing on the way back."

Brent twitched his jaw. "Thanks a lot, bro."

Mark grinned. "Don't mention it."

After stopping at Gwen's house to collect her car and some family mementos, the F-150 headed north on I-95, the Corolla in tow. She drew a deep breath, relaxed back onto the headrest, and closed her eyes. "I've been dreaming about this day for weeks," she murmured.

He reached for her hand. "It's been a lousy December," he said. "No more separations. Ever."

"I have zero plans that don't include you."

"Good, don't make any."

She smiled. "What a great ending though. Who knew Mark would propose like that?"

"I did."

She straightened and turned toward him. "You did?"

"We had a few words before he left with Mona and Sally last night. He said seeing you and me together clicked. He noticed something different about our relationship, the way we treat each other, and it gave him hope." He squeezed her hand. "Apparently, it tipped the scales, and he seized the moment."

She settled back. "Wow."

"It goes to show that people are watching even when we don't realize it. When we went back to his place, we spent a couple of hours talking."

"About what?"

"What he saw in our relationship that impressed him so much. Respect. Consideration. Fun." He smiled. "And no angst. He asked how we managed it."

"What did you tell him?"

"That it's never perfect, but there's someone bigger than us who we dedicated our relationship to."

"God."

He nodded. "I told him how much of a mess we'd made of it, trusting ourselves." He grasped her hand. "Like we did last fall when we were dealing with that blasted steamer trunk."

"Yeah, what a comedy of errors *that* was."

"Comedy without the humor." He talked about the eggshells Mark said he and Cassie always seemed to walk on around each other. Mistakes he'd made, barriers she'd put up. A vicious cycle.

"I understand Cassie much better now. She's got some genuine issues to deal with."

"True, but God has handled worse situations. I saw it time and again overseas. The question is, will she let Him."

"And will Mark."

"I hope so. I left him an extra Bible I keep in my glove compartment. You never know when an opportunity will pop up. Best to be prepared."

Gwen relaxed and looked out the window. As they approached the Sandy River bridge into Farmington, a pristine layer of fresh snow rounded the riverbank, cuddling the dark water like a fleece collar. From a cloudless azure sky, the late afternoon winter sun tinged the surrounding landscape with pinkish highlights that haloed lengthening shadows of soft gray. The trees lining the river bent under fluffy white tufts coating their boughs. She laid a hand on Brent's arm. "Slow down a second."

He downshifted while she reached into her purse for her phone. She snapped a few photos downriver, and he resumed speed onto Main Street.

Tucking the phone back into her purse, she smiled. "I bet Cassie could paint that scene."

"I'm sure she could." He paused. "Would you like to drive past the Octagon House? It's not very far out of the way."

335

Gwen thought for a moment, then shook her head. "Thanks, but not yet." She folded her hands on her lapped and looked at him. "So, tell me about this 'Wild Bill' thing."

He rolled his eyes.

71

Gwen curled up on the couch and watched Brent coax the log fire to a roaring blaze. Firelight danced across the rough-hewn ceiling beams and walls, enlivening glass ornaments and tinsel she'd finished placing around the rustic living room barely in time for Christmas Eve. Evergreen and holly garland draped the fireplace's rock facing, framing an array of scented candles on the mantel. She drew in a deep breath of winterberry and pine garnished with the sweet aroma of cocoa steaming up from the mug cradled in her hands. She released a dreamy sigh.

"What?" asked Brent as he settled onto the cushion beside her and lifted his mug from the coffee table.

"Nothing. Just loving life." She reached for his hand. "I was so afraid the problems in Medford were going to rob me of my first Christmas with you."

He squeezed her hand. "No way was I going to let that happen. I am a cop, after all, and robbery prevention is one of my things."

She laughed. "Good point, Wild Bill."

He peered at her from the corner of his eye. "You promised when I told you the story of roping that goat in Kandahar, it would be the last time I'd hear that name."

"Oops." She touched fingertips to her lips, eyes sparkling. "I did, didn't I?"

"Yes, you did." He smiled and took a sip of cocoa, returning his attention to the crackling fire. "Unless you'd like me to call you 'Annie Oakley'."

She straightened. "You wouldn't dare."

The smile spread to a grin. "Wouldn't I? My lucky throw with a lasso didn't come close to your expertise with a gun. It would only be fair."

Gwen laughed. "Touché! You've outdone yourself this time."

Brent reached for her hand, keeping his gaze on the fire. "Speaking of outdoing oneself, Pastor Dave was brilliant at the candlelight service this evening, wasn't he?"

She intertwined her fingers with his. "He was. I'd never thought about the Advent story ending with a beginning. It's easy to leave the baby Jesus cute and cuddly in a manger, and lose sight of the reason he was born, to grow into a man who would change the world."

"Beginnings are good."

Gwen stared into her cocoa mug. "It made me think of Sally."

"How so?"

"Her story has ended with a beginning too, with Cassie's gracious offer to take her in." She sipped her cocoa. "What do you think will happen to her?"

"She'll answer for her misdemeanors, but after helping us pull in Mona, I think the courts will be lenient."

"I sure hope so."

"You have a big heart." He kissed her hand. "It's one of the things I love about you."

"Only one thing, meaning there are more? Do tell, and don't leave out any details."

His gaze intensified. "Maybe I can show you instead."

She cocked her head.

He rose and left the room, returning with a large gift-wrapped parcel. "Your Christmas gift."

"That's not fair. We're supposed to wait until tomorrow morning. I left my gift for you back at Margie's."

He stroked the package. "Well, okay. If you really don't want it …"

She set down her mug and held out her hands. "I didn't say that."

He laughed. "So much for tradition."

"It can be taken to an extreme."

She hefted the bundle, squeezed it, frowned. "I can't imagine what it is."

"You're not supposed to imagine. You're supposed to open it."

"Anticipation is half the fun."

"That can be taken to an extreme too."

She slipped her finger into a seam of the wrapping paper. Moments later, a roll of rose-colored fleece lay in her lap. "What on earth … ?"

"Unfold it."

"Oh! It's a snuggle sack." She pressed the soft wool to her cheek, beaming. "I love it. Thank you so much." She inspected the gift front and back, fussing over the color and texture. As she unzipped it, a piece of folded paper safety-pinned to the inside tag came into view. "What's this?" She unpinned it. Handwritten on a piece of stationery bordered with Christmas holly were two words. "Look Up."

Gwen looked up.

Brent stood before her wearing an awkward smile. Lowering himself to a knee, he extended his hand, revealing a small royal-blue box. He cleared his throat. "I've never been great at formality, but … Gwendolyn Rose Kelly, would you do me the honor of becoming my wife? I can't promise—"

Gwen launched herself from the sofa and wrapped him in a tight hug. "Yes, yes, *yes!*"

They collapsed onto the floor. "I didn't finish my speech," he mumbled against her neck.

"As far as I'm concerned you did." Any further protests died beneath a passionate kiss. Or two. Maybe more.

Finally, Gwen disengaged and sat back on her legs at his side. He struggled up to his elbows, exaggerating deep breaths. Laughing, she helped him up to a sitting position. She clasped her hands on her lap and gave him an expectant smile. "I believe you had something for me?"

"I did, but I don't know where it went when you tackled me."

She frowned. "Oh, dear. That part is kind of important."

He searched the floor until he spotted the box under the couch. He ushered her back onto the sofa, and opened the lid. A marquis-cut diamond nestled in a cluster of brilliant green emeralds glittered in the flickering firelight. He looked into her eyes tentatively. "I thought the color matched your eyes."

"Oh, Brent." Her voice quavered. "It's absolutely beautiful."

"Not yet, it isn't." He removed the ring and slipped it onto her finger. "Now it's absolutely beautiful."

Their next embrace lingered. As did their kiss.

They sat back on the couch, and she held her ring finger up to the firelight. "Now I have two favorite pieces of jewelry."

"Two?"

"Yes, I meant to show you. Can you hand me my purse, please?"

He retrieved her bag from the end table. She lifted out the antique jewelry box and withdrew the diamond necklace. "Grandmother Irma bequeathed this to me."

"It's a beauty." He paused. "Wait, you mean she bequeathed to you specifically?"

"Yes."

"But how—"

"I don't know how she knew." Gwen settled against the back of the sofa, studying the heirloom glistening in tandem with her engagement ring. "I guess I'll have to ask her next time we meet."

THE END

AUTHOR'S NOTES

Once again, I tip my hat to the wonderful inhabitants of the great town of Rangeley, Maine, the real-life setting for Marble Falls. Although fewer contemporary scenes in *Sandy River* take place there than in the prequel, *Quimby Pond*, the Mountain nonetheless serves as the entire series' geographic inspiration. Readers who stick with me will see more of historical Rangeley Lakes area in the third and final part to "The Marble Falls Legacy."

Local readers will also recognize, Ron Nobbs, characterized in the story as Howard Dobbs. When I asked Ron if he'd like to appear as a good guy or a bad guy, he opted for the latter. However, knowing Ron as I do, I couldn't bring myself to portray him as a bad-bad guy, so I rendered him as more of — how shall we say? — an annoying character with redeeming qualities. Sorry, Ron, if that disappointed you. But you're just not a bad guy. Oh, and for the non-local reader, Ron's Thursday-night poker games are a genuine institution in the region.

Emily Davis is another character inspired by a real-life person, Taffy Davis, of the Farmington Historical Society. Her indomitable spirit, zeal for Farmington's history, and great personality are caricatured in the story. Being a caricature, some of the more acute actions Emily took are embellished beyond what Taffy's normal response to circumstances might actually be. Still, I pray Taffy is satisfied with Emily, because I sure like her.

In the historical setting, most readers will recognize the name Frederick Douglass, the escaped slave who became a abolitionist writer-orator in New England. Others may recognize Caroline Healey Dall, a noted women's rights advocate of the era. Lesser known, but equally important, is Farmington's own Captain Ebenezer Childs, an abolitionist and leader in the "Liberty Party" antislavery group. Finally, Abner Toothaker, his daughter, Mary Jane, and her betrothed Hiram (Hunter) are true figures in Rangeley's history.

I'm excited to continue Irma's story in the final part of "the Marble Falls Legacy." How does she end up with Francis Jones? What becomes of her family? And how on earth did her Jenny Lind hope chest become a focus of intrigue over 150 years later? Truth be told, I'm kind of curious about all of that myself. But, if you can turn the page, you'll get a sneak preview.

SCENE FROM BOOK 3 OF THE MARBLE FALLS LEGACY

Saturday, June 1, 1861

Today is Mary Jane's wedding day. I pray my gift and letter arrived on time. It would have been wonderful to attend, but alas, it was not to be.

Irma locked a troubled gaze at the open doorway. Dr. Riley's and her father's faint voices drifted down the hall from her parents' bedroom. Too faint to make out the words, but their tone was clear.

She laid down the fountain pen. Over the past year, the diary—a gift from Gerald which she'd first disdained—had evolved from an annoyance to a routine to an indispensable part of her life. Sealing her innermost thoughts on paper had given the journal a life of its own, and she relished reading and re-reading her entries. Touching them up. Adding this and that. But this morning, the lure of its precious confidence failed to soothe her.

A persistent cough, subtle at first, then deepening in coarseness, had settled into her mother's chest after their return from Marble Falls into smoggy Boston three weeks ago. At first, she stoically dismissed it as an allergic bout, assuring her family that she was quite well, that they could stop fussing. Until two days ago when an alarmed Miss Doyle burst into the study, beckoning Irma and her father into the dining room. Kate slouched at the table, a cloth napkin pressed to her mouth. A coughing fit wracked her slender frame, and when she lowered the napkin, it was spotted red. Her head lolled, and Byrne caught her as she tipped toward the floor.

He carried his wife upstairs, barking orders at Gibbons to fetch the doctor. Forty-five eternal minutes later, Dr. Riley arrived. After a cursory examination, he demanded to know why they'd not called him sooner. For once, Byrne was at a loss for words, and Irma could barely speak past the lump in her throat.

"How serious is it, Doctor?"

"More so than if you'd summoned me a week ago, but less than if you'd waited another day. We must act quickly."

"What can we do?"

"There are no medicinal remedies for consumption—"

" 'Consumption?' "

"She needs clean air. The city is not good for her."

The doctor's words faded into a cloud of numbness. *Consumption? It can't be true. Mother is never sick.*

When Irma's tortured thoughts released her back to the present, Dr. Riley and her father had left the room. She gathered her skirts and stumbled to the staircase as the front door was closing. An anguished interrogation of her father yielded nothing new, and she trudged back to her room.

Dr. Riley had returned twice since her mother's collapse, but found no change for the better. Mercifully, neither had there been a change for the worse.

As Irma closed her journal with today's entry barely begun, a gentle tap came at the door. She looked up at her father's tired face peering at her through the cracked doorway.

She rose unsteadily.

He entered, but before he could say a word, she wrapped her arms around his broad torso and buried her face against his chest. Despite her best efforts, a sob shuddered her body.

"All will be fine, colleen," he whispered into her ear.

She looked up at him. "What did Dr. Riley say?"

"Little more than we already know. Your mother rests, but she labors for breath."

"What are we to do?"

"It's imperative we transport her to more hospitable environs. This wretched city air is killing her."

"Where would we go?"

"I can think of but one place. Marble Falls."

"But how will you manage your business dealings from Maine?"

He responded with a mirthless smile. "Perhaps the board of directors will be spared the formality of censuring me."

"Father?"

He cleared his throat. "Your mother's health is paramount. I won't let something as trivial as business impede her recovery."

"But Father, you built the firm from nothing. I'm shocked to hear you use the word 'trivial'."

He shook his head. "If you think my textile firm occupies a position even remotely equal to that of my family, then how little you know me."

Her cheeks tinged pink and she looked down. "I didn't mean to imply—"

He touched a fingertip to her lips. "You didn't imply anything, daughter. I merely want you to understand that you and your mother are everything to me." He tucked a finger beneath her chin and lifted her face. "And if it means selling the firm and relocating to the wilderness to preserve her, I will not hesitate."

"You believe it has come to that?"

"I've already asked Henry to begin inquiries. The business is lucrative. Offers should not be long in coming."

Irma stared at the floor, mind roiling. As quaint as Marble Falls is, could she thrive—even survive—there? What of Boston's metropolitan culture she'd become so accustomed to? And where would they live? There was the land at Quimby Lake, but there was no dwelling, not even a storage shed. Had her father thought this through?

As though gleaning her thoughts, Byrne took her gently by the shoulders. "This must be a frightful notion to you. To contemplate so different a life, to leave the only home you have ever known. But consider what life anywhere would be like without your mother."

Irma peered up through a sheen of tears and nodded. "We must go."

He kissed her forehead and departed the room.

When his steps had faded down the staircase, Irma dropped to her knees. She folded her hands on her lap and stared at the intricate needlework of her bedroom's Persian rug. A hem that had begun to unravel beckoned, and she absently prodded the loosening thread with a fingertip.

But no amount of tucking and folding would ever make the rug the same.

About the Author

 Bruce Judisch has been writing fiction for over fifteen years. His first work, "A Prophet's Tale," is a two-part novelization of the story of the Old Testament prophet, Jonah ben Amittai, comprising *The Journey Begun* and *The Word Fulfilled*. A third part, *The Promised Kept*, is under construction. More recently, he wrote *Katia* and its sequel *For Maria*, both with complementary present-day and 20th-century historical storylines. Please see the next pages for more information on these works.

Bruce lives in Texas with his wife and high-school sweetheart, Jeannie, and their two Cavalier King Charles Spaniels, Charlie and Raleigh. They are the proud parents of three and grandparents of fourteen.

Also by Bruce Judisch...

Seek the truth, embrace the pain, cherish the freedom.

Spirited Maddy McAllister, a twenty-one-year-old American exchange student in Berlin, Germany, has a journalism career to launch.

Stalwart Katia Mahler, a sixty-year-old invalid from the former East Berlin, has a story to tell.

Enigmatic Oskar Schultmann brings together the journalist and the storyteller.

Maddy's task: to document Katia's story.

Cultures and generations clash as the young American and the German matron strive to understand each other's present and past. Maddy learns more than a personal history; Katia receives more than a memoir. And always in the background is Oskar, who is drawn into the story in ways he never intended.

Peek over the Berlin Wall as Katia's story comes to life through the scribbled notes of a girl struggling to grasp the significance of what she has written for her own life as well as for future generations.

The sequel to *Katia*

December, 1939. When the Gestapo transport Izaak and Maria Szpilmann away to Ravensbrück, their twin infants are left behind to die. Instead, neighbors Gustaw and Ròsa Dudek rescue the babies and flee occupied Poland. They are never heard from again.

Today. Maria Szpilmann has survived Ravensbrück, Auschwitz, and Bergen-Belsen. Now she is grandmother to Madeline Sommers, a young journalist who, despite the odds, passionately clings to the belief that the lost twins are still alive. Her single-minded mission is to find them and reunite them with her failing grandmother—before it's too late.

"A PROPHET'S TALE"
The story you thought you knew...
An ageless tale of danger, redemption, and love

***

Six years ago, Jonah ben Amittai delivered a message of hope and redemption to his beloved homeland of Israel. Now he's called to the hardest task of all: to bring a message of repentance and hope to Nineveh, a city in the land of Israel's archenemy, Assyria. Horrified by memories of brutal warfare in his youth, repulsed by his hatred of all things Assyrian, and spurred on by dark forces who have no intention of letting Adonai's prophet onto their turf, Jonah flees to the seaport of Joppa. But can he flee the memories of betrayed loyalty, broken friendships, and shattered family relationships? Can he escape the all-seeing eye of Adonai?

***

Israel. Dark forces dog a prophet's every step on his journey to deliver a message of hope to evil Assyria.

Nineveh. When a girl's coming-of-age ritual goes terribly wrong, the unlikely love of a young man becomes her only hope.

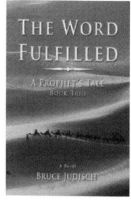

Kalḫu. The Igigi, the great gods of the Assyrian pantheon, are on the move. Their omens of discontent throw a nation into turmoil, and the king and his vizier scheme to evade their wrath.

Relive the world of eighth-century B.C. with Jonah, Ianna, and Ahu-duri as three separate acts converge at a critical point on the stage of history, and God directs them to their grand finale — the fulfillment of His word.

48483150R00214

Made in the USA
Columbia, SC
09 January 2019